Under a Texas Sky

BOOKS BY DOROTHY GARLOCK

After the Parade
Almost Eden
Annie Lash
By Starlight
Come a Little Closer
Dreamkeepers
Dream River
The Edge of Town
Forever Victoria
A Gentle Giving
Glorious Dawn
High on a Hill
Homeplace
Hope's Highway
Keep a Little Secret
Larkspur
Leaving Whiskey Bend
The Listening Sky
Lonesome River
Love and Cherish
Loveseekers
Midnight Blue
The Moon Looked Down
More than Memory
Mother Road
Nightrose

On Tall Pine Lake
A Place Called Rainwater
Promisegivers
Restless Wind
Ribbon in the Sky
River of Tomorrow
River Rising
The Searching Hearts
Sins of Summer
Song of the Road
Stay a Little Longer
Sweetwater
Tenderness
This Loving Land
Train from Marietta
Wayward Wind
A Week from Sunday
Wild Sweet Wilderness
Will You Still Be Mine?
Wind of Promise
Wishmakers
With Heart
With Hope
With Song
Yesteryear

DOROTHY GARLOCK

Under a
Texas Sky

GRAND CENTRAL
PUBLISHING

NEW YORK   BOSTON

Grand Central Publishing
Hachette Book Group
237 Park Avenue
New York, NY 10017

www.HachetteBookGroup.com

Printed in the United States of America

RRD-C

First Edition: August 2013
10 9 8 7 6 5 4 3 2 1

Grand Central Publishing is a division of Hachette Book Group, Inc.
The Grand Central Publishing name and logo is a trademark of Hachette Book Group, Inc.

The Hachette Speakers Bureau provides a wide range of authors for speaking events. To find out more, go to www.hachettespeakersbureau.com or call (866) 376-6591.

The publisher is not responsible for websites (or their content) that are not owned by the publisher.

Library of Congress Cataloging-in-Publication Data
Garlock, Dorothy.
Under a Texas sky / Dorothy Garlock. — 1st ed.
    p. cm.
ISBN 978-0-446-54023-0 (hardcover) — ISBN 978-0-446-54021-6 (trade pbk.) 1. Texas—Fiction. I. Title.
PS3557.A71645U53 2013
813'.6—dc23
                        2012029520

To
Bernadette, Magali, Laurent, and Agnès
with much love

Under a Texas Sky

Questions

Into the forge's fiery glow I thrust the steel
And bend it into the arc of a wheel.
My hammer strikes; my muscles ache.
This is how I make what I make.

My dearest works with the stuff of dreams
Where nothing seen is what it seems.
Her image flickers, and people sigh.
How can she love my kind of guy?

Still she trembles when we kiss.
Is there hope for a match like this?

—F.S.I.

Prologue

Chicago, Illinois
November 1924

Anna Finnegan knew she was being greedy. Even as the biting November wind cut through her ragged clothes and gnawed deep into the bare skin of her hands and face, she knew that the two apples she'd already stolen, secreted into the folds of her threadbare coat, should be enough. Taking another was risky. The longer she lingered, the greater the chance that she'd be caught. But she was so hungry that she couldn't bring herself to walk away.

The corner grocer was busy, even with the weather taking another determined step toward winter. Mothers trudged past Anna with small children in tow, making their way inside through the open door, greeting the shopkeeper, an old woman with a shawl wrapped tightly around her stooped shoulders, her wrinkled cheeks flushed red from the cold. Men tramped up and down the sidewalk behind Anna, some with their noses buried in newspapers, others calling greetings to friends, their voices mixing with the honking horns of automobiles. No one paid much attention to the grubby, twelve-year-old girl standing in front of the bin of apples.

You can do it… Just take one more…

It had been three days since Anna had last eaten. Even now, her stomach grumbled and groaned, making her feel weak and dizzy. She'd done all she possibly could to feed herself, from rooting through every nook and cranny of her mother's apartment for any misplaced scraps, to begging outside of the Chicago & North Western train station; for all of that, the only thing she'd accomplished for her efforts was to be elbowed out of the way and knocked to the ground. She'd ended up hungrier than ever. Anna knew that stealing was wrong, but she no longer had a choice. If she didn't eat something soon, especially with an unforgiving winter approaching, she was as good as dead.

Nervously, Anna licked her lips, took one last glance at the shopkeeper, and, satisfied that the old woman was busy helping customers, shot out her hand, snatched up a particularly tasty-looking apple, and stuffed it down into her coat alongside the others. It was all done in the blink of an eye and no one was the wiser. Now all she had to do was get out of sight and—

"What'n the hell do you think yer doin', girlie?" a man's voice boomed behind her.

Before Anna could even think, a hand grabbed her arm and violently whipped her around. Strands of her dirty blond hair flew into her eyes, but she could still see clearly enough to know who had hold of her; it was the shopkeeper's son. He was a short, squat man, as thick around the chest as a barrel. Glaring at her, his face was twisted into an angry scowl, his eyes narrow and full of fury.

Anna silently cursed herself. She'd spent half the morning waiting across the street until she'd seen the man walk away with a friend. She'd assumed that he would be gone for a while, but her gamble hadn't been a lucky one. She had not watched closely enough; he'd managed to get behind her. He'd seen her snatch the apple. Now she was caught!

"You lousy little thief!" he shouted angrily, pulling Anna closer, dragging her toward him against her will. His breath smelled of tobacco and alcohol. "Ain't nobody steals from my family and gets away with it! Nobody!"

By now, every face in the cramped grocery had turned toward them. Anna saw disgust and disappointment flutter across one woman's features, and a grandfatherly man shook his head.

"Someone get a cop!" the man yelled, looking up and down both sides of the sidewalk, searching for an officer. Glaring down at Anna, he added, "Maybe spendin' some time locked up with the rest a the trash litterin' these streets'll teach you a lesson."

Panic flared in Anna's chest. The thought of going to jail for what she'd done was terrifying. She'd taken the apples only because she was starving. Couldn't anyone understand how hungry she was? Once she was arrested, she knew, no one would come for her, not her brother and definitely not her mother; she'd rot behind bars long before anyone in her family even knew she was missing. After receiving countless beatings at the hands of stronger girls, she'd probably get shipped off to an orphanage. Anna couldn't think of a worse fate. No matter what it took, she had to get away.

Desperately, she tried to pull herself free of the man, but his grip was as tight as a vise; when he felt her struggle, he clamped down even harder.

"Let me go!" Anna screamed.

"Fight all you want," the man sneered. "It ain't gonna do you no good!"

"I'll give them back! I promise I won't do it again!"

"It's too late for all that!"

Anna felt the noose closing quickly around her; if she was going to remain free, she had to do something.

Desperate, Anna raised her foot and drove her heel down onto the man's toes as hard as she could. A sharp yelp burst from his mouth. She couldn't know if it was because she'd actually managed to hurt him, or if he'd just been surprised that she was still defying him, but it was enough to make him momentarily loosen his grip on her arm. Quickly, she threw a sharp elbow into the soft paunch of his stomach and tore herself free. Without a second's hesitation, Anna was off, like a rabbit suddenly freed from a snare, running away from the grocer's as fast as she could.

Behind her, the man bellowed. "Stop! Stop, you good-for-nothin' bitch! Somebody stop her!"

Anna dodged an old man with a cane, slid on the slippery sidewalk, and nearly collided with a fire hydrant before managing to right herself and race on. At any moment, she expected a policeman to suddenly appear before her, ready to snatch her up as she raced headlong into his open arms, or for some Good Samaritan to grab her and drag her kicking and screaming back to the grocer for her punishment.

But nothing happened. The sounds of the city, the shouts of the grocer's son, all faded until the only thing Anna could hear was the pounding of her heart.

"Gimme that!"

Anna had only just bitten into the apple, her teeth piercing the skin, the juice deliciously sweet on her tongue, when it was suddenly yanked from her grasp. Before she could react, she was shoved hard in the chest and sent crashing to the floor, landing awkwardly on her side.

Her brother stood above her in the small, darkened bedroom they shared, staring at his newly acquired prize with a sneer of triumph on his face. Four years older than she, at sixteen, Peter Finnegan was well on his way to manhood, but Anna didn't much like the man he was becoming. While she struggled with the dilemma of stealing food in order to survive, Peter had no such compunction about breaking the law. She'd seen him running around with other boys she knew were up to no good, gambling with a pair of dice in alleyways, and heard rumors of his breaking into people's homes and stealing, and even running errands for one or another neighborhood mobster, the sort of important, dangerous man she knew Peter hoped someday to become. Most nights, she went to sleep in their room alone and woke the next morning to find he hadn't bothered to come home. Assuming that she would be alone to eat her stolen treasure had been a mistake, the second she'd made that day.

"That's mine," she said evenly, doing her best to ignore the throbbing ache in her arm. "Give it back."

"How'd you get this?" Peter asked, nodding at the apple. "You ain't got two pennies to rub together. Did someone give it to you, did you find it, or," he continued, a sinister grin spreading across his face, "did you steal it?"

"It's mine," Anna answered, unwilling to answer his question; she knew her brother would like nothing more than to know she was slowly falling toward the depths to which he'd already sunk.

Peter held out the apple to her. "Come take it."

Anna didn't move. She knew that if she was foolish enough to take Peter up on his offer, to challenge him, he'd use it as an excuse to beat her black and blue. There was a time, not so long ago, when she wouldn't have believed him capable of doing such a thing, but that time had long since passed.

"I didn't think so." He sneered, taking a bite and chewing noisily.

There was nothing for Anna to do to stop him, no one she could call for help. As always, she was on her own.

Anna had only been seven years old the winter her father had gotten so drunk that it had struck him as a good idea to lie down and take a quick rest in the middle of a blizzard. By morning, Patrick Finnegan was dead, as stiff as the bench he'd mistaken for a bed, two blocks from home. Anna didn't remember much more of him than his booming laugh; even looking at the man in the photograph her mother kept didn't rekindle any memories. His sudden absence had started his family on a downward spiral they still hadn't been able to stop.

As much as her brother's life had been changed, Anna was still more horrified by what had happened to her mother. Rather than reacting to her husband's unexpected death by doing whatever it took to provide for her children, Cordelia Finnegan had largely abandoned them, leaving them to care for themselves. Wantonly, she moved from one man to the next, many of them drunks and some of them worse. She was absent from the apartment more often than Peter was. Occasionally, she would come through the door with a black eye or a split lip. Even less frequently, Anna would return home to find her mother had bought groceries, meager though they'd be. Over time, Anna came to prefer the nights her mother was gone; worse were the evenings when she brought one of her men home with her, and Anna had to listen to their drunken goings-on before covering her head with her pillow so she wouldn't have to hear them once they'd retired to the bedroom.

In almost every way, Anna was all alone.

"Thanks for the apple," Peter said with a laugh. At the sound of the door slamming behind him, Anna's lower lip began to tremble and her eyes to fill with tears, but she steadfastly refused to give in and cry. She was no longer a child, hadn't been for years, and besides, what would giving in to her emotions get her?

"Nothing," she whispered.

Not for the first time, Anna swore to herself that she would make something of her life. No matter what it took, no matter how much she had to struggle, to whatever lengths she had to go, she refused to walk down the same path her mother and brother had taken. She'd be better than that. She wouldn't allow herself to be mistreated, live in squalor, or run with the wrong crowd. But that didn't mean she'd allow herself to starve, either; if she absolutely had to, she would steal again if it meant the difference between life and death.

In the dark and silence of her dingy bedroom, Anna pulled one of the other apples she'd stolen from her coat, one of the two she'd managed to keep hidden from her brother, and took a ravenous bite.

I'm going to be somebody.

Chapter One

St. Louis, Missouri
May 1932

Anna Finnegan gasped in both horror and surprise, a hand rising to clutch helplessly at her chest, as the man who'd suddenly appeared before her out of the darkness pulled a knife from the inside of his coat. Even in the gloom all around them, there was still enough light to glint off the long blade. Slowly but purposefully, he moved closer, causing her to take a couple of staggering steps backward.

"Who...who are you...?" she stammered fearfully. "What do you want?"

"I want everythin' you got," the man answered, his voice a deep, threatening growl as he looked her up and down, "and I'm gonna be takin' it."

Anna's eyes grew wide, her breathing ragged, her actions hesitant and panicked. Quickly, she turned one way and then the other, as if indecisive as to what she should do next. She kept slowly moving away from the stranger, but then, suddenly, her heel caught on the ground and she tumbled down, turning sideways to break her fall. As fast as a gunshot, the man raced across the space between them and loomed over her. Cackling devilishly, he slashed the knife back and forth through the air, mere inches above Anna's face.

"Oh, come now!" he shouted, spittle wet on his lips. "You can do better than that! Here I was hopin' you'd be worth a chase! It won't be no fun if you ain't runnin'. How'm I supposed to—"

As hard as she could, Anna kicked out at her attacker with her foot, striking him square in the thigh. With a loud grunt, he lost his balance and fell onto one knee, but he still managed to hold on to the knife. Before the man had touched the ground, Anna scrambled back to her feet, running in the opposite direction.

"Help!" she shouted as loud as she could. "Somebody help me!"

But there was no answer.

"That's it!" the man yelled, filling the silence. "Let me know how afraid you are! Let me hear your fear!"

Anna ran a few steps, stopped, moved tentatively the other way, and then stopped again, all the while looking, unsure of where to go. Finally, she turned and raced back straight toward the man. He was already back on his feet, his arms spread, knife poised, waiting for her. At the last second, she dodged quickly to the side, avoiding him. But for the second time, her foot caught and she fell.

"Now you're mine!" the man bellowed.

Anna watched as he dove toward where she lay sprawled,

bringing the long blade down in a deadly arc. She screamed as the knife landed just short of her, hitting the ground hard enough to make it fly from her attacker's hand, bouncing away into the dark.

Just as it was supposed to . . .

Anna ran quickly off the stage of the Cooper Theater as the heavy curtain began to descend from the rafters, signaling the end of the first act of *Misery's Company* and eliciting a hearty round of applause from the audience. From their place in the small pit in front of the stage, the orchestra began to play a fast, suspenseful piece that masked the sound of her footfalls but couldn't begin to drown out the prideful pounding of her heart. Finally making her way offstage, Anna received warm smiles and praise from her fellow actors.

". . . was just wonderful, Anna!"

". . . made me want to go out there and rescue you myself!"

". . . best performance yet . . ."

Even as she smiled at all of the comments, Anna was already turning to look at the actor hurrying along behind her. Peter Holmes had the role of the production's villain, the man who had attacked her with a knife. Anna was awestruck by how convincingly Peter's normally soft, friendly face could be twisted into that of a blood-crazed maniac. He met her gaze with a smile, once again the soft-spoken man she'd been rehearsing with over the last couple of weeks.

"Are you all right?" Anna asked him with genuine concern. "I didn't kick you too hard, did I?"

"I'm fine," Peter assured her. "It was just like we practiced."

"It felt worse to me."

"What really hurt was smashing that darn knife into the stage." He frowned, wriggling his wrist back and forth in obvious discomfort. "It felt like I almost snapped it clean in two. I shouldn't have brought it down so hard but I wanted everything to look convincing for opening night."

"I thought you were great," she said.

"We both were," he replied, taking her hand and giving it a gentle squeeze before hurrying off to the changing room to get ready for the next act.

All around Anna, the hustle and bustle of the play's production continued: A couple of burly stagehands pushed elaborate backgrounds into place while others arranged a long dining room table and chairs; up in the rafters, men moved enormous riggings of lights to their assigned places; and a woman went from actor to actor, freshening makeup and corralling loose hairs and untidy clothing. Through it all, Dwight Wirtz, the play's director, steered people and props to their positions as calmly as if this was the hundredth time they'd done it for paying customers instead of the first.

Moving to the front of the stage, careful to make sure she was out of everyone's way, Anna pulled the old, worn curtain back just far enough to see out into the theater's hall. In the years since she'd begun acting formally, it had become something of a tradition for her to steal a quick look, an opportunity to gauge the crowd. Tonight's audience was large, but Anna was disappointed to see a scattering of empty seats here and there. She'd hoped for a sellout for opening night, but she consoled herself with the fact that those people who *were* there seemed rapt with the performance; she'd looked out on other nights, in other cities, during other productions, to find people sound asleep, their heads tipped back, snoring loud enough to be heard onstage.

Still, she'd wanted tonight's performance to be different, for there to not be a single empty seat in the house, for there to be people standing in every aisle, shoulder-to-shoulder in the back.

Tonight was special.

This is the first time I've ever been the star of the show...

Anna could still remember that cold November night in Chicago when she'd first stepped onto a stage, the glare of the lights momentarily blinding her, her mouth as dry as cotton, her heart in her throat. As she'd stood there dumbstruck, she'd wondered if she hadn't made a huge mistake. But after those first, hesitantly spoken lines of dialogue, it had all become easier, like the gears of a clock sliding perfectly into place. Over the coming months and years, the stage had begun to feel comfortable, the theater like home.

And it had all led to this night.

She'd worked hard for this moment, spent countless hours going over her lines, practicing all of the ways she would move about the stage, looking into the cracked mirror in her apartment to see how best to portray her emotions, determined to become a better actress. Tonight was the culmination of everything she'd ever wanted.

Finally, the frenzied work on the stage was finished. On cue, the orchestra's tune began to slow, to change its pace, letting the audience know that the performance was about to resume.

Calmly and confidently, Anna strode back out onto the stage to take her rightful place.

"Are you sure you won't come out for a little while?" Marnie Greenwood asked. "I just know you'd have lots of fun. Pretty please?"

Anna swiveled in her chair in front of the large mirror in her otherwise small dressing room and looked at her friend. Through the doorway behind Marnie, all of the other girls in the play were hurrying to change out of their costumes, and Elizabeth Parsons was holding up a compact and carefully applying a fresh coat of lipstick. The room was bursting with laughter and playful shouts as they all prepared to head out for a night on the town.

"I haven't even started getting cleaned up," Anna explained, running her hand across the collar of the costume she was still wearing and then up to her hair, fastened with pins and tied up at the back with a ribbon. "By the time I finally finished, you'd all be mad at me for taking so long."

"You could hurry!"

"It'll take me at least an hour."

Marnie frowned. "Only if you're trying to look perfect."

"I don't want to look like a clown," Anna said with a laugh, thinking about how much makeup she was still wearing. "People would start to wonder if the circus was in town!"

"Just come out for one drink," her friend insisted. "Sarah has this friend who knows of a place near the railroad station that's supposed to be great. A quiet speakeasy with room for dancing, too. Besides, if there was ever a time to go out and celebrate, it's opening night!"

"It sounds like you'll have a great time."

Marnie realized now that she wasn't going to get the answer she wanted. "All right," she groaned. "I may be stubborn but I'm not a fool, either. I know when I'm licked. But next time, you're coming. No excuses!"

"I promise," Anna replied.

"Don't think I won't be holding you to that!"

Within minutes, Marnie and the rest of the girls had raced out of the dressing room, taking all of the noise and commotion with them, and leaving Anna in silence. She watched them go, making a few more apologies, waving and telling them to have fun. Finally alone, she turned back toward her mirror.

"It's just you and me, now," she whispered to her reflection.

Slowly, Anna began the long process of cleaning herself up. She started by untying the silk ribbon and then taking out her hairpins, letting her long blond hair cascade down onto her shoulders. Then, she opened a container of cream and started removing her makeup. Swabbing across the peaks of her high cheekbones, she traced a path down along the smooth curve of her jaw line, dallying for only a moment on her chin before moving on to her thin, dainty mouth and upward toward her nose. This face was her livelihood, was what she used to convey emotion, from fear to sadness, glee to worry. She cleaned her face automatically, watching her movements with her deep green eyes, her thoughts elsewhere.

Anna had always assumed she'd be going out to celebrate, rejoicing in having finally become the leading actress in a play. Even if it was a small production in a run-of-the-mill theater in St. Louis, far from the bright lights of Broadway, playing the lead role was still an accomplishment. But instead of feeling triumph at what she'd done, she instead felt hollow, empty, even a bit disappointed.

"This is what I wanted," she muttered to herself. "So why am I not happy...what's missing...?"

Thinking back on the struggles and heartaches she'd had to endure to escape the hard, squalid life in her mother's apartment back in Chicago, all she'd overcome, Anna was sometimes surprised she'd managed to survive. After that fateful day she'd almost been caught stealing, she'd decided to return to panhandling; begging had seemed a somewhat safer way of making what she'd need to get by. It hadn't been easy, but she'd made do.

But then, one early summer day the following year, she'd had a moment of inspiration; instead of simply standing around looking forlorn, holding out a tin cup and wearing a frown, hoping that some passerby would take pity on her, Anna started singing songs, dancing little routines, or acting out bits of any story she could remember, making up just as many, trying to attract attention. She'd tell jokes, mime whoever happened to be walking past, and offer to read fortunes. With some practice, she even managed a good impression of Chaplin's signature walk, which drew plenty of laughs. At first, she'd been nervous, but with every passing day, with every impromptu performance, she became more and more comfortable. As she did, the amount of money tossed in her cup steadily increased.

Months later, the chill of fall in the air, she'd been standing on a corner across the street from the vaudeville district and the Waxman Theater. It had seen better days; its marquee was missing a few letters here and there, half of the light bulbs were either dead or flickering. Scarcely a night went by when there wasn't at least one drunken brawl in front of the ticket booth. Still, it drew big crowds. Anna serenaded the passing audience with a tune she'd learned by pressing her ear against a nightclub's window.

> *Shoot my man, and catch a cannonball*
> *If he won't have me, he won't have no gal at all*
> *See See Rider, where did you stay last night?*

When she'd finished to a warm round of applause, Anna began picking up the coins tossed onto the sidewalk. She was stuffing them into her pockets as quickly as she could when a man approached her.

Carlton Bleaks had been hired by the Waxman to provide opening acts of entertainment in order to warm up the crowd. He hired singers, jugglers, comedians, animal bits, pie and knife throwers, clowns, performers of every imaginable stripe. He was always in search of something new; it didn't take long for an act to get stale. Months later, he explained to Anna that he'd been watching her from the edge of the crowd while he enjoyed a well-deserved smoke, when he'd had a thought that would change her life forever.

"Oh, what the hell," he muttered to himself, stamping out his still-smoldering cigar beneath the toe of his shoe.

At first, Anna had had her doubts; she'd feared that he was lying, manipulating her in order to lure her into trouble. Trust was not something she gave easily. Still, there was something in her gut that told her to listen. In the end, whatever risks there might have been were outweighed by the rewards; the promise of a meal every night and, most important, more money than she was making on Chicago's streets. Carlton even held out the possibility of her using one of the back rooms in the Waxman as her own. Finally, Anna had accepted his offer.

Now, years later, it was hard for her to believe that that one decision could have had such a profound impact on her life. Everything that had happened to her since had occurred because she'd met Carlton. If not for him, she never would have performed in—

Anna was startled by the sudden sound of knocking on the dressing room's door. Before she could respond, it slowly opened, the hinges loudly squeaking in the silence, and a man's head peeked inside. When he noticed her, he smiled broadly.

"There you are!" he exclaimed enthusiastically. "I was afraid that I'd missed you when the rest of the girls left. Is it all right if I come in?"

Still surprised by the stranger's appearance, Anna struggled to answer. "Yes, I was just...just..." she stammered, stumbling, her hand waving toward her reflection in the mirror, looking at herself as if that other self might be better put together, more collected.

"Excellent!" the man replied, hurrying inside.

The first thing that Anna noticed about her visitor was that he was carrying a bouquet of flowers, at least a dozen roses colored a deep, dark red. He strode toward her confidently, as if there was nothing remotely unusual about his being inside a woman's dressing room. Tall and broad-shouldered, he had dark eyes that sparkled as brightly as his smile. He seemed to be about Anna's age, but the dabs of white that colored the temples of his otherwise coal black hair revealed that he was considerably older. Even as he stopped in front of her chair, Anna had a nagging feeling she'd seen him somewhere before.

"These are for you," he said, holding out the roses. Looking over at her cluttered-yet-flowerless table, he frowned. "Don't tell me that I'm the only person impressed enough to have brought a congratulatory gift? After seeing a performance like I just witnessed, that table should be buried in bouquets!"

"Thank you," Anna replied, taking the flowers while doing her best to stifle the flush of color she felt rising in her cheeks.

"I hope you don't mind my intruding like this," he continued, "but Dwight said it would be all right to knock."

"He did?" Anna asked, surprise in her voice; the mercurial director of *Misery's Company* could be difficult at times, demanding that his actors meet his high expectations, but he was also very protective of them, especially his stars. It seemed remarkable to Anna that he would just let someone wander into her dressing room, especially when he knew she'd be alone.

If only I could remember why he seems so familiar…

The wattage of the man's smile increased. "Well, I assume he wouldn't do it for just *anybody*," he explained with a chuckle, "but we've met a number of times over the years and he understood right away why I was asking."

"And why is that?"

"You don't know?" he asked, looking genuinely surprised.

Growing a bit frustrated at the fact that she was clearly at a disadvantage in their conversation, Anna said flatly, "You haven't even told me your name."

"Now wherever are my manners?" the man asked. Extending his hand, he said, "I'm Samuel Gillen, the head producer for Valentine Pictures out in Hollywood. It's a pleasure to meet you."

Anna felt like a complete fool. As soon as she heard his name, she knew *exactly* where she'd seen his face before; back when Samuel Gillen famously acted in dozens of silent movies, it had been plastered on movie posters, billboards, and on the covers of every gossip rag at the newsstand. Once he'd quit acting, he'd gone on to become one of the most powerful figures in the movie business, making and breaking careers, smashing box office records, and producing films that made Valentine Pictures rich. Anna wanted to apologize for not recognizing him, but instead found herself tongue-tied.

"But what... what are you doing *here*?" was all she could manage.

Samuel laughed out loud. "Isn't it obvious?" he asked. "I want you to be the lead actress in my new movie."

Chapter Two

ONE OF THE FIRST THINGS Anna had learned about a life spent performing on a stage was that it was full of surprises. One time in St. Paul one of the heavy sandbags used as ballast for the curtain suddenly fell, landing with a big crash, exploding no more than three feet from where she stood. On a winter's night in Milwaukee, someone accidentally set fire to the men's restroom, sending thick black smoke billowing through the theater as panicked audience members and performers alike raced for the exits. A year ago, while fighting a bout of the flu, she'd suddenly frozen while on stage in Indianapolis, unable to remember her next line; only after furiously ad-libbing for what felt like hours was she able to recover and go on. She wasn't even safe in her sleep. A couple of months earlier, she'd woken with a start, her chest heaving, shocked by the remnants of a dream in which she'd been on the stage of a packed theater, looking down into the orchestra pit. All of the musicians had been playing their instruments just as expected, but something was still glaringly wrong. The conductor was stark naked! But even with all of those experiences, real or sleep-induced, her time in the theater had never managed to overwhelm or completely dumbfound her.

Until now.

"Your...your movie..." Anna somehow managed, unsure of what she was supposed to say.

"It's going to be my masterpiece!" Samuel exclaimed.

The future suddenly, shockingly danced before Anna. What she knew about Hollywood and the movie-making business was limited, little more than what she'd read about in the gossip magazines and the glitz and glamour she'd watched in the newsreels. The prospect of going there felt unreal, unbelievable, like a dream. "You want me to be in a movie? To go to California...?"

Suddenly, Samuel's smile faded, the thin crease of a frown marring his forehead. "Actually, no," he said. "I don't."

Anna could only stare at him, now more confused than ever; before the flower of her daydream had even been given the time to properly bloom, it had been abruptly cut off at the stem.

"But I thought you said..." she managed.

"What I'm talking about is something completely different," he continued, his earlier enthusiasm returning. "You see, everyone in the movie business always does exactly the same thing. They find a script they like, hire some actors, build whatever sets they need right there on a lot in Hollywood, and start filming. Even I've done it more times than I can count! It works but I've always been left wanting more. Just once, I want to make something real!"

Still dazed, Anna nodded and offered a weak smile.

Samuel kept right on going, his enthusiasm growing so great that he began pacing back and forth in the small dressing room as he talked. "Of course, that showboat Howard Hughes has done location pictures for years, marching around in the desert with his casts of thousands while he fills the skies with his precious planes, but that's because he's got money to burn. What difference does it make to a millionaire like him if he wastes a hundred canisters of film?"

"None . . . ?" Anna answered hesitantly.

"Exactly!" Samuel exclaimed. "No, what I want is something more modest." With his hands, he framed a shot, swiveling his makeshift camera until it focused on Anna. "I'm going to make a picture that transports the audience somewhere they've never been, someplace special. And now, after years of planning and endlessly waiting for the right script, I've finally got it!"

Anna couldn't keep from smiling; his excitement was infectious.

"All this time, I've been missing only one thing," Samuel explained as he resumed his pacing. "I've managed to find the right script, the right location, even the right director, but so far I've never been able to discover the actress who would bring it all to life." He spun quickly on his heel to look right at her, his eyes sparkling. "Until tonight."

Anna knew exactly what Samuel meant; that *she* was the muse he'd been searching for and finally found. But everything still felt so *impossible*, like a fleeting dream. It even occurred to her that this was a joke. Maybe someone thought it would be funny to play a prank on the occasion of her first starring role. But just as soon as she'd had the thought, Anna dismissed it; Samuel Gillen was far too important, far too much of a star to be enticed to travel all the way to some ramshackle theater in St. Louis for the likes of her unless there was good reason. As incredible as it all seemed, it was real. She was being offered the chance of a lifetime.

"You want me to be in your movie?" she asked cautiously, as if by giving such a thought voice, she would cause it to fade away.

"Yes," he answered. "That is exactly what I want."

Anna shook her head, struggling to come to grips with what was happening. "I can't believe you came all the way to St. Louis because of me."

"I didn't," Samuel answered with a laugh.

"But . . . but . . ."

"What I mean is that I didn't come here tonight because I knew *you* would be here," he explained. "I came because of the *hope* of you."

"I don't understand," Anna said with a frown.

"Whenever I've imagined finally making this picture, I've always known that the line of actresses vying for the starring role would be a mile long. Clara Bow, Claudette Colbert, Jean Harlow, Greta Garbo. If any one of them chose to accept the part, it'd mean success. They'd look great on the posters and with their names on the marquees. They'd sell tickets by the tens of thousands and maybe win awards." Samuel paused. "But even with all of that, I'd never consider hiring a one of them."

"But why not?" Anna asked incredulously. "They're all famous!"

"And that's precisely why I won't use them," he explained. "When you see Jean Harlow on the screen, you already know that she's a huge star, you remember her from another movie, something you loved her in, and it transports you out of the movie you are watching, if only for an instant. But I'm not a fool. There need to be some familiar faces in the picture. Audiences love movie stars. That's why I hired Montgomery Bishop and Joan Webb." Anna's eyes widened at the mention of such famous names. "Still, that's not what I want for my lead actress.

"What I've been looking for is a fresh face, a woman who's unknown to the audience. I want them to see the action through *her* eyes, without any of the Hollywood baggage of *who* she is. I don't want them distracted, especially not by the star of the show. And if I have things my way, that actress will be none other than you."

Anna's heart fluttered. "But if you didn't come here tonight because of me, then why *are* you here?"

"Because I got lucky, I suppose." Samuel shrugged.

"Lucky," she repeated.

"From the moment I decided that this was the next picture I was going to make, I've kept my eyes open, searching for just the right girl," he said. "Wherever I traveled, I loitered in train stations, stood on street corners, and sat on park benches in the hope that someone would catch my attention." Laughing, he continued. "If there's one thing I've discovered in my looking, it's that there are plenty of beautiful women to be seen. Heck, they're practically a dime a dozen. But I didn't become as successful as I have in this business without learning that it requires a hell of a lot more than looks to be a star. You need talent. And that's why, no matter what city I'm in, I always stop at the local theaters.

"I've stood in the back of dives in Cleveland and Charleston, Minneapolis and Montgomery, Denver and Davenport, all in the hope that I'd find an undiscovered diamond in the rough. Most every night I go away empty-handed and as disappointed as a panhandler fishing in a played-out stream. But tonight I think I've found her."

"And you think that's me?"

"I do."

"But why?" Anna asked. "What do you see in me?"

"Someone I can believe," Samuel explained. "When you were scared, I worried. When you cried, I hoped you'd find happiness. When you finally discovered what you were looking for, I rejoiced. As I watched, all I could think about was what you would look like up on the silver screen. I think that the audience will find you every bit as genuine as I have."

Anna felt herself blushing. "But what would have happened if I hadn't been to your liking?"

Samuel shrugged. "I would've gone on to the next town carrying my dwindling hopes along like a hobo's satchel," he explained. "Maybe I would've had better luck in Tulsa or somewhere else down the line. Maybe not," he added, smiling mischievously. "If I hadn't discovered someone to my liking, I could always have picked up the phone and called Garbo's representatives. Either way, I would've had to make a decision soon."

"Why?"

"Because shooting starts in a little more than a month," Samuel answered. "That doesn't leave a lot of time."

Anna agreed. She'd thought that there would be time to consider the movie producer's offer and that, even *if* she accepted, there would be weeks spent in poring over the script, meeting with her costars, and getting fitted for her wardrobe, all things she assumed were similar to the preparations that went into putting on a play. From what Samuel was saying, things would be rushed.

"It sounds like you're cutting things awfully close," she said.

"Don't worry," he assured her. "There's still plenty of time to get you where you need to be. I have people at Valentine Pictures working to make sure everything will be in its proper place by the time you get off the train down in Texas."

"Texas?" Anna repeated, wide-eyed.

"It's a location picture, remember?" Samuel explained. "We've practically taken over this town called Redstone near the Mexican border."

"I've never heard of it."

"No one has. That's why it'll be perfect. As authentic as it gets."

Anna fell silent. Her head was spinning. Looking around the Cooper Theater's cramped dressing room, she imagined what it would be like to walk away from it all, to turn her back on all that she'd worked for just as soon as she'd achieved success. But could she really turn down such an unbelievable offer? If she didn't take it, would she regret her decision for the rest of her life?

"You still haven't made up your mind, have you?" Samuel asked suddenly.

"It's such a big decision..."

The movie producer leaned against the edge of Anna's changing table, took a deep breath, and turned to her while flashing his ten-thousand-watt smile. "I'm not about to tell you what to do, but I can give you some advice," he said. "When I was an actor, I was considered to be something of a risk-taker. I took roles that challenged me, some that didn't put me in the best light or even those that paid less but seemed interesting. Now that I'm a producer, I've taken my share of chances and had plenty of flops to show for them, movies I expected to be successes but weren't. I've squandered money and fame but even if I had the chance to go back and make different choices, I wouldn't."

"Why not?" Anna asked.

"Because life is a journey down a long, winding river," Samuel explained. "Sometimes, you just have to let the current take you where it will."

And, just like that, Anna made up her mind.

* * *

Anna took a step back, folded her arms across her chest, and looked at the belongings she'd packed into her steamer trunk. She frowned; it certainly didn't amount to much, little more than what passed for her wardrobe and a few mementos she'd picked up over the years since she'd left Chicago. She'd considered her clothing stylish, if a little thrifty, but she suddenly worried that it would be laughably shabby by Hollywood standards. The luggage was just as worn as what was in it; she had purchased the trunk from a fellow actor and it showed every one of the many miles it had traveled, with deep chips and gouges marring the surface; it had one clasp that was always popping loose. Tomorrow, it would be on its way to Texas, and so would she.

I'm going to be in a movie!

Outside, darkness had fallen. Laughter and shouts mingled with honking car horns, the hustle and bustle of a city that never slept, the sounds rising up and through the window of her tiny apartment. Light from her lamp, another hand-me-down, cast dark shadows dancing across the walls.

Even now, almost a month since there'd been that fateful knock on the door to her dressing room, Anna couldn't believe all that had happened.

Glancing over at the clock, Anna saw the time and startled, her heart pounding. If Samuel Gillen hadn't entered her life and made his incredible offer, she would have been on the stage of the Cooper Theater at that very moment, screaming as Peter chased her with the knife, laughing maniacally. She would have been reveling in her newfound stage stardom, earning a standing ovation from the audience, maybe even making plans to take Marnie and the other girls up on their offer of a night on the town to celebrate. Instead, she was about to turn her back on everything she'd worked for.

But it was a decision she'd made willingly.

Listening to Samuel talk about the chances he'd taken, as well as the successes that had come with them, had been the final push she'd needed. He was right; when opportunity knocked, she owed it to herself to answer the door. Whatever happened next, she had started the ball rolling. Even if she failed, it was still better than spending the rest of her life wondering what would have happened.

Of course, Samuel had been delighted that she'd accepted, his eyes practically glowing, his smile as bright as a spotlight's beam. He'd then rushed off to tell the news to Dwight Wirtz, Anna's director, and to make the necessary arrangements for her to leave the production. When he returned twenty minutes later, still smiling, she hadn't moved from her chair, had done nothing but stare in a daze at her own reflection.

Until that very moment Anna had not realized something important; in all of the craziness since Samuel had knocked on the door, she'd yet to ask him what his dream production, the very movie she'd just agreed to travel hundreds of miles to star in, was called.

Laughing, he answered, "*The Talons of the Hawk.*"

She liked it right away.

"You're going to be perfect," he added with a wink.

Since that day, Anna had been getting ready for her new career. Rather than traveling to Hollywood, Samuel had brought the movie business to her; his explanation for keeping her out of the public eye was that he wanted to be able to reveal her at a time of his choosing, one that would most benefit the picture. So the Valentine Pictures photographers traveled to St. Louis to take her picture for publicity stills. Makeup artists daubed her with different shades of color, searching for just the right look. The wardrobe department fitted her with outfit after outfit, standing back to admire her as if she were a mannequin in a store window.

Through it all, Samuel traveled in and out of town, smiling his approval and frowning his dislike at different stages.

Anna had yet to see an actual copy of the script. Whenever she asked, Samuel gave her another of his bright smiles and promised that he'd eventually get her a copy, explaining that his writer was not only brilliant, but a perfectionist who was always making changes. He said that it was a story of romance, of intrigue and adventure, and that she would need each and every one of the emotions he'd seen her portray on stage in order to pull it off.

As they neared their date of departure, Samuel promised to take care of everything. From the train tickets to the taxi ride to the station, the only thing Anna had to concern herself with was packing her things. Bright and early, she'd be headed to Texas, to the site of Valentine Pictures' latest feature film, off on the greatest adventure of her life. And it was for that very reason that she was having trouble quieting the storm brewing in her chest, weighing her down, filling her with both fear and exhilaration.

"This is what you always wanted," she muttered, turning back to her packing. "You're going to be a star."

Anna stepped out of the taxi and onto the sidewalk in front of Union Station, shutting the door behind her. People hurried in every direction, travelers embarking on their voyages mixing with those just arrived, enthusiastically greeting loved ones. Newspaper men and street vendors hawked their wares. An elderly woman panhandled before the station's enormous doors, her eyes flashing expectantly from face to face, filled with a small thimble of hope that seemed to diminish with every second Anna watched.

Not that many years ago, I would've been standing there...

After Samuel hailed a porter to help them move their baggage to their waiting train, they headed inside the station; on her way past, Anna slipped the old woman a couple of coins. Even though Anna had been in Union Station a dozen times over the course of her acting travels, her eyes were still drawn to the familiar sights. The high, vaulted ceiling was decorated with thousands of ornate tiles. Cascading staircases rose high, leading to other concourses. Looking over her shoulder, Anna marveled at the huge stained-glass window above the doors that sunlight spilled through, sending colors dancing over everything it touched. The sounds of her shoes click-clacking on the marble floor joined the hundreds of other noises echoing around the enormous space.

"Nervous?" Samuel asked, giving her his easy smile.

"A bit," Anna admitted. "I suppose I'm still having a hard time believing that all of this is actually happening."

"Don't worry," the movie producer said with a short laugh. "It'll take us a couple of days to make it all the way to Redstone. You should have more than enough time to put it all in its proper place."

Traveling the length of the Midway, they finally arrived at their platform. The train was already there, its imposing engine black as night, an occasional puff of smoke billowing from its stack. Anna wondered if, when she had become a star, there would be throngs of people coming to see her off, reporters' bulbs flashing while fans asked for her autograph.

Maybe someday, she thought.

Samuel extended Anna a hand to help her on board, then led the way down a long corridor, finally stopping at the open doorway to her compartment in the sleeping car.

"I know it's hardly a room at the Ritz-Carlton," he said with a grin, "but I hope it will be enough to make you feel comfortable."

The space was more than she'd expected. With a raised bed, a small lavatory, a table with two chairs, all framed by a curtained window that looked out on the bustling station, it was certainly better than any rail car she'd ever ridden in before; when she'd traveled for a play, Anna always considered herself lucky if there were only four girls wedged into a space intended for two.

"It's perfect," she replied.

"Then I'll leave you to get settled while I take a quick look around," Samuel said.

Alone in the room, Anna began putting away some of her belongings, but her attention soon wandered. Pulling the curtains open as far as they would go, she watched as late-arriving passengers raced past her window, running down the platform so as not to be late. Suddenly, the train's shrill whistle blew. The conductor pulled out his pocket watch, nodded at the time, and boarded. There was a gentle shuddering, and then Anna could feel the train start to move, and like her life gaining speed with every second.

In a matter of a couple of weeks, everything in her life had suddenly, shockingly changed. Leaving the play, giving up all that she had worked so hard for, was a risk, an undeniable one, but even though she was nervous, Anna knew that it was time for her to stop looking backward. Instead, she needed to concentrate on what lay ahead. She wanted to be the best actress she could be, to prove that Samuel's faith in her wasn't misplaced. It was time to become the star she'd always dreamed of being.

Her journey had begun.

Chapter Three

ANNA HAD JUST put away the last of her belongings when there was a soft knock on the door. Samuel had returned, but this time, he wasn't alone. A short, heavyset, balding man stood beside him, beads of sweat dotting his ample forehead and the roll of his double chin. He looked at her with a smile as he pushed his enormous glasses farther up his beak of a nose. He clutched a thick sheaf of papers against his wrinkled suit coat.

"I'd like you to meet Jonathan Willoughby, one of the people most responsible for making my dream so close to coming true," Samuel said, introducing the man. "Jonathan, this is Anna Finnegan, the girl I told you about on the telephone."

"How do you do?" Anna said, taking his offered hand.

"It's a pleasure to meet you," Jonathan answered. Glancing over at Samuel, he added, "She certainly looks the part."

"That she does."

"I can see it in her eyes," the other man said, staring intently at Anna. "There's something there that speaks of Claire."

Seeing the confusion in Anna's face, Samuel said, "Claire is the name of the character you'll be playing."

"Oh," Anna replied, suddenly happy that she'd unintentionally pleased them. "Then I'm happy you think I look like her."

Jonathan stepped farther into the room, stopping just in front of Anna. Reaching up, he took hold of several strands of the blond hair that cascaded down and over her shoulders. He held it carefully, lifting it up and turning it this way and that, looking at it in the sunlight pouring through the window like a seamstress regarding new material for a dress. Anna didn't find it the least bit uncomfortable; she'd been looked at that way many times before by play directors thinking of casting her for a part. Finally satisfied, Jonathan let go of her hair and stepped back, smiling broadly.

"Everything about you is perfect, my dear," he exclaimed. "You're exactly like who I wrote you to be."

"You wrote the movie's script?" she asked.

"But of course!"

"Jonathan is the very best of the best," Samuel explained. "Everything that rolls off his typewriter is sure to be a hit and win an award or two. I've been trying to get him to work for Valentine Pictures for years."

"I've been busy." Jonathan shrugged.

"What matters now is that he wrote the script for *our* movie," Samuel said, walking over and taking the pile of papers from the writer's hands. "This is everything I've ever wanted in a script and more." He held it out for Anna. "Once you've had a chance to read it, I know you'll feel the same."

Anna took the papers. There on the top page, with Jonathan's name beneath it, was the movie's title.

The Talons of the Hawk.

"We'll leave you to your reading," Samuel said, smiling.

They were at the door, ready to step out into the hallway, when Jonathan paused. Looking back, he said, "I can't wait to hear what you think of it."

"I'm sure I'll love it," Anna answered.

"Just lie to me if you don't." He winked, shutting the door behind him.

Alone, Anna sat down at the table beside the window, glanced out at the dwindling buildings whizzing past on the outskirts of St. Louis, took a deep breath, and turned the first page. It held a synopsis of the plot.

The Talons of the Hawk told the story of Claire Hawkins, a young woman struggling to make ends meet in the rough-and-tumble town of Macalister in rural Texas, just north of the Mexican border. The year is 1895 and the land is unforgiving, particularly for the Hawkins family. Having lost her mother in childbirth, Claire had been raised by her father, Walter, the town's blacksmith, an alcoholic. Year after year, she'd somehow managed to make ends meet by scrimping and saving, only leaning on the benevolence of the church when things got particularly tough. A beautiful girl with long, blond hair, Claire had her share of suitors, the most persistent of whom was Cornelius Baines, the son of Macalister's banker and the richest man in town, but in her heart Claire knew that she'd only be a possession to him, something that was hard to get but, once had, would be quickly discarded in favor of the next bauble to catch his eye. She said "no," even though by saying "yes" she would improve her and her father's lot in life. No, what she yearned for was *real* change, for things to get better without her having to sacrifice her pride, and to meet a man who might take her away from all of her suffering and fill her heart with love.

What she never expected was *where* such a man might come from.

Life along the border is a constant struggle. With the ever-present fear of both crippling droughts and flash floods, combined with the daily worries of rattlesnake bites and illness, danger was everywhere. But the biggest threat to the people of Macalister are the hordes of bandits who roam across the Rio Grande, stealing whatever they can get their hands on. Rumors of a new leader, a mysterious figure who went by the name of El Halcón, the Hawk, a man determined to take all he can from the despised Americans, descend upon the town like a swarm of locusts. But Claire pays the chatter little mind; she has plenty of concerns of her own.

Until one fateful night...

Without warning, the bandits strike! Out of the cover

of darkness, flaming torches race past the windows of the Hawkinses' meager home. Gunshots and shouts split the silence of the night! It is terrifying. But the men of Macalister refuse to let themselves be attacked without returning the fight, rising in their nightshirts to return fire. Claire watches it all, panic-stricken, until suddenly the window she stands before explodes into shards of glass. Scared out of her mind, she does the only thing that makes any sense to her; she runs blindly into the darkness, away from her father, away from the only home she'd ever known, away from the men who have come to terrorize. Claire has no idea how long she runs, how far she has come, but when she finally stops, her chest heaving and her legs burning, she is surprised to find a lone horse standing before her in the moonlight, its midnight-black coat shining bright as it snorts and whinnies, pawing at the ground with its hooves.

But what truly shocks Claire is that a man is slumped across the horse's broad back.

Though she is still frightened, Claire musters her courage and approaches the horse. When the man sees her, he hisses through clenched teeth as he clings tightly to the horse's mane, blood streaming from a bullet wound in his shoulder. He regards her with hard eyes, as if he expects her to pull out a gun and finish him off. Instead, Claire rushes to his side, her earlier fear forgotten. Up close to him, their eyes only inches apart, Claire feels a spark suddenly ignite in her chest; even in the inky darkness, Claire sees clearly enough to know that he is the handsomest man she's ever met. Knowing that he needs medical attention, and without any regard for her own safety, she does the only thing she feels she can.

She guides the horse carrying the wounded stranger back to Macalister.

What follows over the course of the next few days will forever change the path of both their lives. Beginning with the gruesome task of digging the fragments of the bullet out of his shoulder, the stranger refusing to scream, his eyes remaining on Claire at all times, she soon discovers that he is really El Halcón, the leader of the bandits. He tells her that the reason he and his men had attacked Macalister was in retaliation for raids being led against their own people, vicious acts orchestrated by none other than Cornelius Baines, all in an effort to gain access to mineral deposits he hopes to sell for an enormous profit. But what is even more shocking is the way her heart flutters uncontrollably whenever she is near him, the way his voice sings in her ears. When his eyes search her face as if she were a priceless work of art in a museum, she begins to understand that El Halcón might feel the same way about her. Then, in the light of the last embers of the fireplace, he kisses her, and she has no more doubts.

But, after they are almost found out by Margaret Woermer, Macalister's biggest snoop and gossip, the night comes when El Halcón has to leave her. Despite her objections, he insists that he has to try to get across the border and put a stop to the war between their two peoples. Standing in the doorway, the moon framing his face, he holds her in his arms and makes her a promise, one born out of love, that they will be together someday, somehow, no matter what it takes. Even as he vanishes into the night, Claire can still feel his lips against hers.

A week passes, but nothing happens. Claire has begun to worry that he hasn't made it home, that she's been a fool to let him go off to his death, his remains to be picked over by buzzards somewhere in the sandy scrum, when suddenly the afternoon is split by the sound of gunfire high on the ridge south of town. Claire knows who it is. Running as fast as she can, her heart pounding, the air whizzing with bullets, Claire throws herself into the midst of the gun battle, trying desperately to stop the men. Racing straight for El Halcón, the man she's come to love, she throws up her arms and closes her eyes, expecting the next bullet to pierce her heart. But it never comes. Instead, she falls into the bandit's arms as silence descends on the ridge. Opening her eyes, Claire watches as bandits and townspeople alike lower their guns, surprised by what they have just witnessed. As tears roll down her cheeks, the desert breeze stirring her blond hair, she knows that everyone is watching her.

"I didn't want you to be hurt," she says.

The bandit leader smiles. "I promised you that we would be together," he says softly, whispering into her ear. "And I always keep my promises."

In the end, it is their unexpected love that brings an end to the conflict between their people, that brings them all together, and creates the flame that burns in her heart.

* * *

Anna turned over the last page of the synopsis, the train car swaying slightly as it rolled along the rails. She'd been enthralled by every word she'd read. The story was captivating, full of action, suffering, and forbidden romance. She could see herself as Claire, becoming the character in a way that would be believable to the audience. It would be hard work, a challenge unlike any she'd faced before, but Anna had confidence in her abilities as an actress.

She would *become* Claire Hawkins.

Starting from the beginning, she read the actual script. Claire's true character began to shine through, making Anna giddy with anticipation. Memorizing a few lines, she began to act scenes out, moving her hands and working on her facial expressions.

Later that night, sitting in the dining car, sharing a meal with both Samuel and his writer, she told them how much she'd enjoyed the script, how excited she was to try to bring Claire to life, and how she couldn't wait to get started with filming. Both men smiled broadly, clearly pleased with her enthusiasm.

Day darkened into night and then slowly brightened back into day. Anna spent her time reading and rereading the script, memorizing her lines and acting out important scenes in the small window of her train car. Bit by bit, Claire came into clearer focus. She ate her meals with Samuel and Jonathan, asking them about their experiences in the movie business, still amazed that she was having some of her own.

Outside the train's windows, the landscape sped by, slowly growing unfamiliar. Anna had spent her whole life in cities like Chicago and St. Louis, traveling only from performance to performance. Still, she'd never left the Midwest. She was used to broad lakes, thick stands of tall trees, with towns sprinkled in among the rolling hills; a lush greenness in spring and summer that turned into a kaleidoscope of colors in fall and a blanket of snow in winter.

But when she went to sleep the night before they crossed over into Oklahoma, she woke to find the landscape outside her window so changed it was almost unrecognizable. The soil was no longer black but red, spotted here and there with stingy clumps of dry grass. A creek trickled along under the already blazing morning sun, running with so little water that Anna wondered if she could even fill a cup. Herds of steers, their enormous horns caked with dust, lazily lifted their heads as the train raced past.

It was only then, realizing that she was so very far from familiar surroundings, that Anna truly began to feel nervous. Questions began to gnaw at her. *What if I forget my lines? What if the director hates me? Would Samuel be so disappointed that he'd regret choosing me? What if I ruin the movie?* Feeling completely panic-stricken, the only thing Anna could do to quiet the fluttering of her heart was to go back to studying her lines.

The next morning, Anna woke just as the sun was beginning to peek over the horizon, its light beginning to bruise the few drifting clouds black against an otherwise clear sky. Outside her window was Texas, a land she'd only read about. Because of the sun's position, she understood that sometime during the night, the train had turned toward the west. Redstone was located in the far southwestern part of the state, just along the border. The nearest city was El Paso, but Samuel had assured her that where they were going was completely isolated from civilization; from the desolate view outside her window, Anna knew that the producer had been telling the truth.

For the next couple of hours, all Anna could do was watch the barren landscape, captivated. Towns drifted by like pieces of wood bobbing on the surface of a river. Names blurred, one after the other; Marietta, Simon, Los Rios, Muddy Creek, Marathon. Even when they made an occasional stop, she never saw anyone get on or off the train.

Shortly after noon, the engine gave two shrill whistles and Anna felt the train begin to slow. Samuel appeared in her doorway.

"This is it," he said with a smile, excited that they were finally arriving. "I don't know about you, but I'll be glad to get off this train!"

Samuel joined her at the window and together they watched as Redstone came into view. At first, there was only a scattering of houses, long ranches built of wood, each of them surrounded by a fenced-in corral in which horses and cows swatted their tails at irritating flies. Occasionally there was a barn; at one, a woman was reaching into a chicken coop, gathering eggs, but when she saw the train, she stopped and waved; reflexively, Anna waved back. The landscape here was hilly, but the train began to descend a slow rise, and the ground leveled. Shriveled trees mixed with stunted cactus and wildflowers, their bright yellows and purples in stark contrast to the dark ground.

"Pretty land, isn't it?" Samuel said.

Anna nodded. "I've never seen anything like it," she answered.

"That's why people will love it on the screen."

"Have you been here before?"

"I paid my first visit a couple of months ago, back when we were out scouting for just the right location," Samuel explained. "There were other towns we liked, but I took one look and knew this place was perfect."

"It looks like one of those places you see on newsreels where people are barely making do."

"That's Redstone," he answered. "It's out here in the middle of nowhere without any industry or any other reason for people to visit. Without ranching, I have no idea how they'd make it. Most of the town is struggling mightily to make ends meet."

"It doesn't matter where you live," Anna replied, thinking about the troubles she'd faced nearly every day of her young life. "There's evidence of that problem everywhere you turn."

As the train's speed slowed further, more and more buildings began to appear. Houses lined meager streets, many of them with sagging porches, weathered boards, and people looking just as beaten down. The rail line passed to the north of the main part of Redstone, offering only a quick glimpse of its Main Street; there were businesses Anna recognized, a hardware store, a bakery, a blacksmith, and a barbershop, but they all looked run-down, as if they were on the verge of closing. Just off the tracks, a lone dog howled, full-throated and loud, welcoming them to town. It was hard to believe that somewhere out there, waiting for her to arrive, were famous people like Joan Webb and Montgomery Bishop. Anna didn't know what she had expected to see, but there was something about the place that surprised her nonetheless.

Unlike the rest of Redstone, the train station was buzzing with activity. Porters stood at the ready to unload baggage, while men and women waved expectantly with notebooks poised. There was even a photographer set up next to the depot. Anna realized that they were all there because of the movie, because the film's producer was on board and, to some extent, they were also there for *her*.

"Don't worry about your things," Samuel told her, placing a warm, comforting hand on her shoulder. "They'll be taken to where you'll be staying. As you can see, we've been expected."

As if she were in a trance, Anna followed Samuel down the hallway of the passenger car and toward the exit to the platform. Jonathan Willoughby exited ahead of them and was practically swallowed up by the throng of people.

Sensing her unease, Samuel stopped just before the door and turned to her. "Whatever worries you're feeling right now, just put them away," he said. "Regardless of what anyone else might say, *you belong here* and are going to absolutely dazzle up on the screen. Trust me," he added with a smile. "I've been doing this long enough to know a star when I see one."

With that, Samuel stepped out onto the platform and immediately, dozens of voices began shouting his name, holding bundles of paper in the air, everyone vying for his attention. It was as if Clark Gable himself had disembarked. The camera's bulb flashed, blindingly bright even in the sunny afternoon. Through it all, Samuel smiled confidently.

Anna took a moment to compose herself, repeating Samuel's words of encouragement over and over in her head. She tried telling herself this was just like being on stage, another performance in which she had to play a part, recite dialogue, and win over the crowd. *You can do this!* What happened next would place her on the path to stardom, not just in a down-on-its-luck theater, but Hollywood, in the movies, her name in lights and on the lips of thousands of people. Taking a deep breath to steady herself, Anna stepped from the train.

But she'd no more than put both feet on the platform when a man's voice thundered loud in her ear.

"Look out, lady!"

Before there was even time to turn her head, Anna was suddenly, unexpectedly struck in the side. The blow was so hard that she winced in pain as she was lifted from her feet and sent crashing to the ground.

Chapter Four

DALTON BARNES PAUSED beneath the bank awning, tipped back his worn cowboy hat, and wiped the sweat from his brow, loosening a lock of his unruly black hair that had become stuck to his forehead. The day was already a scorcher, just like the day before and the one preceding. Waves of heat shimmered off the road and the light reflected off the storefront windows was blinding. The faint breeze that blew did little to cool the blazing afternoon, stirring up a chalky dust that stung his eyes. With a heavy sigh, he walked on.

"Damn it all," he muttered to himself.

The heat wasn't the only thing making Dalton uncomfortable; he was both disturbed and confused by the small amount of money he'd just deposited. Ever since the movie people had come to town, his family's blacksmith shop had been booming, along with most every other business in Redstone, a welcome respite in trying times; it seemed there was no end to the things they needed, the items requiring repair, or the contraptions that they were tasked with inventing. The work forge was lit morning, noon, and night. Dalton's hands were covered in a tapestry of tiny nicks and burns, and were heavy with calluses. Things had gotten so hectic that there'd even been talk of hiring on another man to meet the orders.

But if business is booming, then why do we have so little to show for it? Where did all of the money go?

Deep down in the pit of his stomach, Dalton knew the answer to both questions, and it made him sick to his stomach.

George Barnes was many things: a man who knew the meaning of a hard day's work; had a good sense of humor; was a regular churchgoer; abstained from tobacco and alcohol; and loved his family. But Dalton knew well that his father wasn't without a vice; in fact, his was so bad that it threatened to destroy the ship his family's fortunes sailed upon, with George down in the boat's hold, drilling the hole that would sink it. His father had an itch that he couldn't keep from scratching.

George was addicted to gambling.

It made no difference if it was the spin of a roulette table's wheel on a riverboat, a hand of cards in the back of a seedy bar, or picking which horse would run the fastest around a well-trodden racetrack, George was drawn to the intoxicating thrill of chance as surely as a moth to an open flame. No bet was too big, no risk too great. Twice, he had nearly succeeded in his hell-bent quest for ruin, a catastrophic loss of everything he owned, a result that would have left him and his family out on the street with little more than the clothes on their backs. But somehow, he'd managed to hold on through charity and a minor stroke of the luck that so often failed him when his wager needed it most.

Every time he inched away from the precipice, he swore that he'd learned his lesson, that he'd never take such foolish risks again. And, for a while at least, he would be true to his word. But then the itch would strike again. It never took long, a month or two at most, and George would start making excuses about having to travel to Marathon or El Grande on business. Or one moonless night he'd step out for a walk and Dalton would hear him slinking back into the house just before dawn. When confronted, he'd either be evasive, lie through his teeth, or admit what he'd done and immediately turn defensive, insisting that this time was different, that he had it under control.

Dalton knew better.

Through it all, Betty Barnes, Dalton's mother, stood by her husband no matter what hell he brought down on them. Regardless of how angry Dalton became, or how often George disappointed, she was always willing to believe his promises and offer forgiveness. Still, her son noticed the wrinkles of worry that lined her face, the way her hair had turned prematurely gray, and how her jaw clenched tight when he told her there was far less money than expected. If she let him, her husband would destroy all they'd struggled to build.

Dalton knew it didn't have to be this way. All of the business the movie people brought with them should have signaled the end of all their problems, an opportunity to pay back all they'd borrowed over the years, even a chance to squirrel enough away to make ends meet when everyone went back to Hollywood and the tough times returned. But what if this was the calm before the storm? What if his father couldn't resist the temptation of the money that had unexpectedly found its way into his pocket?

What if the bank comes calling? Or worse, what if he owes money to that no-good son-of-a-bitch Vernon Black and his flunkies?

What then?

Dalton frowned as he neared the Stagecoach Hotel, crossing the street well before reaching it in order to give it a wide berth. Even at the hottest hour of the day, movie people milled about, talking or smoking out on the long wrap-around porch. Occasional snippets of conversation and laughter drifted toward him.

"Once the cameras start rolling, we can—"

" . . . still think that the third costume we tried looked the best."

. " . . . be up half the night building sets, but . . ."

Though plenty of Valentine Pictures money had been spent at the blacksmithing business, Dalton knew that Curtis Grohl, the hotel's owner, was one of the happiest people in Redstone about their new visitors; his building was overflowing with paying customers. There'd even been some talk about constructing an addition to overcome the shortage of rooms, but then the good townspeople had starting opening their own homes . . . for a fee, of course.

"Anything for money," Dalton muttered angrily.

While it was hard to imagine now, there had been a time when Dalton had loved everything about motion pictures. When he was a boy, he'd looked forward to accompanying his father on his monthly drive to Marathon. As George bought and bartered for what he needed, or stopped off for a quick game of cards, Dalton used to sit in the Pine Theater, mesmerized by the silent images flickering across the screen. As the piano accompaniment soared, he'd marveled at the daring of Rudolph Valentino, the hilarious antics of Charlie Chaplin and Harold Lloyd, as well as the beauty of Mary Pickford and Lillian Gish. He used to fantasize about being up there himself, running along the roof of a moving train, kicking down the door of a burning building, and even getting the girl in the end.

But now, both older and wiser, he saw it for what it was; a sham. What happened up on the screen was fantasy, no different from the fairy tales his mother had read to him when he was a child. The movies, despite the added realism of sound, had nothing to do with the day-to-day struggles he faced in Redstone. They could never accurately portray the painful rumbling of an empty stomach, the disappointment he felt when his father lied to his face, or the reproachful look in the eye of the banker he'd just left, wondering whether he was ever going to be repaid. In the movies, the bad guy always got what was coming to him, the lovers always found a way into each other's arms, and everyone walked out of the theater with a smile.

What a load of manure!

When Valentine Pictures had first come to town, Dalton soon came to understand that the people who made the movies were every bit as disconnected from reality as the product they filmed. From the moment they disembarked from the train, he'd seen plenty of sneers of disapproval. Immediately they began to make unrealistic demands, wanting things done far faster than could have ever been expected. When the director and the head of set construction came to the blacksmith shop, Dalton had tried to reason with them, to make them comprehend how quickly he and his father worked, but he'd been scoffed at, threatened that, if they didn't fill orders on time, the studio would bring in someone who could. The worst part was that everyone in town desperately needed the money and therefore went above and beyond to please their new guests. It sickened Dalton, but he also had no choice but to comply.

Another of Dalton's complaints about the Hollywood people was their softness. Over and over, he'd heard them grumble about Texas, about the unrelenting heat, the food, their accommodations, anything and everything. He had watched them saunter out of the hotel on a day just like this one and come to a sudden stop, one hand shielding their eyes as they gazed up at the noonday sun, sweat glistening on their skin, paralyzed by the oppressive warmth. After a moment, they'd stagger back under the fans inside, showing about as many brains as a cow seeking a tree's shade. Sure, some of them were nice enough, willing to make small talk here and there, but most of these out-of-towners were so full of themselves, already counting down the days until they could leave this desolate, godforsaken excuse for a town, that they couldn't be bothered to give the local people the time of day.

Which suited him just fine.

Before he reached the hotel, Dalton heard the shrill whistle of the afternoon train as it pulled into town. No doubt, it was full of movie people; more annoying Hollywood folk seemed to arrive each day. Unfortunately, his family's shop was located just across the railroad tracks from where he stood. If he was going to avoid dealing with the crush at the depot, he'd have to hurry.

Quickening his stride, Dalton ducked into an alley between the mercantile and bakery, a shortcut he'd used many times before. The shade cooled him, a welcome respite from the oppressive heat as he picked his way through old, weathered crates and a pile of discarded milk bottles. He was practicing the conversation he already dreaded having with his father, piecing the words together in his head, trying to control his rising temper, when a voice spoke from the opposite end of the alley.

"Gonna have a word with you, boy."

Dalton froze. Even in the gloom of the alley, he recognized the wiry, muscular build and stringy hair of the man before him. Creed Cobb meant trouble. For as long as Dalton could remember, his parents had warned him to avoid reckless, hard men like Creed, a thug who had been in and out of jail, who'd been accused of burglary, arson, assault, and worse, and who had been a blight on Redstone since the first day he'd set foot in town. Even now, pushing forty, he was still as dangerous as ever, a rabid dog looking for a leg to bite.

Creed pushed off the wall against which he'd been leaning and took a couple of steps closer, his narrow eyes unreadable.

"I'm not looking for any trouble," Dalton said.

"I ain't never said I was bringin' you any," Creed said with a flat, threatening chuckle. "Did I, Audie?"

Dalton looked back over his shoulder at the mention of Creed's brother. Behind him, lumbering into sight, was Audie Cobb, as tall and wide across the shoulders as a doorframe, stronger than an ox and not a whole lot smarter. Quite a few folks in Redstone thought Audie was a gentle soul, someone who would've been pleasant to be around if it wasn't for the corrupting influence of his brother. For better or more certainly worse, the two were inseparable. Creed had coaxed, threatened, and shamed Audie into taking part in his robberies, ordered him to beat people to within an inch of their lives, and even left him to take the fall for schemes that had gone bad. Dalton felt like a fool; he should've known that wherever Creed lurked, Audie was sure to follow.

"Nope," Audie answered simply.

"But that don't mean you ain't gonna get some," Creed said with a grin that made Dalton's blood run cold.

The alley wasn't narrow but it was cluttered; boxes and trash and who knew what else in the darkness. Making a run for it would be risky; if he tripped... Shouting wouldn't do him much good, either; even *if* there was someone out in the heat, it wasn't likely that anyone would be brave enough to come down the darkened alley to help him.

Dalton knew that the only way he could get by the two thugs was by using his fists.

"I haven't done anything to you," he said, trying to buy some time and figure out what he was going to do.

"Ain't got much to do with you," Creed answered simply.

"Then why?"

"'Cause Mr. Black said so."

"Mr. Black," Audie echoed, sounding like he'd moved closer.

Redstone wasn't much, a town of only nine hundred when it wasn't swamped by movie people, but in some ways it wasn't that different from a city like San Francisco or New York; they each had their own fat cats, too. In Redstone, Vernon Black was the man who took advantage of the less fortunate, offering loans at ridiculous rates of interest, bringing in liquor during Prohibition to sell illegally in his tavern, all while owning most every building in town. For anyone unlucky enough to get on his bad side, he sent goons like Creed and Audie Cobb to collect, with the broken arm or chipped tooth they left behind an effective deterrent to anyone else thinking about reneging on their debt.

Still, it didn't explain why they were after Dalton.

"I don't have anything to do with Vernon Black," he said.

"You ain't listenin' to what I'm sayin'," Creed replied. "See, when a man likes to gamble the way your old man does, there usually comes a time when he ain't got the money he'd like, so he has to borrow it."

"No," Dalton hissed through clenched teeth.

"When that happens," Creed continued, "he's expected to pay it back just as he promised. When he don't, well, then there's consequences."

"Con...quences..." Audie mumbled.

Even as the two men spoke, Dalton struggled to come to grips with what had been said. His earlier suspicion that his father had taken money from the till seemed to be just the beginning of the problem. It shocked Dalton to think that gambling had such a hold on George Barnes that he'd borrow from a snake like Vernon Black. Once a man got in deep with Vernon, he'd never get free, not completely. He'd be sucked dry, as if he had a bloodthirsty leech stuck to his belly. And now, in order to make an impression, George's own son was set up to serve as an example.

Creed ambled over and stopped an arm's length from Dalton. "Most times, Mr. Black'd go right to the source a his problems," he explained. "But sometimes a message is heard clearer if it's given to someone else, someone who matters to who done the borrowin'. It helps 'em make up their minds 'bout repayin' what they owe. Hurries it up."

"And that example is me," Dalton said, not really asking.

Creed nodded as Audie chuckled.

"How much does my father owe?"

Creed shrugged. "We got to this point, it don't matter much."

Now it was Dalton's turn to nod. Clearly, the time for talking had ended. It was no longer a matter for flight, but for fight. Slowly, he prepared himself, tightening his fist as he looked for just the right moment.

"Don't take it personal," Creed said with a grin. "We just gotta—"

Before Vernon Black's thug could say another word, Dalton struck. His punch slammed hard into the side of Creed's jaw, the man's smile instantly transformed into a look of shock, as his head snapped hard to the side and his knees wobbled. The sound filled the confined alleyway, as sharply as a gunshot. Creed's eyes widened further as Dalton's second blow struck his stomach, forcing the air to whoosh from his lungs. This time, he couldn't remain upright, plummeting facedown into the dirt.

Dalton had hoped that the suddenness of his attack would give him an advantage against both men, but when he turned to face Audie, a fist that loomed as big as a side of beef clipped the end of his chin and sent him careening backward. Almost immediately, his vision swam and the ground became unsteady beneath his feet. Audie gave him no respite, landing a clubbing blow against his shoulders that knocked him to the ground.

"Hurt my brother!" he roared.

Even as he struggled to tell up from down and right from left, Dalton knew he'd have to act quickly to keep from getting the beating intended for him; undoubtedly, it would be even worse for what he'd done to Creed.

Audie stood above him, shaking with rage. Just as the man bent down, reaching for him, Dalton lashed out, kicking his much-larger attacker squarely in the knee as hard as he could. With an audible crack, the leg shifted inward, as a deafening howl filled the alley. Audie grabbed hold of his leg with both hands as he fell backward, crashing to the ground like a tree felled in the forest.

Dalton rose to his feet, his head still a bit muddled; he almost fell back down when he retrieved his hat from where it had landed. Both of the Cobb brothers moaned and groaned, but Creed was already trying to get back up.

"...gonna...gonna pay..." he whimpered.

Walking out of the alley as he'd intended, Dalton knew that what had just happened was only the beginning of his troubles.

By the time Dalton reached the depot, the afternoon train had already pulled in. Steam hissed from the engine as the passengers disembarked and the baggage was unloaded. Even with the heat from the blazing sun overhead, there were more people milling around than he'd ever seen before. There was even a lone photographer set up just in front of the main building. Whoever had arrived must be important.

For a moment, Dalton considered walking farther on and crossing the tracks in front of the train, avoiding all of the commotion. But he quickly reconsidered. Redstone was *his* town. He'd lived there his whole life. Just because strangers had descended on it like locusts, treated everyone they met like servants, and acted like they were doing them all a favor by coming from Hollywood to make a movie, that wasn't going to make him act any differently. He'd march right through the crowd and dare any of them to say a word.

Dalton made his way up the depot's steps and out onto the platform. It was packed with people, but not a one of them so much as glanced in his direction. Every head was turned to the nearest train car. Just then, a man stepped out into the sunlight. The crowd erupted in shouts and cheers, and the photographer's bulb flashed. The man smiled broadly, as if he was performing up on a movie screen.

"What a welcome!" the man crowed to the crowd hanging on his every word. "And just wait until you meet who I brought with me!"

The sight made Dalton even more bitter and angry. No one had ever looked at him that way. He wanted to walk right on past the man without acknowledging him, to maybe bump shoulders, to knock him off his high horse. But the crowd was so dense, so focused on the man, that he would have had to shoulder his way through, which would have been too obvious. So instead of retreating and bypassing the depot, he worked his way over to the train and inched along the platform's edge, moving among the porters and the few other disembarking passengers. Absently, he rubbed his stubbled chin, wincing in discomfort at the spot where Audie had hit him.

In front of him, two stooped porters hauled an enormous trunk off the train and dropped it down with a thud on the platform; one of the men pulled a handkerchief from his pocket and began wiping sweat from his brow. Instead of going around, Dalton sprang into the air, leaping over it. But suddenly, as if in slow motion, a woman stepped off the train and stood right in the spot where he'd expected to land. He didn't have time to notice much about her; blond hair billowing to her shoulders, flower-print dress, and fair skin. No matter how desperately he wanted to, he couldn't stop.

"Look out, lady!" Dalton shouted.

Before the woman could turn her head, he collided with her, knocking her to the ground where she lay in a heap. Without looking, Dalton knew that every head in the depot had turned toward them; he'd stalked onto the platform determined to gain the Hollywood people's attention, but now that he had it, he wondered if he hadn't made a huge mistake.

Oh, hell...

Chapter Five

ANNA LAY ON HER BACK on the train platform, stunned, the world strangely and suddenly not where it was supposed to be, a dull ache making its way down the length of her arm. An odd mixture of confusion and embarrassment filled her. *What had happened?* One moment she was getting off the train, her stomach clenched tight with nervousness, ready to face the crowd, there'd been a shout, and then she'd been struck.

"Ouch," she said with a wince, rising on an elbow.

A man stood before her, a cowboy hat slightly askew on his head. Because of how close he was, as well as the way everyone in the depot was staring at them, Anna knew that he was responsible for knocking her to the ground. Instead of offering her an apology or extending his hand to help her back to her feet, he stared at her silently, his mouth slightly open, his eyes never leaving hers. But rather than being angry at what he'd done or at his doing nothing to make it right, she just returned his stare.

It was his looks that disarmed her.

Broad across his shoulders, the taut muscles on his fore-arms both pronounced and tanned by the sun, his simple blue shirt marked across the chest with a streak of grime, he looked powerful. Her eyes roamed his face, noticing the curls of black hair that peeked out from beneath his hat, the curve of his whiskered jaw line, and even the hint of a mark on his chin, the skin swollen and red. But it was his eyes that drew her in and refused to let go. Narrow and dark, they looked to Anna like jewels, hidden pools in which she could drown; even as the seconds ticked past, they never wavered from hers. The sudden, desperate need to know his name filled her. But just as she was about to ask, Samuel was beside her, his hand carefully gripping her by the elbow, and easing her back to her feet.

"Are you all right?" he asked with concern.

"I'm...I'm fine..." Anna managed, her gaze flickering from the movie producer to the stranger. "I'm not hurt."

Relief washed over Samuel's face, but then, just as quickly as it had appeared it vanished, replaced by a barely restrained anger as he turned on the other man. "What in the blazes were you thinking?" he snapped. "What ir-responsible fool knocks a woman to the ground and then isn't enough of a gentleman to offer his hand? You should be ashamed of yourself!"

For a moment, Anna was certain that the only response Samuel was going to get was to be punched in the face. A dark cloud passed over the stranger's face, his eyes narrow-ing, his hand bunching into a fist, his nose flaring. But then his attention wandered back to her and she could see the tension drain from his body.

"It was...an accident..." he said, his voice deep.

"That's all you've got to say for yourself?" Samuel barked, unwilling to let the matter drop so easily.

The stranger sneered. "I'll show you what I've got to say for—"

"That's enough," Anna quickly interjected, stepping between the men, placing a hand on the stranger's chest, and once again calming his rage; feeling the heat of his skin beneath the fabric of his shirt made her heart race. "He's apologized," she said, giving the stranger a faint smile before adding, "even if he wasn't very eloquent doing it..."

The man's eyes narrowed a bit as the faintest hint of a smile teased at the corners of his mouth. He looked as if he was going to say something, but before he could, Samuel grabbed Anna's elbow, turned her back toward the depot and the Hollywood people waiting for them, and started leading her away.

"Be more careful next time," the producer growled over his shoulder even as his famous smile had once again begun to shine.

"But I—" she protested weakly.

"Everyone's waiting," Samuel replied.

Anna looked back at the stranger. He returned her gaze for a moment, his eyes mysteriously unreadable to her, before tipping his hat and walking away. Almost immediately, he was swallowed from sight by the throng of people showering her with questions and words of concern.

"Ladies and gentlemen!" Samuel's voice boomed over the crowd. "I apologize for that scene but I suppose it goes to show that you never know what can pass as a welcome in these little backwater towns!" Laughter rose into the hot afternoon. "But now it is my great honor and pleasure to introduce to you Valentine Pictures' newest star! The woman who is going to be on every poster and magazine cover from Los Angeles to New York and back again! The actress who will bring *The Talons of the Hawk* to life before your very eyes! I give you Anna Finnegan!"

Even as Anna listened to the round of applause that followed, as she answered the many questions that were asked while wearing the smile that had served her so well up on the stage, her mind kept wandering and wondering.

Who was that man with the dark eyes?

Samuel led the way out of the depot and down the streets of Redstone. To Anna, the town seemed much as it had from the train; hard up and more than a little bit beaten down. Though shops were open, with a few customers wandering in and out, what she noticed were the cracked window panes, the walls caked with dust, and the signs in bad need of a new coat of paint. Maybe it had something to do with the heat; she could feel the sweat beading on her bare skin and running down her spine.

"It's only a short walk to our sets from here," Samuel explained, as if sensing her discomfort.

"Is it always this hot?" she asked, wiping her brow.

"Well, it is Texas after all," he answered with a laugh.

Before they'd reached their destination, Anna could hear the loud, rapid pounding of nails, the back-and-forth sawing of wood, and the shouts of workmen. Rounding the corner across from the barber's shop, the entire group came to a stop. Everywhere Anna looked, there was activity. Men scaled up scaffolding as they worked to put up a new, two-story building. Others positioned lights and laid track that the cameras would roll along. Still more lathered paint against the bare boards of another finished set. There was even a group of workers sitting on a post used for tethering horses, dipping their bare feet into a water trough, laughing as they ate their lunch and smoked cigarettes. The whole scene reminded Anna of an ant colony, where everyone was busy, all working toward the same end.

"There are a couple more buildings being put up at the edge of town, including the one that we'll use as the home your character shares with her father," Samuel explained to Anna. "I wanted someplace that had good, clear sight lines that extended off toward the horizon. Audiences love that sort of thing."

"I thought the reason you chose Redstone was that it was authentic as it was," Anna said. "Doesn't making alterations to it change all that?"

"I told you that this place was ideal," he replied. "Not perfect."

As the group strolled around the set, marveling at all that Valentine Pictures had accomplished, Anna noticed that Samuel still retained many traits of an actor. With the photographers snapping pictures and the reporters from the Hollywood gossip magazines eagerly taking notes, the movie producer was in control of everything: his loud, clear voice explained the purpose of each set, patiently answering any questions; his eyes twinkled as he laughed out loud at a man's lame attempt at a joke, so believably that she doubted anyone would question the laugh's sincerity; and with the gentle turn of direction, his hand on a woman's elbow, he guided the group just where he wanted them to go, as if he was a director positioning his actors. Through it all, his smile never wavered. It was masterful.

For Anna, the stroll through Redstone was also the first moment when she began to understand what it meant to become a movie star. Photographers posed her in front of sets. Reporters asked her about her background, her acting experience, and especially her thoughts about *The Talons of the Hawk*. Though it was different from the brief bit of fame she'd had in the theater, it was comforting, a welcome validation of what she had sought for so long; to be somebody important.

Now just don't screw it up...

Once Samuel and Anna had left the others, the movie producer offering his dearest thanks for their company, he led her toward a run-down, dilapidated building located beside the mercantile and within earshot of all of the construction. From the sagging awning that looked like it would collapse in a stiff wind, the broken floorboards of the long porch, the missing window panes, and especially the badly faded sign that announced the place as PORTER'S SALOON, it was quite the eyesore.

"It's much nicer on the inside," Samuel said.

"I can't imagine that it could be a whole lot worse," Anna replied.

But surprisingly, he was right. Two dozen tables and sets of chairs had been neatly arranged to fill the long room, fronting a small stage at the far end, its brilliant red curtain pulled shut. Along one wall, a long bar waited for thirsty customers. A line of liquor bottles reflected off the enormous mirror that ran the bar's length. Everything was spotless; the bar's dark wood shone even more brilliantly than the immaculately mopped floor.

"It's amazing!" Anna exclaimed.

"It should be for what I paid to make it this way," Samuel replied.

"Was it being used for anything?"

The producer shook his head. "It was abandoned," he explained. "The owner practically jumped out of his chair to shake my hand when I offered to buy it from him. I got it for a song. Still, it took a pretty penny to change it into something we could use."

Anna wandered over to the bar and peered at the row of bottles. "Is that real alcohol in those?"

Samuel grinned. "I like things to be authentic, remember?"

"Aren't you worried about Prohibition?"

"We're using this bar to shoot a movie, not to sell drinks. As long as I don't sell it to anyone, we're in the clear. Besides, I get the impression that here in Redstone, they don't pay too close attention to laws they don't like."

Samuel's words unwittingly drew Anna's thoughts to the man who had knocked her to the ground at the depot. He was different, almost exotic, in his own way rougher in appearance than any man she'd ever known, even from those difficult years she'd spent on the streets of Chicago. She recalled the stubble peppering his cheeks, the unruly curls of dark hair, but she especially remembered his eyes and the way they'd looked upon her. She had no trouble believing that he was the sort of man Samuel was talking about, a troublemaker who cared little for law and order.

Then why do I wish that I knew his name?

Suddenly, the door beside the stage burst open and two men entered. One of them was tall and thin, his shoulders slumped as if he were carrying an oppressively heavy weight. His face looked worried, his eyes darting nervously around the room.

"But what if we—" he said meekly.

"No, no, no, no!" the other man shouted. He couldn't have looked more different from the fellow he was berating. Short and heavyset in build, he had white hair that stuck out in awkward tufts, as if he had been pulling on it. Sweat beaded his brow and dotted the rolls of his double chin. His face was colored a dark, angry red. "Only a fool would do it the way you've planned," he continued to rant. "The lights in here have to be placed either straight above the bar or high and just off to the side! Do you have any idea what would happen if you put them on the opposite side of the room and behind the camera like you're suggesting?" Angrily grabbing hold of the other man's arm, he pointed toward the bar. "All of the light that reflected off that glass would ruin everything! You might as well burn all our film before we even load the cameras for all the good it would do us!"

"It's just that I thought that—"

"It doesn't matter what you think!" the heavyset man exploded. "When I tell you to do something, I expect it to be done!"

The tall man walked over to the bar and looked straight up at the ceiling. "I don't know if I could do any work up there. It looks like it'd just collapse if I pounded in a single nail."

"I don't care *how* you do it, just that it gets done!"

Throwing up his hands in surrender, the tall man said, "All right, all right. I'll see if I can't make it work."

"If you can't, I'll fire you and find someone who can!" With that, the heavier man stalked out of the saloon, slamming the door behind him so hard that Anna feared the whole dilapidated building might fall down.

"Who was that?" she whispered to Samuel.

"That," he replied with a grin, "was Frank Dukes. Your director."

Anna frowned. In the years she'd spent in the theater, she had worked with plenty of difficult people: actors who were disgruntled that they hadn't received the billing they thought they deserved; still other performers who mistakenly believed that they had talent they actually didn't have;

orchestra conductors who thought that the audience came for the music and therefore played at the wrong moments and much too loudly; light operators who got drunk and snoozed, unconscious in the rafters; and even promoters who didn't care a whit for the performance as long as they made their expected cut at the box office. She had witnessed plenty of wild accusations, firings, and even fist-fights. Still, the confrontation she'd just witnessed startled her. If that was the man who was going to be her first film director, someone who flew wildly off the handle about the positioning of lights, Anna knew she was going to have to pay careful attention to her every move.

"I'd hate to be on the receiving end of a tongue-lashing like that."

"He's not *always* that way," Samuel said.

"That's reassuring."

"Some days," he continued, giving her a smile and a wink, "he's even worse."

Samuel showed Anna a couple of the other buildings and sets they would be using before taking her back to the center of town. Her head was spinning; it was overwhelming. She'd met so many new people, smiling as she'd shaken their hands, that she worried she wouldn't be able to keep all of their names straight. Just the prospect of lying down for a while in her hotel room, alone and away from all of the fuss and commotion, seemed heavenly.

To Anna's eyes, the Stagecoach Hotel looked only slightly better than Porter's Saloon had. Both were weathered and worn, but the most noticeable difference between them was that the hotel was full of people. Samuel explained that Valentine Pictures had rented every room. Men and women sat on the porch, drinking and talking, out of the relentless heat. When she and Samuel climbed the rickety steps, people practically leaped up to greet them.

"How was your trip?"

"...think you picked the hottest place in the whole world to make a movie!"

"You'll want to talk to Bonnie about the costumes if—"

By the time they'd finished shaking hands, answering an endless stream of questions, and introducing Anna to everyone, she felt as if an hour had passed. Eventually, they made their way through the front doors and into the hotel's lobby. Anna waited as Samuel went over to the desk clerk to get their keys; the hotel employee looked harried, his tie loosened and hanging limp, his eyes those of a man who hadn't slept well for quite some time.

The hotel's lobby bustled with activity: People filled the sitting room, gossiping about the latest Hollywood news; a woman wearing an elaborate hat was cackling with laughter on the telephone beside the front desk; and a couple of stewards strained to haul an enormous chest up the tall staircase that led to the second floor of rooms. Anna watched as the men grunted and groaned their way to the top of the stairs, wondering where her own belongings were. But then, suddenly she froze, her eyes growing wide and her heart pounding. She couldn't believe what she was seeing.

There, starting to descend the stairs, was Joan Webb.

For as long as she could remember, Anna had marveled at Joan's acting. While she'd never had much money to go to the pictures, on those rare occasions when she had, it was Joan who'd most captivated her. Whether the actress was playing a kidnapped socialite who had been tied to the railroad tracks by the villain, a country girl pining hopelessly for the man she loved to notice her, or a nurse bravely tending to the sick and wounded on the battlefield, she was magnificent. Anna had even incorporated some of the other woman's more famous roles into her own street-corner routine.

Even though she was now in her late forties, Joan still looked like a Hollywood starlet. Her emerald dress hung perfectly from her small frame, giving the impression that she was off to a high-society gala, far from the streets of Redstone. Her dark hair was cut stylishly short, framing a face defined by her small green eyes. Even the way she carried herself was elegant; she walked down the staircase as if a camera was trained on her, her shoulders back, lips pursed while her fingers trailed down the railing, the huge diamond on her hand sparkling in the light. It didn't matter to Anna that there were a few more wrinkles around Joan's eyes than she remembered, or that the skin on the older woman's neck had begun to sag a bit. She was still beautiful. What really *did* matter was that Anna was going to star in a movie alongside one of her favorite actresses.

Me and Joan Webb!

Ever since Samuel had told her that Joan was going to be

sharing the film's spotlight with her, Anna had been anxiously awaiting this moment. With butterflies fluttering in her stomach, she stepped over to the foot of the stairs.

"Miss Webb?" Anna said, smiling from ear to ear.

"I don't sign autographs anymore," Joan replied coldly, her eyes staring off into the distance as she made to walk brusquely past.

"No, no, I'm not a fan, well, I am, but..." Anna stammered.

Joan stopped and turned around, clearly annoyed. In a way, Anna completely understood; she could only imagine what it was like for a star with as big a name as Joan to be constantly hounded by fans wanting her attention, the blinding flashbulbs of the gossip magazine photographers going off in every restaurant, train depot, and hotel she entered, never to have a moment of privacy. It had to be maddening. Maybe the day would come when Anna would know exactly how she felt...

"I'm sorry to bother you," she said quickly. "It's just that I thought that I should introduce myself. I'm Anna Finnegan," she explained, smiling as she extended her hand. "I'm going to be in the movie with you."

Joan's eyes widened as she took a step backward. With her brow furrowed deeply and a sour look on her face, she crossed her arms over her chest while slowly looking Anna up and down. "You?" she asked incredulously, a short laugh punctuating the word. "*You're* the girl Samuel has been raving about, the one he's been telling anyone who'll listen that you'll be a star? *You?*"

Anna felt the flush of embarrassment rising to her cheeks, but there was also something else, an emotion she never would have expected; a twinge of anger. Still, she was so dumbstruck that she couldn't say a word.

"I swear," Joan continued, a sneer curling at the corners of her mouth. "Things have certainly changed since I entered this business. Seems that just about anyone can be picked to be in a movie, even if they don't have the looks or the personality for it."

"Now wait just a minute," Anna said, finally finding her voice. "Don't you—"

"Let me guess," Joan said, cutting her off. "He found you in some old theater in Indianapolis?"

Anna frowned. "St. Louis..."

"Close enough," Joan said with a triumphant chuckle. "First Samuel develops this crazy notion to make a movie in a dump like this," she complained, waving her hand around the hotel lobby, "and then he casts some plain newcomer as the star. With you here to ruin things, he'll bankrupt the company in no time flat!"

Anna couldn't believe what she was hearing. She would never have imagined being spoken to in such a horrible way, least of all by a woman she idolized! But then, just as she was about to give the older actress a piece of her mind, Joan's sneer disappeared faster than a snap of her fingers and was replaced with a beaming smile.

"Samuel!" she cried, gently pushing her way past Anna to take the producer by the arm as he approached with two sets of keys. "I was just telling our new starlet what a wonderful choice you made! She's perfect! With her here, we'll make this movie a hit for sure!"

"I'm so glad you think so," Samuel replied.

"I just know we'll work together beautifully. There's no doubt in my mind," Joan added. "Don't you think so, my dear?"

For a moment, Anna was too flustered to respond. Joan's transformation had been so sudden that it had taken her completely off guard. *What a lying, conniving snake!* But her acting was so good, so utterly believable, that Anna knew Samuel didn't suspect a thing.

"Absolutely..." she finally managed.

"Now let me tell you about a couple of ideas I had for my introductory scene," Joan said as she led Samuel toward the sitting room. But they'd only gone a few steps when she looked back over her shoulder at Anna, venom in her eyes.

What have I gotten myself into? Anna asked herself.

Chapter Six

DALTON LEANED AGAINST the doorway to the workroom of his family's blacksmithing shop and watched as his father tended a piece of metal. Over and over, George brought his hammer down, striking the white-hot bar with a loud clang and sending a shower of sparks spilling onto the dirt floor. Protected by heavy work gloves, he gripped the metal with a pair of tongs, turning it one way and then another, pounding and prodding it into the shape he wanted. The sounds of his labor reverberated around the small space, dim with thick shadows, the walls lined with the instruments of the trade, and the heat oppressive even with the wide back doors thrown open to capture any passing breeze.

For as long as Dalton could remember, he had taken pleasure in watching his father work. George had pride in his craftsmanship; he never put down his tools until he was satisfied that the job had been done right. All of the back-breaking work in the heat had shaped him just as surely as he shaped the metal. Even now, in his midfifties, his salt-and-pepper hair thinning a bit on top, with wrinkles around his eyes, his father was still as strong as an ox. All of the years spent swinging hammers, positioning anvils, and hauling metal had broadened his shoulders and chest, and made his arms as thick as the iron he held. Unfortunately, it hadn't made his will to resist the lure of gambling as strong as the rest of his body.

Clenching his jaw, Dalton felt the dull ache from where Audie Cobb had hit him; he was going to have one hell of a bruise. If he hadn't struck Creed first, if he hadn't managed to knock the man's oversize brother off his feet, who knew what kind of beating they would've given him. He could have been *killed*. The worst part was knowing that it was all his father's fault. He hadn't been able to resist the lure of a hand of cards or the roll of a pair of dice. To make matters worse, he'd been foolish enough to borrow money from Vernon Black. Just thinking about it made the anger in Dalton's chest smolder as hot as the iron in his father's hand.

When George finished working the metal, he brought it over to a long trough filled with water and dropped it in, sending a hissing cloud of steam rising up toward the low roof. Absently, he wiped sweat from his brow with the back of his hand, leaving a small streak of grime behind. When he turned around to see his son watching him, he smiled so broadly, so genuinely, that for an instant Dalton considered waiting to confront him about his gambling debts. But then he thought about all the other times they'd been here before.

"I'm gonna need your help to get this order filled," George said before taking a ladle of water from a bucket and drinking deeply, a trickle running down his chin and onto his chest. "Them movie people don't know what the heck they want, just that they want it fast as lightning. One order gets done and another comes in the door. Might be we're gonna need to hire that other hand like you said."

"Could be," Dalton mumbled.

"We keep getting business like this, we're gonna have more money than we'll know what to do with."

"Sure we will."

His father regarded him warily as he took another drink. "Something bothering you?"

Dalton held the older man's gaze, his own eyes narrowed, the anger slowly building to the point where he knew he'd have to let it out or he'd explode. "Why'd you do it?" he asked, the words low and drawn out, as if they were knives being slowly eased from their sheaths. "After all the trouble you've caused, why couldn't you have kept your word?"

"What're you talking about?" George asked.

"You know damn well what this is about," Dalton spat, the dam that had held back his emotions finally giving way. "I just had a run-in with the Cobb brothers because you can't control your urges! It wasn't enough that you've been taking money out of the till, money that should've been deposited at the bank to pay off all we've borrowed to stay afloat," he snarled, his words growing sharper and louder, "but then you had to go and make it all the worse by getting in deep with Vernon Black? What the hell were you thinking?"

His father stared at him silently, sweat trickling down his forehead; Dalton wondered if it was on account of the heat coming off the forge or from the shame of being found out.

"It isn't as bad as you're making it out," George muttered.

"Creed said you hadn't repaid your debts and that they had to hurt me in order to teach you a lesson," Dalton answered. "How much worse could it possibly be than that?"

"I'm going to pay them back," his father insisted.

"How? You gamble away every extra dime we manage to squirrel away! If you keep this up, we'll be out on the street! Is that what you want?"

George frowned. Absently, he walked back over to the water trough and retrieved the metal bar he'd been shaping. Holding it up, he turned it one way, then another, examining it closely. Dalton wondered if his father was ignoring him, hoping that their argument would just go away if he paid it no mind. But then, suddenly, he threw the piece of iron back into the trough with a loud splash.

"You don't understand," he protested faintly, staring at his feet.

"No, I don't," Dalton agreed.

His father shook his head. "No, what you don't understand is that I had been winning! One hand right after another. There I was, sitting at this card table some of the movie fellas had set up, riding a hot streak the likes of which I've never been on before! The more I bet, the more I won! I was raking it in! I was being dealt hands I've been wishing for all my life. I thought that if I just kept on playing, I could make all our troubles go away for good." George's face soured. "I was all in, everything I'd won, I just needed one more card, for a Jack of any color to come up and I'd have needed a wheelbarrow to get my winnings home..."

"But you didn't get it," Dalton said, knowing how the story ended.

George shook his head.

"How'd you end up borrowing from Vernon Black?"

"To make up for what I lost the last time I played," his father explained. "What I started winning on was the money Vernon loaned me."

For a long moment, neither man said a word; Dalton was so disgusted by his father's weakness that he was nearly trembling with anger.

"You don't know what it's like," George finally explained, breaking the silence between them. "There's this calling...this feeling...when you just know deep down in your gut that things are gonna pan out like you've been dreaming..."

"It looks like a nightmare from where I stand."

"I've tried to do better."

"Not hard enough," he replied. "Not damn near hard enough."

The venom in Dalton's words appeared to stoke a fire in

his father. "A son shouldn't speak to his father that way," George groused.

"A son shouldn't *have to*."

The last word had scarcely left Dalton's mouth before he started to wonder if he hadn't gone too far. The pain on his father's face was as obvious as the sun in the sky. Seconds ticked by slowly. The silence that lingered between them was deafening. But before there was a chance for Dalton to apologize, to try to talk about what had happened without so much anger, George walked over to the blazing furnace, pulled out another piece of metal, its end glowing white hot, took it to the anvil, and started to work on it. This time there was no doubt; as far as his father was concerned, their conversation was over. Dalton turned and left, knowing that there was nothing left for him to say.

It was too late. The damage had already been done.

"You're late for lunch," Betty Barnes said.

Dalton planted a kiss on his mother's cheek as he entered the kitchen, mumbled an apology, and stepped over to the icebox to root around inside. He grabbed a plate of roasted chicken, poured himself a tall glass of milk, snagged an apple out of a bin on the counter, and then sat down opposite her at the worn table by the window.

"There was a line at the bank," he lied, taking a big bite of chicken, chewing slowly, trying to think of an explanation for his tardiness that didn't include his alleyway brawl with the Cobb brothers or the discovery of his father's latest gambling debts. "Then on the way back there was a big to-do down at the train depot. More of those damn Hollywood people coming to town."

"Dalton!" his mother hissed. "How many times do I have to tell you to watch your language? I'll not have it under this roof!"

"Yes, ma'am," he grumbled, taking another bite.

The way Dalton had heard it from folks around Redstone, there was a time when Betty Barnes had been the prettiest face in town. Even now, years since her youthful beauty had begun to fade, every once in a while, she still managed to turn a head or two as she walked down Main Street. Her auburn hair was curled at her shoulders, marred here and there by streaks of gray. Though there were wrinkles crisscrossing her face, more than might be expected for a woman in her late forties, her eyes, a deep green with flecks of brown, still shone. But more than anything else, it was her smile that had remained young and vibrant, regardless of any troubles her husband might have brought to her marriage and family. Admiring her as she sat at the kitchen table, crimping the edges of a crust for an apple pie, with the afternoon sunlight streaming through her hair, Dalton could easily imagine how she should have been, if only things had been different; happy, unconcerned with bills, gambling debts, or the thought of losing all she owned.

Dalton thought about everything his mother had been through, all of the indignities she'd had to suffer because of her husband's gambling addiction. Other women would have left or, at the very least, threatened to leave unless there was a change. But not Betty. Every time that George made a mistake, gambled away all of their savings, sneaked in late after a night of losing at the card table, or forced her to face an irate shopkeeper over an unpaid bill, she smiled her bright smile and accepted his vows to do better. When those very same promises were broken time and time again, she held steadfast to the hope that *this time* would be different. Even when Dalton ranted and raved about the destruction being done to them, and tried to suggest a radical solution, she never wavered in her support for George. In the end, it was really all quite simple; she loved the man, faults and all.

.It was then, thinking about his mother's beauty and the love for his father she stubbornly clung to, that Dalton remembered the way the woman he'd knocked down at the depot had looked at him. He'd been dumbstruck by the look in her eyes, the soft curve of her cheek, and even the way her blond hair tumbled across her shoulders. He'd been around other attractive women before, some that could have been called stunning, but he couldn't ever recall being struck mute, frozen in place, his heart pounding in his chest, all at the same time. *I must've looked like an ass!* There was no doubting that she was one of those detestable Hollywood people, but it didn't diminish his desire to see her walking down the street, to be able to apologize without tripping on the words, to learn her name. If only he hadn't—

"What happened to your chin?"

Dalton looked up to find his mother staring intently at him.

"It's nothing," he mumbled, looking back down into his plate.

"That certainly doesn't look like nothing," Betty replied. Reaching out, she lifted her son's chin; when he winced, she frowned.

"I hit it with a hammer this morning," he lied, once again turning away, hoping that his fib wouldn't be too obvious. "We've had so many orders to fill that I was in a hurry and not paying attention. Hurt like a son-of-a..." he began, catching himself before he cursed. "It smarted pretty good."

"Looks like it."

Dalton thought there might be more from her, a question about his improbable story, looking for cracks, or at the least some medical advice on how to care for his wound, but instead she went back to working on her pie; like her husband's gambling problems, it was easier to ignore than address.

"How's Walker these days?" she asked with a smile.

"Same as always," he muttered.

"I haven't seen him around much lately," Betty continued. "Although I'm sure he and his family are just like everyone else in town, so busy with the Hollywood people they don't have time to think! Why I bet that..."

Dalton was barely listening to a word his mother said, the familiar anger once again building inside him; anger at her for how easily she ignored the trouble all around her, the warning signs that would be obvious even to a blind woman, but also at himself for holding his tongue, for not saying a word about how his father's addiction had very nearly cost him much more than a bruise on his chin, about how it might end up costing the both of them everything. In the end, staying silent meant that he was just like her.

Disgusted, he got up from the table, dropped his plate and glass into the wash basin with a clatter, and headed to the door.

"Dinner will be at six," his mother said, ignoring his anger.

"I'll be there," he said.

"There'll be pie!" she called just before the door swung shut behind him.

Vernon Black sat back in his chair, placed his hands together, his fingers forming a steeple, and looked over his large desk at the two men standing before it. A trickle of sweat slithered down his brow but he made no move for his handkerchief. A glass of whiskey sat before him, but he left it untouched. He'd learned a valuable secret a long time ago; silence was a weapon, as effective as one that drew blood. So now he let the seconds slowly tick by without a sound save for the whirling of the ceiling fan above them. Not until he was sure of their discomfort did he finally speak.

"He jumped the two of you..." Vernon said, his voice deep and gravelly.

"That's right, Mr. Black," Creed Cobb agreed, nervously switching his weight from one foot to the other and then back again, over and over. "We was just doin' what you told us, followin' him so that we could get him alone, send our message, but we must a done somethin' to give ourselves away, 'cause when we made our way down that alleyway, he was waitin' for us."

"So you said."

"Honest, that's what happened," Creed pleaded, elbowing his brother hard in the side, the dumb lug nodding on cue.

"And you said that he had a weapon..." Vernon prodded.

"Must a been a steel pipe or a piece a wood, as hard as he was hittin' us. I can't say for certain, on account a how dark it was in that alley. The only way that son-of-a-bitch was gonna get the better a us was just the way he done it."

"Even with your brother there?"

"He done went after him first, ain't that right, Audie?"

The huge man once again nodded enthusiastically.

There was no denying that *something* had happened between the Cobb brothers and Dalton Barnes. Both of the thugs were sporting bruises. Creed's chin was an ugly mottle of purple and brown, while his brother had entered the office with a noticeable limp. Still, Vernon doubted that events had occurred just as Creed had explained them. More than likely, they'd been overconfident, had assumed that the young blacksmith would be easy pickings, and had gotten their clocks cleaned for lack of diligence. It was unusual for them to have failed; the two brothers were ruthlessly efficient, doling out whatever punishment was demanded of them, especially when the message needed to be sent in the form of broken bones. Regardless of their having let him down, Vernon still took some pleasure from watching a hard nut like Creed Cobb lie and squirm; it was a reminder that he held power over the man.

"You just say the word and we'll give Barnes the beatin' he's got comin' to him," Creed offered enthusiastically, wanting to do right by his boss, but desperately wanting revenge of his own, as well. "No mistakes!"

"None!" Audie shouted, the first time he'd spoken since entering the office.

"That won't be necessary," Vernon answered.

"It won't?" Creed replied, clearly surprised.

And why wouldn't it be? One of the ways in which Vernon Black had taken control of Redstone, amassing wealth and power, was by enforcing his will by whatever means were necessary, by claiming each and every red cent that was rightfully his, and by making everyone around him fear what would happen if he didn't get it. Even though he'd done so by using plenty of brawn, employing ruthless thugs like the Cobb brothers, that didn't mean he never used his head.

Vernon reached forward and picked up the letter that lay on his desk, the expensive ruby ring on his chubby finger catching the late afternoon sunlight. The message had arrived sometime in the night, pushed underneath the door; the envelope it had been delivered in, still full of money, had been placed in his office safe hours ago. Bringing it close, Vernon once again peered at the typewritten words, skimming over the contents he'd long ago memorized.

The letter was an offer. After a few lines spent praising Vernon as the man to go to in Redstone if you wanted something to get done, it laid out a plan in which the filming of Valentine Pictures' new movie would be ruined. Each step was more violent and destructive than the one before. If followed, the plan guaranteed that Hollywood and the rest of the country would *never* see *The Talons of the Hawk* on the silver screen. Hundreds of thousands of dollars, plenty of jobs, and maybe even a few lives would be lost. The money had been a first taste, a substantial one at that, with the promise of much more to come with every bit of mayhem wrought. While Vernon had already grown richer from the movie business coming to town, the possibilities from this scheme would make that look like absolute chicken feed in comparison.

The only thing that bothered him was that the note was unsigned. Whoever was orchestrating this plan, his identity was a mystery. It meant that, if something happened and it all went south, Vernon would be the only fish caught wriggling on the hook. Not that it worried him; his word had passed for the law in Redstone for decades. Still, he was a cautious man. The first act of sabotage wasn't much, something that could be easily written off as an accident. If everything went off without a hitch, he could wait to see if he was paid before committing any other crimes. What did he have to lose?

Normally, he would've had the Cobb brothers make sure

that George Barnes's kid never walked again, but there was now riper fruit to pick. Eventually, the blacksmith and his family would get what was coming to them, but it would have to wait. Looking at Creed and Audie, he smiled a mess of stained teeth.

"Something else has come up."

Chapter Seven

ANNA AWOKE EARLY, washed up, spent too much time trying on outfit after outfit in the desperate hope of finding one that wouldn't make her look like she'd just stepped off the train from St. Louis and working on the stage of a run-down theater there, and then headed downstairs. After her awkward encounter with Joan Webb, she was a bundle of nerves, once again wondering if she truly belonged on the set of a Hollywood picture. In the already bustling lobby, she felt as if every eye was on her, judging her every move, waiting for her to make the mistake that would send her back to wherever it was she'd come from.

"There's just the young lady I was looking for!"

The sudden sound of Samuel's booming voice startled her, but Anna managed to recover, doing her best to match his bright smile.

"Here I am," she managed.

"How did you sleep?"

"Fine." She nodded, although the truth was that she'd had a hard time drifting off, not just because of nervousness or her run-in with Joan, but also because she couldn't seem to get out of her head the face of the stranger who'd knocked her down at the depot. For a couple of long hours, she'd lain in her bed, staring up at the ceiling, thinking about how his eyes had wandered over her face.

"Good, good!" Samuel exclaimed. "I always worry about everyone else. With all the traveling I do, I can sleep almost anywhere. If I had a blanket to keep warm, it wouldn't matter if I had a rock for a pillow or was up on top of a moving train car, I'd be out like a light!"

After they had had a quick bite to eat, the movie producer led the way onto the streets of Redstone and off toward the edge of town. Even at such an early hour, the sun was already beating down, hot. As they walked, Samuel explained that they were scheduled to start filming her scenes beginning the next morning.

"Because I thought that you'd want to be as prepared as you can be," he said, "it might be a good idea for you to have some time to rehearse, maybe work out some of your nerves before going in front of the camera."

"That would be wonderful."

"Excellent! Fortunately, you have a costar who also likes to be well-prepared."

Though she was smiling on the outside, Anna's head was filled with worrisome thoughts. Her first assumption was that she'd be rehearsing scenes with Joan; maybe it wouldn't be enough to have humiliated her in the hotel lobby, now the older actress might try to upstage her in front of Samuel. With every step she took, a sickening feeling spread in Anna's stomach.

They passed a church in bad need of a new coat of paint, a lone bird watching them intently from its nest in the tall steeple, then a row of small houses, their tin roofs soaking up the summer sun. Finally, they neared a cabin. It sat off on its own, well away from the other buildings, as if it were a child's toy that hadn't been picked up with the others when playtime ended. Like most of the other houses in Redstone, it was worn and weathered, standing in a state of disrepair.

"This is the building we'll be using as the cabin your character lives in with her father," Samuel explained.

"It's just as I would've imagined it," Anna replied truthfully.

"As authentic as it gets."

Samuel led the way up the creaky stairs, carefully pointing out where to step in order to avoid a board that was nearly rotted through. Inside, the cabin's furnishings were sparse; a table and pair of chairs, a dry sink, a worn mattress and a ratty-looking bedroll were the only personal belongings in the cabin's single room. What *was* in plentiful supply was filmmaking materials. Lights had been set up in the front corners to fully illuminate the small space. Canisters of film were neatly piled next to the short track that would be used as the camera moved from one side of the room to the other. There was even a director's chair, ready to be filled. There was so much clutter that Anna almost didn't notice the figure staring out the cabin's rear windows. A man stood with his back to them, his hands clasped behind him. Slowly, he turned to face them, causing Anna to stifle a gasp when she saw his face.

Montgomery Bishop!

Even more than Joan Webb, Montgomery Bishop filled Anna's childhood memories of going to the movies. Once upon a time, he'd been one of the biggest stars in all of Hollywood's silent era, burning nearly as brightly as Valentino or Chaplin. There wasn't a role he couldn't make his own; whether he played a swashbuckling pirate, a sinister gangster, a wounded soldier, or even a down-on-his-luck farmer, Montgomery owned the screen and his audience's rapt attention. He'd been even more famous than Samuel. But with the advent of the talkies, as well as the advancement of years, his star had dimmed. The roles had gotten smaller, the billing lower on the posters and marquees.

None of that mattered to Anna in the slightest; to her, he was still every bit as impressive as ever. Like Joan he had aged; there were more wrinkles on his face, his formerly lustrous black hair had thinned and gone gray, and the piercing eyes that had looked down at her in the movie theater now seemed duller. None of that mattered to Anna; she still found herself enchanted. He looked exactly like what he was: a movie star. For the second time since she'd arrived, Anna couldn't believe that she was going to share the screen with such a famous actor. The only thing tempering her excitement was the fear that he'd disappoint her as Joan had.

"Monty!" Samuel called in greeting. "I see you're early as usual."

"Of course," the actor replied, his voice still as strong and vibrant as Anna remembered from his films. "And this must be Miss Finnegan," he said as he took a step toward her and extended his hand. While his smile wasn't as intense as Samuel's, it was undeniably charming; instantly, Anna found herself liking him.

"Please, call me Anna," she answered.

"Only if you call me Montgomery," he said, throwing a look in Samuel's direction for the earlier use of his name. "I thought we might rehearse the scene just after the bandit's first attack on the town, where Tom suffered an injury. Do you have your script?"

"I don't," Anna frowned. "I wasn't told I'd need it."

"That's perfectly all right. I brought an extra."

"Actually," she interjected, "I've practiced the lines so often that I've already memorized them."

Montgomery smiled, nodding in approval.

"Then let's get to it," Samuel said gleefully, lowering himself into the director's chair and clapping his hands together. "I might never have been on this side of the camera, but I've sure seen it enough to know what to do. Just tell me when you're ready and I'll yell 'action'!"

"You'll do nothing of the sort," Montgomery replied. "We're not going to practice a single line until after you leave."

"What?" Samuel asked, looking honestly surprised. "Why not?"

"She doesn't need the added pressure of you watching her every move. You'll get your chance to see it tomorrow with everyone else."

"But it's *my* movie!" the producer exclaimed.

"I told you to go," his actor insisted.

"It's fine," Anna interjected, stepping between the two men, smiling as broadly as she could. "Montgomery's right. Having you here would probably be a bit distracting. Let me flub all my lines and turn the wrong direction today," she said with a laugh. "That way you'll get a perfect performance tomorrow."

Samuel looked as if he wanted to argue further, but instead his smile returned and he nodded. "Then I suppose I'll leave you." Just as he was about to pull the front door shut behind him, he turned back to Anna. "Don't forget that you need to meet with Bonnie Trubee to make the final alterations to your costume."

"I won't," Anna replied.

"All right then," he smiled. "Happy rehearsing."

Once the door had closed, Montgomery said, "I hope you don't mind my sending him away. It's just that, in my experience, a little privacy can help two actors get to know each other better. I didn't mean to offend."

"I'm sure no offense was taken. He seemed fine."

"That's because you don't know him like I do," he said with a frown, his voice so soft it was as if he was speaking only to himself. But like turning the page of a book, his unease vanished, replaced with a smile. "Let's get started," he continued, taking his mark by the window. "I want to see just exactly what sort of an actress you are."

"Well, I must say *that* was impressive."

Anna couldn't keep herself from smiling at Montgomery's words of praise. Acting out the scene had been exhilarating, the dialogue sharp and the chemistry between them stronger than she would have expected. At first, she'd been quite nervous, worried she would disappoint him, but within seconds she'd relaxed, easing into her character as if she'd been playing Claire for years.

But as happy as she'd been with her own acting, Anna had been mesmerized by Montgomery's. With no more apparent effort than turning on a light switch, he'd shed his sophisticated, movie-star air to become a broken-down old man, poorer than dirt, who was addicted to drink. All his dialogue was spoken with a thick Texas twang. Even his physical appearance changed; his shoulders slumped, his face hung slack, and his hand occasionally twitched in a most convincing manner. The strength of his acting was somewhat intimidating. It challenged Anna, made her strive to become better. His comment made her feel as if she'd succeeded.

"Don't forget that this isn't the same as performing in a theater," Montgomery said. "You always have to be aware of the camera. It's the only set of eyes watching you. There were a couple of times when you turned your back toward it instead of the other way around. Always remember where your attention should be focused."

Anna nodded, knowing what part of the script he was talking about.

"Other than that," he continued, "you were excellent."

"I thought so, too."

"It can still be better. Both of us can be," Montgomery said. "Let's start again from the beginning."

As Anna took her mark, preparing herself to once again become Claire, remembering the advice she'd been given and noting where the camera would be positioned, she was so absorbed that she never noticed the stranger standing at the cabin's window, watching her every move.

Anna looked at herself in the long mirror of the dressing room, angling first one way and then the other, finally turning her back to it and glancing over her shoulder. The clothes she wore were simple, a long-sleeved white blouse adorned with ivory buttons that could lace all the way up to her neck but were now undone to her collarbone, and a plain, long black skirt that was tightly cinched around her waist. Neither of the items of clothing, or even the shoes that felt slightly too small, bunching up her toes, looked new. In fact, it seemed as if they had all been worn for a long time, yet had been well cared for thanks to a few stitches here and a patch there. Anna felt that her clothes were exactly what a young woman like Claire would have worn.

"I think it all looks perfect," she said.

Bonnie Trubee looked closely at Anna, her eyes narrowed, her arms crossed over her chest, with one hand raised so that she could nibble disinterestedly on a finger-nail. Middle-aged, with curly strawberry-blond hair, she had green eyes that were like pinpricks on an otherwise impassive face. With her high cheekbones, tightly pursed lips, and the thin-framed glasses she wore on a long chain hung around her neck, she had reminded Anna of a librarian since the day they'd met.

"I'm not happy with this," Bonnie replied. "Not at all."

"Why? What's wrong with it?"

Walking over to Anna, a frown on her face, the seamstress pulled at the fabric on the elbow of the blouse. "Right here," she said. "There's something here that isn't right. I want it to be looser instead of so form-fitting."

"Are you sure?" Anna asked, moving her arm. "It looks fine to me."

"It might be if you were shot standing still, but the moment you reached for something, it'd be obvious. I'd be a laughingstock."

Bonnie had worked for Valentine Pictures' costume department since the company's inception. It was her job to oversee the creation of all of the outfits that would be worn in the studio's films. She'd created a wardrobe for characters ranging from Arthurian knights, dapper gentlemen and elegant ladies on their way to a gala ball, farmhands struggling through a drought, and even Indian braves on the warpath. Everything sprang from Bonnie's mind before being put together on her staff's sewing machines. She was also something of a perfectionist. When she and an assistant had come to St. Louis to take Anna's measurements and to have her try on a few sample outfits, she'd diligently checked every stitch, run her finger down every seam, and looked over her newest actress from every angle. Not once had she appeared satisfied.

"I can't believe that this is all newly made," Anna commented, hoping that a few well-placed compliments might bring a smile to the seamstress's stony countenance. "It looks homespun."

Bonnie frowned. "It's not easy making things that look authentic but won't fall apart after a few takes." Sighing, she pulled a dress off a hanger and handed it to Anna. "Try on what you'll be wearing for the big love scene while I see if I can fix that sleeve."

Anna stripped off the blouse and handed it to Bonnie, who quickly left. Undoing her skirt, Anna slid it down her legs and into a heap on the dressing room floor. Once she'd taken off her boots, she slid the dress up and over her head, pulled it down over her breasts, and wiggled her hips into its snug fit. She was just pushing back a few strands of her loose blond hair, turning slightly for a look at herself in the mirror, when a voice spoke from behind her.

"Looking at you is making my heart pound awfully fast."

Gasping, Anna spun around to find a man leaning against the door frame. She had no trouble identifying who stood before her.

Milburn Hood was one of the fastest-rising stars in Hollywood. Though he had only a couple of movies to his credit, his good looks graced the covers of several magazines, making women swoon from coast to coast. Up close,

Anna could see that much of the praise for his looks was warranted; he had broad shoulders, thick dark hair, a chiseled jaw, and a smirk of a smile that some women would undoubtedly find irresistible. The look in his dark eyes made him seem both exotic and mysterious, but the way that he was staring at her made Anna nervous. It didn't help that she had no idea how long he'd been standing there, watching.

Did he see me while I was undressed?

"You startled me," she said tersely, her hand rising to the bare skin of her chest that showed above the dress's collar.

"I've been told I have that effect on a lot of women," he replied slyly.

"I must not have heard you knock."

Milburn acted as if he hadn't heard her. "You're Anna, aren't you?" he asked. "Anna Flannagan."

"Finnegan," she corrected him.

"Sure," he replied, smirking. Moving away from the door frame, he walked slowly over to where she stood, stopping only inches in front of her; feeling uncomfortable with his closeness, Anna took a half-step back.

"So you're the lucky lady who'll be playing my lover," Milburn said softly, his eyes dancing hungrily across her face. "Gillen didn't do half bad when he picked you," he continued, one finger rising to trace a path down her cheek.

"Don't touch me like that," she replied, repulsed. She tried to squirm away, but that only brought him closer, pressing her back against the mirror.

"I like a little fight in a gal," he said, his breath hot in her face. "Makes for a bit of fun, but eventually you'll end up fighting to get closer to me instead of away. That's how things always go."

"I don't think so," Anna replied forcefully, moving to push past him, but as soon as she tried, he reached out and grabbed her by the arm, squeezing hard enough to make tears well in her eyes.

"Ah, ah, ah," he said as if he was talking to a naughty child. Pulling her forcefully against him, Milburn added, "After watching you slip that dress on, there's nothing that could stop me from making you mine."

Instantly Anna went pale. He *had* seen her change! Anger mixed with revulsion and fear. How was she going to get away? What could she do to fight him when he was so much stronger than she was? But just as she was about to scream, to try something, anything, to make him let go, she heard, "What do you think you're doing in here?"

Milburn turned to find Bonnie staring hard at him, Anna's repaired blouse clutched in her hand.

"No men are allowed in this dressing room," she added firmly.

"I was just introducing myself," he replied with a broad smile, simultaneously letting go of Anna's arm. Turning to face her, he gave her a wink and said, softly, "I'll be seeing you soon." With that, he walked out of the room without a glance back.

"Why I never!" Bonnie complained. Handing the blouse to Anna, she said, "But enough of all that. Let's see if this fits better."

Even as she complied, Anna's thoughts churned. Now that she'd met Milburn Hood, she knew one thing for certain; if audiences in movie theaters across the country were going to believe that she loved the man's character, it was going to take every ounce of acting ability she had, and maybe even some she didn't.

Chapter Eight

Anna stood back in the corner and watched as the movie's crew prepared the set for filming. They had gathered inside one of the buildings Valentine Pictures had built from the ground up. Samuel had wanted to work in a familiar environment before moving outside for the more authentic scenes. Men stood on ladders to position lights, a woman busily arranged items on the fake mercantile store's counter, while a pair of cameramen blocked the shot. All around was hustle and bustle, but Anna remained still and quiet, even though butterflies filled her stomach. Today was the start of shooting, the day she would step before the camera for the very first time, and, she hoped, start down the road to becoming a star.

"Bring that over here so we can..."

"...we don't get that set right, Dukes is going to have a fit!"

"All right, all right! I'm comin'!"

The one thing Anna wished was that she had gotten a better night's sleep, but her thoughts had been racing. After her run-in with Milburn, she'd spent the rest of the day agitated, wondering if she shouldn't say something to Samuel. There was little doubt that the young actor's behavior warranted it. But in the end she'd decided to stay silent, at least for now. Shooting was just starting and she didn't want to be seen as difficult. Besides, it wasn't as if this was the first time she'd ever been propositioned. Most times it was harmless, an unfortunate part of the business. Fortunately, Milburn had been absent from her dreams, although the stranger from the train had made another appearance.

While Anna was glad that Milburn wouldn't be a part of the day's filming, Joan would be. She stood on the opposite side of the room, her face set in stone, glaring at her younger costar. After the way she'd spoken in the hotel lobby before Samuel arrived, Anna didn't put *anything* past the woman. She was just wondering what malicious thoughts were running through Joan's head, when Frank Dukes suddenly stalked into the room, Samuel right behind him, smiling. The director glowered at everyone, as if he'd managed to catch them doing something inappropriate, instead of the tasks he'd set them to.

"Enough dilly-dallying around!" he barked. "It's time to start making this damn movie!"

"Cut! No! No! No!"

Anna froze as Frank stopped her line of dialogue midsentence, leaped out of his director's chair, and stomped toward her. She hadn't finished her second line, had only said a handful of words, and already he was upset with her. Looking at the redness in his face, the narrowing of his eyes, and the spittle that shone on his lips, she felt as if she'd ruined the whole picture just as they'd started making it.

"Where do you think you are, still back in that miserable little theater in Milwaukee?" the director ranted.

"I believe it was St. Louis," Joan corrected him.

Frank paid her no mind. "You don't have to worry about the poor drunken slob in the back row of the third tier hearing you anymore," he explained. "If you go on talking so loudly, the audience will run out of the theater with their hands over their ears, half-deaf from all the shouting!"

"I'm sorry," Anna offered, embarrassed that she'd already made such a ridiculous mistake. "I'll speak more quietly."

"See that you do!"

Once everyone was back in position, Frank called for silence and, once he had it, called, "Action!" Anna resumed her acting, careful to keep her voice at a normal level, but she hadn't made it much further than the first time she'd been stopped when the director again cut her off.

"Was I still talking too loudly?" she asked nervously.

"Your voice was fine," he snapped, "but the way you were waving your hands around, it was like you were trying to signal a boat at sea! Stop exaggerating everything you do! You're not up on the stage anymore!"

"She'll do better if you stop yelling at her."

Every head in the room turned to the sound of the

voice, most of their mouths open wide at the thought of someone speaking out against the hot-tempered director. Montgomery stood just out of the camera's view. He was supposed to enter the scene midway, Claire's father bringing news of another bandit attack against the town, and had been watching from the beginning. Though Anna had been frightened by Frank's outburst, Montgomery didn't seem the least bit bothered, his eyes never leaving the other man's.

"She keeps making mistakes!" Frank shouted.

"Yes, she does," Montgomery agreed, "but that's to be expected. You belittling her isn't going to make it better. The only thing you're going to accomplish is to make her too nervous to act. She's a good actress. Tell her what it is you want and she'll give it to you."

"I just want things done correctly," the director said.

"So does she."

Frank looked at Anna, raised his finger as if he wanted to chide her some more, but instead lowered his hand and sulked back to his chair. Anna looked quickly over at Montgomery, who gave her a thin smile and a subtle nod of his head, as if to say *the rest is up to you.*

This time, when filming resumed, Anna felt relaxed, even a bit confident. Rather than worrying about the director pouncing on the next thing she said or did wrong, she followed the script, became Claire, and acted. Her movements were natural and the dialogue she spoke flowed smoothly, without a single mistake. When Frank finally shouted a halt to the scene, the camera whirring to a stop, he grudgingly gave her a nod of satisfaction; by contrast, Samuel was beaming ear to ear.

Walking over to Montgomery, Anna said, "Thank you for what you did."

"You would've done the same for me," he replied.

Anna laughed. "I'm sure it's been an awfully long time since you made as silly a mistake as I did."

"But not so long that I don't remember it, either. Just like you, I had a background in the theater, vaudeville, to be precise, so I had all the same misconceptions. I'd talk too loudly, turn the wrong direction, and do too much with my hands. Quite frankly, I should've given you better advice during our rehearsal yesterday."

"I appreciate it all the same."

Montgomery gave her an easy smile. "Just remember to pass it along when *you're* the big star. I doubt it will take long."

Now that the first scene of the day had been filmed, the set was prepared for the next. The camera's position was moved and changes were made to the lighting. Once again, Anna's character would be the lead, but this time she would be interacting with Joan. She had no idea what to expect. After their initial, awkward meeting in the hotel lobby, as well as the way Joan had been glaring at her all day, Anna was nervous. When Frank called them to their places, readied the cameras, and counted down to filming, she couldn't help but expect the worst.

Surprisingly, she didn't get it. As line after line of dialogue passed between them, Joan remained a complete professional. Gone was the petulant, jealous woman whose every word had been meant to cut Anna to the quick; in her place was the same strong actress who for years had lit up screens across the country, the one whom Anna had marveled at when watching her years before. Everything was going so well that she actually began to enjoy herself.

Maybe this is all some misunderstanding and we just got off on the wrong foot. Maybe I'm not being fair.

But then, at almost the exact moment when Anna had given thought to her hopes, they were dashed. The script called for her to take Joan's character a pitcher full of water. She retrieved it from the mercantile's counter, walked to where Joan sat, the two of them speaking their lines, and made to hand it over. At the last possible moment, Joan's hand moved. It was such a slight movement that it was almost imperceptible; Anna was sure she was the only person in the room who noticed. The effect wasn't equally well hidden. The pitcher fell, hit the table, and spilled its contents down the front of Joan's clothes, before dropping the rest of the way to the floor with a clatter. It all happened so quickly, so suddenly, that for a moment, no one in the room made a sound.

Frank had just grumbled for the camera to stop rolling when Joan spoke. "I know you're nervous, darling," she said, looking straight into Anna's eyes, "but that's still no excuse to let go of it before you put it in my hand."

Anna was beside herself. With only a few words, Joan had squarely deflected all the blame for what had happened. To everyone in the room, *she* was at fault. Although Anna knew that voicing what she'd seen, that Joan had purposely moved her hand, would sound like whining, it was a struggle to hold her tongue. There was no doubt in her mind that Joan had orchestrated the whole thing to make her look like a fool. The worst part was that it had worked.

"I'm sorry..." Anna managed, swallowing her pride, as well as her anger. "It was an accident."

"Unfortunately, an apology won't do a thing to dry out this outfit," Joan replied, holding the soaked fabric of her blouse between her fingers. "If there isn't a replacement, you may have ruined the whole day's schedule."

"We can move on to something else if we have to," Samuel said.

While Bonnie ran off to see if there was a duplicate costume or, at the least, a suitable alternative, the crew began resetting the shoot, while Frank and Samuel conferred beside the camera. That left Anna and Joan alone.

Hazarding a glance at the older actress, her heart still roiling with anger, Anna was surprised to see Joan motion her closer. Deep in her heart, Anna knew that nothing good could come of it, but the temptation to hear what the other woman had to say was too great to ignore. She leaned down.

"No matter what it takes," Joan said, her voice an angry whisper, the words hissing out as they competed against the commotion in the room, "I'm going to make sure that the only acting job you can get is on a street corner!"

This time, Anna knew there was no way she'd be able to stay quiet. While Joan had no way of knowing how close to the mark her vow had come, that her new rival had actually performed on street corners, struggling to make enough money to put a roof over her head and food in her stomach, that ignorance wouldn't keep Anna from making her regret her words. No matter how big a scene she made, no matter how much embarrassment she caused herself, she was going to give Joan a piece of her mind, make her regret what she'd callously said, and cause her to think twice about ever crossing her path again!

But just as Anna was about to finally let her anger out, the door to the set flew open and a man spilled inside, his face dotted with sweat and worry. He looked exhausted, bent over, his hands on his knees, sucking in huge gulps of air while pointing back the way he'd come.

"What's the meaning of this?" Frank bellowed, once again full of anger, annoyed that anyone would dare to interrupt his work.

The man looked up, his eyes wide, steadied himself, and said, "Fire..."

For the second time that day, the room seemed to freeze in surprise, no one moving or saying a word, but the spell didn't last long.

"What did you say?" Samuel said hurriedly. "Did you say fire?"

The man nodded furiously, still winded. "One of the... buildings we put up...just down from...the hotel..." he struggled to say. "It's burning..."

Without hesitation, Samuel ran for the door. Immediately the rest of the crew followed, Frank included. Anna glanced down at Joan; the actress was smiling triumphantly, as if she'd just been given an award. But with all of the commotion, Anna had lost her anger, at least for now; any confrontation between the two of them would have to wait. So off she ran, wondering what she might find.

Anna had just reached the door when Joan called after her.

"Have fun out there!"

Anna raced down the street, heading toward the center of town. As she ran, people began to come out of their houses and businesses, looking to see what all of the commotion was about. Shouts drifted toward her from off in the distance, growing increasingly louder. A tendril of ominous black smoke snaked up into the clear afternoon sky, expanding with every passing second. The sharp, acrid smell of burning wood filled the air.

Men raced past her carrying empty buckets. Running hard, Anna rounded the corner near the Stagecoach Hotel and suddenly, right there before her eyes, was a raging inferno.

The building that was on fire was one that Samuel had proudly shown her just after their arrival in town, built by Valentine Pictures to serve as one of the movie's sets. But it was now nearly unrecognizable. Flames licked hungrily up the walls, danced just beyond the broken windows, and roared out of the hole that had been burned through the roof. Wood, glass, and metal were being consumed, creating a symphony of destruction, roaring louder than a train's engine. Where earlier there'd been a pleasing palate of colors painted onto the structure, there were now only the angry shades of flame; red, yellow, orange, and the ever-growing black of ruin. Here the smoke was thickest, stinging her eyes, while the stench of the blaze burned her nose.

All around her was chaos.

Samuel suddenly ran past her, visible for only a moment, like a ship in the morning fog. He was frantically waving his arms, one way and then another, desperate to organize some sort of effort to save the building. Shouts rang out all around, faint in the overpowering rage of the fire.

"Get every man you can find!"

"...afraid it looks hopeless..."

"...we can do now is keep it from spreading!"

Even with the intense heat and choking smoke, Anna found herself drawn toward the burning building. Pressing the sleeve of her blouse against her nose, she peered into the smoky gloom, wondering what, if anything, could be done to save it. Ahead of her, she noticed that a line of men had formed. Moving closer, she found that they were running a line of buckets from a nearby pump, each man passing one to the person in front of him and so on until they reached the fire; Anna recognized Montgomery standing near the middle. Without giving it a second thought, she took a place in line right behind her fellow actor.

It took a couple of passes of the heavy buckets, water

slopping over the rim and soaking the hem of her skirt and shoes, before Montgomery finally noticed her. When he did, he frowned.

"You shouldn't be here!" he shouted to be heard over the blaze.

"I want to help!" she replied.

"This isn't the place for you!" Anna knew that he meant it was because she was a woman.

"I can do this!" she insisted.

Montgomery still didn't look happy about it, but he nodded, taking each bucket she passed to him without further protest.

It didn't take long for Anna to get completely soaked, or for her shoulders and hands to ache and throb from passing the heavy buckets. Still, she didn't complain or beg out, but instead gritted her teeth and kept doing her part. But no matter how much water was passed forward, she soon realized that it was all for a lost cause; the building was going to burn to the ground.

"What do you suppose caused the fire?" she shouted to Montgomery.

"I don't know!" he answered. "It could've been anything!"

"It was probably a cigarette some fool tossed to the ground without thinkin'!" the man behind Anna interjected. "What with the way things are so dry 'round these parts, wouldn't take much for it to catch!"

"That's terrible!" Anna said.

"The worst part is that ain't nobody ever gonna know for

sure!" the man continued. "There ain't no way someone's gonna come forward and admit to bein' that stupid! He'd be fired on the spot! Whoever it was'll just keep his trap shut and his head down! Hell, he's gonna get paid to rebuild what he just burnt up!"

"As bad as it may be, he's probably right," Montgomery added.

The man shrugged. "Best thing to do now is worry 'bout the surroundin' buildin's!" Nodding his head forward, he added, "Looks like someone up there's got the same idea!"

Anna followed his gaze to see that the buckets of water were no longer being fed to the burning building, but being splashed against the side of the nearest structure instead; even though it wasn't on fire, she understood that people were trying to soak the wood in order to make sure that it stayed that way.

Ten minutes later, the burnt-out building collapsed into a pile of broken beams, shattered glass, and billowing ash. The crash echoed all around the center of town and loud in Anna's ears. Through the efforts of the townspeople and movie crew, it was the only structure destroyed.

Because of the fire, Samuel canceled the rest of the day's shooting. Even with the destruction, he still wore a broad smile as he went around shaking hands and thanking everyone who had helped try to put out the blaze. His hands and forehead were streaked with soot when he approached Anna to tell her that although he wished she had stayed safely away, he appreciated what she'd done nevertheless.

Optimistically, he'd declared it to be only a minor setback and that they'd just rebuild the building, bigger and better than ever.

Walking back to the hotel with Montgomery, her blouse soaked through with water and sweat, Anna wondered how angry Bonnie would be when she saw the state of her costume.

"Is making movies always this exciting?" she asked Samuel.

"Just give it another day or two," he answered with a wink.

By early evening, the sun had started to dip down to the horizon, slowly vanishing for the night but daubing the sky in brilliant hues of orange and purple as it left. Watching out the window of her hotel room, Anna was exhausted. She had blisters on both thumbs from passing the water buckets and her shoulders throbbed painfully. Still, she was so worked up by the excitement of the day that she could hardly stand still.

I can't stay cooped up in here...

Bouncing down the hotel's tall staircase, Anna headed through the front doors and out into the early summer evening.

Chapter Nine

YOU GOT AWAY FROM BOTH OF THEM?"

Dalton looked over at Walker Duncan and gave his friend a nod. The two of them sat on the back steps of the hardware store, the business Walker's family owned, as they watched the day slowly turn to night. Dalton had been talking about all the crazy things that had happened the day before, from discovering the extent of his money troubles at the bank, to colliding with the beautiful blond woman at the train depot, to discovering how deep his father's gambling debts ran; but the only thing Walker wanted to discuss was his fight with the Cobb brothers.

"I didn't say it was *easy*," Dalton explained with a frown. "Those two are bad news. The only reason I escaped with nothing worse than this," he said, thrusting out his chin and pointing at the mottled bruise of brown and purple, "was because I threw the first punch. Creed didn't see it coming. Lord knows what would've happened if he had, or if Audie had been a step quicker."

With the cuff of his worn, long-sleeved shirt, Walker wiped clean the piece of slate balanced on his knees, snatched up a nub of chalk, and began to furiously scribble his response.

Walker had been born mute. Even as a baby, he hadn't cooed, hadn't cried out, hadn't giggled at the silly faces his mother made, desperate for her only son to make a sound, *any* sound. As he grew older, most people in Redstone dismissed him as simple, but Walker was anything but. He watched everything and everyone around him like a hawk, quietly listening and learning. To the surprise of his parents, he flourished when he went to school; though he couldn't stand up in front of the classroom and recite his ABCs, he had long since committed them to memory, and from there, he'd found a way to communicate.

Everywhere he went, Walker took a piece of slate with him. As fast as he could, his hand flew across it, writing out questions, making statements, an odd declaration or two, even making comments about the weather, things that everyone else took for granted when they spoke. There wasn't a person in Redstone who wasn't familiar with his big, block-lettered script. Rather than waste paper, constantly wadding it up and throwing it away once he'd filled every line, he used the erasable slate so that he could start over in an instant. His pockets were always caked in chalk from fishing out a new piece, and his sleeves were equally dusty from wiping the slate, but he was able to have his say.

"I'M GLAD AUDIE DIDN'T FALL ON YOU. AS BIG AS HE IS, YOU'D HAVE BEEN SQUASHED FLAT!" he'd written, holding out the slate so that Dalton could read his reply.

"It wasn't his rump I was worried about."

"WHAT IF THEY COME AFTER YOU AGAIN?"

"I'll fight," Dalton answered matter-of-factly, his fist involuntarily tightening as the taut muscles of his forearm twitched. "I won't run away." His grim look softening, he looked over at Walker and asked, "If it comes down to a brawl, you'd stand with me, wouldn't you?"

"I DON'T THINK I'D BE A LOT OF HELP."

"Sure you would be. I reckon that Audie would take one look at you and run away as quick as he could. He'd hide behind his momma's skirt!"

"HA HA... VERY FUNNY..."

Dalton slapped his friend on the shoulder, doing the laughing for both of them, as usual.

Despite his claims to the contrary, Dalton knew that if it actually came down to it, Walker would fight beside him to the end. After all, that was how their friendship had begun. One day, when they were boys, a couple of the older lads had started picking on Walker because of his handicap, but Dalton wouldn't stand for it. He'd waded into the bullies with his fists flying, had soon gotten his nose bloodied, and expected that he was going to take a beating for his defiance. But it never came. Suddenly and surprisingly, the older boys tucked their tails between their legs and ran. When the dust settled, Dalton had found Walker right beside him, bleeding from a split lip but smiling all the same. They'd been close ever since.

There were many ways in which the two of them were different, the most obvious of them physical. Where Dalton was tall and broad-shouldered, thickly muscled from the long hours he spent shaping metal as a blacksmith, Walker was thin and wiry. He looked as if he might blow away in a stiff breeze. He had a head of sandy blond hair and a sprinkle of freckles across the bridge of his nose. Where Dalton was moody, often expecting the worst in life, Walker was more optimistic, even in the face of his handicap, meeting each obstacle as something possible to overcome.

Even with these differences, much was similar about them. They were both about the same age; Dalton was only two years older. They both enjoyed reading books, although Walker devoured them three times as fast as Dalton. Where their lives most closely intersected was that they both had fathers who struggled with addiction. Richard Duncan couldn't resist the lure of a bottle of alcohol, so both young men had been thrust early into roles of responsibility. While it was hard for both of them, they had each other.

"DID YOUR FATHER SAY HOW MUCH HE OWES?"

"I didn't ask," Dalton answered with a frown. "But even if he'd told me, I'd be a fool to believe a word he said. I've heard too many lies already. I reckon the only way I'd ever know for certain would be to go ask Vernon Black; but after what happened with the Cobb brothers, I can only imagine the welcome I'd get."

"SO HOW ARE YOU GOING TO PAY IT BACK?"

"Damned if I know."

For a moment, they sat in silence, the quiet broken only by the steady rhythm of a cricket's chirp and the barking of a faraway dog. Then Walker once again cleared his slate and started writing. When he finished, it read, "FOUND MY PA'S NEW HIDING SPOT."

"Where was it?" Dalton asked. He knew that Walker was deflecting their conversation from his friend's father's troubles and onto his own. While it did nothing to improve Dalton's sour mood, he appreciated the attempt.

"UP ON A RAFTER IN THE STOREROOM."

"How'd you know it was there?"

Walker laughed silently, his shoulders shaking. "ALL OF THAT WHISKEY MUST MAKE IT HARD TO REMEMBER THINGS." He cleaned the slate, then added, "HE USED THE SAME SPOT THREE MONTHS AGO."

Dalton had to laugh at that. "Did you confront him?"

"I POURED IT OUT AND FILLED IT BACK UP WITH WATER. HE PROBABLY ALREADY KNOWS. I DOUBT IT TASTED THE SAME."

One of the things Dalton enjoyed most about his time with Walker was the ease they felt around each other. It took time for them to communicate; Walker had to erase his slate and write out his message. But Dalton never felt impatient or hurried. Quite the opposite, it was nice not to rush; maybe it cut down on all the useless chatter other people spoke. With the two of them, everything had its time and place. On days like this one, when there was so much turmoil in his life, there was rarely anywhere else Dalton would want to be.

"WHERE WERE YOU DURING THE FIRE? I DIDN'T SEE YOU."

"I was working the forge," he explained. "With all the fire and smoke in there, I never noticed a thing. I didn't know about it until later, when Sam Chamberlain came in to pick up his weathervane."

"I DOUBT YOU WOULD'VE MADE MUCH DIFFER-ENCE."

"I'd have come if I'd known. How bad was it?"

"IT WAS A MESS. I HELPED PASS WATER BUCKETS."

"Serves those Hollywood people right, if you ask me." While Dalton was happy no one had been hurt in the fire, he wouldn't have given a damn if every one of their build-ings, *if all of Hollywood*, had burned to the ground.

"THERE YOU GO AGAIN."

One thing that Dalton and Walker disagreed about was the arrival of Hollywood in Redstone. Where Dalton saw the movie crowd as a nuisance, a pack of snobs who flaunted their success with their noses held high in the air, Walker looked at them differently; he saw opportunity. Since he knew their time in town would be short, he wanted to make as much from them as possible. The Dun-cans' hardware store, just like the Barneses' blacksmith shop, had never been busier. The difference between them was that Walker was happy to take their money with a smile instead of a frown. He found most of the newcomers to be nice, even if they talked a bit funny and their clothes were flashy. Only one or two of them had looked at him as if he was a monkey in the zoo.

"THERE WERE PLENTY OF MOVIE PEOPLE TRYING TO PUT OUT THE FIRE."

"Of course there were," Dalton replied. "It's *their* building that burned. Anything that costs them money is worth fighting for."

"YOU MAKE IT SOUND LIKE THEY'RE ALL BAD."

"Finding a good one's like plucking a needle from a haystack."

"WHAT ABOUT THE WOMAN FROM THE TRAIN? I'M SURE SHE'S FROM HOLLYWOOD, TOO."

Though it pained him to admit it, Dalton knew Walker was right. A blind man could've seen it. It was all there in the way she'd been dressed, her hair, the way that blowhard had rushed to help her up and make Dalton look like a fool. Everyone had been at the depot for *her.* She was Hollywood through and through. He knew he should despise her like all the others...

Then why can't I stop thinking about her?

Even with all that had happened, she still flitted in and out of his thoughts. Morning, noon, night, and especially in his sleep, he never knew when she might appear. He'd only been around her for a couple of minutes, but she'd managed to captivate him. When he'd first told Walker about her, he'd tried to hide his interest, but his friend had read him just as easily as one of his beloved books.

But then, just as he was about to say something, to offer up some ridiculous explanation for why she didn't deserve his ire, the words froze in his throat. There she was, turning off Main Street and coming closer, the setting sunlight catching her blond hair and lighting the strands as if they were made of gold. Dalton's breath caught and his heart thundered.

Walker followed his gaze, looking first at the woman, then back at his friend, and then once again to her. "IS THAT HER?" he wrote, underlining the last word.

Dalton could only nod; it was hard enough to take his eyes off her long enough to look at the slate and Walker's response.

"I SAW HER TODAY. SHE WAS HELPING WITH THE FIRE."

With every step she took, coming closer and closer, Dalton felt his stomach being slowly twisted into knots. It wasn't a feeling he was used to. He had no shortage of opportunities; women stopped him on the street or came by the blacksmith shop, their hands lingering on his arm for a moment longer than necessary. But in a town the size of Redstone, no one had ever caught *his* eye. Maybe it was because of all the time he'd spent watching his parents as they struggled to make ends meet, but he'd often wondered if a woman could ever come along and turn his head, make him want to get married and raise a family. There was no denying, however, that *this* woman was making him feel something he'd never felt before.

I wonder what her name is…

Suddenly, Walker hit him in the arm and thrust the slate in front of his face. "GO TALK TO HER!"

Dalton shook his head; she was too different, too cultured, too Hollywood. "She wouldn't have anything to do with a guy like me."

"WHY NOT?"

"Look at her," Dalton said, glancing up to see that she'd already started to walk past, her back to them.

"IF YOU DON'T GO AFTER HER, YOU'RE A FOOL!" Walker jabbed one finger against his slate for emphasis.

The strength of his friend's conviction made something change inside Dalton. Maybe she wouldn't give him the time of day, or maybe she was still angry about what had happened at the depot, but he'd never know unless he spoke to her. Because of the way she was haunting his every moment, he knew he owed it to himself to try. At least he'd be able to give her a real apology.

And maybe, just maybe…

With his chalk, Walker underlined the word "GO" three times, his eyes imploring, the edges of his mouth turning up in the faintest of smiles.

Dalton stood up.

Anna walked out the front door of the Stagecoach Hotel, smiled at a cameraman she recognized from the day's filming, and headed off down the street. She stopped for a moment to look at the still-smoldering wreckage of the building that had burned down; only the frame of one wall remained standing, reaching up toward the sky like a skeleton. A group of men still hauled buckets of water over and poured them on the charred remains, sending clouds of steam and ash billowing. But with all of her restless energy from the day's excitement, Anna didn't stay to watch for long. She needed to move.

Since she'd arrived in Redstone, Anna hadn't had the opportunity to see much of the small town on her own; Samuel had given her a tour of the studio's construction work and sets, and she'd had company every time she'd gone to and from the hotel, with Bonnie after her run-in with Milburn and with Montgomery after the fire. This was the first time she'd been able to explore by herself.

She made her way down Main Street, pausing to look in store windows. Businesses had long since closed for the day; everyone had shut their doors to come see the fire. While Redstone still looked to her a bit rough around the edges, with a few broken windows here and a cracked board there, as run-down as it had appeared when she'd arrived on the train, Anna began to notice some of its charm, too. As she walked, she saw crisp American flags rippling in the breeze, potted flowers on windowsills, but what interested her most were the townspeople. She saw people laughing, waving, and even helping their neighbors, part of that same sense of community that had sent everyone running to help battle the fire. It wasn't like the anonymous hustle and bustle of the city, a place where you didn't know the person living just across the hall.

This is nice, she thought to herself. *Just what I needed.*

As she walked under the awning of the bank, watching as a pair of children ran down the sidewalk ahead of her, a boy chasing a girl with long pigtails, both of them laughing among the first fireflies of the night, Anna couldn't completely escape the things that weighed heaviest on her mind. Joan was clearly trying to sabotage her movie career before it really ever got started. Causing her to drop a pitcher of water was undoubtedly only the beginning of Joan's plans. Anna was almost thankful for the fire; it had kept her from confronting Joan, something she feared would only have made matters worse. There was also the matter of Milburn's unwelcome advances. At least she'd managed to survive being yelled at by Frank Dukes and, with Montgomery's help, had even seemed to please the difficult director with her acting.

And there's still the stranger from the depot...

Shaking her head, her golden hair tumbling across her shoulders, Anna couldn't suppress a laugh. "One problem at a time," she muttered to herself.

The sun was steadily dropping and the sky darkening as the first stars began to shine in the east, so Anna decided to start heading back toward the hotel. Passing the bakery, she turned at the corner, wanting to take a different return route in order to see more of the town. It was then, staring up at the beveled windows of the nearest house, thinking that life in Redstone was a far cry from anything she'd ever known in the city, that she heard a voice behind her.

"Excuse me."

Anna turned around quickly, jolted by the suddenness of the sound. She was even more shocked to find out who had made it; it was the stranger from the train, the man who'd knocked her down and had been drifting in and out of her thoughts ever since.

"I'm sorry," he said, holding up his hands. "I didn't mean to scare you."

"You just startled me a bit, that's all," she replied.

"I saw you walking past," the stranger explained, glancing back over his shoulder, "and I thought I should come talk to you. I wanted to apologize for what happened at the depot."

As he spoke, Anna could feel her heart start to beat faster. Just as she had earlier, she found herself responding to the man's handsome, rugged face. His eyes searched hers, drawing her in. "That's all right," she managed, desperately trying to steady her nerves. "It was an accident."

"I'd like to say I'm sorry all the same."

"Apology accepted."

For a moment, there was an awkward silence between them, neither speaking. But Anna didn't feel uncomfortable or self-conscious. On the contrary, she felt oddly at ease.

"I'm Anna Finnegan," she said with a smile, holding out her hand.

Returning her smile, he reached out and took her offered hand, his dwarfing hers in size, his calloused fingers rough against her skin. "I'm Dalton," he said. "Dalton Barnes."

"It's nice to meet you."

"Likewise." When he let go of her hand, the warmth of his grasp lingered. Strangely though, his smile faltered for an instant; he looked uncomfortable. "I suppose it's not much of a leap to guess you're here with the movie," he said.

"Yes, I am," Anna answered. She thought about telling him that she was the lead actress, but the words remained unspoken; she didn't want him to think that she was bragging. "I haven't had a lot of time to look around, so I thought I'd take a walk and see the town."

"There isn't much to see," Dalton said with a chuckle. "Towns like Redstone are a dime a dozen."

"I don't think it's so bad. I've only ever known life in the city, people everywhere you turn, crowded streets and buildings, noise at all hours of the night and day. Sometimes it's nice for things to slow down a bit."

"You've only been here for two days. Tomorrow you'll be bored to tears."

Anna laughed. "Maybe you're right."

"Of course I am. I've lived here my whole life."

"Then you must be thrilled that the movie's come to town and brought a little excitement." As soon as she'd said it, Anna knew that she'd touched on a sore subject. The look was there again, the same flicker of dislike, a sign of *something* wrong. But it lasted for only an instant.

"I reckon that there're a couple of things about Redstone that aren't all bad," Dalton explained. "A few places worth visiting." He paused, looking directly at Anna, his eyes searching her face as if he was weighing what he should say. "Would you like to see one?" he finally asked.

Anna knew that the right thing to do was politely decline, that she should go back to the hotel, practice her lines, and get a good night's sleep so she'd be well rested for the next day's filming. She knew she should try to come up with a plan for the next time Joan tried to ruin her. She even knew that, after what happened with Milburn, she should be cautious around strange men, but even though she'd only spent a matter of minutes with him, there was no doubt in her mind that Dalton was nothing like Milburn. Despite it all, the truth was that she wanted to see where he'd take her. She wanted to spend time with him.

"Yes," Anna said, a smile slowly spreading across her face. "I'd like that very much."

Chapter Ten

ANNA FOLLOWED as Dalton led the way toward the edge of town. Houses began to thin out as the landscape became more and more barren. All the while, the sun continued its steady descent. They skirted a meandering creek, the water barely a trickle, before taking a worn path that weaved between tufts of dry-scrabble grass. What few sounds emanated from Redstone began to fade, soon vanishing altogether. As they walked, Dalton took the time to point out interesting sights; a hawk slowly circling on the warm winds high above, a pair of prickly cactus that had intertwined as they grew, and a group of lizards sunning themselves on a rock, catching the last heat of the day.

"They only come out when it starts to cool a bit," he explained. "If the sun's straight up in the sky, they keep to the shade."

"Sounds like good thinking to me," she replied.

Dalton stayed on the path as it wound down a hill and into a small depression, then held out his hand to Anna to help her up and onto a large outcropping of rock. They climbed up, soon reaching the top. Even with the cooler temperature, sweat began to bead on her forehead from the effort. They crossed the summit, then stopped. Dalton turned her away from the sun and pointed.

"There it is," he said.

Anna stared in amazement. Off in the distance, a couple of hundred feet from where they stood, were two huge rock formations, their red stone shining like fire in the setting sunlight. That by itself was impressive, but what was most amazing was the natural bridge that linked them, a stone overpass, wide at the ends and tapering toward the middle, high above the sandy ground below. With the sun behind them, shadows had begun to climb the stone, stretching farther and farther with every passing second, dancing in the fading light.

"It's beautiful," Anna said.

"I thought you might like it," Dalton replied.

"How did it get that way?"

"Hundreds and hundreds of years of wind and water, I reckon," he explained. "It must've been hollowed out over time. I've been coming here ever since I was a little boy, sitting right in this spot and watching the sun go down, and it's always looked the same."

"I suppose it makes sense that water *could* do that, but here?" Anna asked, "As hot as it is?"

"That right there's the reason why," Dalton answered.

"Just because it's as dry as a bone most of the time, doesn't mean we never get any rain." Holding his hand out toward the horizon, he said, "Every summer there'll be a storm that comes rolling in, the sky blacker than night with lightning flashing across the sky and thunder shaking the ground. When the rain comes pouring down, the ground's too dry to hold it so it just races around on the surface. It cuts down through these depressions and up against those rocks. Sometimes it comes so fast that it sweeps up anything unlucky enough to be in its way, livestock, fence posts, buildings and occasionally people. The land can be flooded for miles around."

Anna looked back at the naturally made stone bridge and the rough, desolate landscape that surrounded it and tried to picture what it would look like, surging with water while the sky bellowed and roared, rain pouring down from the heavens. It was almost impossible to imagine.

"I've never seen anything like this before," she said. "It sure doesn't look like this where I'm from."

"And where's that?" Dalton asked.

"St. Louis," Anna answered, "but I grew up in Chicago. Things there are so different, so tall and bold and brash, like night and day compared to here. Even doing something like this," she said, holding her arm out toward the sunset, "is a lot harder than you'd think because of all the buildings and people. Trees are few and far between. The smoke that billowed from the stockyards, the smell of it, could be overpowering. Growing up in my mother's apartment, I never would've imagined that there was a place like this out there, waiting for me to find." Turning to face Dalton, she added, "I can't imagine what it must've been like to grow up here and see it every day."

Dalton shrugged his broad shoulders. "When you see something all the time, it doesn't take long to lose that special feeling. It works the other way, too. The biggest town I've ever set foot in is El Paso, which isn't saying much; but if I were to visit a city like Chicago, I suppose I'd be feeling about the same way you are right now, maybe more so. Besides," he continued, "Redstone is plenty short on excitement."

"I beg to differ," she said with a smile. "The fire this afternoon was nothing if not exciting. I even got to help pass buckets."

"So I heard."

"You did? From whom?"

"A friend of mine saw you there and told me."

Immediately Anna understood that Dalton had been talking about her. Maybe that meant that the way he'd been drifting in and out of her thoughts ever since their collision at the depot wasn't so unusual after all. Maybe she wasn't the only one their meeting had had an impact on.

"I hope you don't think that sort of thing happens every day," Dalton said.

"If it did, I don't think the town would still be standing," Anna replied with a laugh. "Did you get to see it?"

Dalton shook his head. "I was busy working."

"What is it you do?"

He gave her an easy smile before staring down at his

hands, as if they would provide an answer. "I'm a blacksmith, just like my father and his before him."

"I'm afraid I don't really know what that means, not exactly," she said. Anna was surprised that she had no worries about admitting her ignorance, no fear that Dalton might consider her stupid for not knowing what he did for a living. There was something about him that made her want to be honest, even if in doing so she wasn't painting herself in the best light.

"Being a blacksmith means that I work with metal," Dalton explained, not seeming the least bit put out. "I build things and I tear them apart. I do it over a hot forge with a hammer and an anvil." Spreading his fingers wide, he held up his hands to the light, examining them. "I have plenty of nicks, cuts, and burns to show for it, but it's all I know how to do."

"Do you like it?" Anna asked.

He paused for a moment, the look on his face making Anna wonder if anyone had ever asked him before. "I reckon I like it well enough," he finally answered.

"It sounds like hard work."

"I'm used to it." Dalton paused, watching as the shadows crawled farther up toward the stone bridge. "What about you?" he asked. "Do you like being an actress?"

"So far," she answered.

"I can't imagine what that must be like. Seems strange to have to stand there and pretend to be someone you're not."

"Actually," Anna said with a smile, "I don't think our jobs are all that different, when you get down to it."

"How do you figure?"

"Well, when I'm acting, it's all about creating something out of what I have," she explained. "I need to be believable, so I search through my own experiences or those of someone close to me, maybe a story I've read or heard on the street. Sometimes it's easy, just a few little knocks to get it all in place, but other times it's a struggle, like when you really have to hammer a piece of metal into shape."

"I never would've thought of it that way," Dalton replied.

"I hadn't either, until you started talking about being a blacksmith," Anna answered. Still, she couldn't help but notice a change in Dalton's mood. He faced away from her, his eyes avoiding hers. He looked tense, his jaw clenching occasionally. She'd noticed a similar cloud pass over him back in town and hadn't said a word. But this time, she couldn't hold her tongue.

"Is something the matter?" she asked. "Did I say something wrong?"

Dalton gave a scarcely noticeable flinch, as if he'd just been caught doing something he shouldn't. "No," he said, working a smile onto his face. "Everything's fine."

Anna couldn't help but feel a twinge of disappointment. She knew he was lying. What she couldn't understand was why.

Dalton was a man who worked with his hands. He pounded on rods of steel, twisted pieces of iron, shaping the metal over the forge. Most days were spent alone, but even when his father labored beside him, they never said much, often only a word or two when one of them needed help. The sounds of his profession were the sharp clang of a hammer against hot metal and the hiss of steam after it was dropped into water. There definitely wasn't a script or dialogue to recite. No scenes to perform or costumes to be worn. No audiences rising to their feet to clap their approval or stampeding to the exits as they booed their dislike.

Dalton was most definitely not an actor. And that was why, the moment he'd lied to Anna, he knew she hadn't believed him.

Up until then, he'd felt as if their time together was going better than he could have hoped. It'd been a touch awkward in the beginning; walking up behind her on the street, he'd been surprised to find that his stomach was full of butterflies, but once they'd started talking, his nerves had quickly calmed. Learning her name felt like being trusted with a secret. It had been bold to ask her if she'd like to see more of Redstone, but he'd been thrilled when Anna had accepted.

He'd known right where to go. The stone bridge had always been his favorite spot. Whenever his father had gambled away too much money, or if he'd had a bad day, Dalton sat and watched the sun slowly set against the rocks. He liked the solitude, the chance to be alone and straighten out his troubled thoughts. Gazing at the stone bridge never failed to soothe him. Holding Anna's hand had sent a shiver of excitement racing through him, but it was the way her face lit up as she saw the bridge for the first time that told Dalton he'd made the right choice in bringing her.

But then she'd started talking about the movie she was filming and everything began to unravel.

For some reason, Dalton had it in his head that any woman who worked in Hollywood couldn't be very bright, that an actress got her position solely because of her looks. But Anna destroyed that myth. She certainly *was* beautiful, far more so than he remembered, but she was also charming, funny, and smart. Listening to her talk, captivated by what she said and how she said it, Dalton soon understood how foolish it was to hope something could develop between them. She was an actress, from the city, with opportunities and dreams far beyond anything he could aspire to. Why would a woman like her be interested in a blacksmith like him?

It made him feel frustrated and angry.

What Dalton felt wasn't directed at Anna, even though she represented Hollywood just as much as the rich jackasses who traipsed into his business. His anger was directed at himself. He was stuck in Redstone. Stuck with his father's gambling. Stuck with no present and no future. He was born here and, more than likely, he'd die here. People from a far-off place like Hollywood, where money and fame seemed to grow on trees, would never understand the struggles he faced.

"Tell me what's bothering you," Anna pressed.

"It's nothing," Dalton said again, his lie even less convincing than the first time he'd uttered it.

"No, it's not. Clearly, it's more than that. Don't take this personally," she said, a smile teasing at the corners of her mouth, "but you're not a very good actor."

But when Dalton didn't return her smile, Anna's faltered.

With the sun behind her, her blond hair blazing orange in the fading light, Anna stepped closer and placed her hand on Dalton's; almost immediately, he was filled with the same electric feeling as before. When Anna spoke, her voice was soft. "If it's because of something I said or did wrong, I'm sorry."

"It's not you," he replied, his voice low, his mouth feeling as dry as the ground at his feet.

"Then tell me what's bothering you. I'd like to try to understand."

Later that night, when Dalton had had time to think about what happened next, he realized that it had been that one word, *understand*, that had set loose the anger he'd kept dammed up inside. He knew then that he'd made a mistake, that he'd lashed out at someone who didn't deserve his ire, someone who was only trying to help.

But that was later.

"I don't have to explain myself," he growled, snatching away his hand. "I don't need your pity."

"Dalton, wait," Anna hurriedly replied, her eyes wide, the shock she felt written plain on her lovely face, wondering where this sudden, unexpected anger was coming from. She held up her hands as she took a tentative step back, trying to recover the smile that had completely slipped away; it came back, but only for a second, then vanished for good. She didn't look afraid, not exactly, but very confused. "I didn't mean to offend you," she said. "I'm sorry if I did. Really, I am."

But it was too late for Dalton to let it go. Even if he'd wanted to stop, he couldn't have; his anger was picking up steam like a stone rolling downhill. It was like the dominoes his father occasionally gambled with, the ones George used to set up on the kitchen table to entertain his young son; when one teetered over, it collided with the next, then the one after, and on and on until the table was littered with them. He wouldn't be able to stop until there was nothing left to say.

"What do you have to be sorry about?" he asked. "Look at you! You're an actress! With the way everyone fawned all over you at the depot, I would've thought Eleanor Roosevelt was on board!" Pointing at her clothing, he said, "You're wearing a blouse that probably cost more than I make in a month, while mine's got so many stains on it I don't know what color it is anymore."

"Now wait just a minute," Anna said, "That's not—"

"All of you Hollywood people come here and walk around like cocks on the walk, flaunting your fame and money," Dalton continued, cutting her off. "Folks around these parts barely make ends meet and you all act like we should be grateful for whatever scraps you throw our way. But that doesn't make you better than us! It doesn't!"

Ever since Valentine Pictures had come to Redstone, Dalton had fantasized about giving someone from the company a piece of his mind. But he never would've imagined it would be Anna. He'd always expected it would make him feel better, relieved that he'd unburdened himself, but now, watching her stare at him, he felt sick to his stomach. Right then and there, he wished he could go back and swallow every vicious word he'd spoken. But before Dalton could muster up the words to express how horrible he felt, to stumble his way toward an apology, Anna's jaw clenched, her eyes narrowed, and she walked straight up to him and jabbed her finger right in the middle of his chest.

"How dare you talk to me like that!" Anna snapped, punctuating every word with another poke at his sternum. "You don't know the first thing about me or how I was brought up! Nothing! You don't have any idea what I had to go through to get where I am today! Not a clue!"

"But, I—" he managed before she again cut him off.

"And why would you assume that every person who's working on this movie thinks the same?" she asked with a sneer. "How would you feel if I thought that every person in this town was an ignorant, ill-tempered, insensitive, loud-mouthed jerk?" With every derogatory word Anna used to describe him, there was another jab of her finger into his chest. "You said before that you didn't want my pity. Well, too late! With the way you go around looking at the worst in people, you've got it!"

For a long moment, neither of them said a word. Dalton knew that if Walker could see what sort of mess he'd just made of things, he would've written one word on his slate; "STUPID!" The worst part was that Dalton knew he deserved it. To think, there'd been a moment when they'd first started their walk when he wondered if the night might end with a kiss; now he'd be lucky to escape without being slapped.

"Anna, I'm sorry..." he finally managed.

"Take me back to town," she snapped.

Dalton thought about pleading his case some more, but instead held his tongue, nodded, and started to lead her back the way they'd come. With every step he took, he felt like an even bigger fool. Here he was with the first interesting woman to come his way in longer than he could remember, the beauty who'd been weaving in and out of his thoughts ever since they'd met, even in his dreams, and he'd already ruined any chance he might have with her.

Chapter Eleven

VERNON BLACK TOOK a quick look at his gold pocket watch as he crossed Main Street, heading toward his office. It was early, just a few minutes before six, and Redstone felt deserted. Above, the sky was just beginning to lighten, the sun peeking up in the east, setting the horizon aglow. In the west, the remaining stars of night clung tenaciously to the still-dark sky, as if they weren't quite ready to let go. There was even a slight chill lingering in the air, though it would be gone soon enough as the day began to heat up.

Even though he had a hand in businesses that didn't shut down until far into the night, particularly taverns and gambling dens, Vernon preferred to rise early instead of sleeping late. The morning was a time for him to be alone, to avoid the distractions that cluttered most of his days. He hadn't amassed his wealth and power by resting on his laurels. He liked to go to his office, to think of new ways to get what he wanted, to make plans about taking what others had, to roll up his sleeves and get dirty.

Some days were dirtier than others.

Vernon turned down an alleyway between a cobbler's shop and Redstone's biggest tavern, his most profitable business. Stairs rose up the outside of the building, leading to his office. There was another entrance inside the bar; he wasn't stupid enough to have only one way to escape, should the need arise. Climbing the stairs, he fished out his key, turned it in the lock, and pushed open the door. He'd taken only a couple of steps inside when he kicked something with his foot. In the faint morning sunlight spilling in the door, he saw that it was an envelope. Without opening it or even picking it up, he knew what it was.

Stepping back onto the landing, Vernon looked down the length of the alley behind him and then toward the street, but no one was around. He wasn't surprised; whoever it was who'd left the envelope wouldn't be lingering, watching to see if delivery had been received. Whoever it was behind all this mischief was much smarter than that.

After locking the door, Vernon picked up the envelope and placed it on his desk. Pulling the shades tight, he turned on a lamp, poured himself a short glass of whiskey, and settled into his chair. For a long moment, he stared ahead, leaving the envelope untouched, and thought.

The first job he'd been contacted for had been an easy one, just as promised. Creed had sneaked into the newly constructed building, lit a kerosene-soaked rag, gotten out before anyone noticed the rapidly growing blaze, and then watched from afar as it burned to the ground. Ever cautious, Vernon had waited, wondering if anyone had seen Creed, but no one had reported the fact. Creed could blend in when necessary, unlike his brother, whose sheer size drew attention; that was why Audie had been kept out of the crime.

Once this job was finished, Vernon knew that another envelope would be coming, he just couldn't predict when. He'd mentioned it to Creed, told the man to keep his eyes on the office door, had tried to do so himself, but had been fairly certain that he wouldn't see the next package's arrival. Once again, whoever was behind all this was no fool; Vernon even suspected that a patsy had been hired to slide the packet under the door, so as to better insulate its author from discovery. Regardless of the how and why, here it was.

Now, what in the hell's inside it?

Vernon picked up the envelope, tore off one end, and dumped the contents out onto his desk. What he saw shocked him. There was enough money, in huge bills, to make him suck air back through his clenched teeth. Slowly, he counted it. There was twice what had been sent with the first envelope. There was also another letter. Unfolding it, Vernon began to read.

The letter opened with congratulations on a job well done. It praised Vernon for following instructions perfectly and explained that the money included in the envelope was payment as promised. It then outlined the next step in its author's plan. Vernon read it through once, then again, and then a third time. While burning the building down had been simple, what the letter now asked of him was more complicated. Much more risk was involved. Still, the potential reward was incredible; the letter stated that he would get double what he'd just received. Vernon looked back over at the pile of money; twice *that* meant that whoever slid the money under the door was going to need more than one envelope.

Ever since Hollywood had arrived in Redstone, Vernon had been raking in money hand over fist. But if he followed the letter's instructions, everything would be jeopardized. As devious as the plan was, Vernon doubted that it'd be enough to make Valentine Pictures pack up and leave town. For now, it made sense for him to go along and get richer in the process.

There was other money to be made, too. Creed kept pressing him about George Barnes and his kid; Vernon knew that his flunky would never get over his wounded pride if he wasn't given a chance to earn it back. It would soon be time to give him the opportunity to do just that.

Vernon put down the letter and again picked up the money, enjoying the heft of it in his hand. While he couldn't deny that this was the oddest business relationship he'd ever entered into, he was starting to like it.

"I wonder who you are," he muttered.

He wondered what it would take to find out.

"Does that feel too tight?"

Anna pushed a few wind-blown strands of hair away from her face and looked down at Bonnie. The seamstress knelt in front of her as she made a few last-minute alterations to Anna's costume. The cuffs of Bonnie's shirt were littered with pins and a few were even pressed between her lips; they made her mumble when she talked.

"It's fine," Anna answered.

Bonnie frowned deeply. "I still don't like the look of that hem," she said. Unsatisfied, she began to make more changes.

Shading her eyes, Anna looked around the outdoor set. It had been erected at the far southern end of town, a couple of blocks away from Main. A pair of older houses stood nearby, the last noticeable signs of civilization before the landscape disappeared into a mess of stunted grass, rocks, and a few lonely trees. It looked desolate, which was just the authentic feel Samuel had been seeking.

Even though one of the movie company's newly constructed buildings had unexpectedly burned to the ground the day before, Samuel showed no signs of distress. He was once again full of energy and excitement, walking beside Frank as the scene was laid out. Anna was to be among a group of townspeople, mostly women and the elderly, who were to cheer on the men as they all rode out on horseback to chase down the Hawk and his bandits. Over a dozen horses lazed about in the meager shade, eating from feedbags as their tails shooed away pesky flies. The whole scene would last only a matter of seconds, the camera focusing on the posse. Later, a close-up would be added of Anna's fretful, worried reaction. This was an important shot, one that would be used to sell the wild majesty of Texas to the audience. But Anna was too preoccupied to give it much more than a passing thought.

All she could think about was Dalton.

She had been up half the night replaying their conversation over and over again in her head. Everything had been going so well. He was unlike anyone else she'd ever met, rough in appearance yet kind in word, scruffy but handsome. She'd felt something between them, an unexpected spark. But then they'd started talking about her being an actress and it had all fallen apart.

No matter how hard Anna tried, she still couldn't understand why he'd become so upset. The way he'd talked about Hollywood, about how those connected to the place were snobs who looked down their noses at people like him, had been bad enough, but to think that *she* would think that way was ridiculous. If he knew her background, how much she'd struggled and sacrificed to get to where she was, he would have understood how wrong he'd been to say such things. There was a part of her that had wanted to tell him, to set him straight, but he'd made her so angry that she could hardly think clearly. Once she'd demanded that he take her back to town, Dalton had silently complied, the two of them walking back the way they'd come, different people from those who'd gone out. By the time they'd come within sight of the hotel, neither of them had spoken a word. When Dalton had stopped in his tracks, Anna had the impression he'd wanted to say something, maybe apologize, but she was still so put out that she just kept right on walking.

She'd never once looked back.

But now, after thinking about Dalton all night and day, Anna wasn't completely willing to write him off. Part of it was that she'd never been particularly lucky with men. In all her years working in vaudeville and then traveling around with theater troupes, she hadn't had one significant relationship. That wasn't to say there hadn't been suitors; she'd been pursued by fellow cast members, stagehands, there'd been the memorable time the orchestra's trombonist had serenaded her with his instrument, and she'd had more than her share of love letters written by members of the audience. But Anna had turned them all down. She'd always been so driven to succeed, so focused on her acting career, that no one had ever penetrated the barrier she'd put up around herself. Somehow, she'd convinced herself that she had no time for love and that a man in her life would only get in the way.

But there was something about Dalton that was different, that spoke to her in a strange, unfamiliar way. No man had ever introduced himself less elegantly than he had; that was for certain. Even as Samuel had chastised the man for not only knocking her down, but also failing to apologize for it, Anna hadn't been angry. The truth of it was, from the first moment they'd met, she'd been intrigued by Dalton. Maybe it was because they were so obviously different. Or maybe it was because after spending time with him, there was clearly more to the small-town blacksmith than met the eye, although she wasn't sure if discovering what he was hiding inside might be a good thing.

Still, Anna *was* upset about what had happened. Normally she would've completely written him off and never spoken to him again. Surprisingly, she felt like doing the opposite; she wanted to see him again, to find out if there was an explanation for his anger. She wondered if she might even be able to help him.

"There!" Bonnie said triumphantly, leaning back on her heels to look at her work. "It finally looks right!"

Anna looked down at her skirt and couldn't really see any difference. Regardless, she said, "I think you're right. That is better."

Just then, Frank's voice rang out from his director's chair. "Places, everyone!" he shouted. "Places!"

Lifting up the hem of her long skirt, Anna hurried to join the other actors, with Bonnie trailing along to see how her costume looked when she moved. Though Dalton still filled her thoughts and she was no closer to deciding what, if anything, she should do, it was time to get to work and stop wondering.

For now...

For the next couple of hours, the cast repeated the scene again and again, trying to get the action just right. Under the relentless sun, Frank made the riders race their horses past the camera, their hooves thundering over the hard ground, the leather of their saddles creaking, and the men sweating. Through it all, the director remained unsatisfied. On several occasions, he threatened to fire riders for offenses that ranged from going too fast to going too slow, or, first, for looking directly at the camera, then, before the next take, looking away too intently. Anna was thankful that Frank's ire wasn't aimed at her. Still, she was tired from standing around in the heat. But finally, a take ended without a tirade. Both Samuel and Frank smiled broadly.

The day's shooting was over.

Anna was walking back toward town with a couple of the other actors from the day's shoot when she saw Milburn just ahead. The young actor was leaning against the back of a pickup truck, one foot on the bumper, watching her. Another man stood beside him, talking animatedly with his hands, a lit cigarette between his fingers, its smoke yanked one way and then the other, but Milburn didn't seem to be listening. His eyes met hers for an instant before Anna looked quickly away.

This was the first she'd seen him since his unwanted advances in the dressing room. Even though her mind had been full of thoughts about Dalton, she never completely forgot what Milburn had done; every time she recalled the feeling of his hand clamping down on her arm, refusing to let her go as he spoke his lecherous words, his breath hot on her face, it made her sick to her stomach. She'd hoped to keep avoiding him for as long as she could, at least up until the point where they would start filming together and she wouldn't have a choice. But now, out of the corner of her eye, she saw him push off the truck, leaving the other man confused by his abrupt departure, and start walking toward her.

He stopped right in front of her, forcing some of the other actors to move out of his way, and said, "I want to talk to you."

Anna stared at Milburn, refusing to look away. She considered just walking past and ignoring what he'd said, but something inside her wouldn't allow it. Maybe it was because she wanted to stand up for herself and show him that she wasn't afraid, or maybe it was because she wanted him to apologize for what he'd done. Either way, she wasn't going to back down. Besides, they were standing in the middle of town; surely he wouldn't do anything untoward.

Not until she'd said her good-byes to her fellow actors did she finally turn and speak to Milburn. It repulsed Anna to see one of the women conspiratorially wink at her, as if she should consider herself lucky that such a handsome man wanted her company. "I'm listening," she said simply.

"You're looking nice today," he said, surveying her up and down, the tip of his tongue darting swiftly between his lips like a snake.

"What do you want?" she asked, not in the mood for any of the games he might want to play.

Milburn acted slightly taken aback. "Am I not allowed to pay you a compliment?"

"Not after what you pulled in the dressing room, you're not."

"You're still sore about all that?" He moved a half-step closer; Anna had to fight the urge to back the same distance away, not wanting to show weakness. "We just got off on the wrong foot, that's all," he continued. "It's just a misunderstanding. I'll tell you what, why don't you come on up to my room tonight, we can have a couple of drinks, and then I'll make it up to you."

"Is this your idea of an apology?" Anna asked with disgust.

"What do I have to be sorry about?" he answered her question with one of his own. Anna could see that he honestly did not understand.

Even though her evening with Dalton had ended badly, Anna was shocked by the differences between Milburn and the blacksmith. While there was no denying that Dalton had problems, there was still a kindness inside him; she remembered his laugh, as well as the way his eyes lit up when he first talked about the stone bridge. But there was nothing but malice inside Milburn. He was selfish, rude, egotistical, and honestly believed that every woman he met should want nothing more than to become his lover. Just because he was a star, he expected Anna to do anything he wanted, including going to bed with him. Looking back, her first instinct had been right; she should've just walked away without a word.

In fact...

"I'm leaving," she said as she started to go past him. But as he had in the dressing room, Milburn grabbed her hard by the arm and angrily yanked her closer.

"You're not going anywhere," he snarled, his voice low.

"Let go of me," she insisted.

"Not until I'm done with you."

"What do you think you're doing?" Anna couldn't believe his daring. Desperate, she looked around, thinking that someone must be watching them, must have seen what Milburn had done, but the streets were empty. Once again, she tried to pull herself free, but he only squeezed harder.

"I'm the only one who should be asking that question. Maybe I didn't make myself clear enough the last time, but I always get what I want," he explained, speaking the last words slow and sharp, his eyes staring daggers into Anna's. "I didn't get to be such a big star by letting people give me 'no' for an answer, and there's no way in hell I'm gonna start now. So when I tell you that you're coming up to my room, you don't ignore me and start to walk away," he growled as he dragged her close enough that her chest was pressed up against his, "you ask me what time I want you to be there."

This time, Anna wasn't going to quietly allow Milburn to hurt and demean her. But just as she was about to scream, to shout and shout until someone came to her aid, she looked over Milburn's shoulder and saw Montgomery. He was walking up the street alone, late to leave the afternoon's filming and looking at the two of them quizzically. When he saw the distress in Anna's face, he began to hurry toward them.

"Just what is going on here?" he demanded.

Milburn spun around and glared at the older actor, angry for the interruption. "Nothing for you to worry about."

"That hardly looks to be the case to me," Montgomery answered, seeing that Milburn still held Anna by the arm.

Sensing her chance, Anna yanked as hard as she could. "Let go of me!" she yelled; this time, Milburn did as she asked. Once free, she moved quickly away, stepping closer to Montgomery.

Though Milburn still had a sneer on his face, it was obvious to Anna that he was uncomfortable with the added attention. It reminded her of bullies she'd known as a girl; when push came to shove, they were often more bark than bite. "We'll continue this talk later," he grumbled before swiftly walking away.

Once Milburn was well on his way, Montgomery turned to Anna. "Are you all right?" he asked. "Did he hurt you?"

Though she could still feel where Milburn's fingers had clutched her arm, Anna said, "I'm fine."

"What was that all about?"

"He seems to think that we should be having some sort of . . . relationship . . ." she explained, the words bitter in her mouth. "This is the second time he's approached me and both times he hasn't much liked the answer I've given."

Montgomery looked back up the street to where Milburn was just rounding a corner and escaping out of sight. "I've heard that about him," he replied. "Whenever someone is a problem in the industry, word eventually gets around. Quite frankly, I was surprised Samuel hired him."

Anna hated to think that Milburn might have done this sort of thing before.

"You said this was the second time this has happened?" Montgomery asked.

She nodded.

"Then I think you have no choice but to talk to Samuel about it. Milburn might be a bastard and a louse, but if our producer has a word with him, I'm quite certain he'll be on his best behavior. The last thing he'd want would be to lose his job."

Anna thought about it for a moment. There was no denying that Milburn deserved to pay for what he'd done, but it was more complicated than that. She didn't want to be a troublemaker. She already had a problem with Joan. As Montgomery said, word got around the movie industry; she didn't want to be stuck with the label of being difficult to work with.

Still, what Montgomery was suggesting made sense. Milburn couldn't just keep getting away with things. There needed to be consequences. Still, she hesitated.

"Do you really think it would be best?"

"I do," he answered.

Finally, Anna nodded her agreement. She had no choice. Besides, it made her shudder to think what Milburn would do if he got his hands on her a third time.

Chapter Twelve

DALTON BROUGHT HIS heavy hammer down with a clang, the vibrations from striking the long piece of steel reverberating up the length of his arm. Sweat slicked his taut arms, beaded on his forehead, and dripped onto his work; any droplets that landed on the scorching hot metal instantly turned to steam. He was trying to shape an addition for the track that the movie company used to move their camera, a curve that would allow them to alter their shot without any break in filming. It was delicate work, the angle had to be just right, but Dalton had been struggling to focus on his task all day.

All he could think about was Anna.

Looking back, he realized that he'd made an ass of himself. What had he been thinking, ranting about Hollywood like that? He knew it was unfair to generalize that way, and it was even worse that by doing so he was including Anna, but once he'd gotten started, he just couldn't stop. All night, he'd replayed every harsh word she'd said to him once he'd finally finished. He'd deserved them all. On the long walk back to town, there'd been a dozen times he'd wanted to stop, to apologize, but he couldn't find the words. By the time the hotel was in sight, he knew that it wouldn't do any good even if he could locate them. It was too late.

He'd already destroyed whatever might have grown between them.

In between blows of his hammer, Dalton heard a loud knocking. He looked up to find Walker standing at the open double doors of the workroom.

"Give me a minute to finish and I'll be out," he said.

Dalton hammered the piece of metal into shape, dropped it into the trough to cool, and fetched himself a ladle of water, the excess pouring down the front of his work shirt and making it stick to his heaving chest, before he finally stepped outside. The high afternoon sun actually felt cool on his skin after the sweltering heat of the shop.

Walker sat up on one of the fence posts behind the shop, already holding out his slate and looking impatient. Dalton knew what his friend wanted to talk about; he had known this conversation was coming the moment he'd left the Stagecoach. Sure enough, as he neared he read, "SO WHAT HAPPENED LAST NIGHT?"

Dalton frowned as he leaned against the fence, but didn't answer.

Wiping the slate clean, Walker quickly wrote, "WHAT DID YOU DO?"

Taking a deep breath, Dalton told him everything. He talked about first approaching Anna, of how she'd accepted his offer, and of how excited she'd been to see the stone bridge. He paused for just a second before plunging on; admitting to frowning when she'd started talking about her job, and then how he'd erupted when she'd pressed him about it. He left nothing out, all the way up to and including taking Anna back to the hotel; what good would it do him to lie now?

Through it all, Walker sat and listened, scowling. When Dalton finished, his friend still made no move to write on his slate, and the two of them sat in silence beneath the sweltering sun. Dalton could tell that Walker was angry from the way he kept lightly whacking his slate against his leg. Finally, Walker wiped it clean, dug a fresh piece of chalk from his pocket, and began to write.

"STUPID!"

This was just the word Dalton had expected Walker to write. And, just like everything Anna had said to him last night, he deserved it.

"I TOLD YOU THAT THEY'RE NOT ALL BAD PEOPLE."

"I know, I know," Dalton grumbled.

"AND SHE'S ONE OF THE GOOD ONES."

"I didn't take her out to the bridge just so I could give her a piece of my mind," he explained, trying to defend himself a bit. "It just happened. I wish I could take it all back, but I can't. I blew it."

"MAYBE IT'S NOT TOO LATE."

"Believe me, it is," Dalton disagreed, remembering that Anna had not once looked back as she'd walked to the hotel.

"THE ONLY WAY YOU'LL KNOW FOR SURE IS IF YOU GET UP OFF YOUR ASS," Walker wrote, holding up a finger to show that he wasn't finished, showing some frustration that he couldn't clean his slate any faster. He then added, "GO TO THE HOTEL AND APOLOGIZE!"

"I'm supposed to just wait outside the Stagecoach for her to show up?"

"YES, THAT'S EXACTLY WHAT YOU SHOULD DO."

"Someone will call the sheriff," he said, adding a bitter laugh. "They'll say some degenerate is lurking around. Besides, I don't think Anna wants to listen to anything more I have to say."

"IF THAT HAPPENS, THEN SO BE IT. BUT JUST MAYBE..."

"That sounds like crazy talk."

Walker shrugged.

"What are the odds? One in a hundred? A thousand?"

"THAT ONE HAS TO COME UP SOMETIME, DOESN'T IT?"

Dalton thought about what Walker was arguing. Odds were, Anna wouldn't talk to him and that, even if she did, she'd do so in order to give him an even bigger piece of her mind. Still, if she lashed into him and screamed at him to get lost, at least he'd know for certain how she felt. He wouldn't have to spend the rest of his life asking the same question over and over.

What if…?

Walker tapped him on the shoulder. Dalton looked at the slate. It read, "EVEN IF YOU END UP LOOKING LIKE A FOOL, DON'T YOU THINK SHE'S WORTH IT?"

Dalton thought about it, but it didn't take long for him to come up with an answer. The truth of it struck him like a rock right between the eyes. Anna Finnegan was special; there was no other way for him to say it. If he somehow managed to get another chance to talk to her, he wouldn't waste it. Instead, he'd do everything he could to make her see him in a different light; not as some hothead itching for an argument, but as he truly believed himself to be inside.

"Yeah…she is…" he said.

"THEN WHAT ARE YOU WAITING FOR? GO!"

Dalton leaned off the weathered fence and gave Walker a friendly pat on the shoulder. He'd just started back to the shop to close up when he heard the sound of snapping fingers behind him. He turned to find Walker smiling mischievously and holding out his slate.

"THIS TIME, TRY NOT TO BE SO STUPID."

After tidying up a bit and putting on his cleanest shirt, Dalton headed toward the Stagecoach Hotel. The sun had started its steady drift downward, the dark shadows of the late afternoon stretching farther with each passing minute, although the day was still plenty hot. Looking down Main Street, he saw people milling around on the hotel's long porch, talking and laughing. A few still looked to be in costume, their clothes harking back to an older time. Dalton recognized only one or two faces. With every step he took, he grew more uncomfortable. Deep down, he understood what Walker had told him, that not all the people from Hollywood were as bad as Dalton assumed them to be, but he struggled to let his prejudices go. Stopping just across the street from the hotel, he began to feel paranoid, as if every eye was watching and judging him.

Just remember why you're here...

For Dalton, one of the worst parts about his coming to the hotel was that he had no idea how long he was going to have to wait for Anna. For all he knew, she was already inside, not that he was about to go to the front desk and ask. If she wasn't there, he hadn't the slightest idea when he might expect her to return. He remembered some of the movie people who'd come to the blacksmith shop talking about filming at night; Dalton wondered if she might not be back before dawn. Loitering outside the hotel seemed ridiculous, but what choice did he have? Absently, Dalton began to pace in an attempt to calm his jumpy nerves, but it seemed a futile effort.

Still, the problem of where Anna was paled in comparison to trying to figure out what he was going to say to her when she finally did appear. He'd so muddled things between them that a simple apology might not make much of a difference. For the briefest of moments, Dalton's determination wavered. Maybe this was a bad idea.

Dalton walked back and forth, ten paces one way and then the same number back, his hands jammed deep into his pockets and his eyes on his feet. But suddenly, something caught his attention. Glancing up, he was startled to find a man barreling toward him almost at a run. The stranger looked nervous. With his head twisted around so that he was looking back in the direction from which he'd come, he hadn't even noticed Dalton. A collision looked unavoidable.

There was only enough time for Dalton to shout, "Hey, buddy, look—" before the man slammed into him.

Though they hit each other hard, Dalton managed to stay upright, staggering backward a couple of steps. The other man wasn't so lucky. He careened off Dalton and crashed onto the sidewalk in a heap, landing hard on his side, his elbow cracking against the bricks. But the man didn't stay down long. With an ugly grimace of pain and anger, he shot back to his feet, glaring daggers, his hands balled into fists. Dalton had seen this look many times before; the stranger was itching for a fight.

"Why don't you watch where the hell you're going," he snarled.

Looking at the man, Dalton had no doubt that he was from Hollywood. His hair, though disheveled from running and the fall, had just the right look. It was there in the chiseled jaw and bright eyes. But mostly it was the way the stranger carried himself, as if he were better than everyone else, as if all he encountered should just get the hell out of his way.

He was just the sort of man Dalton hated most.

"Well?" the man kept on. "Don't you have anything to say for yourself?"

"You ran into me," Dalton replied, his voice low and

menacing. With everything that had happened with Anna, with how big a fool he'd been, the idea of a brawl suddenly wasn't so unappealing. The fact that he'd be squaring off with some dandy from Hollywood who fancied himself to be tougher than he really was made it all the sweeter.

In as little time as it would've taken him to snap his fingers, Dalton saw all the air go out of the man's sails. The two men were about the same height, but the blacksmith's arms and chest were more hardily built, thick from lifting and shaping metal all day. Dalton saw the stranger's eyes widen slightly as he came to understand that, if it came to a fight, he was going to come up lacking.

"You should've... should've been paying more attention..." he stammered, still not completely willing to back down from the challenge he'd made.

"How do you figure?" Dalton asked, taking a step closer to the man; immediately, the stranger moved a step back.

"You just should've," the man continued to protest. "Next time, be more careful!" With that, he turned on his heel and started rushing toward the Stagecoach. All the way to the hotel, even as he was going up the front steps, he kept looking back over his shoulder.

"What an idiot," Dalton muttered under his breath.

Still, he was glad for the distraction. Strangely enough, nearly getting into a fight had calmed his nerves. He still didn't have any idea what he was going to say to Anna when he finally saw her, but he was no longer worried about the moment arriving.

I wonder why that guy was so worked up...

Walking up to the corner, Dalton looked down the street in the direction the stranger had been coming from. Shading his eyes, he saw something that made his heart start pounding. There, no more than fifty feet away, was Anna.

She was walking with another man, a slightly older fellow, whom Dalton pegged as part of the movie production. When Anna noticed him watching her, she stopped short. To Dalton's eyes, she looked a bit out of sorts; he could only assume that she was still upset about last night.

Without any hesitation, Dalton walked toward her. He no longer cared if he had an audience. He didn't care if he got slapped in front of the whole of Hollywood. He was going to do his damnedest to set things right between them, no matter what.

After what had happened with Milburn, seeing Dalton standing at the top of the low rise that led to the hotel was enough to stop Anna in her tracks. For a moment, she wondered if she wasn't imagining things, if Dalton wasn't some sort of mirage, but then she noticed Montgomery looking at him, too. When Dalton started walking toward her, her heart began to beat a bit faster. She'd spent much of the day thinking about how badly things had ended between them the night before and wondering what she might say to him if she ever got the chance, but she never would have expected that such an opportunity would present itself so soon.

"Is there going to be a problem?" Montgomery asked before Dalton was close enough to hear.

Anna looked at the older man, thankful that he was still watching out for her. "No," she said simply. "I know him. It's all right."

Dalton stopped just short of Anna. With the sun behind her, shining brightly just over her shoulder, it lit up his face, making his eyes dance and his dark hair shine. "Can I talk to you for a minute?" he asked. Anna noticed that he'd never once looked in Montgomery's direction; he was so focused on her that it was as if the other man wasn't even there.

"I suppose I've been an actor long enough to know when I've been given my cue," Montgomery said, starting back toward the hotel.

"Thank you," Anna called after him. "For everything."

"Any time, my dear. Any time."

Once Montgomery was out of earshot, Anna turned back to Dalton. He stared at her silently, his eyes searching her face. Once, she thought he was about to say something, but he remained quiet. Anna did the same; she was determined that *he* would be the one who would talk first, so she crossed her arms over her chest, returned his stare, and waited as the seconds slowly ticked by.

Then finally, he spoke.

"I know that there's nothing I can say or do to make up for what happened last night," he said, his voice soft and sincere. "I understand that. But that doesn't mean I'm not going to try."

When he again fell silent, Anna didn't say a word. Dalton looked uneasy, even miserable as he searched for the right words, and a small part of Anna was enjoying his discomfort.

"I was up half the night thinking about it," he continued, "and it's been bothering me all day. No matter where I go or what I do, I can't stop thinking about you. I know there's no reason for you to hear me out, but I'm asking all the same."

After a pause, she nodded.

"When I saw those hotel doors close behind you last night, I thought I'd destroyed any chance I might ever have to..." he began before faltering, his eyes looking away, "...to get to know you better. What I said was wrong. I never should've accused you of anything. It wasn't fair. There are just some things that have happened to me...some problems that..." When he stumbled this time, he seemed more frustrated, almost undone. Dalton sighed. "I shouldn't have come here and bothered you."

"Yes, you really *should* have," Anna corrected him, reaching out and touching his arm, feeling the heat and sweat on his skin. "And I'm glad that you did."

"Anna," he began, moving closer, and, unlike her response when Milburn approached her, she had no desire to move farther away. "I *am* sorry for what happened."

"You should be," she answered. "Just because I'm glad that you came to see me doesn't mean I'm not still mad at you."

"What I did was stupid." He smiled before adding, "At least that's what my friend Walker told me."

"He sounds like a smart guy."

"He is," Dalton admitted. "Just don't tell him, because if you do, I'll never hear the end of it."

Both of them laughed. Now, instead of focusing on what had already happened, they might just be able to go forward.

"Would you like to go for a walk?" Dalton asked.

"Isn't that what got us into trouble the last time?"

He shook his head. "We don't have to say a word. To tell you the truth, I'd be happy just to have your company."

"In that case, I accept."

As they started walking, Anna wondered if all they would do was walk, silently enjoying themselves as he showed her more of Redstone. But she doubted it. Maybe, just maybe, she might even get some answers to some of the lingering questions she still had about Dalton Barnes.

Milburn stared out the window of his hotel room, the sun bright in his eyes, unable to believe what he was seeing. There was Anna, the slut who kept on denying him what was rightfully his, walking off with the same bastard who'd knocked him down on the street. *What's she doing with him? Where are they going? She couldn't possibly be interested in him, could she?*

Snatching up a half-full glass of whiskey from the dresser top, Milburn took it down in one quick, burning gulp, and then threw the glass against the door, shattering it and sending shards of glass flying around the room. His blood thundered in his temples, his anger raging out of control.

Since he'd first laid eyes on Anna Finnegan, he'd known

that she was a trophy he had to have. He'd already slept with two of the movie's bit-part actresses, trollops who hoped to hang their fortunes on his rapidly ascending star, girls whose names he'd quickly forgotten. To him they were nothing more than a night's dalliance, something to do until someone better came along.

And that someone was Anna.

Didn't she know that he was one of the hottest young stars in Hollywood? Couldn't she understand how big a mistake she was making by turning him down, especially if it was for some small-town bumpkin who couldn't spell "movie" if you spotted him four letters out of the five?

And what about Montgomery? That old has-been had better keep his mouth shut if he knew what was good for him.

Milburn took a long pull on the whiskey bottle he'd brought with him from California, Prohibition be damned. Already, an idea was forming in his head, a plan to get Anna Finnegan into his bed, regardless of whether she wanted to be there or not. He'd make her see things his way. He'd hurt her and that son-of-a-bitch she preferred over him.

"No one turns down Milburn Hood," he snarled. "No one."

Chapter Thirteen

IT DIDN'T TAKE LONG for Dalton's suggestion that they walk in silence to fall by the wayside. As they first drifted back down the street the way Anna had come, then crossed eastward over Main Street and into a part of Redstone she'd not visited before, they talked and laughed easily, so much so that it was possible to imagine that the previous night had never happened. Anna asked Dalton about his day, and he grew animated describing how he'd labored to build the addition to the camera's rail, pushing and prodding the steel until the angle was just right; it was obvious that he took pride in his work. Still, Hollywood remained a sore subject; he never asked her about her own day of filming, and she didn't volunteer any information, either.

They tramped down a dusty dirt road, crossed over a rickety bridge that spanned a dried-up river bed, and then descended into a soft depression with a scrum of rocks, patchy grass, and gnarled trees, whose parched limbs stretched skyward in a futile plea for water that wouldn't come.

"Where are we going?" Anna asked.

"You'll see," he answered with a grin.

Dalton led the way along a crude wooden fence, its posts and planks weathered by years under the sun. The going was rough, loose rock and the dry earth gave way beneath her feet, and she occasionally had to steady herself by grabbing the fence. Finally, he stopped.

"We're here," he said.

Anna looked out at the horizon as Dalton leaned back against the fence. The land here was different from that around the stone bridge; it was flatter, with sporadic rises and boulders, dotted with patchwork clusters of trees, tall grasses, and hardy flowers, running away for miles and miles, all lit from behind by the slowly setting sun in the west. It was certainly pretty, but she looked at Dalton expectantly, knowing that there had to be something more; his easy smile told Anna that her guess was right.

"What am I looking at?" she asked.

"Nothing yet, but sometimes wild horses pass through here," he explained. "Because of the way the ground settles on this side of town, the grasses grow faster here so there's more for them to eat." Seeing her growing excitement, he added, "I'm not making any promises that we'll see them, so don't get your hopes up too high."

"I won't," she said, even though she already had.

For the next couple of minutes, Anna's gaze darted among the few outcroppings of rock and the scant trees, hoping for a glimpse of any horses, but she didn't see any. But then, just as she was about to give up hope, Dalton grabbed her by the arm and pointed. From behind a clump of cactus, two horses emerged. One was burnt orange in color, with a few splotches of white on its flanks, its mane trailing behind it as it ran. The other was breathtakingly beautiful, midnight black with only a diamond of white centered on its muscular chest. It chased after its companion, dust rising every time its powerful hooves drove into the ground, whinnying as it snorted the early evening air. The two animals stopped and ate the tall grass, just as Dalton said they would.

"They're amazing!" Anna exclaimed. "I've never seen anything like them."

"You've never seen a horse before?" Dalton blurted in surprise.

"Not wild ones," she answered, giving him a playful frown. "I used to see cart horses every day when I was a little girl in Chicago. They hauled milk drums and other heavy things down the busy streets. I can still hear the sound of their feet clopping on the bricks. But they were nothing like these two. They weren't this lively. And none of the movie horses are quite like these."

"I expect I'd be like those cart horses if I ever had to live in a city," he said, watching the animals as they ate. "When I think about all of those people so close together, fighting for jobs, for something to eat, a dozen people crammed into a room made for a third that number, I'm sure I'd end up just as broken as those horses you used to see."

Anna shook her head. "Not everything about cities is like that. There are lots of beautiful things there, too."

Dalton turned to look directly at her, his gaze intense. "There was a time when I wouldn't have believed you," he said, his voice low. "But now I do."

The meaning in both his words and his stare was enough to make Anna turn away, a blush rising in her cheeks.

Silence descended between them, so they turned their attention back to the wild horses. After a while, the black horse raised its head and looked directly at them, as if it'd just noticed them for the first time. A couple of minutes later, the pair scampered off, going back the same way they'd come. But just before they vanished out of sight, both animals stopped and turned back for one final look; Anna wondered if they might have been saying their good-byes.

"Why do you hate everyone from Hollywood so much?" she suddenly asked, giving voice to the question that had been lingering in her thoughts the whole day. She knew that she was bringing up a delicate subject, one that might cause a repeat of what had happened the night before, but she also knew that, if they wanted to go forward, it was something that needed to be answered.

But Dalton remained silent.

"You said that everyone connected to the movie looked down their noses at people like you," Anna pressed, not willing to let the matter go. "Why? Did someone do something? Did they offend you? Tell me."

Dalton frowned. But just when she'd accepted that he

was never going to answer her, his features softened. "Times here in Redstone have been tough for years," he began. "You'd have to be blind not to see it. Houses in disrepair. Jobs lost. For plenty of folks, the only solace they can find is in a bottle, legal or not. Every day's the same, one right after the next."

Anna remembered how things had looked on the train coming into town. She'd seen the poor conditions Dalton was talking about.

"And then, in the midst of all that, here comes Hollywood to save the day, swooping in with bucketfuls of money to give to those willing to bend over backward and provide them with whatever they need," he growled, bitterness punctuating every word. "Sad thing is, most folks in town are glad you all came."

"But you're not," she finished.

"I've got my pride," Dalton said passionately. "I don't need someone showing up at my family's business and making me feel like they're doing me a favor just by walking in the door. Especially when it's coming from some fat cat, dressed to the nines, who looks like he's never worked a real day's labor in his life. *That* makes me mad as hell."

"And you think that all of us, everyone who's involved in making this movie, we're all the same, all so despicable?"

"Not all," he admitted, "but most." When Dalton turned to face her, he held out his hands, palms up. "Look at these."

Gently, Anna took Dalton's hands and looked closely at them in the fading light. They were rugged, worn, with calluses, nicks, scrapes, and several scars; even if she'd only been allowed to touch them, she would've known that they belonged to a man who worked with them for a living.

"Most folks don't have hands like mine," he said. "Those Hollywood people, theirs are all soft and pampered, the kind that belong to rich men who're used to giving orders instead of taking them."

"That's not fair," Anna answered, letting go of his hands. "Looking at people from the outside doesn't mean that you know them," she explained. "You can assume all sorts of things, but you have no idea how they got there, how hard they had to struggle, or what obstacles they had to overcome. To think otherwise is foolish."

"None of you know what it's like to suffer. Not like folks do here."

Anna was shocked. "Is that what you think of me, too?"

Dalton held his tongue.

She nodded, knowing that his silence meant that he did. Taking a deep breath, she steadied herself before she began talking. "My father died when I was a little girl," she explained. "I don't remember much about him other than that he was a drunk, the sort of man who couldn't wait to cash his paycheck so that he could go to the tavern. My mother was little better. After her husband died, she'd latch on to any man who showed an interest in her, anyone who'd provide her with drink and drugs, even if that meant she had to let him beat her in order to get them. Needless to say, mothering wasn't something she was very concerned about."

Dalton stared at her, his eyes wide with surprise. "Anna, I'm—" he started, but she just talked right over him; now that she'd started, he was going to listen to every word until she'd finished.

"One day, when I was twelve, my mother stopped coming home altogether. I looked and looked for her, asked around to a few people who I thought might've known where she'd gone, but no one knew. I never saw her again. I don't know if she's still alive or dead."

This time when she paused, Dalton remained silent.

"While all of this was happening, my brother started to run with the wrong crowd. He idolized the toughs and gangsters in the neighborhood, men who got ahead by stealing, running their rackets, and cracking heads when someone wouldn't pay. There was no one around to tell him different. I tried, but he wouldn't listen. I don't know what happened to my mother, but I know exactly what happened to Peter. He was shot and killed one night outside a nightclub. I used every cent I had left to make sure he had a proper burial.

"After that, it was a struggle to live. I begged on street corners and at the train station during the day, and then tried to find somewhere safe to sleep at night. Every time the police came around, I hid, afraid that they'd send me to the orphanage if they caught me. But then one day, a miracle happened. I was outside an old, run-down vaudeville theater when a man saw me performing for change. He took pity on me, gave me something to eat and a place to sleep, as well as an opportunity to act on the stage. He saved my life. If it hadn't been for him, I'm sure I'd be dead. Ever since, I've worked as hard as I could, acted when I was sick, put up with hecklers and drunks snoring in the audience, all so that I'd have the chance to be someone, to be a star."

Anna took a step closer to Dalton. "So the next time you look at someone and think that you know them," she said flatly, a tear balancing on the end of her eyelash, "you'd better think again."

Dalton stared at Anna, dumbstruck by what he'd heard. He had no idea what to say. Listening to her talk about her life had been gut-wrenching; when he thought her story couldn't get any worse, it did. What she had described was almost unfathomable, much more difficult than the problems he faced. Shame tightened his chest and made him look away from her. Remembering all of the hurtful things he'd said to her the night before, how he'd blindly assumed that she was like everyone else from Hollywood, made him sick. Anna hadn't been born with a silver spoon in her mouth. She didn't spend money without a moment's pause, and she also didn't look down on those who didn't have any. Thinking otherwise had been a terrible mistake. Instantly he knew that he could never look at her the same way again.

"I'm nothing but a damn fool," he muttered angrily.

Anna stepped forward and again took hold of his hand. "I hope that you're an awful lot more than that."

Something sparked in Dalton's chest, a feeling strong enough for him to raise his eyes to meet hers. "You do?"

"I suppose I must," she answered, a small smile spreading across her beautiful face. "After what happened yesterday, what other reason could I possibly have for agreeing to go for another walk with you?" she said, laughing into the darkening sky. "It either means that I'm a glutton for punishment, or that I see something inside you that I like." Anna paused, giving his hand a gentle squeeze. "So far, I think it's the latter."

Dalton felt the strong, sudden urge to tell her about his own troubles, to unburden himself about his father's gambling problem. He had a feeling that, because of all the things Anna had overcome, she would understand. But something stopped him. He didn't know if it was his stubborn pride or the irrational fear that by telling her he'd be admitting weakness.

"I . . . I just can't believe what you've gone through . . ." he finally managed. "It sounds like it must've been horrible."

"It was, but there were some good times, too," Anna explained. "Besides, it was a long time ago. I'm not the same person I was then. My point in telling you what I went through wasn't to gain your sympathy, but so you'd understand that until you get to know who someone is inside, where she's come from, you don't *really* know her." Tenderly, her thumb rubbed the hard skin of his palm; it sent shivers racing the length of Dalton's spine. "Maybe now you know me a little better," she added.

It was true. Listening to her history, Dalton *did* know her better. He'd also come to understand that they were more alike than he'd imagined; she'd faced more than her share of hardship. She was also inspiring; Anna had overcome every obstacle put in her way to make something of herself. Even though he remained wary, Dalton had begun to think, to hazard the hope, that the idea that there could be something between them wasn't as impossible as it had once seemed.

Anna looked up at Dalton, watching the way his gaze moved across her face, drifting for a moment to her mouth, darting over to her hair as it fell past her ears and onto her shoulders. But always returning to her eyes. In turn, she gazed intently back, longing to touch his curly dark hair, glancing at the small creases that marked the corners of his mouth, and noticing the stubble that darkened his cheeks and jaw. No matter how good an actress she was, it would have been utterly impossible to deny that she was attracted to him. Though neither of them said a word, Anna still felt as if they were speaking. By talking about her past, by revealing the grim fate that had befallen her family, she understood that she'd forever changed something between them. They'd shared an intimacy. She couldn't say for certain where they were going to end up, but she had to admit that she liked the direction they were headed.

She had been bold to reach out and take Dalton's hand, maybe too forward for a lady. But Anna didn't regret a thing. Earlier, when he'd offered his hands for her to touch, she'd let go of them in anger, but now she held on long after what would have been considered proper. Even though his skin was rough, she was comforted by its warmth; it made her heart race. When she traced a path over his palm with her thumb, it was clear from the look in his eyes that her touch moved him.

No matter how honest she'd been, how much they had shared, Anna knew there was still something that Dalton was holding back. She'd noticed the look that had crossed his face, the hesitation in his eyes. He'd wanted to say something, to confess some closely guarded secret, but whatever impulse he'd had to reveal it, it hadn't been strong enough. When she'd pressed him, he swallowed it back down. Anna decided to be patient; she knew the time would come when he'd tell her the truth.

Somewhere in the distance, an owl hooted. The sky had darkened to shades of purple and black. A breeze stirred the hem of Anna's skirt and rustled the grass. With every passing second that the sun dipped farther, more and more stars twinkled into sight, but they scarcely noticed.

"I wish I could take back yesterday," he said, and he moved an almost imperceptible bit closer, but nearer all the same.

"I don't," she answered.

Dalton frowned with confusion.

"If we hadn't had yesterday, for better and most certainly for worse," Anna explained, squeezing his hand, "there's a good chance we wouldn't be standing right here, right now, together like this."

"I hadn't thought of it like that."

"That doesn't mean I'm not still sore about what happened."

"Any chance I can make it up to you?"

"How?" Anna asked.

"I might have an idea."

Before Anna could ask what that might be, Dalton leaned down and placed his lips against hers. The suddenness of it surprised her, but her shock lasted for only an instant. Eagerly, she rose up onto the tips of her toes and returned Dalton's kiss, her mouth parting slightly. She lifted her arms to circle his neck, burying her fingers in his thick hair, and Dalton drew her by the waist and gently pulled her closer.

Anna knew that what was happening between them was real. It wasn't like the scenes she acted out before the cameras. It wasn't like the overblown lines in one of the dime novels she liked to read. No, this felt new, strangely different, and more than a little exciting. The emotions that were threatening to consume her came straight from her heart.

Anna had no idea how long their kiss lasted, only that she had closed her eyes and given herself over to it, completely. When it ended, she stepped back and found Dalton smiling at her.

"That was nice," he whispered.

Yes...yes, it was...

Chapter Fourteen

OH, COME NOW, DARLING!" Joan cooed. "I know you don't know any better, only having worked in quaint little theater plays, but you'd better start taking this more seriously if you hope to have any measure of success in this business!"

Anna bit her tongue as Joan smiled at her, triumphant now that she'd finally gotten what she wanted; for her rival to make a mistake.

She'd been trying to cause one all morning. First, she'd stomped down hard on Anna's foot, claiming that the younger actress had wandered into her mark. Then, Joan had jumped her line of dialogue while she was obscured from the camera, talking before Anna had had time to move past, accusing her of being too slow and causing another halt to the filming. Finally, with Anna now nervously watching every word she said and step she took, Joan had managed to make her so self-conscious that she'd garbled a line. When Frank angrily shouted "cut," half the room groaned.

"How many times are we going to have to do this?" Frank grumbled loudly enough for all the cast and crew to hear.

"Don't be angry with *me*, Frank. I'm just trying to give you the best performance I can," Joan argued, pleading her case with a fake, honey-tongued voice. "I only want to do what's worthy of a film under your direction. It's just a shame that not everyone shares that sentiment."

It was a struggle, but Anna managed to keep quiet.

Strangely enough, the day had started out fine. Filming had originally been scheduled for outdoors. Anna had been dreading it because it was the first scene she was supposed to film with Milburn. But sometime in the night, the sky had been darkened by ominous-looking clouds. So far, they'd yet to let loose any rain, but Samuel had decided not to risk being caught in a downpour and changed the day's plan. Unfortunately, dodging working with Milburn had meant that Anna would now be paired with Joan.

Still, Anna wasn't as worked up about Joan's shenanigans as she might have expected to be. She supposed that was due in no small part to her night with Dalton. After their first kiss, they'd sat wrapped in each other's arms as he pointed out constellations she'd never seen before under the bright lights of the big city. Finally, Dalton had insisted on walking her back to the hotel, although he once again stopped well short of escorting her all the way to the Stagecoach's front door. After they had kissed their good-byes, Anna had been up most of the night, replaying their evening together, wondering when she would see him again.

Her lack of indignation seemed only to encourage Joan to push harder, desperate for a reaction that would embarrass her young rival. "Maybe you should have the makeup girl come up here and give poor Anna a touch-up," she said, putting on an overblown air of concern. "I think she's developing some sort of blemish on her nose. Why, it would look as big as an automobile up on the screen!"

"That's it!" Frank snapped, practically leaping out of his chair and tossing his copy of the script onto the floor in disgust. "Everyone break for lunch! Filming picks up back here in an hour!"

People began filing off the set. Anna got quite a few looks of sympathy from men and women who saw through Joan's pathetic attempt to frame her as the real trouble-maker, but she noticed a few who glared angrily, not blaming her necessarily, but not seeing a distinction between two divas fighting over a whole lot of nothing when all *they* wanted was to make a movie worth watching. Anna felt bad she'd become caught up in it all.

Joan was one of the last to go, pulling her diamond ring out of her pocket and slipping it back on her finger, no longer an *actress* but a *star*. Before she left, she glided over to Anna and whispered in her ear.

"Believe me when I say that this is only the beginning of what I have in store for you," she said cruelly. "Only the beginning…"

* * *

After her run-in with Joan, Anna hadn't felt much like eating, so instead of going to lunch with the rest of the crew, she lazily wandered around Redstone. Briefly, she considered trying to find Dalton's blacksmith shop and pay him a visit, but she had no idea where it was. The thought of asking for directions embarrassed her, and besides, there really wasn't enough time before filming was scheduled to resume. So after only twenty minutes, escaping indoors just as the first fat drops of rain began to fall from the heavy clouds, she made her way back to the set.

Most of the crew was not yet back from lunch. A young technician was up on a ladder, changing a bulb on one of the light stands while two cameramen were laughing as they swapped out a spool of film. Anna was surprised to find that Samuel had returned, too. He leaned against the far wall, staring out the window. When he saw Anna enter, he smiled and waved her over to join him.

"You're back early," he said. "That must've been a quick lunch."

"I didn't eat," she admitted. "After what happened this morning, I didn't have much of an appetite. I went for a walk to clear my head instead."

"Joan's a bit of a handful, isn't she?"

Still not wanting to be seen as a troublemaker, Anna only nodded.

"Don't worry," Samuel said gently, seeing her unease. "No one's blaming you for what happened. I know I'm not."

"I screwed up my lines, too," she confessed.

"Only because Joan wouldn't stop needling you. I'm not blind, you know." Smiling as he folded his arms across his chest, Samuel said, "But I have to admit I'm a touch sympathetic to Joan's plight. You have to understand how hard all of this is for her. People in this business spend years struggling and scraping to reach the top of the ladder. All they want is to be famous and have their names up on the marquees. But someday, no matter what they try to do to stall it, they no longer are as famous as they once were. Trust me, I know all about it."

Anna accepted his explanation. Once, he had been one of the biggest stars in Hollywood, the type that made men want to be *like* him and women want to be *with* him. Even though he was still a big shot in the movie industry, one of the hit producers in Hollywood, it wasn't the same.

"The worst part is having to watch all the actors coming along behind you," he continued. "They're scratching and clawing for what you have. They want to be right there on the pedestal you've grown comfortable on. They're younger, prettier, and hungrier. Actors like Joan and me who came up during the silent era find that maybe the new producers and directors don't like the sound of our voices. You are an old lion still fighting to be king of the pride. All Joan wants is to hold on to what she's earned. She's still a star, just not as big as she was or wants to be. To her, you're out to steal her spotlight, nothing more and nothing less. You could be anyone. It's jealousy, but it isn't personal."

Anna had never thought of Joan's dislike for her quite like that. In some ways, it was understandable. Still . . .

"I just wish she wasn't so mean about it," she said.

Samuel laughed. "Just remember that when the time comes when you're the famous star approaching the end of the line and you have to share your spotlight with a beautiful young costar."

"I'd hate to think I'd be so bitter."

"You won't be," he said, giving her a wink. "Still, if having to put up with Joan's nonsense is the worst part of your first movie shoot, I'd say you're doing pretty well."

Immediately Anna thought about the problems she'd been having with Milburn. Up until now, she'd been reluctant to say anything about the actor's inappropriate advances for fear that she'd be labeled a complainer or troublemaker. But after how Samuel had just spoken to her, she knew that she could finally unburden herself. The producer was a good man; she knew he wouldn't dismiss her concerns or think less of her for voicing them.

But then, just as she was about to start telling Samuel about what had happened, a man burst through the set's door and hurried over toward them. Anna recognized him; it was Bill Mayhew, Frank's primary assistant. "Mr. Gillen!" he half-shouted. "Mr. Gillen, I need you to come with me right away!"

"What is it, Bill?" Samuel asked. "What's wrong?"

"It's Frank. There's been an emergency!"

Anna saw the wave of concern wash over the producer's face. "My God! What happened? Is he all right?"

Bill shook his head. "It's not him. Frank's fine, well, he's not...it's not his health. It's the film. Frank says that it's ruined!" He whispered the last bit so that no one else in the room heard him.

"What?" Samuel exclaimed in surprise. "What are you talking about? What does he mean it's ruined?"

"It's better if you just come with me and see for yourself."

When Samuel went running out the door with Bill at his heels, Anna knew that there was no way she could stay behind. Her curiosity was so great it was irresistible. Lifting the hem of her skirt, she raced after him.

Valentine Pictures' offices in Redstone were located in a building once occupied by a lawyer's office, a couple of doors down from the hotel. Anna followed as Samuel and Bill dashed through the front door and climbed the rickety staircase up to the second floor. A couple of desks had been set up, equipped with typewriters and telephones, but none of them were staffed; Anna assumed that everyone was still at lunch. To her eye, nothing appeared to be amiss. But then she heard shouting coming from a door at the back of the building.

"Damn it! God damn it all to hell!"

The three of them hurried to the room and looked inside; Anna couldn't help but gasp at what she saw. Frank Dukes stood among an avalanche of destruction. Papers littered the floor and every other surface. A projector had been tipped over, its bulb smashed and lying in fragments on the ground beside it. Canisters of film were everywhere, more than a dozen of them, many of them open. The director was clearly livid; his face was flushed an angry shade of red and his hair stood up in odd tufts, as if he'd been trying to pull it out.

"It's ruined!" he screamed, spittle forming on his lip. "It's all ruined!"

"What…what happened here…?'" Samuel asked, struggling to keep his voice calm and to quell the panic he most surely felt.

"I found it like this," Frank explained. "I was so angry with the way filming was going this morning that I thought I'd come back here and take a look at some of what we'd already shot, but when I opened the door, this is what I found." He waved toward the devastation like a carnival barker showing his audience a freak show exhibit.

"But the door should've been locked."

"It was. But that didn't stop someone from getting in and destroying everything we've done so far."

"It's a mess all right, but surely we can pick this up and put it back to right."

"No amount of cleaning is going to fix this," Frank disagreed. He grabbed a canister of film and tossed it down on the table in front of them; its lid wobbled before it tipped over and fell into the jumble of paper at their feet. Anna could see that something was wrong with it. The film looked warped, as if the celluloid had been burned, shrunken in places. An odd, pungent smell filled the air.

"What…what happened to it…?" Samuel finally managed.

"Acid of some kind, I suspect," Frank growled, struggling to contain his anger. "Nearly every canister has had the same thing done to it, even the ones we haven't used yet. They're all ruined beyond repair."

"But...but who would do such a thing...?"

Frank sneered. "If I knew, I'd have already strung the son-of-a-bitch up by his—" he said, stopping only when he finally noticed that Anna was present. Changing direction, he instead said, "I would've killed the bastard by now!"

"We have to call the sheriff," Samuel said.

"Fat lot of good some small-town tinhorn is going to do," Frank countered. "This isn't Los Angeles or some other city with a police force used to dealing with this sort of thing. What passes for The Law in these parts probably isn't sure which end of his gun is supposed to go in the holster first!"

"Frank's right," Bill added. "I've seen the sheriff around town a time or two and he looks old enough to already have one foot in the grave. I don't know if he'd know who committed a crime even if the person who did it came up and confessed."

"Then what do we do?" Samuel asked.

His question was met with silence. Suddenly Anna had a thought, something that had been nagging her since she'd entered the room.

"What about the fire?" she asked.

Everyone turned to look at her. "What about it?" Bill asked.

"Well, since what happened in this room was clearly

done on purpose, who's to say the building wasn't intentionally burned down, too? We've been treating it like an accident, but what if it wasn't? After this, I think it'd be a mistake to assume anything."

"Sabotage," Frank said, spitting out the word as if it were poison.

Samuel was silent for a moment, but he soon started nodding. "I hate to say it, but that makes sense. I have no idea why, but it looks like someone's trying to ruin our movie."

"But who?" Anna asked. "Why would they do such a thing?"

"It has to be another studio," Frank declared. "Those bastards over at Flyover Films have always been jealous of me!"

"No, I don't think that's it," Samuel disagreed. "Even though I've made more than my share of enemies in this business, another studio trying something like this doesn't make sense. There's far too much to lose if they were ever caught. It'd be suicide. This is something different. Maybe even personal."

"Surely it's not someone in the picture," Anna said.

Samuel thought about it for a moment before answering. "I suppose it's possible, but it just doesn't feel right. Because this is a location picture, everyone on the crew is getting more than the usual rate," he explained, "and why would someone who was trying to further his own career in the movie business do something that would damage his prospects? Who could possibly be crazy enough to do something like that? It wouldn't make sense."

Everyone involved with Valentine Pictures had been so nice to Anna that she couldn't help but agree. Even Milburn and Joan, the two people who *hadn't* been kind to her, seemed beyond suspicion of committing sabotage; both of them had already proven themselves more than capable of doing harm to *her*, but it seemed ridiculous to think that they'd inflict harm upon their own careers, even if they were heading in opposite directions on the ladder of success. But if it wasn't another studio or someone working on the picture, who was it? Who was responsible?

"How about a local?" Bill asked. "Most folks around town seem pretty happy to have us, but that doesn't mean there aren't one or two others who're bent out of shape. Maybe their grudge got so big they decided to do something about it."

Anna felt almost faint; she was sure that all of the color had instantly drained out of her face. *Dalton!* Could it possibly be? She didn't want to believe it, but it was plausible at first glance. The hatred he felt for Hollywood was so intense that it had nearly driven them apart before they'd had a chance to get started. She'd listened to him rant about the bigwigs and fat cats that he felt disrespected him and others who weren't as fortunate. But was his hatred so great he had acted upon it?

It was then, just as Anna was beginning to consider whether Dalton could actually be involved, that she felt ashamed. In her heart, she knew he could do no such thing. It was impossible. The man she'd shared kisses with was angry, undeniably so, but Anna refused to believe that his indignation was enough to make him burn down a building or destroy the studio's film. Still, she had to wonder if he might know of anyone else in Redstone who shared his dislike for Hollywood and, if he did, whether they could have committed the crime.

"We need to start asking questions," Frank said.

"Actually," Samuel answered, "I think that's the last thing we should do."

"What?" the director sputtered. "Why not?"

"Because right now there are reporters from the Hollywood gossip magazines staying at the hotel," the producer explained. "If word gets out that we're suspicious of foul play, the rumor mill will run wilder and hotter than the fire that burned down our building. Bad publicity is the last thing we need. For now, we should keep it between ourselves," Samuel said, looking to each of them in the room. "We keep our eyes and ears open and hope that we can catch whoever's behind this before they strike again. If you see or hear anything, anything at all, you come and tell me immediately."

"What about the footage that's been lost?" Anna asked.

"We'll reshoot it."

"Even though we've only lost a couple of days' worth, don't you think folks are gonna be a bit suspicious why we're doin' it all over again?" Bill asked.

"We'll blame it on Frank," Samuel answered, turning to look at his director. "Everyone in the business knows that he's brilliant but difficult to work with. We'll just say that he wasn't satisfied and demands that we shoot it over. There'll be plenty of grumbling, but no one will refuse."

Anna thought that Frank might complain about being portrayed as a tyrant, but the director just shrugged his shoulders. "Samuel's right," he said with resignation. "Besides, there *were* a few scenes I thought could've been better."

"Let's go back and finish today's work like normal," Samuel said. "We'll start posting a guard here at the offices and start filming backward tomorrow. Everyone be on the lookout. We'll catch whoever's responsible."

Even as she prepared to head back to the set and resume shooting, Anna knew the first thing she was going to do when the day's work was completed.

She was going to find Dalton.

Chapter Fifteen

DALTON SWEPT THE BROOM back and forth, pushing around the many bits and pieces of metal and scrap that had accumulated during the day's work. Every pass of the bristles sent up a cloud of dust. Outside, a soft rain fell, drumming steadily against the shop's tin roof, a loud but soothing sound. Dalton whistled as he cleaned. Though a blacksmith's job was messy, full of grime and dirt, he still believed that there must be an order to things. At the end of every day, he made sure to pick up after himself, putting away all his hammers and other tools, making sure there was plenty of material for relighting the forge the next morning, and removing any mess he might have made. He usually spent this time thinking about the work he'd done that day, as well as what was scheduled for the next, but today was different.

All he could think about was Anna.

He hadn't gone to her hotel or asked her to go for

another walk so that he could kiss her. In truth, it had been the furthest thing from his mind. He'd gone to try to make things right between them. Still, Dalton couldn't deny his happiness at what had happened. Feeling the heat of her lips against his, the way their bodies had been pressed tightly together...It had been unexpected ecstasy. And even though she was still an actress from Hollywood and he was still a blacksmith from Texas, he wasn't as bothered by it, at least not as badly as he'd been before Anna had told him about her past. She was right; they weren't all that different in the end. He still couldn't believe that she'd endured and overcome so much. It'd taken courage to tell her story.

So where's my courage? Why didn't I tell her about my father?

Things between George and him hadn't improved. Ever since he'd discovered the gambling debts to Vernon Black, Dalton had been giving his father the cold shoulder. After their initial confrontation, they'd hardly spoken a word to each other. Today hadn't been any different. Even though they had needed to work closely together, shaping a large piece of metal that had required two sets of hands, they'd spoken mainly in grunts, with a few points of the hand and nods of the head passing as directions. Dalton hadn't enjoyed it much; from the pained expression on George's face, his father hadn't either. Still, Dalton couldn't ignore the anger he felt. No matter how much he tried, he still couldn't come up with a solution for how they were going to pay back Vernon, although he was surprised that the bloodsucker hadn't sent the Cobb brothers after him again. He knew it was only a matter of time.

He supposed he hadn't told Anna about his father's gambling problem because he was ashamed. But in his heart, Dalton knew she wouldn't judge him for it. With all Anna had faced, he thought she'd understand. All he needed to do was come clean, but that was easier said than done. He just had to find the words.

Just as he was finishing his sweeping, Dalton heard a knock on the door behind him. He thought it might be Walker, but when he turned around he found Anna smiling at him, her hair and blouse wet from the rain. Strangely enough, he wasn't surprised to see her. Even though he'd never told her where he worked or lived, he had hoped that she'd seek him out; now that she had, it told him that her desire to spend time together was as great as his own.

"There you are," she said. "I was beginning to think you were hiding."

"Like an ogre living under a bridge," he answered, holding up his hands so that she could see all of the dirt and grime covering them after a day's work. "It's best to keep all the monsters out of sight, you know."

Anna frowned, although she did so playfully. "I was thinking more along the lines of a piece of jewelry," she said. "The kind that's kept safely locked away and only brought out so that it can be shown off."

Dalton laughed loudly. "Now that's a good one! No one's ever mistaken me for a diamond before!"

"Beauty's in the eye of the beholder, I suppose."

I couldn't agree more...

"So this is where you work," Anna said as she looked past Dalton and deeper into the blacksmith shop. Her heart was pounding and her skin, dotted with beads of rainwater, tingled with anticipation. Standing near him was exciting, almost intoxicating. Anna half-expected him to reach out and pull her close so that they could resume their passionate kisses from the night before.

But instead Dalton stayed still, smiling.

"It's not all that different from when my grandfather opened it just after he moved to Redstone. A few changes here and there, but not many."

"It's so dark," she commented, peering into the gloom. Besides the way she'd come in, she could see a larger pair of doors on the opposite wall; one of them stood open, to the cloudy late afternoon beyond. Even with the fresh, rain-scented breeze that managed to make its way inside, the room still held the sharp odor of smoke.

"When the forge is lit, it's bright enough to work by."

More than a dozen hammers and several long tongs hung on one wall, balanced in place between nails pounded into the wood. Beneath was a large worktable, its thick wood surface deeply scarred by gouges and nicks, the markings of years of use. Anna knew that these were the tools of Dalton's trade. Unable to resist taking a closer look, she reached up to take hold of a hammer, its wood handle smooth to the touch, the metal head blackened. But no sooner had Anna touched it than it slipped free, falling onto the worktable with a loud thud.

"I'm so sorry," she said, embarrassed.

"There's no need to be," Dalton answered with a smile. "I doubt you could damage it if you tried. Those things are made to take a pounding."

Happy that he hadn't been upset with her, Anna picked up the hammer with the intention of putting it back where it belonged, but was surprised that she had to struggle just to lift it off the table. It had looked formidable up on the wall, but she never would have guessed that it was so heavy. She didn't consider herself to be a weakling, but just holding the hammer in place was making her arm tremble. As she was about to use both hands, Dalton stepped over and took it from her, placing it back between the two nails as easily as if he were lifting a feather.

"I've got it," he said as their hands touched.

"How do you lift something that heavy all day long?" she asked.

"It wasn't easy back when I started, but I'm used to it. Since I use one of those hammers most all the day, they've become a part of me, like an extension of my hand. I don't really notice them anymore."

Looking at the thick cords of muscles that ran the length of Dalton's arms, rising up and underneath his shirt and spreading across his chest and shoulders, Anna could see the truth of his words. Before meeting him, she'd no idea how strong a blacksmith would need to be, but now she understood. The thought of once again being held in those arms, enveloped by them, was suddenly very appealing.

From the look in Dalton's eyes, he was thinking the same thing.

"I've thought about you nearly all day," he said, moving a little closer, his eyes smoldering like the embers in a forge.

"You have?" she teased, answering heat stirring inside her. "I'm flattered."

"I didn't say what I thought was all good," he teased in return.

"Oh, really? What could you possibly be holding against me?"

"I hate to admit to it, but I was disturbed by your kisses. After last night, I'm not sure how I feel about them." When Anna stepped back, her hands on her hips and a playful scowl on her face, Dalton added, "What I mean is that I'm not sure if I've had a large enough sample to form an opinion. If I could just figure out a way to have some more..."

"No harm in asking," Anna suggested.

"That's what my mother always told me," he replied.

"Sound advice."

Dalton stepped closer and Anna did the same, gently placing her hand on his arm, waiting for his kiss. Even though she'd hurried across town after asking at the Stagecoach's front desk about where she could find the town blacksmith, all with the intent of asking Dalton if he had any idea who could be responsible for what had happened to the studio's film, she wasn't going to stop him now. Everything else could come later.

But just as Anna was about to close her eyes, tilting her head slightly as she rose onto her tiptoes, she saw someone standing in the doorway behind him, watching them. Giving Dalton's arm a gentle squeeze, she nodded in the stranger's direction.

A man leaned against the door frame, grinning as he tapped a piece of slate against his thigh. He was about Dalton's age, but thinner, his sandy blond hair shaggy and a bit wild, his smile mischievous. To Anna, it didn't look as if he was embarrassed by what he'd seen, but rather amused.

"How long have you been standing there?" Dalton asked him.

The stranger shrugged. He started digging in his pocket. Anna thought he might be looking for a watch to give his answer, but he pulled out a piece of chalk instead. With his shirtsleeve, he wiped the slate before beginning to write on it. When he'd finished, he held it out as he walked toward them. Anna peered at it through the shadow, finally seeing the words. "I DIDN'T SEE A THING. HONEST. I THINK."

"You better know for certain," Dalton said. "Otherwise, I'll get one of those hammers down and do some convincing."

The stranger again cleaned the slate. "DON'T WORRY," he wrote. "YOU ALREADY HAVE MY SILENCE!"

At that, both of them laughed, although only Dalton did so out loud; the stranger's shoulders shook but no sound came from him. Anna understood immediately that the man was mute; she'd known a woman in Chicago who'd had the same affliction, although she hadn't compensated with a chalkboard, but had rather just made do with points and grunts. The other thing she instantly knew was that the two of them were friends, and close ones at that.

"Anna, this is Walker," Dalton introduced the two of them. When they shook hands, Anna ended up with a big handful of chalk dust, which she didn't mind in the slightest.

"He's talked about you," she said. "He said that you told him he was stupid for how he treated me out at the stone bridge."

Walker smiled. "THAT I MOST DEFINITELY DID," he wrote. After wiping the slate, he added, "STICK AROUND FOR A BIT...IT WON'T BE THE WORST THING I SAY ABOUT HIM."

"Maybe we should share secrets."

"THAT SOUNDS LIKE A GREAT IDEA."

"All right, that's enough fun at my expense," Dalton protested.

Walker gave him a friendly shove then turned back to Anna and wrote, "SO YOU'RE AN ACTRESS?"

She nodded. "This is the first time I've been in a movie," she said. "Before this, I acted in the theater."

"EVERYBODY HAS TO START SOMEWHERE," Walker scribbled with his nub of chalk. Once he'd cleaned the board, he added, "WHO KNOWS? SOMEDAY YOU MIGHT BE THE STAR OF THE SHOW!"

The smile on Anna's face faltered, if only for a second. This was the moment she'd been tiptoeing around ever since she discovered Dalton's dislike for everything Hollywood. She'd purposely neglected to mention that she was already "the star of the show," the woman whose name would be featured on theater marquees, billboards, and movie posters, whose picture would soon be gracing the covers of gossip magazines. She hadn't wanted to be seen as bragging, but now she knew she must to set the matter straight.

"Actually," she said a bit awkwardly, "I'm the lead actress."

Both of the men's eyes grew wide; Dalton seemed the more disturbed of the pair, frozen in place, his mouth dropping open a bit in surprise. Anna didn't know which of them was the more uncomfortable.

"THAT'S INCREDIBLE!" Walker wrote, his own shock quickly overcome by excitement. "YOU'RE THE FIRST STAR I'VE EVER MET!"

"I'm hardly a star," she corrected him. "Right now, nobody knows who I am. Even when the movie is finished, there's no guarantee that it'll be a hit. There's an awfully long list of actors and actresses who've made movies that no one remembers."

"TRUST ME! YOU'LL BE FAMOUS! I JUST KNOW IT!"

While Walker wrote, Anna had taken a quick glance at Dalton. He still looked dumbstruck, staring at her intensely, as if he was still trying to digest what he'd heard. She wondered what he was thinking, if he thought she'd held out on him or, even worse, lied. After everything he'd said about the movie business, did knowing she was more deeply involved make him think less of her?

Lost in her thoughts, Anna jumped a little when Walker smacked his friend on the arm with his slate. Dalton flinched, his eyes blinking rapidly, as if the trance he'd been under had finally been broken. He didn't appear annoyed, but rather confused, as if he'd just woken up to unfamiliar surroundings. He looked down to find Walker holding out his board; both he and Anna had been so focused on each other that they hadn't noticed him writing. "ARE YOU READY TO GO?" it read.

"Oh, I'm sorry," Anna said. "I didn't realize I was delaying your plans."

"You didn't know," Dalton replied. "Walker's family owns the mercantile in town. I promised that I'd help him move some things in the storeroom. We arranged the time a couple of weeks back."

"I understand."

"I didn't know you were coming," he insisted.

"I DON'T NEED HIS MUSCLES FOR VERY LONG," Walker added.

"That's all right," Anna said. "I should probably get back to the hotel and go over my lines. I had a long day and we're starting early in the morning."

"Are you sure?" Dalton asked. "I could come over once I'm done."

As tempting as spending more time with him was, Anna turned the offer down. With everything that had happened, from her late night with Dalton to the excitement and uncertainty of what had happened in the film room, she was starting to feel run down; she really did need some rest. Discussing it with Dalton might take some time; it could wait a day.

Besides, the anticipation of a few more of his kisses would surely make the time go fast.

"YOU HAD NO IDEA SHE WAS THE STAR OF THE MOVIE, DID YOU?" Walker wrote after Anna had left.

Dalton shook his head. "She never told me," he replied. "I mean, I knew she was an actress as soon as I saw her, but from the way she talked, I just assumed she had a smaller part. I never would've guessed..."

Try as he might, Dalton was having a hard time coming to grips with what Anna had revealed. Thinking back, it made sense; remembering all of the press at the depot, the flashbulbs going off, he knew he should have put it all together. She was beautiful, the sort of woman who wouldn't look out of place up on a movie screen, but he hadn't had a clue that she was the *star*. Maybe she would have told him sooner if he hadn't ranted and raved about how much he hated Hollywood. In the end, Anna Finnegan was full of surprises. It made the fact that she was spending time with him, a lowly blacksmith living in the middle of nowhere, all the more perplexing. Eventually, she was going to leave for Hollywood and her career. What would happen then? It seemed crazy to imagine that she'd settle for him with so much spread out before her.

Still, he couldn't deny that he'd been happy she'd come to see him. If Walker hadn't interrupted, they would have kissed. Even the way she'd treated his friend had pleased him. Unlike those who couldn't get past Walker's handicap, Anna had taken it in stride, treating him just like anyone else, enjoying him for the person he was, not for what he wasn't.

It made Dalton like her all the more.

"IF YOU WANT, THE CELLAR CAN WAIT," Walker wrote.

"No," Dalton answered. "We made plans so we should stick to them. Besides, I'm so worked up that I'm afraid I'd say something stupid to her. Hopefully by tomorrow I'll know what to do."

"GOOD IDEA. THAT THERE IS A WOMAN WORTH KEEPING."

Dalton couldn't have agreed more.

When Anna left Dalton's blacksmith shop, the rain had finally stopped. Rainwater was everywhere, dripping from rooftops, pooling on the ground in puddles and making the earth muddy. Lifting the hem of her skirt, she watched every step she made, careful not to get dirty as she started back toward the hotel.

It was then, just as she rounded the corner of the shop, her head down, thinking about how Dalton had reacted to learning she was the lead actress in the movie, that Anna suddenly slammed into something, hard. It was almost enough to cause her to lose her balance and fall down in the muck, but she managed to keep to her feet. She assumed that she'd hit a post or barrel, but when she looked up, an enormous man stood before her. He looked back impassively, his long, muscled arms hanging slack at his sides.

"I'm so sorry," Anna apologized. "I wasn't watching where I was going."

The man remained mute, a silent stare his only reply.

"Are...are you all right...?" she asked, immediately realizing how ridiculous her question must have sounded; she wondered if the stranger would have noticed being struck by a train.

"My brother ain't much of a talker," another man said, stepping out of the shadows of a nearby alley.

Anna was startled. This man wasn't nearly as large as the one she'd run into, but there was something about him that was even more threatening. Anna didn't know if it was the tension that seemed to course through his wiry body, the gravelly sound of his voice, or if it was the way he looked at her, as if he was sizing her up, that made her the most uncomfortable.

"You're one a them movie people, ain't you?" he asked.

Anna hesitated. "Yes," she finally answered.

"Me and Audie," he said, nodding toward the hulking figure beside her, "we don't get much chance to see any a them picture shows, but you sure ain't like none a the girls we got 'round these parts. You look like you done jumped outta one a them magazines I seen up in El Paso. You're too damn pretty for a place like this."

Listening to the man made Anna's chest tighten. All she wanted was to get away as fast as she could. "Well..." she started, taking a step back. "I should really be getting back to the hotel. There are people expecting me," she lied.

But the man made no move to stop her. "You just run along then, darlin'," he nodded, smiling. "I ain't gonna stop you."

Without any hesitation, Anna did exactly what the man suggested, hurrying away without the least bit of attention to whether she stepped in the mud and rainwater or not. She never once looked back.

Creed watched the woman rushing away and knew that he'd frightened her, which pleased him no end. He and Audie had been keeping a close eye on Dalton Barnes, even though Mr. Black would disapprove. Creed had done as he'd been instructed, first burning down the building and then jimmying a lock and pouring acid all over the film housed in the old lawyer's office, but he still couldn't get over what had happened between him and Barnes in the alley. It didn't sit right with him and it wouldn't until he got his revenge. He wanted the bastard begging, bleeding, and then broken. Nothing else would do. But now, watching the blonde hurry away, Creed thought that he just might have figured out a way to get his revenge.

"You know, Audie," he said. "I think I just got me an idea."

Chapter Sixteen

FILMING RESUMED the next morning. But unlike the original schedule, which had called for an indoor scene between Anna and Montgomery in which their characters were to discuss the toll the bandit's raids were taking on the town, Samuel announced that they would be outdoors, reshooting the wild horseback ride out of town. At first, there was plenty of grumbling. When someone finally worked up the nerve to ask Samuel what had happened, why they were going back to something they'd already filmed, the producer replied that Frank hadn't liked the look of the rushes and wanted to do it over.

Out at the film site, the welcome respite of the previous day's rain was long gone and the blazing sun had returned, just as it had the day the scene had originally been shot. Anna waited with the rest of the cast and crew as the camera track was laid out and the path of the horses replotted. Frank played it off perfectly, as per plan, scowling and shouting, kicking at the dirt and making anyone watching see just how difficult he could be.

For her part, Anna tried to be supportive, yet not reveal that she knew the real reason for the reshoot.

"I can't believe we're back out here," one of the extras grumbled.

"There's nothing we can do about it," Anna answered. "I'm just going to do what Frank asks and get it over with. The sooner it's done, the sooner we'll be inside and out of this heat."

"But who's to say we won't just be right back out here in a couple more days? What if he's still not happy?"

Not if the guard outside the film room does his job, Anna thought.

Once the horseback ride had been filmed, the cast took a break for lunch as the cameras were positioned for another scene that had to be reshot. This one was the first Anna had ever done, in which she'd worked alongside Montgomery and Joan on the mercantile set. Since Anna had been nervous, as well as unbalanced by her fellow actress's antics, she thought this take might be better the second time around, although she doubted Joan would make it any easier for her.

As she had during the morning's filming, Anna heard a few complaints here and there, but they didn't last long. Anna even detected a bit of excitement among the stage-hands; since they were paid by the day, any reshoots meant that they'd be paid extra wages. Up until then, Anna hadn't thought about the extra cost that Valentine Pictures would bear because of the sabotage. She had no way of knowing how much it totaled, but it had to be significant. Still, when she looked at Samuel, walking beside Frank as he growled and occasionally roared, he was still flashing a smile bright enough to say he didn't have a worry in the world. Anna knew that she shouldn't be surprised; he was an accomplished actor, after all.

While Montgomery appeared to be taking the reshoot in stride, shrugging his shoulders and looking amused that they were right back where they'd started, Anna noticed that Joan wasn't as willing to let the matter go without complaint. While the set was being prepared, she rolled her eyes, tapped her foot impatiently, snapped at the unlucky girl who had been tasked with freshening her makeup, and occasionally gave voice to her frustrations.

"It's a shame that Frank wasn't satisfied with my first take," she loudly declared to no one in particular. "Personally, I think it would've been good enough to win an Academy Award. Who's to say I can do as well a second time."

Anna also noticed that Joan kept staring at her. Even though she'd been doing her best to make Anna feel as uncomfortable as she could ever since they'd first met, this was different; this felt like suspicion. Somehow, Joan seemed to sense that her younger rival knew something about why they were refilming. No matter how hard Anna tried to act as clueless as everyone else, every time she looked up, Joan's eyes were on her.

But fortunately, nothing ever came of it. Even during the filming, Joan acted professionally, much more so than she ever had before.

Maybe I was imagining things...

Anna sat in front of the dressing room mirror, slowly pulling a brush through her long blond hair. She was so tired that she had to stifle a yawn. The day's shoot had been hard; she didn't know if Frank was acting or not, trying to maintain the subterfuge Samuel had concocted, but on the set he'd been an unforgiving taskmaster. Anna thought that there was a good chance she'd hear the director shouting in her sleep. She was thankful that the day was finally over.

Except for her, the room was empty. After the trying day of filming, everyone had been in a hurry to get cleaned up and leave. Since Anna had been the last to finish on the set, it meant that she was the last woman to use the dressing room. Still, as exhausted as she was, she didn't hurry; she took her time removing her makeup and changing into her own clothes. Earlier, Bonnie had instructed her to hang up her costume beside the sewing machine; the seamstress said she wanted to make a few alterations in the morning. All Anna needed was to finish her hair and then she could go. Maybe then she could speak with Dalton about all that had happened.

And I can ask a few questions.

Throughout the day, Anna's thoughts had drifted back to the destruction in the film room. It hadn't been an accident. Someone had purposefully ruined the canisters and, more than likely, burned down Valentine Pictures' newly constructed building. But who? Why? Was there someone out there who had a deeper hatred for Hollywood than Dalton did? Was it intense enough for someone to act on it? What was planned next? She'd wished that she and Dalton had been able to talk about it yesterday, but Walker had unwittingly interrupted. She hoped today would be different.

Suddenly, Anna was startled by the sound of the doorknob turning. Panic gripped her chest. Ever since her terrible encounter with Milburn, she'd tried not to be alone in the dressing room, and in those times when it was unavoidable, she always made sure to lock the door. But this time she'd forgotten. Quick as a flash, she sprang up out of her chair, but she was only halfway to the door when it opened. Anna's breath caught in her throat, but instead of Milburn's leering face, she watched as someone else entered.

It was Joan.

"What were you trying to do, get up and lock the door before I could get inside?" the older actress asked with a sneer.

"No, I was just—" Anna started to reply.

"Whatever," Joan cut her off, barging past and taking a seat at the mirror beside the one Anna was using.

For a moment, Anna thought about just walking right out the door without another word or glance back. The last thing she wanted right then and there was to spend time with a harpy like Joan Webb. Still, she also didn't want to give the woman the satisfaction of knowing she got under her skin. What could possibly happen, anyway? She'd just sit back down in her chair, finish brushing her hair, and *then* she would leave.

But soon after she'd taken her seat, picked up her brush, and resumed stroking her hair, Anna noticed that Joan was acting a little oddly. She'd expected to hear a few snide comments, but the older actress sat silently still in her chair, lips tightly pursed, making no move to take off her makeup. Occasionally, her eyes wandered to Anna's in the mirror, but quickly looked away. The more time that passed, the stranger it all seemed. For one thing, it didn't make sense that Joan was still wearing her costume. She'd left the set well before Anna, had been one of the first to go, and should've been cleaned up and changed long before now. What explanation could there be? Where had she been until now?

"What's going on around here?"

Anna jumped in surprise; Joan's voice held an undeniable threat of menace running through it, like an animal's growl. When Anna looked over at her, she could see how tense she was; she was gripping the arms of her chair so tightly that her knuckles were white.

"I don't know what you're talking about…" Anna replied.

"Don't you play games with me!" Joan snapped, swiveling in her chair toward Anna, her face twisted with fury. "You think I'm a fool, don't you? Just some washed-up old actress who doesn't understand her fame's passed her by. Well, listen to me, sweetheart! I didn't get to be a star in this business without knowing when the wool's being pulled over my eyes!"

"Joan, I don't know what you're talking about," Anna said forcefully.

"Why are we filming the same scenes over again? And don't give me that garbage about how Frank didn't like what had been shot and wanted to do it over. That's the tripe you shovel to the peons in the crew. *You* know the truth! I saw the way you were looking at Samuel when he changed the shooting schedule. You weren't the least bit surprised by what was happening."

"That's because he told me this morning before he made the announcement," Anna said, giving what she thought was a believable explanation.

"He told you first..."

"Yes," Anna insisted.

"I suppose it's because you're the *star*," Joan said with a sneer.

"I met him in the hallway before breakfast and he thought I should know so I'd be able to go over my lines. That's all." Even though what she was saying wasn't the truth, Anna knew she didn't have a choice. Everyone who saw the wreckage of the film room had been sworn to secrecy. Joan *couldn't* know.

"Oh, just stop all the lies!" the older woman snapped, her face growing red in anger. "I see it right there in your beady little eyes!" she said, pointing so close to Anna that she had to lean away. "You're Samuel's new favorite! His new find! Valentine Pictures' next big star! It's enough to make me sick to my stomach!"

"You're out of your mind!"

"Am I? What did you have to do to get this job anyway?" Joan asked. "How much of that body of yours did you have to show in order to land the lead?"

Anna's eyes widened with shock and disbelief. "How *dare* you!"

A cruel smile coursed across Joan's face as she saw that her spiteful words had cut close enough to draw a reaction. "How long a train ride is it from St. Louis to Redstone, anyway?" she asked. "I'm sure there was plenty of time for you to show Samuel just how grateful you were..."

Her hands trembling, Anna was so stunned she could only gasp.

"Don't act so surprised," Joan kept on. "It's not as though I never took off my skirt for a job. At least Samuel is holding on to his looks as he gets older. It could've been some slob pawing at your tits. Here's a little secret," she added, her voice lowering into a conspiratorial whisper. "When he's busy pumping away on you, just keep thinking about all the money you're going to get out of it. Who knows, you might even end up liking it."

No longer able to contain her anger, Anna started to rise out of her chair. She didn't know what she was going to do, only that Joan wasn't going to like it very much. But just as she was getting to her feet, the older actress suddenly reached out and shoved her in the chest with both hands.

Anna rocked backward, her arms uselessly pinwheeling in the air for a moment, before she finally lost her balance. She crashed back down hard into her chair, the force of Joan's push propelling her over and onto the floor. Pain filled her; her head cracked the floor and her elbow stung so badly that tears filled her eyes. But pain wasn't the emotion that filled her.

It was anger.

Livid with both fury and embarrassment, Anna scrambled back to her feet, her hands balled tightly into fists, ready to show Joan that she wasn't some weakling who would keep taking abuse without ever fighting back. This called for much more than giving the woman a piece of her mind. Maybe a split lip and a black eye would teach her a thing or two.

But then, just as Anna was about to rear back and throw a punch, she suddenly stopped. Joan was still sitting in her chair, but she didn't seem frightened, or even angry.

She looked excited.

It was then that Anna finally understood. *This* was why Joan was still wearing her costume. *This* was why she'd waited until she was sure that everyone else had gone before entering the dressing room. *This* was why she had shoved Anna to the floor and, instead of raising her fists to fight, stuck out her chin. She *wanted* Anna to hit her, to hurt her, to mark up her face. She'd come to goad her rival into a fight, earn a few scars she could show around, and get Anna fired from the picture. If she managed to get Anna to do all of the work, to not inflict any noticeable damage of her own, the brawl would be seen as one-sided. Everyone would know that Joan had been the innocent victim of a jealous attack. What price was a bloody nose to pay for that kind of reward? Anna had been manipulated from the second the door opened. The worst part was that she'd almost fallen for it.

Almost...

As quickly as Anna had raised her hands, she lowered them; the smile on Joan's face immediately started to wilt. "I'm not going to play your game," Anna declared.

"Come on, you little slut!" Joan shouted, growing desperate to get the response she wanted. "You whore! Tramp! Hit me, bitch! Hit me!"

If she hadn't figured out Joan's plan, the actress's words might have been enough to make Anna lash out, but now it was too late. "You can yell until you're hoarse, but I won't give you what you want," Anna said. Even though she'd decided not to hurt Joan with her hands, she still had words to use as weapons. "I can't believe you'd stoop to something like this," Anna added. "To think, there was a time I idolized you, but no more. You're pathetic."

As if she'd touched a match to a candle's wick, Anna's words lit a fire in Joan. "Don't you dare pity me! Don't you dare!" she shouted, rising out of her chair and narrowing the distance between them. Anna wondered if this would be the moment when Joan snapped, throwing punches regardless of the consequences, but the woman held herself in check, though her body shook with rage. "You think you've bested me?" she snarled. "You think that I'm just going to let you walk away from this so easily? Let me show you how wrong you are!"

With that, Joan stormed over to the dressing room door, turned the key in the lock, and looked back to Anna with a sickening smile.

"What are you doing?" Anna asked.

In answer, Joan snatched up a lamp from a side table near the door, tested its heft in her hand, and then hurled it at the mirror Anna had been using. Smashing with a loud, almost deafening crash, the glass exploded into countless shards that rained down on the floor, the chairs, and the tabletops, landing everywhere and on everything. Anna thought that she couldn't possibly have been more surprised than she was at that moment, but she was wrong.

She was struck mute, frozen in place, so completely shocked that she had no idea what to say or do, the moment Joan started screaming.

"Help! Somebody please help me!" she shouted at the top of her lungs, shrill and loud in the small dressing room. "She's trying to kill me! Help!"

Quickly, Joan stepped over to the changing tables and, with one violent brush of her arm, swept everything onto the floor. Shards of glass, lipstick containers, jars of cold cream, and brushes of all shapes and sizes went flying. With a malevolent smile on her face, she kicked the chair she'd been sitting in and sent it caroming up against the wall. Gleefully, Joan rushed over to the standing rack of costumes and began to tear them from their hangers, tossing them every which way. Through it all, she never stopped yelling.

"Stay away from me! Don't hurt me! Please, please don't hurt me!"

Anna was so flabbergasted, so completely unable to believe what she was seeing, that all she could do was stand and stare. She'd long since determined that Joan was unhinged, that she desperately wanted to ruin her new costar's career before it even began, but she never would have imagined that Joan would resort to something as insane as *this*.

But then she took things even further.

Snatching up a small wooden jewelry box from one of the changing tables she hadn't yet destroyed, Joan paused for only a second, sneering at Anna, before she brought the box up and smashed herself in the face with it. Anna gasped in horrified disbelief. Almost immediately, blood began to trickle from a small cut on the woman's cheek.

"What are you doing?" Joan shouted; her voice was full of shock and pain. "Whatever I did, I'm sorry! Don't hit me again!"

And then, contrary to what she'd just pleaded for, she once again smacked herself with the jewelry box. This time, the blow landed more flush with her nose; a steady stream of crimson began to gush, spilling across Joan's lips and darkening her chin. Anna was convinced that the crazed woman had broken something. Joan's eyes watered with tears.

But this time, Anna wasn't frozen in place. She rushed

over and tried to wrestle the jewelry box from Joan's hands, but the older actress clung to it tenaciously, as if it was a prized possession instead of a weapon.

"What are you doing?" Anna asked. "Stop hurting yourself!"

"Someone help me!" Joan continued to shout, turning her head toward the locked door. "She's trying to kill me!"

Still struggling to stop Joan, Anna nearly leaped out of her skin when the dressing room's door suddenly rattled. From the other side, a man's voice shouted, "What's going on in there?"

"Help me! Help!" Joan screamed even louder, giving Anna a smile smeared with her own blood. "Stop her before it's too late."

"Hold on! I'm coming!" the man yelled back. Unable to open the door because of the lock Joan had engaged, her would-be rescuer decided to break it down instead, pounding at the door as he threw his weight against it. Over and over he tried. Anna knew it wouldn't take long before he succeeded.

"Are you insane?" she pleaded, trying to make Joan see reason.

"Let's see how perfect everyone thinks you are now," the older woman said, her voice no longer a shout but a low, menacing whisper.

With a sudden, almost deafening crack, the door frame snapped at the hinges as the man outside finally managed to break through. Just as the noise came roaring through the room, Joan finally let go of the jewelry box; Anna had been pulling on it so hard that the sudden lack of resistance almost caused her to fall over. Joan collapsed onto the floor in a hail of tears, crawling backward through the debris of her evil plan, looking pleadingly at the man, a stagehand Anna recognized, as he stepped into the room, his eyes wide with shock.

"Oh, thank God! Thank God!" Joan cried. "She was trying to kill me! She was..." she went on but dissolved into tears.

Anna could only stare at the chaos all around her; the weapon Joan had used to hurt herself now in *her* hands, the other woman's face a disaster while her own was unmarred, and the look on the man's face telling her that he already believed her guilty.

How am I ever going to get out of this one...?

Chapter Seventeen

I KNOW IT SOUNDS CRAZY, but it's the truth! I swear it is!"

Anna sat with Samuel in the office across the hallway from the room in which the studio's film had been destroyed. In the aftermath of Joan's self-inflicted beating, the movie's producer had been the first person called, but he'd hardly been the last. With the speed with which news traveled, especially gossip as scandalous as this, coupled with the fact that Joan had never once stopped screaming about what she claimed to have happened, it hadn't taken long for a crowd to gather outside the dressing room. Some of the murmurs that reached Anna's ears were enough to make her weak in the knees.

"...nothing but jealousy is all!"

"...never know what'll set one of these so-called stars off! Why I once..."

"She'll be lucky if she doesn't end up in jail for this..."

The wounds on Joan's face were ugly. Even though she'd

only hit herself twice, she'd inflicted plenty of damage; her cheek was already swollen and discolored, a horrible mess of purple and black, and her nose still dripped blood. Joan winced as the doctor treated her, but whatever discomfort she felt, it wasn't enough to keep her from continuing to lash out at her "attacker."

"I want her fired for what she's done!" she said, pointing at Anna, as she somehow managed to bring fresh tears to her eyes. "She tried to kill me!"

Though Anna was the real victim of the woman's scheme, she had to admit that it had all been an impressive performance, even for an actress as accomplished as Joan Webb.

Eventually, Samuel had had enough of listening to Joan's relentless screed. Taking Anna by the arm, he cut a path for them through the milling throng and out the dressing room door, then outside, and across town to the studio's office. The whole way, he never said a word, and Anna knew better than to add any of her own. Finally, with no small amount of anger peppering his words, he ordered all of the secretaries out of the building, led the way up the stairs and into the back room. Even though he'd told everyone to leave, he still shut the door behind them, wanting to avoid any curious eavesdroppers. Once they'd both taken a seat, he leaned forward, laced his fingers together, and asked only one question.

"What in the hell happened?"

Anna told him everything, not leaving out a single detail. When she began to recount how Joan had locked the door and proceeded to trash the room before picking up the jewelry box and hitting herself with it, she expected to see a reaction on Samuel's face, but he sat there impassively, his mouth pinched tight, listening. Even when she got to the part where Joan insinuated that she and Samuel had to be sleeping together, that that was how she'd gotten the role, he never flinched. When she finished, he remained still and silent for a long time, before finally sighing and rubbing his hand along his jaw.

"You're telling me that...that Joan did that...to *herself*...?"

All Anna could do was nod; she knew that if she opened her mouth, she was going to start crying. She knew it sounded crazy, like some unbelievable lie someone would concoct to keep from getting into trouble. In her heart, she understood that Joan had succeeded, that she'd finally managed to drive away her rival. Anna was going to be fired. She was going to lose her chance to be in the movies, to become a star, to be somebody. She'd leave Redstone in shame and disgrace. But worst of all, she'd leave Dalton. This was the thought that paralyzed her, that made her want to scream. She didn't know where things between them were going, had no idea where they would end up, but she desperately wanted to drive down that road. It wasn't fair! She wanted more kisses, more touches, and more opportunities to give voice to the feelings that were threatening to burst her heart. She'd never known love before and had started to wonder if what she was experiencing with Dalton wasn't a part of it, a first step that would lead them to something special and new. But now it had all been ruined, destroyed by a bitter, jealous woman's hatred.

"I believe you."

Anna's head shot up; she moved so abruptly that a tear was dislodged to run down her cheek. She couldn't believe what she'd heard. "What?"

"I have to believe one of you, don't I?" Samuel asked, leaning back in his chair, suddenly looking tired. "In the end, I have to choose which of the two explanations is the *least* crazy," he said. "That Joan smashed up her face and destroyed the dressing room on her own, or that you attacked her. I may not have known you for long, but I just can't see you doing it. What for? To what end? I've seen the way she's treated you on the set, how jealously she's behaved, but I never would've thought something like this could happen."

"I should've left as soon as she opened the door."

"Yes, that's exactly what you should've done," Samuel said. He sighed and rubbed the bridge of his nose. "Why, on top of all the other headaches I'm dealing with, did I have to get saddled with another?"

Anna didn't know what to say. Samuel was right. Just yesterday the producer had discovered that someone was trying to sabotage his dream project. Now, one of his actresses had been badly hurt and was accusing another of his stars of having done it. Even though Anna hadn't meant for it to happen, her latest run-in with Joan had made life for Samuel even harder.

"This won't be the end of it, you know," he explained.

"Yes, it will be," she disagreed. "Other than when we have to work together on the movie, you won't find me within a hundred feet of her. I promise."

"That's not what I mean. What happened today isn't just going to go away because you avoid Joan. Even if she somehow manages to keep from blabbing about this to anyone who'll listen, word is going to get out. I wouldn't be a bit surprised if it ended up in one of the gossip magazines within a week."

"But that's not right! It didn't happen! It's all a lie!"

Samuel shook his head. "None of that matters. Even if there had been a witness, someone who could back up your side of the story, those hacks in Hollywood would find a way to make you out to blame."

"But why?" Anna asked.

"Because Joan Webb is old news. You, on the other hand, are fresh, an exciting and pretty new face who's on the way up. Writing it so that you're at fault is juicier, more of a scandal. Plastering your picture underneath some headline that says you attacked your costar will sell rags from New York to Los Angeles and back again."

Anna knew he was right. It was just another form of entertainment. She was as guilty of feeding the gossip mill as anyone; she herself had stood in front of the newspaper stand back in St. Louis and browsed the headlines looking for some unseemly tidbit about a celebrity. Everyone loved a good scandal, even if it didn't have a shred of truth connected to it.

"This is the sort of thing that could follow you the rest of your career."

"What do I do about it?"

"I don't know if you can do anything," Samuel answered.

"That doesn't seem fair."

"It isn't," he admitted. "But think about it for a moment. Obviously, you're not going to admit to something you didn't do, but if you go out of your way to deny it, there are plenty of people out there who'll twist your words until they're unrecognizable, even to you. The only other option you have is to ignore it and hope it just goes away, which, in the end, might be the best course to follow. Unfortunately, you won't be the only person who's going to be hounded about this, and I'm not talking about Joan."

"They'll come after you, too?" Anna asked.

The producer nodded. "I bet that there are writers already camped out in the hotel lobby even as we speak, like vultures ready to pick the carcass clean. Everywhere I turn for the next couple of days, there will be someone with a notebook, a pencil, and a bunch of questions I don't want to answer, not that they'll give a damn."

"I'm sorry for the trouble, Samuel. I really am."

"It's all right. Because I've chosen to believe your side of the story, I also know it's not your fault."

"I apologize all the same."

Samuel gave her a thin smile. "The one thing that really chaps my hide about all of this is that I'm going to have to deal with it while trying to figure out this sabotage business at the same time. I don't like having too many eggs in the air at once. Eventually, one of them is going to fall and break."

Listening to the producer, Anna knew that it was not the time to tell him about what had happened between her and Milburn. Even though the young actor's advances had become bolder and more upsetting, she couldn't bring herself to add to Samuel's burden. As a solution, she'd take the same tack with Milburn that she was planning to use with Joan, and besides when they were on the set together, she'd stay as far away from both of them as possible. That way, she'd ensure that nothing bad could happen.

"Are you going to talk to Joan?" she asked.

"Don't worry about her," he replied. "I'll get things straightened out as best as I can. Maybe I can convince her that keeping her mouth shut would be in everyone's best interests." Then, he added ironically, "I'm not holding my breath."

When Samuel got up from behind the desk and opened the door, Anna understood that their meeting was over. She thanked him for everything and started for the stairs. She'd almost reached them when he asked, "Are you still glad you accepted my offer?"

She stopped and turned back at him. "Even with all this, I'd never regret saying 'yes.'"

For the first time since Samuel had rushed into the dressing room and discovered the destruction that had been wrought, Anna finally saw the return of his trademark smile. "That's what I was hoping you'd say."

* * *

Anna stepped out of the studio's office and paused beneath the awning. It was still early in the evening, about half past five, and the sun shone brightly, with a few hours left until it vanished in the west. People milled about on the street; a shopkeeper locked up his store for the day, tipping his hat to an older woman as she walked by. A truck rattled past, belching a few puffs of dark smoke. Though everything looked the same, to Anna, after what'd happened between her and Joan, it all felt strangely different.

Nowhere would that be more true than at the Stagecoach. The last thing she wanted to do was go back to the hotel and face the crowd. Everyone would be staring at her. By now, who knew what rumors had spread? Though Anna knew she was innocent, others wouldn't believe her no matter what she said or did. Another horrifying thought filled her; what if some of the gossip magazine writers Samuel had been talking about were waiting to pounce on her the moment she walked through the door? Just thinking about it was exhausting. In the end, there was only one person she wanted to be with.

Dalton.

Without any hesitation, she set out to find him. Taking a roundabout way toward the blacksmith shop, she crossed Main Street before turning down a side street. A couple of times, she couldn't keep from being noticed by someone connected to the movie; opposite the post office, she saw a woman who worked with Bonnie on the film's costumes, who, when she saw Anna, pointed and then whispered excitedly to her companion. Anna was leery of the shadows, too, after what had happened the day before with the dangerous-looking pair of men; she doubted that another run-in with them would end so innocently.

Finally, after what seemed like forever, Anna arrived at the blacksmith shop only to find that Dalton was gone, the door shut and locked for the day. She looked around helplessly; he'd never told her where he lived, but she assumed that it had to be close by. Wandering behind the shop, her head turning every which way in the hopes of spotting him, she was suddenly rewarded with a glimpse. Dalton was walking away from her, skirting a worn-looking fence and heading toward a house set at the rear of the lot. His back was to her, but she would have recognized him anywhere.

"Dalton!" she shouted, running to reach him.

When he turned to look at her, a flicker of surprise rippling across his face, Anna did something she felt like she hadn't done in ages.

She smiled.

Dalton had been walking back home after another long day of pounding, bending, and building things for the movie studio. Absently, he'd been wiping the grime and sweat from his hands with a work towel when he heard Anna's voice shouting his name. When he turned to find her hurrying toward him, he was both surprised and thrilled. But when she threw herself into his arms, leaping from the ground to wrap herself around him, clinging so tightly that she seemed afraid to let go, he knew something was wrong.

"Are you all right?" he asked, delighted to be so close to her, especially after the short time they'd been able to be together the day before. "Did something happen?"

When Anna pulled away from him, she tried to smile her way through whatever it was that was bothering her, but it soon faltered, her lip trembling and her eyes growing wet. "I had a bad day, that's all," she admitted. "Worse than I ever could've imagined. It was so bad that you were the only person I thought might be able to make it better. I hope you don't mind my coming like this."

Dalton shook his head. "Not at all," he said.

"I'm glad," she said with relief.

"Look, I just closed up the shop, so let me grab a clean shirt and then we can go somewhere and you can tell me all about it."

Anna nodded. "I don't care what we do. I just want to be with you."

But just as Dalton turned back to the house, his mother stepped out of the back door, giving a start of surprise as she saw them. To her son, it all seemed so fake as to be comical; he was certain that she must have been standing at the window, watching them.

"Oh, I'm sorry," Betty gushed. "I didn't mean to interrupt."

"You're fine, Mother," Dalton answered, a vein of irritation in his voice. "As soon as I change, we'll be leaving."

"Right now? But I just put dinner on the table," Betty

replied. Suddenly, as if inspiration had struck her like a bolt of lightning, she added, "I know! Why don't you join us, my dear! You haven't already eaten, have you?"

"Well, no I haven't," Anna replied.

"Then it's settled!"

"We've already made plans," Dalton interjected.

"But surely it's something that can wait until after dinner," Betty insisted. He knew that his mother was just being nosy, that seeing her son with a woman as beautiful as Anna was impossible to resist; she just had to know more. For Dalton, the worst thing of all was noticing that Anna was starting to buy into it; she was smiling now, charmed by his mother's enthusiasm. She looked at him and shrugged, as if asking "Why not?"

Why not, indeed...

"I'm Betty," his mother said, extending her hand before adding, "since my son hasn't bothered to introduce us."

Anna gave her name with a smile; Dalton could see that she was growing more involved with Betty by the second.

"Are you one of the actresses in the movie that's being made?"

"I am," Anna answered.

"I knew it!" Betty exclaimed. "Obviously I've never seen you around before, but you're far too beautiful to be putting on someone else's makeup or getting coffee. Is acting as exciting as it seems?"

"Some days more than others," she answered, glancing at Dalton.

"Well, you'll just have to come in and tell me all about

it," Betty said as she took Anna by the arm and began to lead her toward the house. "I've always wondered what it would be like to be famous!"

Dalton sighed as the door shut behind the two women. Because of his mother's insistence, whatever it was that Anna had wanted to talk about was going to have to wait. But what really unsettled his stomach, what made him a little nervous, was the one topic he'd been avoiding with Anna.

Even though she'd told him so much about her own past, had explained to him all that she'd overcome to get to where she was, he hadn't been nearly as forthcoming. In particular, he had never spoken a word about his father's gambling problem. George Barnes's failing embarrassed his son, even though he knew that Anna would never blame him for it. Ever since the day he'd been attacked by the Cobb brothers, it had been a struggle for Dalton to be around his father. He'd had to really work at keeping his temper in check. But now, he was going to have to try harder than ever.

His father would be at dinner.

Chapter Eighteen

SITTING DOWN TO DINNER with the Barnes family, Anna was more than a bit nervous, but it didn't take long for the good company and delicious food to make her feel completely at ease. Betty had prepared a roast with carrots and onions, as well as a pan of cornbread. An apple pie cooled in the kitchen. Conversation and the occasional bit of laughter filled the small room, mixing with sounds of silverware clinking against plates and bowls.

"Tell me: What's it like seeing yourself up on the big screen?" Betty asked, placing another helping of meat on Anna's plate, her smile bright, her eyes practically twinkling with excitement.

"I don't really know yet," Anna answered. "This is my first movie. I worry about what I'll look like up there. It might not be as flattering as I hope.'"

"Nonsense! You're beautiful! It'll make you look even more so!"

Dalton's parents were much as Anna had expected them to be: down-to-earth, similar to their son. Betty was a chatterbox, an attractive older woman who wanted to know anything and everything she could about the movie business. Her son had inherited much of her looks, especially around the eyes. She was so friendly, so welcoming, that Anna couldn't help but take an immediate liking to her. But with Dalton's father, George, things weren't quite so easy. Being a blacksmith like his son, he had the same large frame and beaten hands. Unlike his wife, he appeared distant. Though he was polite enough to smile and nod periodically, he pushed his fork aimlessly around his plate, eating little and saying less. Every so often, she noticed that he'd glance at his watch, as if he was worried about being late for something.

Surprisingly, the person who seemed to be enjoying dinner the least was Dalton. He sulked as he sat beside Anna, across from his father, adding little to the conversation. He'd hardly eaten a bite. When they'd first sat down to eat, Anna had wondered if he was upset with her. Even though she'd desperately wanted to tell him about her confrontation with Joan, she'd found Betty's gesture to be too sweet to turn down. It would have been rude not to accept. There'd be time for them to talk later. Still, Dalton's mood continued to sour. Whenever she managed to catch his attention, he'd raise his eyes to hers and offer a weak smile before once again looking away.

What's going on here? Why is he so upset?

"These carrots are delicious, Mrs. Barnes," Anna said,

complimenting Betty on her cooking. "I can't remember when I last had any this good."

Dalton's mother smiled, pleased by the praise. "Thank you, dear," she replied, "But this is nothing compared to what you get back at the hotel. Claudette Gibbons told me that they brought in some fancy chef from Hollywood. Flew him all the way to Redstone! I can't imagine that this meal could match his cooking."

"You'd be surprised."

Anna meant what she said. While the meals that the studio provided were good, sitting down to the table as a family struck her as special. After all, this was something that she'd never had the chance to experience, something that had been denied her because of her father's death and the hard paths her mother and brother had taken. She'd always wondered how different her life could have been, and this, just maybe, provided a glimpse. Regardless of why he was so unhappy, Dalton was lucky to have this.

"A chef isn't the only thing you people have brought to town," George suddenly offered. "You've brought plenty of business, too. There isn't a person in Redstone who hasn't profited because of it."

"I can think of a couple," Dalton replied, his voice low.

Noticing the look that flickered across Betty's face, Anna suddenly understood the source of Dalton's unease. While she didn't know the reason why, something had gone wrong between father and son, something that still festered, worming its way between them and causing Dalton to sit and stew through dinner. With the white-knuckled way Dalton was gripping the edge of the table, Anna also knew that if she didn't change the subject, things were about to get ugly.

Turning back to George, she said, "Dalton told me that the studio's asked you to make all sorts of things. That must be hard work."

"It sure is," he replied, warming to the conversation, ignoring the warning signs coming from his son. "Except when we stop to eat and sleep, the shop forge is lit pert' near the rest of the day. As soon as we finish one job, some fella comes by with the next. Working with you Hollywood people has been nothing but profitable for this family."

"Has it now?" Dalton snapped angrily, his eyes rising from his untouched plate to stare daggers at his father. "It might be working out fine for one of us, but it's the rest of us I'm worried about."

"Dalton, please," Betty soothed, trying to play peacemaker. She glanced over at Anna and gave a faint smile. "I don't think this is the time."

"When would be the right time, then? How about when the bank comes and hauls away everything we've got so that they can put it up for auction?" Dalton asked sarcastically. "Or should we wait until the next time Vernon Black sends his goons to beat me senseless in order to send a message about paying our debts?"

"What?" Betty exclaimed, her eyes wide with shock. Turning to George, she asked, "What's he talking about? We owe money to Vernon Black?"

"It's nothing to worry about," her husband answered, raising his hands as if he were trying to fend off a punch. "I've got a handle on it. It's just a misunderstanding, is all. It'll all get straightened out."

Turning back to her son, Betty asked, "Is this why you had that bruise on your chin? Did someone hit you?"

Dalton didn't say a word in reply, but his silence gave as clear an answer as any words could have done.

Through it all, Anna sat shell-shocked. If she'd known that there was so much tension between Dalton and his father, she never would have accepted Betty's invitation. But in all the time they'd spent together, Dalton had never talked much about his family, certainly not the way she had about hers. If there was this much discord, this much anger, especially if it was about money, it was easier to understand why Dalton could fly off the handle.

"Ask him how much he owes," Dalton said to his mother. "After the Cobb brothers jumped me, I couldn't get it out of him. Hell, who knows, maybe he'll even tell you the truth, although he's gotten so good at lying over the years, I wouldn't be too quick to believe him."

"I told you before," George said, his temper clearly rising, "a son shouldn't talk to his father that way."

"And *I* told *you*," Dalton countered, "a son shouldn't have to."

"You best hold your tongue."

"Or what? You'll disappoint me some more?"

"Dalton!" Betty hissed; Anna could see tears welling in the woman's eyes.

"It's all right, sweetheart," George said. He pushed back his chair slowly, the legs scraping hard against the floor. "As angry as he is at me, I reckon I should be glad he hasn't said worse. I think it's best if I just up and go." Turning to Anna, he smiled weakly. "It was real nice meeting you," he said. "Keep a close eye on my son for me, would you? He can be a handful."

With a touch of sadness in his eyes, George dropped his napkin onto his plate and left the room. Moments later, they heard the front door shut, the hinges squeaking as it closed behind him. Just when Anna began to wonder what she might say or do next, Dalton suddenly stood up from his chair. Without a word, he stalked out of the dining room in the opposite direction from the one his father had taken, slamming the back door so hard that Anna imagined it could be heard at the Stagecoach.

Anna made no move to stop him; she simply let him go. What had happened between Dalton and his father was troubling, but she didn't fully understand it or know if Dalton wanted her to get involved. If he hadn't mentioned it to her yet, there had to be a reason.

Still, she couldn't deny her curiosity.

Glancing over at Betty, Anna found her still staring after her son. She looked as if she was struggling to control her emotions. Anna expected her to burst into tears, so she was momentarily stunned when, seconds later, Betty turned back to her with a smile on her face, as if nothing had happened.

"Well then," she said cheerfully. "How about some pie?"

* * *

Dalton kicked disgustedly at a rock, sending it flying. Absently, he ran a hand through his hair as he stared toward his family's blacksmith shop; he'd been so angry that he'd forgotten his hat back inside. The sun hadn't completely gone yet, streaking the sky with its remaining light, but the shadows were growing longer by the second. Soon it would be pitch black. But as dark as the encroaching gloom was, it was nothing compared to his mood.

Once again, he'd let his temper get the better of him. After Anna had accepted his mother's offer to join them for dinner, Dalton had tried to make the best of it, but as soon as he'd sat down and looked across the table at his father, all the familiar feelings of disgust and resentment had come bubbling back. Part of it was because of the roles his parents had assumed before Anna, acting as if they were the perfect family. He'd managed to hold his tongue for a while, but as soon as his father started talking about how happy he was for the money the movie company was spending, it had become too much. Memories came rushing back, especially of his run-in with Creed and Audie Cobb, as well as of the sleepless nights he'd spent wondering how the family would manage to make ends meet. He just couldn't take it anymore.

Then he'd opened his big, fat mouth...

Dalton felt that he hadn't been wrong to blow up at his father. His mistake had been to do it in front of Anna. She'd come to him to talk about something bad that had happened to her, but she'd never had the chance. This latest outburst, combined with the first time he'd lost his temper out at the stone bridge, would surely be too much for her.

Behind him, he heard the back door open.

"Dalton?" Anna called to him.

He froze, unable to answer, embarrassed by his behavior. In the quiet twilight, he heard her come down the stairs and cross the distance between them. When she touched his arm at the elbow, her fingers lightly holding him, it sent shivers racing across his skin. Still, he was too humiliated to even look at her.

"Are you all right?" she asked.

Somehow, after a short pause, he was able to find his voice. "I've been better."

"I imagine you have."

"I never wanted you to see that."

In reply, she gave his arm a gentle squeeze.

For a long moment, they stood together silently, side by side, and stared out into the darkness. Dalton was surprised by how comforting it was to have her with him, even if neither of them said a word. He could only imagine how confused she must be by what she'd seen, as well as how many questions she must have.

"Don't you want to know what that was all about?" he asked.

"Of course I do," she admitted with a smile. "But I'm not going to pry. It's up to you. If you want to tell me, I'll listen."

"I don't want to burden you with my troubles."

Playfully, Anna hit him on the arm. "Have you forgotten why I came to see you tonight?" she asked. "I had one of the worst days of my life today and you were the first and only person I wanted to share it with."

"Why?" he asked.

"Because you're special to me," she answered, sliding her hand down the length of his arm, eventually intertwining her fingers with his. "I meant what I said before. It might not look like it from the outside, but the two of us are more alike than you might think. I wanted to be with you because, if there was anyone who might be able to make me feel better, it'd be you."

Dalton stared down into Anna's eyes, the green catching the last, fleeting rays of sun, and knew that she was right. He felt exactly the same way. For more years than he could remember, he'd held the burden of his father's addiction inside him, sharing it only with Walker. No matter how hard he struggled to deal with it, first pleading with his father to stop and then squirreling away money when he didn't, nothing seemed to work. All that had done was make him distrustful. It had taught him to keep his distance from people so that he wasn't disappointed when they inevitably let him down. But then along had come this woman, from Hollywood of all places, and she'd somehow managed to reach through the barrier he'd put up around himself and take him by the hand. It was almost too good to be true. How could a woman as beautiful, funny, and charming as Anna was find love with a man like him? His life had started to resemble one of those romantic movies he'd once enjoyed but had come to consider far from true to life as he knew it.

Anna Finnegan was a miracle.

"My father has a gambling problem," he said.

Dalton watched her face, wondering if he would see a look that betrayed her feelings. But she remained silent, listening. Recalling her manner when she'd met Walker, Dalton understood that she wasn't the type of person who leaped to conclusions or was quick to pass judgment. The stirrings in his heart were so loud, so insistent, that Dalton struggled to resist the urge to take her in his arms and hold her close.

But then, before Dalton could act, the sound of his mother washing dishes drifted out of the kitchen's open window. He couldn't talk about his problems here, not now, not when Betty was probably straining to hear every word they said.

"Why don't we go for a walk," Anna suggested.

Dalton chuckled. "You took the words right out of my mouth."

"One of the earliest memories I have of my father is him sitting at the table in the kitchen, the sun streaming through the window behind him, playing with a weathered deck of cards. He'd show me how to snap them over my fingers, turning them so fast that the edge of the card scraped my thumb. It was like magic. When I was a little older, we'd take turns throwing them into a hat. We'd bet a penny on who could make the most. At the time, I thought it was great fun."

Anna listened to Dalton as they walked down the near-dark streets of Redstone. For a long time after they'd left his family's house, they'd drifted in silence. After his initial revelation about his father's gambling problem, Dalton had held back, but she could tell that he was only measuring his words, searching for the right order and time to let them out. She never prompted him, but waited, content just to be beside him. When he'd finally started talking, the words came out as a torrent.

"It all seemed so innocent, but it wasn't," Dalton added. "If I could go back, I'd snatch those cards out of his hands and tear them all in half."

"It sounds like a wonderful memory to me," Anna disagreed. "Just because what's happened since hasn't turned out well, it doesn't mean that what came before is ruined. I have a couple of recollections of my mother that I cherish; one when she took my brother and me to the park, and another when she sat down with my dolls for tea. Even though she eventually chose to go down a path that took her away from me, her actions didn't spoil those older memories. On the contrary, it makes me cherish them that much more."

Dalton shook his head, frowning. "It's just so damn hard to accept what he's become. It's even worse when I remember what he was and what he gave to me. He taught me how to hold a hammer and how to work the forge until the metal was just the right temperature. He showed me what it meant to be a man. The first time I really became friends with Walker, I stood up to a pack of bullies who were teasing him because I thought that it was what my father would've done. I'm who I am because of him."

"From where I stand, it looks like he did a good job."

"You really think so?"

Slipping her arm into the crook of his elbow, Anna said, "I do."

Having made their way to Main Street, they walked past the closed shops, their windows darkened. There were a few people here and there, but Anna decided that she didn't care who noticed the two of them together.

"Maybe more than angry, you're disappointed in him," she said.

Dalton thought it over for a moment. "I'm still plenty mad, but I do feel like he's let me down."

"In that case, maybe what you ought to try is to—"

Suddenly Anna was nearly yanked backward and off her feet. Stumbling, she somehow managed to keep from falling, but was confused over what had happened. It took a second for her to realize that Dalton had come to an unexpected stop and, with her arm laced in his, had merely kept her from continuing forward. He stood staring into a window, the low sound of music drifting lazily toward them, his eyes wide and his chest heaving.

"What is it?" she asked. "Dalton, what's wrong?"

He didn't answer.

Following his gaze, Anna looked inside. There, seated at a table in a tavern, was George, holding a handful of cards.

Chapter Nineteen

I'LL KILL HIM!"

Anna wondered if that wasn't exactly what Dalton intended to do. Seeing his father inside the bar, gambling over cards, smiling and laughing as he chanced losing everything his family had left, had enraged him. She knew that Dalton's reaction had been made all the more violent by the fact that they'd just been talking about how much George Barnes had once meant to him, raising the hope, no matter how slim, that he could still reach him. But seeing George at his addiction had wiped that all away in an instant. Dalton's muscled arm flexed, straining against the fabric of his shirt. Heading toward the tavern's door, he was full of bad intentions, and didn't seem to care or even notice that he was dragging Anna with him.

"Dalton, wait!" she shouted. "Just wait!"

Her pleas fell on deaf ears. Though she held on tightly, he moved as if she wasn't even there, stomping across the wooden planks. She tried to plant her heels, but she couldn't gain purchase. His strength was too great. How was she ever going to stop him?

"Please, don't do this! Please!" she pleaded.

Desperate, Anna looked around for something or someone who might be able to help. Ahead of them, a couple came out of the bar, the man looking a little the worse for wear, unsteady on his feet and leaning heavily against his female companion. They took one look at Dalton's face and size and quickly hurried in the opposite direction. Anna thought about yelling after them, but decided that it wouldn't do any good. She had to stop Dalton herself.

Before it was too late.

Squeezing his arm as hard as she could, she dug her fingernails so deeply into the tough flesh that she was sure she'd drawn blood, but to no effect. She considered hitting his arm or slapping his face, but he was too far gone. She remembered when they'd met at the train depot, after he'd knocked her to the ground. When Samuel had chastised him for not helping her to her feet, Dalton acted as if he was about to slug the producer. She'd stopped him by placing her hand on his chest, but when she tried it now, nothing happened. She was running out of ideas, as well as time. Dalton only had a few more feet to go until he reached the door; once he was inside, all hell was going to break loose. Desperate, she could only think of one last thing to try.

She let go.

Dalton had gone a couple more steps when Anna took

a deep breath, her heart pounding, and said, "I think I'm falling in love with you."

While her actions hadn't had the slightest effect, Anna's words succeeded, stopping him as surely as if he'd run into a brick wall. Slowly, Dalton turned around to look at her, his nostrils flaring, his chest heaving, the anger and disappointment and embarrassment still roiling around inside him, only momentarily held back, but still there at the surface. He looked at the bar, then at Anna, back toward the tavern, and once again at her, conflicted about what he should do next. Her words had stunned him, just as she'd known they would. Quickly, Anna stepped to him and took his hands in her own; she was surprised to find that they were trembling. Slowly but deliberately, she led him down the sidewalk and away from the bar. For his part, Dalton followed without any complaint. When she was sure they were alone, she stopped.

"Nothing good will come of you going in there and confronting him," she said.

"I can't let him get away with it! I can't!"

"Listen to me! If you—"

"Let me go back there and—"

"And do what?" Anna cut him off, her voice rising. "Are you going to walk over and flip the card table?" she asked insistently. "Will you hurl a couple of chairs and glasses against the wall? Scream and curse? Grab him by the arm and drag him home against his will? If you do anything of the sort, all you'll accomplish is to cause a scene the whole town will be talking about tomorrow. Walking through that door as angry as you are would be a terrible mistake you'd quickly regret. You have to walk away."

"I can't believe you're taking his side!" Dalton exclaimed.

"I'm not doing anything of the sort," she corrected him. "What I'm saying is that this is neither the time nor the place, not the way you're feeling."

Dalton could only stare in response.

"I spent years trying to help my mother and brother," Anna explained patiently, hoping that he was listening closely. "But I was a child. I didn't know what to say or do. I couldn't reach them. I never had the chance that you have right now. You need to talk to your father with the love in your heart, not the anger in your blood. If you just yell at him and carry on, you'll only succeed in driving him away. You have to make him *want* to quit."

He shook his head, scowling. "I've tried all that."

"Have you? Or is it that every time you've tried, that temper of yours has gotten in the way?"

"He just makes me so damn mad! My mother, too!"

"Betty?" Anna asked, surprised. "How?"

"She always makes excuses for him. Even if he robbed a bank for money to gamble, she wouldn't leave."

"Then why did she look so upset tonight?"

"Because Vernon Black, the piece of trash my father borrowed money from, sent his two thugs after me. She knows all about them. Everyone in town does. They're as dangerous as rabid dogs."

Anna thought for a moment. A suspicion needled her, making her ask, "*Two* men attacked you?"

"Yeah," he said. "Why?"

"What do they look like?"

A look of concern rippled across Dalton's face. "Why are you asking?"

"Just tell me."

Listening to Dalton describe the men made Anna queasy. There was no doubt in her mind that they were the two she'd encountered outside the blacksmith shop. She was sure they'd been there keeping an eye on Dalton; unfortunately, that also meant they'd been watching her.

"I saw them," she said. "I literally ran into the big one. Audie, was it?"

"You met them?" he asked, shocked. "Where? When?"

"The other day when I left you and Walker at the shop. I turned a corner and there they were. The other one, Creed, did all the talking."

"What did he say?" Dalton asked insistently, his temper rising. "What did he do? Did he put a hand on you?"

"He didn't touch me," Anna reassured him. "He talked to me is all, although I admit it was all quite frightening."

Dalton looked around the dark streets, as if he expected the Cobb brothers to come after them at any second.

"These are the men your father owes money to?" she asked.

Dalton nodded. "They work for that man."

"How much money is it?"

"I have no idea. It's like I said at supper, when I asked him, he wouldn't tell me. Even Creed Cobb wouldn't say when he came to collect."

"If you don't know, how will you ever pay it back?"

He shrugged. "There've been other times when things were bad," he said. "We've always managed to find a way."

"But what happens when the movie leaves town? If business goes back to what it was before, how will you come up with it?"

Dalton frowned in response.

A sudden bit of inspiration struck Anna. "What if I were to give you the money?" she asked. "I'm getting a fair amount for the movie, more than I ever got in the theater. We could go to this Vernon Black and I can—"

"No! No way!" Dalton snapped. "I won't take your money. I won't do it! I'll come up with it somehow, but I'm not getting it from you."

"That's your pride talking."

"So what if it is? I won't do it and that's final!"

"If not from me, then how?"

Anna tried to catch Dalton's eye, but he wouldn't look at her. If was clear that he felt ashamed. She also understood that this was a burden he'd been struggling to carry for a long time. Although he desperately wanted his father to change, he'd never been able to reach him, to convince him of the error of his ways. George Barnes seemed like a good man; with a son as principled as Dalton, he couldn't have been a bad father. She could only imagine the arguments they'd had over the years, the shouting matches and harsh words that cut deep. Looking at Dalton and seeing the way his head hung low and his shoulders slumped, she witnessed the wounds of George's addiction. But maybe it didn't have to stay that way. Maybe honey could work where vinegar so clearly did not. There were no guarantees that his father wouldn't go right back to his gambling, but at least Dalton could say he'd tried everything.

They stood in silence for a while before Anna gently took Dalton by the hand and tugged him away from the tavern. "Come with me," she said.

With one last, forlorn look back at the bar in which his father sat gambling, he did as she asked.

This time, without a fight.

Leaving the tavern and Dalton's father behind, they walked along in silence as night fell, blanketing the town in darkness, but eventually he asked about her bad day. Anna had tried to sidestep the question, thinking that it could wait, but he'd been insistent. Reluctantly, she told him what had happened, beginning with her first meeting with Joan in the hotel lobby, and everything up to and including the actress's self-inflicted beating that afternoon.

When Anna finished, Dalton was quiet, clearly shocked. "That's the craziest thing I've ever heard," he finally said.

"I don't have the slightest idea what I've done to make her so angry. She was one of my favorite actresses when I was a girl."

"She's jealous, plain and simple."

"Of me?" Anna asked incredulously. "She's famous! I'm no one!"

Dalton shook his head. "You're younger, prettier, and on your way up the ladder, while she's headed in the opposite direction," he said, using the same explanation Samuel had. "She's holding on with everything she's got, and then here you come, stepping on her fingers as you go past."

"I'm not doing anything of the sort!"

"All that matters is that she thinks you are," Dalton explained. "The only thing that chaps me is that producer fella wanting to act like nothing happened. The way I see it, he should fire Joan."

"He can't do *that*."

"Why in the hell not?" he asked. "She deserves nothing less."

"Samuel's got too many other things to worry about without me adding another," Anna said.

"Like what?"

Anna knew that the time had come for her to tell Dalton about the sabotage against the film. Taking a deep breath, she recounted how the film had been destroyed and shared her suspicion that the fire might've been set intentionally. She told him how Samuel had dismissed her suggestion that the instigator might be another studio out to ruin a competitor, and refused to believe that the culprit was anyone connected to the film. Finally, Anna asked Dalton whether he thought someone from Redstone might have been involved.

"Maybe," he shrugged, "but that wouldn't make a lot of sense."

"Why not?" she asked.

"Because everyone in town is making money off the movie being here," Dalton explained. "Unless it's someone who got stiffed or thinks they haven't gotten their fair share, sabotage doesn't make a lot of sense."

"What about the man your father owes money to?" Anna asked. "From what you've said, he's the type to be involved with something shady."

Dalton shook his head. "Vernon Black's a criminal, but he's a businessman, too. He's made as much money off you Hollywood people as anyone. He's focused on profit and nothing else. Why would he want to endanger that?" Walking along for a bit, he then added, "It'd have to be someone who really had it in for the movie." He paused, turning to look at her. "Someone like me."

Anna didn't say a word.

"Did you think it could be me?" he asked her. "Even for a second?"

"No," Anna lied, ashamed that she'd ever suspected him. Even then, standing amidst the wreckage of the film room, she had felt she was wrong, but now, after having had a chance to get to know Dalton better, after meeting his family, learning what burdens he carried, she knew it was impossible that he could be behind the plot.

Then Anna smiled. No matter how many troubles she faced, she was still able to find pleasure in this moment with Dalton. She loved the sound of his voice, his grin, and even the rough feel of her hand in his. Though love was something that had long eluded her, what she was feeling for Dalton surprised her with its intensity. She hadn't lied when she called out to him in front of the tavern; she *was* falling for him, and falling hard.

Amazingly, Dalton seemed to be thinking the same thing. He stopped walking and pulled her into the shadows of a nearby alley, still several blocks from the Stagecoach. Even in the darkness, she could see his eyes roaming across her face; it felt so real as to be almost physical, as if he was actually touching her.

"You said that you were falling in love with me," he said, his voice a whisper, though his words thundered through her.

"I did," she answered.

"That's an awfully bold thing to say."

"It is," Anna agreed.

"No one has ever said that to me before," Dalton admitted. "When you did, it cut through me like a knife."

"I've never said it to anyone before, but I've never *heard* it, either."

"I find that very hard to believe."

Anna smiled. "It's true. I've gotten letters from admirers and some indecent proposals, but no one's ever said it to me for real. Not from their heart, and most definitely not from someone I've wanted to hear say it."

"Like me?"

All she could do was nod.

She could see it in his face, in the way Dalton nervously licked his lips, in the feel of his hand steadily tightening around hers. He was falling in love with her, too. And he was going to say it, to speak the words she'd always wanted to hear. The anticipation was almost more than she could bear. As he opened his mouth, she leaned closer and—

Without warning, a man burst out of the shadows at the back of the alley and rushed toward them. Anna gave a short scream as Dalton pushed her behind him, his fists rising. In her panicked mind, it could only be one of the Cobb brothers finally coming to deliver their message to Dalton's father, as well as to get their revenge on the man's son. And that was why it was so bewildering for her to realize that it wasn't who she'd expected. Not at all. Instead, it was a short, squat man in a worn, checkered suit, armed with only a pad of paper and a pencil.

"Miss Finnegan! Miss Finnegan!" he shouted. "Mitchell Hubert with the *Movie Land News*! Would you care to comment on why you attacked your costar in your dressing room this afternoon?"

The words shot out of the reporter's mouth so fast and with such ferocity and accusation that Anna felt as if she was up on the stand of a packed courtroom, with the prosecutor trying to get her to admit to a crime she hadn't committed. The reporter was relentless. Even faced with a barrier the size of Dalton, he didn't seem in the least bit intimidated, rushing up to the blacksmith and desperately trying to get around him, all the while peppering Anna with more questions.

"Was it because you were jealous with the amount of screen time Joan was getting? Aren't you worried about goin' to jail? There's word goin' 'round it might a been on account of an affair you're havin' with Samuel Gillen! Any chance you've been getting ahead in this business the old-fashioned way?"

This last question clearly enraged Dalton. He grabbed the reporter by taking two fistfuls of his coat, lifted him off the ground, and slammed him up against the wall so hard that Anna swore the man's eyes rolled around in his head like marbles. "That's enough of that talk!" Dalton shouted.

Anna couldn't believe it. It was just as Samuel had predicted; the Hollywood gossip reporters had camped out, waiting for her to come back to the hotel so that they could pounce on her and try to wheedle out any details about what had happened between her and Joan. But instead of just waiting in the Stagecoach lobby, they'd spread out around town, hoping to get lucky.

And now one of them had.

"Just answer a couple a questions," the muckraker insisted. "Can't hurt to give your side of the story before someone starts puttin' words in your mouth!"

"I said shut up!" Dalton threatened.

The warning seemed to focus the reporter's attention on Dalton for the first time, as if before he'd only seen Anna. His eyes narrowed as a mischievous smile spread on his face. "Wait a second here," he said. "Who the heck are you? What're you doin' out and about with our new starlet here?" Turning to Anna, he added, "Don't tell me you're foolin' 'round with a townie!"

"One more word out of you and you're going to be spitting teeth," Dalton growled, raising his fist to show he meant business, but the demonstration of strength only made the man laugh.

"Oh, please!" he said. "Threaten me all you want, but Charlie Chaplin himself once swore he'd drag me down the street behind his car, so don't start thinkin' you're intimidatin' me with the tough talk! I've been cursed by better, and I'm still writin'!"

"I wonder how good you'd use that pencil with a few busted fingers..."

The reporter was still smiling, although it seemed he was growing apprehensive. "Look, all she's gotta do is give me somethin' to work with, that's all. I got a byline in need of a juicy quote!"

"I'm not saying a word to you," Anna said defiantly.

Mitchell shrugged. "Then I guess I'm gonna have to make it up as I go. Maybe throw in a little somethin' about your boyfriend here, too."

Angrily, Dalton tossed the man to the ground where he landed with a thud on his rump. The blacksmith stalked over, took Anna by the arm, and the two of them left the alley in a hurry. With every step, she expected to hear the reporter getting back to his feet and scurrying after them, pencil raised, as he assaulted her with more questions all the way to the hotel doors.

But instead, the only thing that followed them was his laughter.

Chapter Twenty

DALTON PULLED ANNA beneath the awning of the bakery and out of sight, right across the street from the Stagecoach. Through the windows of the hotel, they could clearly see that people were everywhere, filling the lobby and waiting room, and milling about outside. Anna understood why. Even if none of them were reporters, they were all just as curious, hoping to catch a glimpse of her after her now infamous run-in with Joan, desperate for some tidbit of gossip they could savor. If she went in the front door, they'd be on her like a pack of wolves.

"How am I going to get to my room?" she asked.

"Is it on the second floor?"

Anna nodded.

"Come with me."

Guiding her around to the rear of the building, Dalton pointed up at a staircase that rose to the second floor, and a door lit faintly by the moonlight. "Take that and you'll get up there," he explained. "Although there's no guarantee there won't be more of those bastards waiting in the hallway."

"It's the best chance I've got."

For a moment, neither of them spoke. Anna's heart was still beating hard, not only from being confronted by the reporter but also from what had been about to happen between her and Dalton just before they'd been interrupted. It had ended before he'd had the chance to tell her how he felt. Still, she knew. She *knew*.

But something else was gnawing at her, a worrisome feeling she felt compelled to address.

"I don't care, you know," she said simply.

"About what?"

"About whether or not someone knows about the two of us," Anna answered.

He nodded.

"I don't," she insisted. "I wasn't refusing to answer his questions because I was ashamed I'd been caught out with you."

"I wouldn't blame you if you were," Dalton said.

Anna felt as if she'd been slugged in the stomach. "What would make you say such a thing?"

Dalton ran a hand through his unruly dark hair. "A woman as beautiful as you," he said, "with all of Hollywood ready to fall at your feet, might not find it best to be seen spending time with a blacksmith from the middle of nowhere. It could hurt your career. I don't want to hold you back."

"I don't care about any of that," she insisted, stepping closer.

"I'd just hate for—" was all Dalton managed to say before Anna leaned up and kissed him. It didn't take long, a heartbeat or two, for them to come together, his arms pulling her close, their passion growing, as she melted into his embrace. With her eyes closed, his lips against hers, it was easy for Anna to convince herself that there was nothing that could get between them; no film, no nosy reporters chasing after her in the night, no crazed costars desperate to maintain their fame, no family problems, and no dangerous men lurking in the shadows, wanting to do them harm.

It was only the two of them.

When their kiss ended, Anna reached up and placed a hand on his cheek. "I didn't expect this, didn't imagine it was possible," she said, "but I found it here with you. What we have is special. I'm willing to fight for it, no matter what anyone else thinks. If there are people who don't like it, that's their problem, not mine. So I don't want to hear any worries from you, all right?"

Dalton nodded.

With one more quick kiss on his cheek, she hurried toward the hotel.

Anna paused at the top of the outdoor stairs, took a deep breath to steady her nerves, turned the knob, pulled the door open a sliver, and peeked inside. She'd expected to find half a dozen reporters standing outside her door, but to her great relief, the short hallway that led to the front of the hotel was mostly unoccupied; a man and woman leaned against the railing at the opposite end, but they had their backs to her and seemed focused on each other. The door to her room was the third one down on the right. If she could just reach it without attracting any notice...

Quick as a thief, Anna slipped inside the hotel, careful not to make too much noise when she shut the door behind her. Fishing her key out of her pocket, she started to make her way down the hall. Every creek of a floorboard sounded amplified, far louder than it should have been. She kept expecting the couple to turn, spot her, shout, and set off a stampede with everyone in the lobby and waiting room rushing up the stairs to ask about what happened with Joan. But somehow, she made it to her door without being noticed. In an instant, she'd put the key in the door, turned the lock, yanked it open, and hurried in.

I made it!

The inside of the room was dark, so Anna reached over to the small table beside her bed and turned on the light. Everything was just as she'd left it. A change of clothes had been laid out on her bed, but she'd never made it back to the hotel to put them on after her talk with Samuel. Her script was on the dresser, the corners dog-eared to the scenes they'd soon be filming. The window was open, the faint evening breeze causing the curtains to flutter. Anna smiled. Everything seemed the same, but after sharing her feelings with Dalton, after learning his family's secret, running from the reporter, and especially after receiving another kiss, everything somehow felt different.

Anna walked over to the window and looked out. Dalton stood just where she'd left him, staring up at the hotel. She would have understood if he'd already started for home, but she had been hoping he'd waited, wanting another look, just as she had. It took only a second for him to find her, but when he did, he gave no sign, no wave or nod, didn't call her name, but only watched. Anna didn't mind; even from so far away, she could feel the passion in his gaze.

Raising her fingers to her lips, Anna gave them a gentle kiss before holding them out to Dalton and blowing. When he reached up his open hand, quickly snapping it shut before placing it against his chest, her heart pounded and she wobbled, suddenly weak in the knees.

This is something special…

Leaning back, Anna's thoughts turned to getting ready for bed, but before she could so much as move, she heard the faint sound of a creak behind her. There wasn't even time for her to grow curious before a hand clamped down on her mouth and another grabbed her arm, dragging her backward. With her eyes wide with fright, she tried to scream, but she'd been muffled and the noise was little louder than a whimper. Desperately, she lashed out, struggling with all of her might, knowing that Dalton was just outside her window, but her attacker's grip never lessened. Her fear rising, she scratched and clawed, squirmed and wiggled, stomped and thrashed, but it had no effect.

Slowly, deliberately, she was pulled toward the bed and a fate she was too horrified to imagine. Her assailant pushed her onto the mattress, letting go of her arm just long enough to shut off the lamp, plunging the room into darkness. Immediately a hand began roaming across her chest, pulling hard at her blouse, not caring whether it was torn, only that it was open.

Through it all, her attacker didn't say a word.

Dalton watched as Anna backed away from the window. He couldn't keep from smiling. Though much of their evening had been a mess, especially his outburst after discovering his father playing cards, it had ended better than he could have expected. He still didn't understand how he'd managed to attract the attention of a woman like Anna, or why she was willing to risk being seen with him, but he was glad all the same.

I suppose every dog has his day...

Finally turning to head home, Dalton stopped in his tracks, groaning at what he saw. Walking toward him was the reporter from the alley.

"Whoa, whoa, there, big fella! No need to get upset," the man said, raising his hands in a gesture of good faith. "I stayed out a sight so you could say your good nights with your sweetheart. But now that she's off to bed, I thought you and me might be able to talk."

"I don't have anything to say to you," Dalton growled.

"Look, pal. You might think you got a good thing goin' here, but I've been a part of this business long enough to tell you that there ain't gonna be a happy endin'," the reporter explained. "These actresses fall in love as easily as droppin' out of a boat. It's all promises and fun till it's time for the movie to pack up and leave town. When that happens, you'll be forgotten so fast it'll make your head spin. Trust me, I seen this more times than I can count."

Dalton frowned. He really didn't like what this Hollywood reporter was suggesting. Anna wasn't like that; everything about her struck him as genuine, especially the feelings she was expressing for him. It was true that he worried about what would happen when the movie was finished, but he couldn't imagine that she'd just up and abandon him.

She couldn't do that, could she?

"What I'm sayin' is that you could make yourself a buck or two, even while you're havin' your fun," the man continued. He fished a few bills out of his pocket and fanned them for Dalton to see. "You give me a little somethin' now and again and I make sure you get a little money in return. Ain't nothin' but good business. She don't need to ever know a thing, so what do you say?"

Gritting his teeth tight, Dalton had to look away to keep from punching the man. Absently, his eyes drifted back to the window to Anna's room. As he watched, the light was lit for only a couple of seconds before blinking out, but in that short time, he saw something strange. Shadows had been moving frantically across the ceiling and walls. Dalton couldn't help but think it looked like someone was struggling. In his gut, he knew something was wrong.

"All right, all right! I'll double it."

Dalton spun on his heel and slugged the reporter square in his nose. Just before the fist had smashed into the man's face, his eyes had grown as wide as saucers with shock, then shut as he was instantly knocked unconscious. He crashed onto his back in the middle of the street, his pad of paper flopping down next to him as his pencil skittered away. The money he'd been holding fluttered down as if the bills were birds, landing on his chest.

But Dalton saw none of this. No sooner had his blow landed than he was off and running for the hotel.

Panic and fear hammered Anna as she desperately tried to fight back against her attacker. The man kept pawing hungrily at her, his hand roaming across her breasts, sliding down to her legs, and then insistently pushing between them. Over and over, she tried to scream, but with his hand clamped down on her mouth, it did no good; she made so little sound that it was as if her lips had been sewn shut. No matter what she tried to do, he swatted her away. He was much too strong. Eventually, he was going to have his way with her.

Oh, Lord! Please don't let this happen!

Even now, Anna didn't know who was assaulting her. Because of what had happened between them, she'd initially assumed it was Milburn, but something about her guess felt wrong. The young actor was so full of himself, such an egotistical ass, a man who loved nothing more than to talk about how wonderful he was, she doubted that he would've been able to hold his tongue for so long. But there was another possibility...

It could be Creed Cobb, the man who'd made her so uncomfortable outside the blacksmith shop and who was out for Dalton's blood.

Either way, she knew she had to get free before it was too late.

Thrashing her head around, Anna hoped to shake free of his grip long enough to scream, but the man moved with her. But although he kept her from making a sound, she managed to slightly reposition herself. Now, instead of the palm of his hand over her mouth, it was the meaty flesh beneath his thumb. Seizing the opportunity, Anna struck, biting down as hard as she could. Her mouth was filled with the copper tang of the man's blood just before he jerked his hand away in pain.

"Bitch!" the man hissed, his voice unrecognizable to her.

Before Anna could capitalize on her hard-won advantage, the man struck back, slapping her face so hard that the world seemed to go dull at the edges. When he once again clamped down on her mouth, she was even less able to offer any resistance.

Just as she was about to give up all hope of stopping him, a glimmer unexpectedly arrived as someone began to pound on the door.

"Anna! Open the door!"

It was Dalton.

Through the waves of dizziness that washed over her, the stars that twinkled at the edges of her vision, and the man who still seemed determined to rape her, Anna struggled to reach out to Dalton, as if she was a drowning woman desperate to break the surface of the water and breathe again. With what little remained of her strength, she fought.

Suddenly, it sounded as if the whole room shook; Anna understood that Dalton was throwing his weight against the door. Over and over he pounded, ramming into it until the frame finally cracked. At the sound, her assailant gave up on his attack, wordlessly sliding off her and away.

"Dalton," she managed, her voice weak.

The next time the blacksmith hit the door, it finally gave way, opening into the room. Dalton stepped inside, the light of the hallway behind him blindingly bright against the darkness of her room.

I've been rescued!

But no sooner had Anna felt the elation of being saved than a figure leaped out of the shadows at Dalton and drove a heavy fist into the middle of Dalton's stomach. Dalton never saw it coming. Air whooshed from his lungs and his knees buckled. Collapsing into a heap on the floor, he moaned, defenseless. Panic once again grabbed hold of Anna, even stronger than before; with Dalton beaten, her attacker could return his attentions to her. But then, just as the man turned toward her, the light behind him far too bright for her to have any idea of his identity, he hesitated, his head turning at the sound of voices in the hallway; someone must've heard all of the commotion.

"Help!" Anna shouted as loudly as she could manage, still dazed from the attack. "Somebody please help me!"

Before the sound of her shout had had a chance to quiet, the stranger was already racing from the room, whipping around the edge of the door so fast that Anna didn't have a chance to see even one distinguishing feature. He was gone, and she still had no idea who it had been.

"Damn...it..."

Anna looked down to see Dalton writhing on the floor. He tried to prop himself up on an elbow, but the pain was too great and he collapsed back down. Tears filled her eyes at the sight of him, but they weren't born of dismay, but rather elation for what he'd done for her.

"I'm here," she said, sliding onto the floor and draping her arms across his heaving shoulders. "I'm right here."

"Son...son-of-a...bitch got away..." he muttered, gritting his teeth.

Anna shook her head, the tears breaking free. "It doesn't matter," she told him. "You saved me, Dalton. You came back and saved me."

Just then, cradling his head and pulling him close, Anna began to understand what had been about to happen to her. Her attacker had intended to rape her. Remembering the way his hands had felt on her body made her involuntarily shiver with fear and revulsion. Once he'd finished having his way with her, who knew what he'd intended. She could have been killed.

Somehow, some way, Dalton had realized that she was in trouble. He'd come to her rescue, even at his own peril. He'd saved her. But then, just as Anna was about to place a tender kiss on his forehead, to hold him in her arms and say everything that was rushing to fill her heart, she suddenly stopped at a sound that made the hairs on the back of her neck stand up.

From somewhere in the hotel, a woman screamed.

"My diamond ring! Someone stole my precious diamond!"

Joan stood at the top of the Stagecoach's tall staircase in her blue satin nightgown, her hair disheveled and her eyes wide with shock. Her face bore bruises and cuts from what had happened in the dressing room. At the sound of her voice, everyone in the hotel had immediately fallen silent, every head turning to look at her, watching in amazement and disbelief as the actress continued to wail.

"A thief!" she screamed, almost hysterical. "Someone broke into my room and stole it! They stole my precious ring!"

Anna and Dalton reached the end of the hallway that led to the hotel's lobby. Since Dalton was still a bit winded from the blow he'd received, Anna had slung her arm around his waist and helped him down the hall. Nearing the landing, they hung back behind some of the other people who'd come out of their rooms at the sound of the shouting; once Anna had understood who it was screaming, the last thing she'd wanted to do was draw attention to herself.

"What are you all just standing around for?" Joan screeched, the fire returning to her voice. "Someone call the police! There still might be time to catch whoever did it if we hurry! Quick!"

Suddenly there rose a commotion at the bottom of the

stairs. Anna watched in surprise as Montgomery pushed his way through the crowd. The older actor hurried up the stairs, taking them two at a time, and took Joan by the hands. Witnessing his concern for his fellow performer, Anna thought about all the help Montgomery had given her, rehearsing with her and coming to her defense with both Frank and Milburn; he was clearly a kind man trying to do right. Turning back to the still-dazed crowd, he echoed Joan's demands. "Someone go get the sheriff!" he shouted. "The doctor, too!" Joan's hysterical cries hadn't gotten a response, but Montgomery's words pushed many in the room into action; several men headed for the door and the man at the hotel's front desk grabbed for the telephone.

Turning his attention back to Joan, Montgomery spoke slowly and calmly. "Tell me exactly what happened."

Joan nodded, though she still looked shell-shocked. "I was sleeping," she explained. "I was just so tired after being attacked by that tart that I went to bed early. I don't know why, but I heard a sound and...and..."

"Then?" the actor prompted after she faltered.

"I woke up and my ring was gone!" Joan continued, her daze gone as she reached out and grabbed Montgomery by the hands. "I put it on the nightstand as I always do, but when I turned on the light, it wasn't there! Someone took it! They stole..."

Without warning, Joan fainted. She would've fallen all the way to the floor if Montgomery hadn't caught her, easing her the rest of the way down. Gasps rose from the crowd. From where Anna stood watching, it was a masterful performance, made all the more shocking because it seemed real.

Was the same man who'd attacked her responsible for the theft of Joan's diamond ring?

Still, as sorry as she was for Joan, Anna was relieved that her fellow actress was unconscious. If she'd noticed her rival standing there, watching, Anna had no doubt that she would've been accused of the crime.

"What in the hell's going on around here?" Dalton asked.

Wonder as she might, Anna had no answer.

Chapter Twenty-one

"YOU RECKON IT'S REAL?"

Vernon Black picked the stolen ring up off his desk and held it up between his fingers, its facets catching the morning sunlight that streamed through the crack in the curtains of his office. The bauble sent countless reflections of light dancing across the room, glinting off the doors, his large selection of liquor bottles, the slowly turning ceiling fan, and into the eyes of the man who sat opposite his desk. It bothered Creed so much that he shielded his eyes.

"What makes you think it's a fake?" Vernon asked.

"Just a hunch, I suppose."

"Tell me."

"That broad'd have to be one hell of a fool to bring a ring that size to a place like Redstone. Hell, it'd be worth 'bout half the whole town," Creed explained. "After flashin' it 'round she just goes and leaves it lyin' there on her night-stand like it was nothin' special? Makes more sense to me that it'd be made a glass or some such. Worthless, but lookin' like it ain't."

"Interesting, but I don't think that's how these movie stars think," Vernon disagreed. "If it was glass, it'd defeat the purpose."

"Which is?"

"Knowing that everyone who looks at it will instantly understand that you're worth more money than they'll ever see in their lifetime."

Creed shrugged. "Either way, you got what you wanted."

Vernon nodded his agreement, although Creed wasn't exactly right. It was his mysterious benefactor who'd gotten what he'd asked for, what had been demanded in the last note slid underneath Vernon's door. The pile of money that had accompanied it had made Vernon's heart pound. Even though he wasn't any closer to learning who was bankrolling the destruction of the film, the rewards continued to be well worth pursuing. Yet, this latest note had been different. Instead of detailing one act of sabotage, it laid out plans for two. In order to get an amount of cash that made his head swim with all the possibilities, there was still another task to be completed. It was the boldest yet, something that could easily end with someone dead, and it was scheduled to happen later that afternoon.

What bothered Vernon was that Creed would be the one responsible for carrying out the job. Usually, he was reliable, but looking at the disheveled mess across from him, Vernon wasn't feeling confident. Creed clearly hadn't slept since undertaking the robbery at the hotel the night before. His clothes were dirtier and more rumpled than usual, and there were heavy dark circles beneath his eyes. It was also obvious that the man had been drinking. To put it simply, Creed stank of liquor. While Vernon wasn't opposed to those who worked for him imbibing, since he often got back much of what he paid out in exchange for drinks at his tavern, he wasn't happy that Creed would be getting drunk when he knew damn well that he still had work to do.

"Felt like doing some celebrating last night?" Vernon asked.

"I did," Creed answered, then belched.

"That how come Audie isn't here? He sleeping it off?"

Creed snorted. "My brother might be big as a house, but he ain't never been able to hold his liquor well as I can. Left him snorin' like a bear. Didn't figure he'd be needed."

Vernon nodded. He looked down at the ring, then up at Creed, then back to the stolen jewelry. In the course of becoming rich and in squashing Redstone beneath his thumb, Vernon had long since learned to trust his instincts. "Who was it that saw you at the hotel?" he asked, his voice low and menacing.

The words and the tone in which they were spoken cut through the haze that enveloped Creed. The man looked up quickly, his eyes bloodshot, his mouth hanging open like a busted trap. "Weren't no one, boss," he insisted. "Ain't no one seen me comin' or goin'."

"You sure about that?"

"Honest, I am! I done it just like we talked!"

"Then what's wrong with your hand?" Ever since Creed had walked into his office, Vernon had noticed the way he'd been favoring his hand, keeping it tucked close to his side and out of sight. In the few glances he'd managed to get of it, Vernon thought it looked red and angry.

"Nothin'," Creed answered dismissively, pulling the hand in question even farther out of sight, until he was practically sitting on it.

"Hold it up."

Creed sat there, acting as if he hadn't heard.

"I said hold your goddamn hand up," Vernon growled.

After a moment's hesitation, Creed did as he was told. A series of indentations, many of which looked to have punctured the skin, ringed the meaty part of his palm just beneath the thumb. The flesh was swollen an angry red. Vernon thought the wound looked nasty.

"What is that?" he asked. "It looks like a bite mark."

Creed paused. "It is," he admitted.

"How'd you get it?"

"From the whore I took to bed last night. We'd both been drinkin' a bit and things got a little out a hand. I might a slapped her pretty good in return." All through his explanation, Creed's eyes moved, passing over the desk, the wall, down at his wounded hand, anywhere but at Vernon. He knew his man was lying. Worse, he'd been stupid about it; if he'd just wrapped the thing up in a bandage and said he'd cut it leaving the hotel, Vernon would've been none the wiser.

Creed Cobb... What am I ever going to do with you...?

Not for the first time, Vernon wondered if the end of his business relationship with Creed Cobb wasn't fast approaching. At moments like this, with Creed lying right to his face, Vernon knew it wouldn't be long before he'd have to do something drastic. He thought about pulling out the gun he kept in his side drawer and putting a couple of bullets in Creed, killing him where he sat, but there'd be consequences. First, to murder Creed meant that he'd have to do the same with Audie; the big goon was too loyal to go on without his brother. Second, and more important, he needed the man. In order to pull off what was asked of him in the letter, he'd need Creed's ruthless hand. Besides, it was far too late for him to find anyone else to do it. Vernon knew there was no way *he* could do it. No, if there was to be a reckoning with the Cobb brothers, patience would be needed. Until then, it was better not to rock the boat.

"You should have a doctor take a look at that," Vernon said, sitting back in his chair and smiling.

"I might at that," Creed said with measurable relief.

"Now," Vernon said, picking up the ring and tossing it into the air, snatching it on the way back down. "About this afternoon..."

In the aftermath of the night's drama at the Stagecoach Hotel, it took a long time for things to quiet down. After the doctor arrived, Joan was taken to her room, where upon regaining consciousness, she continued to rant and rave about all the indignities that had been visited upon her, specifically the theft of her beloved ring, as well as the cruel beating she'd received from her jealous young costar. The sheriff showed up much later, a short stub of a man who appeared more than a little put out that he'd been rousted from his bed at such a late hour. He asked only a handful of questions before leaving, grumbling about how he'd be back in the morning. Frank's earlier assessment of the man appeared to have been right; he was worthless. Samuel had been running every which way, trying to deal with the lawman, to settle his employees, to stop the gossip from running rampant, and answering an endless barrage of questions from the Hollywood reporters. It had taken a couple of hours for Anna to finally tell him about what'd happened in her room. The producer had listened closely, nodding here and there, but Anna couldn't help but feel that she was weighing him down with yet another problem.

"Are you sure you didn't get a look at who it was?" he asked; it was the same question Dalton had asked her.

"Yes," she answered truthfully for the second time.

What Anna didn't tell Samuel was her suspicion that it could've been Milburn who had attacked her. As horrible as the actor had been to her, as guilty as he was of behaving inappropriately, she had no real proof that he was responsible for what had happened in her room. She'd looked around for Milburn in the hotel's lobby, but she hadn't seen him; maybe it meant that he'd run far away after punching Dalton, that he was sleeping, or out for the night. It didn't say anything about his guilt one way or the other. Because of that, she held her tongue.

"I should call the sheriff back," Samuel said, "incompetent or not. This isn't the sort of thing to be ignored."

"It won't do any good," Anna said; she could see that the producer was clearly upset and worried about her having been attacked.

"There has to be something I can do for you."

Anna smiled. "Just find out who's behind all of this and stop them."

Eventually, Anna's crazy day caught up with her; stifling a yawn, she finally went back to her room. Despite her protests that she'd be fine, Dalton insisted on staying with her through the night, propping his chair up against the hastily repaired door.

"Stop arguing," he said. "I'm staying."

With her eyelids fluttering, her heartbeat slowing, and her head on her pillow, she allowed sleep to claim her. The last sight she saw before drifting off was Dalton watching her from the other side of the room, still awake, making sure she was safe.

The next morning, shooting was scheduled to resume as planned, regardless of what had happened the night before. As she came down the staircase, Anna noticed plenty of long faces, tired, with bags under their eyes; every other person she met seemed to be stifling a yawn. All throughout breakfast, she listened as people grumbled more than usual, thinking that they should have had the day off. There were even a few who ventured that the film was doomed to fail.

"All I'm sayin' is that there're too many things goin' wrong for it all to be a coincidence," the man seated directly behind her declared to his companion. "Makes me wonder if we shouldn't a just stayed in California."

"Too late now," his friend argued. "Let's just hope nothin' else happens."

Anna couldn't have agreed more.

If there was a silver lining to the night's events, it was that people seemed far more interested in the theft of Joan's diamond ring than the brawl that supposedly took place in the dressing room. Even though there were plenty of stares and whispers directed toward her, it wasn't as bad as Anna had been expecting. A few people even sat down at her table to eat, smiling as they greeted her; she was far from a pariah.

Still, she was as confused as ever about what was happening. Questions raced helter-skelter around her head. Was it Milburn who had assaulted her? If not, then who? Could it have been Creed Cobb? Did it have anything to do with the theft of Joan's jewel? Was it somehow connected to the other acts of sabotage that had been directed at Valentine Pictures?

She'd said as much to Dalton when they'd parted that morning. He'd been there in his chair when she'd woken, still watching, though he looked utterly exhausted. When he noticed her looking at him, he'd smiled.

"Who's doing all this?" she'd asked.

Dalton hadn't answered, which told her plenty.

"You have a suspicion, don't you?"

"That's all it is," he'd answered. "It's just that, whenever there's trouble in Redstone, there's a better chance than not that Vernon Black's involved. He's greedy, rotten, and willing to get his hands dirty. If there's a profit to be made, he'd be on it like a rat after cheese. Lending gambling money to my father is only the beginning of the trouble he's into. I just can't understand why he'd be involved in something like this. He's already making money hand over fist off the movie coming to town. Why jeopardize that?" Dalton frowned, scratching at the dark stubble that peppered his jaw. "There's got to be more to it than we see. Maybe it's a Hollywood thing, something that was brought here."

"We might be missing a piece of the puzzle," Anna suggested.

Dalton nodded, thinking.

When they'd parted, Dalton had promised to come for her just as soon as filming had ended; he didn't want her to be alone. The kiss they shared made Anna hope that the time they'd be apart would pass quickly.

For the first time since the discovery of the ruined film, Samuel had decided to return to shooting new scenes. Today they would be bringing to life one of the script's most action-filled moments, a raging gunfight between the townspeople and the roving bandits. The cast and crew made their way to the southern end of Main Street. Cameras had been set up at various angles and Frank went from unit to unit, looking through each lens and making whatever adjustments were needed. Actors and stunt men stood around in groups, some smoking cigarettes, a few laughing, and most all shading their eyes from the bright sun. Someone had brought a harmonica; its breathy notes floated on the breeze.

Though she was going to spend the whole day under the hot sun, little would be asked of Anna; she'd stand with the other women, huddling together as their fathers, husbands, brothers, and sons fought against the bandits, firing their guns in an attempt to drive them away. Samuel had told her that, at some point, they'd do a series of close-ups where she'd show fear and worry that her father might be hurt, but it wouldn't be much. Glancing at the script, she saw that she only had three lines of dialogue for the day.

Other actors wouldn't be so lucky. One of those was Milburn. As the outlaw chief, he would be right there in the thick of battle, leading his men in a charge, encouraging them to fight harder, before eventually dashing to his waiting horse, relentlessly slapping it with his reins as he tried to make his escape. Looking around, Anna found Milburn alone by the water bucket that had been set out as relief against the heat, getting a drink, his eyes watching one of Bonnie's assistants over his cup, his gaze never leaving the woman's chest.

Swallowing her revulsion, Anna walked over. As much as she hated even the idea of being near the man, she knew that she had to learn the truth about Milburn's possible involvement in her attack. When she reached the bucket, his head was still turned away as he leered at the woman, and he paid her no mind. Carefully, Anna stole a glance at Milburn's raised hand. Last night, she'd managed to fend off her attacker by biting down on his hand so hard that she drew blood; whoever she'd bitten should show the effects. But Milburn's hand hadn't been wounded, at least not the one showing. In the darkness of her room, Anna had no idea which hand she'd bitten, so though the young actor's right hand was unmarred, it didn't mean he was innocent. Unfortunately, his other hand was stuffed down into his pocket. She'd have to stay close to him long enough to check it.

"Well, look who's here." Milburn sneered, finally noticing her. He turned to face her, his eyes running up and down her body, but his hand stayed hidden. "Couldn't stay away, huh?"

Forcing herself to smile, Anna answered, "I just needed some water." When she reached out to grab the ladle, Milburn leaned forward, his hand brushing against her hip; she couldn't help but wonder if that was the same hand that had roamed across her breasts in the darkness. It was a struggle to hold down her anger. "Where were you last night?" she asked. "I didn't see you during all of the commotion after the robbery."

"Would you be jealous if I told you I was in another woman's bed?" he asked, his eyes narrowing mischievously.

"Not at all," she answered unwaveringly.

"You would be if you knew what you were missing."

Did you try to force me to find out last night?

"I would have thought you'd at least be curious about what all the racket was about," Anna said instead.

Milburn stepped closer. "Do you really think I give a damn what little dramas these people face?" he hissed. "What was it? Somebody stole one of the old bitch's rings? Boo-hoo! Cry me a river!"

"That sounds pretty heartless to me."

"Why do you care, anyway?" he kept on. "You're better than all these riffraff. We both are. You sure as hell deserve more than that townie bumpkin you were fawning all over the other night can ever give you."

For an instant, Anna was struck speechless. When she finally found her voice, it came out angry. "How dare you!"

"If you want to be someone in this business, you can't be seen with someone that far below your station," Milburn cold-heartedly explained. "It can't do anything but tarnish your name. You need to hook up with another star on the way up, someone who can make you burn all the hotter. Someone like me."

After what Anna had gone through the night before, after being violently groped no matter how hard she protested, the thought of willingly going to bed with Milburn was almost more than she could bear. For him to speak so poorly of her relationship with Dalton wasn't doing him any favors, either. All she wanted was the truth, to see whether he had a bite mark on his hand, and she was starting not to care what it took to find out.

"For the life of me, I can't see why you keep turning me down," Milburn said, stepping even closer. "If you'd just give me a chance, I'd—"

Sick and tired of listening to his pathetic advances and

having long since lost her last shred of patience, Anna reached out and grabbed hold of Milburn's left hand, yanking it free from his pants pocket. She was instantly filled with disappointment at what she found; it was unmarred, just like the other, lacking any evidence that she'd bitten down on it.

Milburn wasn't the man who'd attacked her.

"If you want to see what's in my pants so bad, all you have to do is ask," the actor said with a leer of a smile, mistaking her actions for attraction; what he couldn't understand was that she no longer had any interest in him at all.

Without a word in response, Anna turned and walked away.

Once everyone had taken his place, Frank settled into his director's chair and shouted for action. Immediately, the sound of gunshots rang out. The actors playing townspeople raced in every direction, leaning around the corner of buildings and crouching behind water troughs, quickly rising to fire pistols and rifles. For their part, the bandits did the same. One man darted across the divide between the two groups before he suddenly clutched at his stomach as if shot, turned theatrically toward the rolling camera, and then pitched over onto his agonized face, as dead as the script called for him to be.

Even though the actors were firing blanks, Anna still found the noise deafening. She'd been around props before while in the theater, but never so many at the same time. She acted just as she was supposed to, frightened and hopeful in equal measure, but her awe at what she was witnessing made it harder than she'd expected. When a bandit on horseback was suddenly felled as he raced past, yanking hard on his reins before crashing down onto the hard ground in a cloud of dust and trampling hooves, it was impossible not to gape.

"Come on, amigos! We'll not be denied!"

As much as Anna hated to admit it, Milburn cut a dashing figure as the Hawk. He moved like a leading actor, his head held high above his broad shoulders, his dark hair lifting a bit in the faint wind. It was easy to see why so many women swooned at the mere mention of him.

Too bad none of them know him like I do...

Anna's eyes followed Milburn; after all, their characters were eventually supposed to fall in love, a prospect that, even while make-believe, made her struggle to keep down her breakfast. Even though the cameras were filming from a good distance away, she wanted to be acting as Claire was supposed to, just in case the cinematographer managed to get a good shot of her.

And it was because Anna was trying to stay in character that she was looking right at Milburn the moment the bullet ripped through his shoulder, his body spasming as dark blood was sent flying into the hot afternoon air.

Chapter Twenty-two

Anna could only stare in horror and disbelief, a scream caught in her throat, as Milburn plummeted to the ground, his face twisted in agony, as the hand he'd pressed against his wounded arm instantly became stained with dark blood. Incredibly, no one else seemed to have noticed; all around the fallen actor, men shouted and ran, firing their weapons, their performance uninterrupted by the very real tragedy in their midst. For a moment, Anna wondered if she hadn't misunderstood the script; Milburn's character was supposed to sustain a gunshot wound to the shoulder, it was what brought the film's two lovers together, but she thought that it was supposed to be in a later scene. But as soon as Milburn let out his first scream, a bloodcurdling yell that turned every head on the set, it was clear that something was horribly wrong.

"Cut!" Frank shouted. "Everyone stop!"

Several seconds passed, with Milburn rolling around in

the dirt, writhing in agony, before Samuel and a couple of other men in the crew ran over to the stricken actor; Anna couldn't help but do the same, drawn to it like a moth to flame. Milburn had turned as white as a sheet, sweat beading on his brow. He clutched his arm tightly, close to his chest, making it hard to see. But the copious amounts of blood that stained his hand, his costume, and the dry earth beneath him left little room for doubt.

"What happened?" Samuel asked, getting down on one knee.

"Somebody shot me!" Milburn hissed through clenched teeth. When the producer placed his hand on the actor's shoulder, the man screamed as if he'd been shot another time. "Don't touch me!" he shouted. "Damn it all, this hurts!"

One of the men who'd been playing the part of a townsman suddenly dropped his rifle, the weapon clattering on the ground; from the look of disgust on his face, it seemed as if he'd discovered he was holding a live snake. "I thought we're supposed to be shooting blanks!" he exclaimed.

"We are," Samuel reassured him.

"That don't look like it was done by no blank," another man commented.

Milburn had finally lifted his hand from his arm in order to take a closer look at the damage he'd suffered. The bullet had ripped out of the muscle of his bicep, leaving behind a hole that seeped blood. One of the women who'd gathered around Milburn turned her head away in disgust, but Anna held fast, staring.

"Someone go get the doctor," Samuel ordered.

"Look what happened!" Milburn shouted, his face registering his shock. "Who in the hell shot me?"

"Weren't me," one man answered.

"How the hell do you know?" another said. "Coulda been any of us."

"It was an accident," Samuel insisted.

"Seems like we're havin' more'n our fair share a those," a man beside Anna grumbled, low enough so that it wasn't clearly heard, although she was sure he wasn't the only one in the crowd thinking it.

Creed walked with his hat pulled down low over his eyes, moving as quickly as he dared so as to not draw any unwanted attention. Even though everyone in Redstone knew him by sight, he'd still chosen a route back to his ramshackle place that wasn't well-traveled. If anyone was unlucky enough to cross his path, he knew they'd stay well enough away. Few were those who didn't understand how dangerous he could be.

He was the sort who could shoot a man in cold blood.

Behind him, he hadn't even bothered to close the front door of the decrepit house he'd been hiding in for hours. No one would pay it any mind. It had long since been abandoned, like many others in Redstone, with its floorboards rotted through and most of its windows broken. The gun he'd fired was stashed on an outcropping of stone inside the fireplace; he'd go back for it after nightfall.

Since leaving Vernon Black's office that morning, Creed had done as he'd been ordered, getting himself into position and waiting. Knowing where the production was going to shoot for the day, he'd picked a place with a clear line of sight and no neighbors close enough to see what he was up to. Once filming had begun, gunfire split the otherwise quiet Texas afternoon. Creed had smiled to himself; one more gunshot wouldn't be noticed. He hadn't been given a specific target, but rather told that someone had to be shot. It had also been made clear that no one was to be killed if it could be helped, but he'd taken that with a grain of salt.

Whenever a gun was fired, anything could happen.

So it was that when he was watching all of the movie actors running around, Creed had picked a target at random, aimed down the rifle's sight, and then squeezed the trigger. He'd no more than seen the man clutch at his arm in pain before he was moving, stashing the gun and heading out the door.

Finally hazarding a look behind him, Creed saw that no one was following and he could begin to relax. He was glad that Audie wasn't with him; not only did his brother stick out like a sore thumb, but with his bum leg, he wouldn't have been able to keep up. Of course, Audie wasn't the only one licking his wounds.

Creed looked down at his hand and frowned. The bite marks that Barnes's bitch had sunk into the flesh of his palm looked red and angry; the wound had throbbed so badly that he'd had trouble steadying the rifle. He knew he should have done as Mr. Black had suggested and gone to the doctor or, at the very least, wrapped it in a handkerchief, but somehow being able to look at it gave encouragement to his rage, reminding him of how he'd failed.

He'd gone to the Stagecoach to steal the actress's ring, a relatively easy task given that the rich twat had left it right there on the nightstand next to her. Sneaking away would've been easy, but just as he'd gone to the window something had stopped him, a desire to turn a wrong into a right.

He'd have his way with Barnes's woman.

As quietly as he could, careful to keep from being seen, Creed had made his way into the woman's room; popping the lock had been child's play. Once inside, he'd hidden under the bed and waited. When she'd finally entered and gone to the window, he'd felt his blood pump harder. He'd stayed stock-still until she had backed toward him; strangely enough, the creak of the floorboard beneath his foot, the sound that had given him away, only served to heighten his excitement. Clamping his hand over her mouth and dragging her toward the bed, his imagination running wild with what he was about to do, Creed couldn't help but smile. Throwing her on the bed and shutting off the light, he'd proceeded to grope her, his hands sliding over her most intimate and private parts.

But then she'd bitten his hand.

Worse, Barnes had shown up.

Even socking the blacksmith hadn't pleased Creed. It wasn't enough. He needed the man to suffer. Ruining his sweetheart would've done the trick, but he'd been foiled. It had all seemed so foolproof that he still couldn't figure out what had gone wrong, how he'd been seen. To make matters worse, he'd lied to Mr. Black about the bite marks, but he'd felt like he had no choice. His boss was the sort of man who understood the value of revenge, hell, he often encouraged taking it, but never when it could have jeopardized his schemes. Defying Vernon Black was a good way to end up with a bullet in his head and lying in a ditch somewhere in the desert, his bones picked over by coyotes.

Creed knew he had to swallow his momentary defeat. Eventually, this business with the Hollywood people was going to end, they'd all pack up and leave town, and then he could handle his business with that bastard Barnes, one way or another.

It was only a matter of time.

"I'm telling you, Mr. Gillen, it's not possible!"

Samuel stood next to Jack Scott, the man Valentine Pictures had placed in charge of firearms for the film. Piled on the table in front of them was every weapon that had been used that day, their blank cartridges removed and carefully examined. Not a single bullet had been found.

"All I know is that Milburn was shot by one of these guns," Samuel explained, as upset as Anna had ever seen him.

Once the doctor had arrived, Milburn had been loaded into the bed of a pickup truck and taken back to town.

With every bump in the road as the vehicle drove away, the actor let out another curse or shout of pain.

"It's impossible that these guns weren't loaded with blanks," Jack insisted. "I checked every last round!"

"Then how else can you explain what happened?"

The other man stumbled, growing flustered as he tried to come up with something that made sense. "I . . . I just . . . damn it, I can't . . ."

"It was an accident," Samuel said. "Plain and simple."

Though Anna understood what the movie's producer was saying, there was still something about what'd happened that bothered her, some small bit of information that continued to elude her, just out of her reach, but that she nevertheless knew was important.

What am I not seeing here?

"How are you holding up?"

Anna had been so preoccupied with Samuel's conversation that she hadn't heard anyone approach. She was so shocked that she gasped out loud. Her embarrassment was made even worse when, her heart still pounding in her chest, she looked over to find Montgomery looking as upset as she felt.

"I'm so sorry, my dear," the actor apologized. "I thought that you'd heard me. I didn't mean to scare you. As on edge as we all are after the shooting, I should've known better."

"It's all right," Anna replied, her nerves settling. "It's just been such a strange day."

"That it has. Quite frankly, it's gotten me thinking about things that are more than a little morbid."

"Like what?" she asked, curious.

"That it could have been any one of us in Milburn's shoes."

"You mean who got shot?"

Montgomery nodded solemnly. "If there was a bullet loaded into one of those guns instead of a blank, it could've been pointed at any one of us when it was fired. Just as easily as it was Milburn, it could have been me," he explained. Turning to look right at her, he added, "Or it might've been you."

Up until then, Anna had never considered the possibility that it could have been she instead of Milburn. Montgomery was right. One moment she was concentrating on her acting, the next a bullet would end her life as easily as snuffing a candle. She could have been killed; Milburn could have been, any one of them might have been the victim. Shivers ran down the length of her spine.

"Have you noticed how strange things have been around here?"

"What do you mean?" Anna asked, knowing *exactly* what he meant.

"First there was the fire, then the robbery at the hotel, and now this," Montgomery explained. "And that doesn't include your altercation with Joan in the dressing room or your problems with Milburn. To chalk all of this up to co-incidence seems a tremendous leap of faith."

Montgomery didn't know the whole story; he wasn't aware of the destruction of the film canisters or the attack on Anna just the night before. He hadn't been part of the conversation in the film room that had concluded that someone was trying to sabotage the film, and Anna wasn't going to break her vow of secrecy, but it was interesting that he was coming to some of the same conclusions on his own.

"If it isn't coincidence," she said, "then what is it?"

The older actor frowned. "I hate to think that it could be on purpose."

"But what if it was?" Anna pressed.

"If my wild guess *were* right," Montgomery mused, "then if I were you, I'd be starting to wonder if this was somewhere I'd still want to be."

"I'm not just going to run away. I'm not a coward."

"Anyone who saw the way you helped during the fire would know that you're anything but, my dear," he said. "But sometimes courage and smarts don't make the best bedfellows, if you know what I mean. Sometimes when the storm comes thundering up on the horizon, the best thing to do is to find shelter." Giving her a smile, he added, "It would break my heart if anything was to happen to you. I may not have known you long, but I'm fond of you all the same."

Anna felt the same; ever since the afternoon they'd first met, rehearsing their scene, just the two of them, the older actor had stood up for her and had tried shepherding her along through the ups and downs of the movie business. "What about you?" she asked. "After what happened to Milburn, aren't you worried? As you said, it could've been any one of us who got hurt."

Montgomery gave a short laugh. "We're in two different places. While you've got your whole career in front of you, all I have to look forward to are those last few parts, a role here and there on account of what I once was," he said. "Maybe dying on a movie set is the perfect way for me to retire."

"That's not funny," Anna said with a frown.

"No, it wasn't," Montgomery agreed. "But truthfully, I don't know how much longer any of us will be in danger."

"What do you mean?"

He nodded over toward Samuel. "With the way things are going, with all the accidents and gossip about fighting among the cast, there will come a point where the higher-ups at Valentine pull the plug on the shoot. They'll lose money, everything they've sunk into it up until now, but it'll be a price they're willing to pay to keep the bad publicity at a minimum. With what just happened to Milburn, we're probably at the tipping point. Unfortunately, there will have to be a scapegoat. Since this was Samuel's project, there's a good chance that his will be the first head to roll."

Looking over at the producer, Anna could see some truth in what Montgomery was saying. With all of those Hollywood reporters sniffing around, to say nothing about how Joan was crowing about what had happened to her, imaginary or not, word of the film's troubles would get out fast. When the Hollywood big shots found out, it could all come tumbling down. Her first acting role in a movie could be over before it really had a chance to begin.

* * *

Back at the hotel, word about Milburn's accident spread like wildfire; passing through the lobby, it was the only thing anyone was talking about. Fortunately, Milburn's wound wasn't considered life-threatening; the bullet had passed directly through the meat of his bicep, avoiding any bones or arteries, though he'd have a heck of a scar and be in an awful lot of pain. He'd been given a shot of morphine and was sleeping in the doctor's office.

After a bit of waiting, Anna finally caught sight of Samuel excusing himself from the yapping mob and heading toward the back door of the hotel. Pushing her way through the crowd, she followed and found him smoking a cigarette, sitting on the steps that led to the Stagecoach's second floor. When he saw her, he tried to hide his worried frown with one of his trademark smiles, but it faltered, looking almost comical.

"You don't have to put on an act for me," Anna said as she sat down beside him. "You've got plenty of reasons to be upset."

"It's even worse than you think," Samuel replied.

"How could it be?"

For a moment, Anna thought he wanted to hold back, but since she was one of the few who knew about the sabotage, he eventually continued. "After what happened today, the whole movie is in jeopardy. I just took a call from California that suggested we might need to shut it all down."

"That's not fair," she said defiantly.

"Fair or not, all they care about is the bottom line. We might've been able to make it if it weren't for Milburn's injury. But the doctor won't allow him to shoot any of his action scenes until he's healed and the studio doesn't want to go on without him."

"Maybe they don't have to," Anna replied. "What if, while he's healing, we shoot all the scenes in the cabin? According to the story, he's supposed to be wounded and bedridden anyway. We can do the action later."

Samuel shook his head. "It'll be a good month before he's well enough to get back on a horse and ride. We're supposed to be finished by then."

At first glance, the situation seemed hopeless. If Milburn couldn't be counted on to film his scenes, it was all over. What other solution could there be? But just then, an idea suddenly struck her. It was bold and more than a little bit crazy.

And it just might work.

"I might have the answer," she said with a grin.

Chapter Twenty-three

HAVE YOU COMPLETELY lost your mind?"

Anna had to struggle to keep from laughing; Dalton's re-action was exactly what she'd expected. The whole walk over to the blacksmith shop, hurrying as she glanced nervously into every dark shadow, fearful that she'd see someone staring back, she imagined the disgusted look on his face, how he'd spit out his words, and even the way he'd look at her, acting as if she had suddenly sprouted a horn in the middle of her forehead.

"I'm serious," she answered.

"No! Not in a million years! Absolutely not!"

Anna had come around the back to look in the open doors and watch Dalton as he worked. He'd been using the same hammer she'd tried to lift from the wall on her first visit, but for him it looked to be weightless. He swung it down over and over, smashing it onto a white-hot bar of metal, sending orange sparks shooting in every direction.

The muscles on his arms and chest rippled, his bare skin slick with sweat, the sight of which brought a longing to Anna so sharp that she had to bite down on her lower lip. When Dalton had finally looked up to see her, instead of smiling he'd frowned, angry that she would cross town at such a late hour, especially given what had happened just the night before.

He'd liked it even less when she'd told him the reason for her visit.

"It's utterly nuts!"

"No, it's not," Anna insisted.

"Given how much I've carried on about my dislike for anything and anyone from Hollywood, present company excluded," Dalton quickly added, "what could've possibly made you think I'd want to be *in the damn movie*?"

The plan that Anna had suggested to Samuel was that Dalton take Milburn's place in filming the action scenes. They were both about the same size, with dark hair and tan complexions. From a distance, they'd look almost identical. She even played up the idea that casting a native of Redstone would make the movie more authentic; she didn't know if Samuel completely bought her sales pitch, but he'd agreed to give Dalton a look early the next morning.

"At this point," the producer had said with a shrug, "what's the harm in it?"

That left the hard part to Anna: getting Dalton to accept.

So far, it wasn't going very well.

"Give me one good reason why I should say 'yes,'" Dalton demanded.

"You'd get to spend more time with me," Anna answered.

"In front of a couple dozen strangers, a gaggle of those nosy reporters, and half the town, all with a camera recording everything I do and say!"

"You wouldn't have to recite any dialogue," she tried to reassure him. "Milburn can still do that later in a close-up. All that you'd need to do is ride a horse and run around firing a gun. It'll be easy."

"If it's so easy, then how come the last guy doing it got shot?" Dalton asked. "Who's to say I won't end up taking a bullet?"

Anna frowned. What Dalton was saying made sense. She *couldn't* guarantee his safety, not completely. For the first time, she began to doubt her plan; if anything were to happen to Dalton because she'd pressured him into doing it, she would never be able to forgive herself.

Maybe this was the end of her dream.

Dalton stood with his hands folded over his chest, unsure of what to do. Even though he'd been angry at Anna for going out alone, he was also happy to be with her. He never would have imagined the proposal she'd brought with her. He'd been dumbstruck, stunned that she would even suggest such a thing, but then he slowly began to understand why; Anna wanted to be a movie star and, if he turned her down, it was possible she'd never get another chance. After a long moment of silence, Dalton finally sighed heavily. "Is it that important to you?" he asked.

Anna slowly nodded.

Dalton slowly shook his head in resignation. "All right," he said. "I can't believe I'm saying this, but I'll do it."

The smile that lit up Anna's face was brighter than the noonday sun. She threw herself into his arms and buried her face in the crook of his neck. The feel of her, the heat of her touch that was hotter to him than the forge on which he worked, the sweet smell of her perfume, and the tickling touch of her hair against his rough cheek all combined to make Dalton's heart thunder in his chest. But he hadn't given in to her request so that he might receive her affections; he'd done so for a reason.

Taking Anna by the shoulders, Dalton gently pushed her back, looking down into her beautiful face. "I want you to understand that I'm willing to do this because I'm worried about you," he explained, his face and voice grave. "After what happened last night at the hotel, I don't like the idea of you being on your own. This way, I can keep an eye on you."

"I like that idea," she said, with a delighted laugh.

Even though the way she looked at him caused a further stirring in his chest, Dalton managed to keep his composure. "I mean it," he insisted. "There's something not right about all of this. Until I'm convinced that you're not in any danger, I don't want you to be too far out of my sight."

At his words tears rose to Anna's eyes.

"I'm sorry," he said hastily, feeling terrible that he'd upset her. "I shouldn't have talked like that. I didn't mean to frighten you."

"You didn't," she said with a weak smile.

"But you're crying."

"Not because I'm sad or scared or worried," Anna replied, "but because of how happy I am that I found you."

Listening to her, Dalton found himself finally understanding the depth of his feelings for her with a clarity that was a little bit shocking. They came from two completely different worlds. She made a living acting on stage and screen as someone else while he used his hands to shape metal, she came from a city filled with buildings that reached for the clouds while he'd lived his whole life in the middle of nowhere. She was as beautiful as any jewel while he was as rough around the edges as a thistle. Yet they'd somehow managed to find each other. From their awkward beginning had blossomed the unexpected, the unimaginable, with even a touch of the impossible mixed in for good measure.

He was in love with her.

His whole life, he'd never been good at expressing himself, at admitting to the feelings inside him. Love was something he'd seen up on the silver screen or read about in the books he and Walker passed back and forth. It certainly wasn't something he'd ever expected to feel, but now that he had, he knew that it roared hotter than any fire, was more intoxicating than any drink, was stronger than any iron, and more beautiful than any sunset.

"Anna, I...I want you to know..." he struggled, trying to find the words that would tell her how he felt. "I just... I've never..."

Placing her hand on his cheek, she gazed up at him, smiling knowingly. "I know exactly what you're trying to say," she said.

"No," he disagreed. "I don't think you do."

Finally deciding that it would be easier to show her what he seemed unable to articulate with words, Dalton leaned down and pressed his lips against hers. The kiss began tenderly, softly, but it wasn't long before a small moan growled up from deep in his chest. Instead of his hunger for her being sated by their kiss, it grew, burning like the fire in the forge. To feed it, he pulled her to him, held her body tightly against his own. Slowly, tantalizingly, she slid her hand up the length of his sweaty, bare arm, over his taut shoulder, and then to his neck, her fingers burrowing into his hair. Unable to stop himself, he touched his tongue against hers, the two of them entwining, soft and wet.

When their kiss finally ended, Dalton continued to hold Anna close, her head against his chest. Buoyed by what they'd shared, he finally managed to admit his feelings.

"I love you, Anna," he told her, when she raised her head to gaze up into his dark eyes. His heart pounded, but he managed to keep talking. "Ever since we collided at the depot," he said with a smile, "I haven't been able to stop thinking about you, morning, noon, or night. I never could've imagined I could find someone like you, that you could be here in my arms. My life couldn't be any better."

"Yes, it could," she disagreed with a smile.

This time, their kiss was even more passionate than before. Anna's hands tugged at the fabric of his shirt, finally letting go to dig her fingernails into his muscular arm. Dalton felt so aroused that he was afraid he might hurt her by pressing her too tightly against him. He struggled to contain the ardor welling inside him, but even as he worked to hold it back, he began to realize that restraining his desire was the last thing Anna wanted. Up on the tips of her toes, she strained to meet him, her eyes closed, her mouth open, her touch hot against his skin. She showed no signs of stopping, no worry or embarrassment, only a longing for him that rivaled his own for her.

Drawing away and looking into Anna's eyes, he said, "I want you."

Dalton was afraid he'd been too blunt, but as a smile curled the edges of Anna's mouth, hope flared in his chest.

When she nodded, he headed for the door.

Anna watched as Dalton closed the double doors at the back of the blacksmith shop and threw the lock. He took her by the hand and led her past the forge, the workbenches littered with bits of metal and piled high with tools, and over to a makeshift ladder nailed against the wall. It led up into the darkness above; the setting sun's light was no longer strong enough to penetrate the small slats. Peering up, she saw that the ladder led to an attic. Dalton looked at her as if he still expected her to turn away from what they were about to do, not judging or worrying with his gaze, but as if he'd understand if she got cold feet.

In answer, she grabbed a rung and started to climb.

Anna knew what was about to happen. There was a part

of her that had understood the possibility of it as far back as the day she stood outside the shop and watched Dalton pound away at the anvil. It wasn't surprising. They'd shared so much in such a short time, it seemed they had known each other forever. Her desire for him had grown to where she no longer wanted to hold it back. Feeling his hands on her and the passion of their kisses had been wonderful, but hearing him finally admit his feelings had made her long to give herself to him.

At the top of the ladder, Anna stepped off and waited for Dalton to join her. The attic wasn't large, it only covered a third of the space of the shop below, and was used primarily for storage; boxes and sacks were piled in the back, but nearer to where they stood, a bedroll had been laid out on the floor with a couple of blankets folded beside it.

"I put this up here so that I can grab a bit of shut-eye between jobs," Dalton explained. "We've been so busy that I've had to use it a time or two."

"It's perfect," she replied.

Dalton nodded before taking her hands in his and looking at her in the gloom, his face serious. "Anna," he said, his voice soft, "if you don't want to do this, I wouldn't be angry. I'd understand."

She smiled. "If I didn't want to share this with you, I wouldn't be here."

This time when they kissed, she knew that there'd be no holding back for either of them. Anna's hands roamed free, reveling in being able to touch him without restraint, rejoicing in the warmth of his skin. For the next few seconds, there was a flurry of unbuttoning and the unhooking of buckles. When Dalton's shirt was open, Anna's hands dug into the thick hair of his chest and the stony muscle beneath. Once the shirt was over his shoulders, she helped him yank it off completely. He wasn't as nimble with the tiny buttons on her blouse, so she helped him, still unwilling to break their kiss. When his fingers began tracing their way across her collar and down to the soft inner curve of her breasts, she sucked in air through her clenched teeth; startled, Dalton didn't quite understand the reason she'd made the sound.

"I'm sorry," he said, removing his hand. "It can't feel all that nice to have these ruined fingers touching you."

"You don't have anything to apologize for," she insisted, taking his hand and gently pressing her lips against the scars and burns that marked his palm. "It's just right the way it is. It's part of what makes you," she explained, giving him another kiss, "*you*."

Once they'd removed the rest of their clothing, Dalton's heavy belt buckle striking the attic's floorboard with a loud crack, they lay down on the bedroll together. Anna smiled as she looked at the thin sliver of moonlight that came through one of the slats and traced a bright line down the length of Dalton's side. Following it with her finger made him moan. When she returned the way she'd come, she suddenly veered off at his waist, sliding her hand down to touch him between his legs; this time he did more than make guttural sounds; he almost jumped.

Encouraged, he began his own explorations. He brushed

away a few unruly strands of her hair, pushing them out of her face, and then traced the curve of her jaw back down to her chest. When he took her breast in his hand, his thumb tracing a delicate circle across her nipple, Anna gasped and covered his hand with her own.

"Dalton," she moaned into his open mouth.

His hand left her breast, sliding across her ribs, tickling a bit, before reaching the small of her back. He pulled her even closer, their bodies pressed tight as their sweat mingled. Moving across her bare hip, his hand followed a meandering path down her thigh before sliding between her legs. When he caressed her hot, damp center, stars of ecstasy danced before her eyes. In response, she frantically returned his caresses. He'd long since grown hard in her hand, but now he bucked and groaned, like a horse straining against its bit.

"Anna," he breathed hard. "I can't wait much longer..."

"Then don't," she encouraged him.

Rising up onto his thick forearms, Dalton positioned his body as Anna opened herself to him. As he eased between her legs, anticipation mounted for both of them. Anna couldn't deny her nervousness, but that feeling paled in comparison to the excitement coursing through her. Slowly, Dalton began to lower himself, easing inside her. She'd often wondered if there would be pain, had expected it, but he moved so gently that she released and accepted him eagerly.

"Are you all right?" he asked.

Anna nodded. "You feel wonderful."

As slowly as he could, Dalton began to move inside her. Anna breathed out every time he entered, her hands squeezing his side when he backed out. Rhythmically, their bodies began to move in unison. With every thrust, waves of pleasure rolled over her, threatening to pull her under. Whatever discomfort she'd felt soon melted away, like surprise snow on a May morning. Eventually, Dalton began to move faster, growing secure that he wasn't hurting her. Their sweat connected them to each other, hot and slick, but Anna still wanted to be closer, rising to wrap her hands around his neck and kiss him hungrily. The steady sounds of their lovemaking filled the attic as she tried to hold back the cries of pleasure rising in her throat.

"Dalton!" She sighed into his ear.

"I love you," he whispered back, going faster still.

"And I love you," Anna managed before a spasm of ecstasy, an unstoppable ripple of happiness ripped through her, making her shake and twitch.

She hadn't even finished shuddering when Dalton did the same, his body tightening, every muscle in his body clenching as he let loose, filling her with warmth that felt as if it went from her head to her toes. His eyes shut while he jerked, but the moment they opened, they seized hers, holding her gaze and refusing to let go. The smile she gave him in return was as sparkling as the brightest star in the night sky.

When Dalton lowered himself down beside her on the bedroll, Anna nestled into the cradle of his arms. She didn't know if she'd ever been so happy in all her life. If she lived to be a hundred, she might never be able to understand how they came to be together, but she'd always be thankful that they had. For so many years, she'd wanted to be somebody, to see her name in lights and rise above the squalor of her past. But now she felt foolish. *This* was what she should've been looking for.

All she'd been missing was love.

Chapter Twenty-four

DALTON WOKE SLOWLY, his eyes blinking, the last remnants of his dream drifting away as if they were made of smoke. Darkness filled the attic and the only sounds he heard were the steady, melodic sawing of crickets. For a long moment, he lay still, staring up at the pitched roof, wondering if what had happened between him and Anna was also a dream, but when he glanced beside him, she was pressed closely to his side, still sleeping, her blond hair spilling across her shoulders.

Tenderly, he touched her arm, reveling in the feel of her soft skin. Making love to Anna for the first time was something he would always cherish, but falling in love with her meant more. Her beauty, inside and out, was breathtaking. She was a treasure the likes of which he'd never expected to find, but now that he had, he intended to fight for her, to protect her, for as long as she'd let him. That she'd chosen to share herself with him, heart and body, was almost too good to be true.

She was the love of his life.

Too restless to go back to sleep, Dalton got up and dressed, being careful not to wake Anna. He was reluctant to leave her alone, especially after what had happened in her hotel room, but she was sleeping soundly, it was late at night, and he wasn't planning on going too far away, just out for a breath of fresh air. Descending the ladder, he unlatched the door and slipped quietly out.

Redstone was as still as a graveyard. Dalton didn't know what time it was, but he guessed between three and four o'clock. The moon was a little less than half-full, surrounded by countless stars in an otherwise clear sky. A thin breeze blew, just chilly enough to raise the flesh on Dalton's arms, but he wasn't cold.

Circling around the blacksmith shop, he slipped up to Main and turned at the corner. Though the sleeping town looked the same as it always had, Dalton felt different, changed. His life certainly wasn't what it had been that afternoon at the depot. Somehow, Anna had managed to soothe the anger inside him. Instead of worrying about the future, he now felt a bit excited.

It was then, just as Dalton was beginning to wonder if he might not take Anna's advice and have another go at patching things up with his father, that he suddenly stopped. Something had moved up ahead of him. At first, he thought that it must have been a cat or a trick of the moonlight, but as he watched, standing in the shadows of an awning, he saw it again.

It was a person.

Whoever it was wasn't just out for a casual late-night stroll like Dalton; this person was acting strangely, moving quickly from one shadow to the next, stopping to look around as if fearful of being seen. Acting on instinct, Dalton pressed himself up against the side of the nearest building. Fortunately he'd yet to be noticed. Questions filled him.

Who in the hell is that? Where did he come from and where is he going? Does this have anything to do with all the strange goings-on lately?

Right then and there, Dalton made up his mind to follow. Whenever the stranger moved, so did he; when the person froze, he did the same, fearful that the slightest twitch might give him away. The more he watched, the more certain Dalton was that it wasn't anyone he knew; even Creed moved differently than this, less nervously. After a couple of blocks, he felt a tickle at the back of his brain, a suspicion that he knew where the stranger was headed.

In the end, his guess proved right. The person stopped at the base of the stairs that led to Vernon Black's office. In the faint light, Dalton could see that the stranger was carrying something, a package perhaps. Deep in his gut, he knew that this had something to do with the sabotage being carried out against Anna's movie.

But it was then that Dalton made a big mistake. He'd been so intent on learning where the stranger was headed that he'd forgotten to step back out of the moonlight; when the man looked back, he saw Dalton staring at him. If he was surprised, he didn't show it for long; fast as a rabbit, the stranger bolted, running away down the alley. With only a split-second's hesitation, Dalton followed.

Since he no longer had to worry about being quiet, Dalton ran all out, his booted feet pounding on the sidewalk and then down the dirt alley. Up ahead, he saw the stranger in silhouette, moving fast but not so far away that Dalton felt he couldn't catch him. Whizzing through the alleyway, racing across the street, passing from moonlight to shadow and back again, they ran. But suddenly, just as Dalton thought his perseverance was about to be rewarded, he rounded a corner and the mysterious man was gone. It was as if he'd vanished into thin air.

Where in the hell had he gone?

Backtracking a few steps, Dalton noticed a sliver of space that ran between two buildings. Was it possible that the man had squeezed through there? Not knowing what other solution there might be, he tried to follow, but he was too broad and wouldn't fit. As fast as he could, he raced around the buildings and finally came out on the other side, right where he'd expected the stranger had gone. He was only a block from the hotel. Looking in that direction, he saw someone hurrying up the back stairs, the same route Anna had used to get past the Hollywood reporters. He only caught a glimpse of the person before the second-floor door shut behind him, but he knew it was the same man he'd been chasing; he was still clutching his package.

Dalton saw no point in following the stranger into the Stagecoach; whoever it had been was surely safely inside his room. But that did nothing to weaken his belief that he'd found a link between Hollywood and Vernon Black. If he could identify who it had been, he could end both his and Anna's troubles for good. But he wasn't going to be able to do it alone.

He needed to talk to Anna.

When Dalton first shook Anna's shoulder, she'd awoken with a gasp, startled and a touch fearful, but as soon as she saw his face, her heart calmed. Through the numbing fog of sleep, she struggled to hear what he was telling her, his words coming fast and excited. She was still groggy and could see that it was early, well before sunrise. But once she understood what he was saying, she was wide awake.

"You're right," she said, pulling the blankets tight around her naked body, not out of modesty but for warmth. "This has to do with the movie."

"It has to," Dalton agreed. "I just know it."

"Then we have to go to Samuel right away and tell him everything," she said, reaching for her blouse. "He needs to know as soon as possible."

Dalton reached out and took her by the hand, stopping her from gathering her clothes. "I don't think that would be a good idea."

"Why not?" Anna asked, more than a little confused. "It's not like he's mixed up in it. He's not trying to destroy his own movie."

"We don't know that, not for certain," Dalton replied calmly. "As far as I'm concerned, it could be anyone in that hotel. They're all suspects. To just dismiss someone because it seems unlikely he'd be involved would be foolish."

"But if we don't tell Samuel, then who? The sheriff?"

Dalton laughed out loud. "What passes for the law here in Redstone would make the Keystone Cops look like Sherlock Holmes," he said. "The sheriff would be more hindrance than help, although he's bound to play a part before it's all said and done."

"So if we're not telling anyone, what do we do next?"

"We need more answers. Not only do we have to find out who's behind all this, but we need to know what they plan to do next."

Anna thought about all of the acts of sabotage that had been directed at the film, from the questionable origins of the fire to the destruction of the film canisters, and even to the theft of Joan's diamond ring and her own attack. It was then, while thinking about the fluke accident that had wounded Milburn, that she suddenly understood what had been nagging her.

"I think Milburn was shot on purpose," she admitted.

"What makes you say that?" Dalton asked, curious.

"Something's been bothering me about it ever since it happened," Anna explained. "I don't know if it was the shock of it or because of everything else going on, but I wasn't able to put it together until now." She paused, gathering her thoughts. "I was looking right at Milburn when he was hit. When the bullet struck his arm, blood flew forward. That means he was shot from behind, except there wasn't another actor positioned there."

"Which means that someone who wasn't part of the movie pulled the trigger," Dalton said, finishing her thought.

Anna nodded. She remembered what Montgomery had said: that any one of them could've been killed. If Milburn's shooting had been done on purpose, then what calamity would happen next? How far was the person behind all of this willing to go? Murder? No matter what, the scheme had to be stopped.

But how?

"What we need is to get our hands on that parcel he was carrying," Dalton said, answering her unasked question. "I don't know if it was money or the details for the next part of the plan, but if he was bringing it to Vernon Black, it has to be important. We get our hands on the package and we've got him."

"You keep saying that it was a man, but are you sure?" Anna asked. Whenever she ran through her list of potential suspects, she kept coming back to Joan; if the actress went so far as to attack herself in order to be rid of her rival, what wouldn't she do? "Could you tell for certain in the dark?"

Dalton thought about it for a moment. "I'm not one hundred percent sure," he admitted. "I never got that good a look. It's hard for me to believe a woman could be wrapped up in something like this, but you're right, we can't discount the possibility. Either way, what matters now is finding out what's in that package."

"How can we do that? After nearly getting caught, there's no way the person is coming back. It'd be too big a risk."

Dalton shook his head. "I don't think he has a choice," he disagreed. "Why else would he be going to Vernon's office in the middle of the night? Not even the worst drunks in town are about at that hour. It makes me wonder if Vernon even knows who he's dealing with. If he did, they'd just meet in his office during the day."

"Maybe whoever it is doesn't want to be seen. If it's someone famous," Anna wondered aloud, "then they wouldn't want the attention it'd bring."

"But then you'd use a proxy, a go-between. That would take away most all of the risk. No, there's a reason for all of the secrecy."

"Then how do we find out the truth?"

"We watch," he answered simply. "It'll happen at night. We just need to be there when it does. We grab the package or, if we're really lucky, whoever's carrying it."

"That sounds dangerous."

"It could be."

Reaching out, Anna took Dalton by the hand. "I love you," she told him. "I don't want you to get hurt."

"If we don't do something about this, someone else will be."

Anna knew he was right, even if she didn't like it.

"Don't worry," Dalton said, giving her a reassuring smile. "Just because we're not going to tell that Samuel fella, doesn't mean we're going it alone."

For the next two days, Dalton watched for the stranger to come back, but to no avail. Even with Walker relieving him so that he could get some sleep, the stairs outside Vernon Black's office remained undisturbed until morning. Anna began to get frustrated, still arguing that they should go to Samuel, but Dalton insisted that they had to stay patient. He was convinced that whoever he'd chased would return.

In the meantime, having accepted Anna's offer, Dalton became a part of the film. At the first meeting with Samuel, he'd been looked up and down, asked to turn one way and then the other, scrutinized from far away and then up close. He'd felt like a cow being sold at market. The producer nodded to himself and then to Anna.

"This might actually work," Samuel agreed.

From there, Dalton had gone to Bonnie to be fitted for his costume, been introduced to the cast and crew, and even shown the horse he'd be riding. With all the bad things he'd said about Hollywood, it was a bit embarrassing to find out exactly how wrong he'd been; most everyone he met, he liked. When shooting started, the first couple of takes had been rough, but with equal parts of the director's venom and Anna's encouragement, he kept at it until it started to feel natural. By the end of the first day, he was whooping and hollering as he rode his mount for all it was worth. He had to admit that it was kind of fun.

But for Anna, returning to filming wasn't as pleasant. The first day was fine, working with Montgomery, but on the second, Milburn returned. Since the wounded actor couldn't shoot outdoors or with any action, Samuel had decided to take Anna's advice and film their bedside scenes. Milburn had looked terrible; Anna had expected him to be bedridden for at least a week, but there he was, staring at her as she entered the room. At first, their scene had gone just fine; the weakness in Milburn's voice was perfect for the Hawk. But it hadn't taken long before things went south in a hurry.

Anna sat beside the bed in which Milburn lay, tending to his character's injuries as he told her about the life he led across the border. As he talked, she placed a cloth in a washpan, wrung out the water, and pressed it against his brow. But suddenly, she felt something. Struggling to keep her composure, Anna understood that Milburn had slid his finger into the slit of her skirt and was touching the bare skin of her calf. Because of the way she was sitting, she knew that no one else could see what he was doing. She couldn't believe it herself. Even after being shot, he couldn't resist provoking her. She stumbled over her next line of dialogue on purpose, standing up to apologize.

When she sat back down, Anna glared hard at Milburn, but he feigned ignorance. But as soon as the camera started rolling again, he was right back at it, touching her. Even as she continued with the scene, Anna wondered what she should do. Flubbing her lines hadn't worked. If she were to accuse him of anything, he'd just lie and then try twice as hard. What she needed was something bold enough for him to get the hint.

Then it came to her.

Reaching back to put the towel in the basin, Anna wobbled as if she was about to lose her balance. In order to steady herself and keep from falling out of her chair, she grabbed Milburn's arm, right where he'd been shot, and gave it a hard squeeze. The scream that burst from the actor's lips was loud enough to have woken up the dead.

"God damn it to hell!" he roared in agony.

"Oh, I'm so sorry!" Anna gasped, doing the best acting she could. "I didn't mean to! I thought I was going to fall!"

"I've probably popped my stitches!"

As members of the crew rushed forward to see if they could help, Anna leaned forward and whispered into Milburn's ear. "If you ever lay another hand on me," she told him, "you'll end up hurting a lot worse than this!"

The young actor's eyes went wide with both pain and shock.

Though only a small amount of blood seeped through the thick bandages around his arm, Milburn didn't want to leave the set. Over and over, he told Samuel that it had been an accident, and that they should just get back to work. In the end, as drastic as Anna's plan had been, it worked.

Milburn didn't bother her for the rest of the day.

On the third night after Dalton had given chase to the mysterious stranger, Walker sat in the front windows of his family's hardware store and looked out onto the street. The business was perfectly located; it offered a clear view of the stairs leading to Vernon Black's office. For the twentieth time that night, he looked at his pocket watch; by the scant light of the moon, he saw that it was a quarter past three in the morning.

Walker yawned. When Dalton had first told him about what had happened, trusting him with the secret that the movie company feared they were being sabotaged, Walker had been thrilled. When Dalton suggested that they use the Duncans' family store to keep an eye on things, Walker had quickly volunteered to help keep watch. It had sounded like an adventure. Now it just seemed boring.

When Dalton had left for the night an hour earlier because he had to get up early for filming, a fact that entertained Walker no end, he'd written to the blacksmith that he thought Anna might end up being right; almost being discovered had frightened away the stranger for good. Though Dalton had once again preached patience, Walker could see that his friend's was running out.

But then, just as Walker was beginning to worry that he wouldn't be able to stay awake until dawn, he glanced up and saw something that made him leap straight out of his chair. Someone was coming *down* the steps from Vernon's office. He'd been so lost in thought that he'd never seen anyone go *up*. Staring out the window in shock, Walker watched as the person reached the bottom of the staircase and kept right on going into the darkness of the alley, immediately swallowed from sight.

Dalton is going to kill me!

But though he'd lost his chance to learn the person's identity, that didn't mean he couldn't still get his hands on the package.

Once he was sure that the stranger was gone, Walker slipped out the door of the hardware store and hurried across the street. Every step he took up to Vernon's office creaked beneath his foot, sounding louder to his ears in the quiet night than it probably was. At the top of the stairs, Walker tried the door, but it was locked. Then, crouching so that his face was pressed against the boards, he peered beneath it, hoping and praying that luck might shine on him.

And it did.

The gap between the door and the floor wasn't much, but it had been enough for the mysterious visitor to slide something in. But he hadn't pushed it quite far enough; one corner was still visible. As carefully as he could, Walker reached under, fearful that he'd accidentally shove it farther out of reach, and wiggled the package back and forth, manipulating it closer, until he could pinch the paper and finally drag it out.

It was more of an envelope than a package, thick and heavy in his hand, wrapped with twine. As quickly as he could, Walker untied the string; he wanted to act fast lest someone might be coming for the package. The last thing he wanted was to be caught with it. Pulling open the flap, he looked inside. What he found took his breath away. It was full of money, more than Walker had ever seen at one time in all his life.

There was also a note.

Walker pulled it out and unfolded it, holding it up to the moonlight. What he read was even more shocking than the amount of cash. He read it over again, then one more time, careful to memorize each and every word. Once he was sure he had it, he placed the letter back in the envelope, retied it, and again slipped it under the door, making sure it was all the way inside.

Racing back down the stairs, Walker struggled to settle his nerves. What he'd read would've been enough to make him sweat with worry if he hadn't been frozen with fear. He had to get to Dalton and Anna to tell them what was planned for later that day. He had to do his part to stop it.

Otherwise, Redstone would never be the same.

Chapter Twenty-five

Aɴɴᴀ ᴡᴀʟᴋᴇᴅ ᴛᴏᴡᴀʀᴅ the site of the day's shooting, struggling just to put one foot in front of the other, so distraught that she let her skirt drag behind her in the dirt. She felt as if she was about to cry. Though the day was beautiful, yet another hot, cloudless Texas morning, she expected dark storm clouds to come rolling in, or maybe even a fierce tornado, its powerful winds tearing apart her life and leaving it broken beyond repair.

Only a few minutes earlier, she'd been with Dalton and Walker, talking about what they'd discovered in the envelope. While there was nothing in the letter that gave away the true identity of the person who was paying Vernon Black to commit acts of mayhem against Valentine Pictures, it did reveal what the next part of the nefarious plan projected.

At exactly noon, a few short hours from now, the building they'd be shooting in, the rickety old saloon Samuel had shown her when she'd first arrived in town, would be brought crumbling down around their heads, potentially killing each and every person inside. The letter didn't say how the act would be done, but Anna doubted it would take much force; even after it had been refurbished, the saloon still looked unsteady enough to collapse in a stiff breeze.

Reading what Walker had written made Anna feel faint. She had questioned him, wondering if he hadn't misunderstood, but the mute young man insisted that he remembered it just as it'd been written. That she was now walking to the exact spot where the destruction was supposed to take place struck her as insane.

But Dalton had a plan.

He believed that this was their chance to unravel the mystery of the sabotage and make sure that all of the guilty parties were caught. All they had to do was stop Creed and Audie Cobb in the act; Dalton suspected they'd be the ones entrusted with carrying it all out, since they were Black's henchmen. For her part, Anna just had to watch to see if someone tried to leave the scene before the appointed hour. Everyone of importance to the movie was scheduled to be there. With the amount of money stuffed into the envelope, payment for shooting Milburn, the culprit had to be someone high up the ladder, wealthy enough to be able to pay Vernon's price. If the plan didn't come to fruition, Dalton was convinced that Anna would see signs of confusion in the person's face.

"We need to go to Samuel or the sheriff," she'd insisted. "This is too dangerous for us to be playing games!"

"This will work," he'd assured her.

"But what if it doesn't?"

"It will," Dalton insisted. "I promise you that we're going to put an end to this. Trust me."

And she did, but only to a point. Though Dalton sounded confident, Anna couldn't keep from worrying that when she left him, sharing a kiss as Walker looked the other way, she was saying good-bye to him for the last time.

"You've gotta be shittin' me!"

Vernon stared hard over his desk at Creed, his anger rising; if there was one thing he wouldn't stand for, it was backtalk. He'd called in the Cobb brothers to tell them about the latest request being made for their services, as well as to pay Creed for shooting the actor. Creed had been all smiles as he'd picked up his money, but as soon as his boss told him about the planned destruction of the old saloon, the man's mood soured.

"If that buildin' comes down, it'll kill most everyone inside," he said.

"That's the idea," Vernon explained.

"You're talkin' 'bout murder."

"That's never stopped you before."

"That's 'cause every time I done it I been sure I'd get away with it. If more'n a dozen or so a them Hollywood folks die, there ain't gonna be a rock small enough for me to crawl under and hide, they ain't gonna turn it over lookin'. They'll send the damn Pinkertons after me."

"Let them come. There won't be any evidence to link you to a thing," Vernon tried to reassure the man.

Creed glanced over at Audie. His brother stood where he always did, just a few feet inside the door, silent as ever; if Creed had looked to the giant for answers, he'd turned to the wrong man.

"How in the hell're we supposed to knock that damn buildin' down, anyway?" Creed asked, turning back to Vernon. "We supposed to run into it with a truck? Take a hammer to the load beam?"

The letter that Vernon had found shoved under the door, along with enough money to make him go weak in the knees, hadn't been specific about how to accomplish the job. What it had been insistent on was that the task had to be completed that day, a timetable that hadn't pleased Vernon; as a matter of fact, he'd been growing angry that his payment for the shooting hadn't come sooner; he'd started to wonder if he wasn't being stiffed. He'd also never managed to discover the identity of his business partner, a fact that annoyed him. But in the end, the pile of cash now locked in his safe had made his anger vanish. Though he wouldn't have admitted it to Creed, he did have some misgivings about destroying the building, but the lure of the money was too great for him to ignore. Greed was driving him, plain and simple. To that end, an idea had started forming in his head about how to accomplish the task.

"Dynamite," he said simply.

Creed was too stunned to say anything; even Audie looked a little more dumbstruck than usual.

"It wouldn't take much to bring down that mess of a saloon," Vernon continued. "Just a stick. All you have to do is throw it up on the roof, let it blow, and the whole thing will come down. With a long enough fuse, you could toss it and be gone before anyone was the wiser."

"Where'n hell am I gonna get any dynamite 'fore noon?" Creed asked.

"I have some."

Creed's mouth hung open. "You do?"

Vernon nodded. Over the years he'd stockpiled plenty of things he thought might come in handy; some leftover dynamite from one of the many mining expeditions that had tested the area had always struck him as a good choice. He told Creed where it was located, expecting that this would be the end of their discussion. It wasn't.

"I just don't think this is right," Creed mumbled.

"Then it's a good goddamn thing you aren't paid for your thoughts!" Vernon roared, rising out of his chair and startling the men. "You'd do best to remember that you're paid to do, not think!"

The look in Creed's eyes told Vernon that his message had been heard. The man hazarded one quick glance over to Audie, nodded, and left.

As he had the day he'd first run into Anna at the train depot, Dalton stood in the doorway to the blacksmith shop and watched his father work a piece of metal. Today, however, he had no anger in his heart or, if he did, he was mad at himself for letting their relationship deteriorate as badly as it had. Even though his life had been hectic in the days since he and Anna had spied George gambling in Vernon Black's tavern, he'd still found himself thinking about his father from time to time. He'd come to understand that Anna had been right; if he kept yelling, all he'd accomplish would be to drive a wedge between them for good.

If everything went right today, maybe they'd have a chance to talk.

If things went wrong...

Once George had finished, dropping the metal in the water trough, Dalton walked over. "Do you have a minute?" he asked.

"Of course," his father answered.

Dalton nodded. The whole way to the shop, he'd planned out what he wanted to say, had even mumbled it to himself to practice, but now that he was here, the words seemed to have abandoned him. "I...I...just wanted to..." he said, sputtering to a stop. Determined, he took a breath and pressed on. "I came here to apologize for how I've acted lately. Even though I'm still not happy about your gambling, it's no excuse for my behavior." It was painful for Dalton to hold his father's gaze, but he did it all the same. "A son should treat his father with more respect than that."

"A father shouldn't give his son a reason to question that respect," George said, offering a wisp of a smile.

·Dalton clasped his father on the shoulder; as amazing as it was, he already felt that they'd taken a step toward bridging the troubles between them. Unfortunately, with what was about to happen at the saloon, he didn't have time to do more. Reaching into his back pocket, he pulled out an envelope. Inside was a letter detailing everything he'd discovered about the sabotage of the movie; if he was wrong and none of them survived, someone needed to know what was going on. He knew that if he told his father what was happening, he would insist on coming along or, at the very least, going to the sheriff, but Dalton feared that too much attention on the saloon might scare Creed and Audie away, as well as let Vernon know they were on to them. If that happened, they might never learn the truth. The letter would have to do. He handed it to his father.

"What's this?" George asked.

"Something for later," Dalton answered.

"When am I supposed to open it?"

"You'll know when the time is right." Dalton hoped he'd never have to.

With that, Dalton headed for the door. He was just about to leave when his father called out to him. "Does this have something to do with Anna?" he asked, holding up the envelope.

"It does."

"I thought so," George said. "From the moment I saw the two of you together, I knew she was special. To be honest, she reminds me of your mother just a bit. That same kindness." He paused, adding, "She's one of the good ones. I reckon you'd do well to hold on to her."

Dalton felt the same; that was why he was about to risk his life.

When Dalton hurried up the front steps of the Stagecoach Hotel, it didn't take long for him to find who he was looking for. Mitchell Hubert, the reporter with the *Movie Land News*, the same man he'd knocked unconscious the night of Anna's attack, was leaning against the railing on the far side of the front porch, smoking a cigarette. His face was a mess. A bandage had been plastered across the bridge of his nose, a wad of cotton stuffed in one nostril. His eyes were ringed with dark circles, like a raccoon's. When he noticed who was striding over, he looked so nervous that Dalton half expected him to vault the railing and take off running as fast as he could.

"Ain't you given me enough grief?" the man asked, holding up his hands in surrender, making sure to shield his face.

"I didn't come here to slug you again," Dalton answered.

"You didn't?" Mitchell asked in surprise. "I figured you musta read the piece I done 'bout your lady and come after me."

"What piece? What did you write?"

The reporter paused. "That the rumor is she went after Joan in the dressin' room 'cause she was jealous of her looks." He hesitated a moment longer, then added, "And she might be a suspect in the jewel theft."

"That's a pack of lies and you know it," Dalton growled.

"I know, I know! But I told you if you didn't give me somethin' to work with I was gonna have to make it up. Besides, after you whopped me one, I wasn't figurin' on doin' you no favors."

"What if I asked for one now?"

Mitchell's eyes narrowed, like a bloodhound that had

caught the whiff of something worth following. "Like what?"

"If I told you to be at a certain place at a certain time," Dalton said, "and you had to write *exactly* what you saw, would you be there?"

"It'd be worth my time?"

"I have no doubts."

"Then I'd be there with bells on."

Dalton gave the reporter the information and started to leave. He was just about to the steps when the man called out. "Don't hold what I wrote 'bout your sweetheart against me," he said. "Remember, bad publicity sells as much as good."

That was just what Dalton was counting on.

The preparations for filming inside the old saloon were proceeding just as they had every other day on every other set. Technicians climbed on ladders as they made last-minute adjustments to lights and sound equipment. Bonnie went from costume to costume, fussing over the smallest stray stitch or out-of-place seam. Actors practiced their lines while makeup artists hovered like flies, occasionally shooed away. Samuel smiled and Frank growled. Nothing looked out of place, but to Anna, with the fear of what was about to happen gnawing at her, everything felt different.

No matter how hard she tried to remain calm, to believe Dalton's promise, to trust in his plan, she couldn't keep her eyes from roaming from one person to the next, looking for anything, some sign that would give them away. But every time someone glanced in her direction, whether it was one of the cameramen or Frank or even the young woman who took cups of coffee around on a tray, she couldn't help but think that they were watching her, wondering if she was on to them.

Just relax! Don't jump to conclusions!

Trying to steady her nerves, Anna focused on one person at a time. Joan stood on the opposite side of the room, her face caked in powder and cream to hide her bruises. She kept flashing her naked finger, the one that normally would have displayed her diamond ring, to anyone unlucky enough to get too close. Montgomery was beside the bar practicing his lines, his mouth moving silently, his hands weaving through the air as if he were conducting an orchestra. Milburn was absent, but Anna had already exempted him from her suspicion; he certainly hadn't paid to have himself shot. Frank stared up at the lights that had been placed above the bar, just as he'd requested. He grumbled and fussed, wanting everything perfect, going back and forth to the camera to look through the lens, hardly the behavior of someone about to destroy the building. Or was it?

"Are you all ready to go?"

Anna startled so badly that she let out a yelp. She turned to find Samuel beside her, his face full of concern.

"I didn't mean to scare you," the producer said. Looking at her more closely, he added, "Are you all right? You're a little pale."

"I'm fine," she said quickly, forcing a smile. "I just didn't sleep well."

"That makes two of us." Glancing around, Samuel took her by the hand and leaned closer. "You know, Anna," he said. "I've wanted to thank you for the way you've held up with everything that's happened. I know it hasn't been easy, especially since you know more than most. It's a burden I wish you didn't have to carry. I just wanted you to know how much I appreciate it."

Anna nodded. "It must not be too bad," she said. "I still don't regret accepting your offer."

"If you ever do, promise me you won't tell me."

As she watched Samuel walk away, it was hard for Anna not to call out to him and tell him what she knew about the impending sabotage. Unlike Dalton, she could see no reason not to trust him; it was his movie, after all.

But she held her tongue. Was it really possible that Samuel could be involved? He *was* once an actor. Could he be talented enough to pull the wool over everyone's eyes? What reason could he possibly have for doing it? It was impossible, wasn't it? But if not he, then who...?

As a technician walked past her, Anna stopped him and asked him for the time. When he held out his pocket watch, it read half-past eleven.

In thirty minutes, she was going to find out.

"WHAT IF THEY HAVE A GUN?"

"Then we do our damnedest not to get shot."

"YOU'RE NOT MAKING ME FEEL ANY BETTER."

Dalton and Walker stood in the shadows of the alley behind the saloon. From their vantage point, they could watch in three different directions back toward the center of town. The hope was to see the Cobb brothers coming and then go to meet them, keeping them as far away from the building as possible. It was the only way Dalton could think of to keep Anna safe. Sweat trickled down his back, as much from his nerves as the heat. Time felt as if it was standing still, the calm before the storm.

"HOW DO YOU RECKON THEY'LL TRY TO BRING IT DOWN?"

"Knowing Creed, it'll be crafty."

"MAYBE THEY'LL DRIVE A TRUCK INTO IT."

Dalton shook his head. "That'd be too much, even for Creed. Besides, there's no guarantee that it'd be enough to topple the building and, even if it was, there'd be plenty of evidence left behind. Creed won't want to be caught. He's a criminal, but that doesn't mean he's stupid."

"NO, THE STUPID ONES ARE THE TWO OF US FOR TRYING TO STOP THEM."

"You didn't have to come along."

"LIKE HELL I DIDN'T. YOU NEED ME," Walker wrote. Erasing it, he added, "BUT THAT STILL DOESN'T MEAN WE'RE SMART."

Dalton knew that Walker was nervous; he'd been scratching things on his slate all day, ever since he'd come to wake his friend and tell him what he'd found in the envelope. He had every right to be worried; going up against two dangerous men like Creed and Audie Cobb wasn't like facing off against the bullies when they were kids. One of them could be killed, maybe both. But when Walker had volunteered to stand with him, Dalton hadn't been able to tell him no; truth be told, he was glad he wouldn't have to face the two thugs alone.

Suddenly Walker pointed. Dalton looked and saw the sight he knew was coming, but had been dreading all the same; Creed and Audie were slowly making their way toward them. They were taking a backward route, off Main, attempting to stay out of sight for as long as they could. Creed looked to be carrying something wrapped in an oilcloth.

"You ready?" Dalton asked.

Walker nodded, setting down his slate and chalk; with what was about to happen, there wouldn't be time for writing.

Creed's boots crunched over the broken rock of the alley that led to the saloon. When he took off his hat to wipe his brow with the back of his forearm, it came away wet. He didn't need to look at a watch to know what time it was. The dynamite felt awfully heavy in the cloth at his side. It was only one stick, threaded through with enough fuse to give them plenty of time to run, but it weighed on Creed as if he was dragging his own tombstone behind him.

Ever since he'd left Vernon's office, he'd felt misgivings about what he was about to do. It wasn't that he was above murder, even if it meant he'd be killing folks who wouldn't know him from Adam. But somehow this was different. He'd managed to keep himself from prison so far, but when this day was finished, he wondered if he wouldn't be locked up in some hole in the ground and left to rot.

Audie lumbered beside him, as quiet as always. All day, his brother hadn't said a word one way or the other about what they'd been ordered to do. Creed assumed that Audie went along with it because he had. But what choice did they have? They'd never gone against Vernon before, never had a reason to. The businessman had always done right by them, had lined their pockets with far more money than they ever could have expected to earn on their own. Deep down, Creed understood that he was no leader. He needed someone to steer him, to pull his trigger. So even though he'd considered defying Vernon today, the fact that he and Audie were right here, right now, proved that he never would.

"Creed!"

The sound of someone calling his name stunned Creed. He was even more shocked to look up and see Dalton Barnes and the dummy from the hardware store step out of the shadows and directly into their path. All four of them stood still, staring at each other under the hot sun.

"I know why you're here," Barnes said.

"If you did, you wouldn't be within a mile of this place," Creed answered.

"We read the letter, the one that was slid under Vernon's door. We know someone's paying an awful lot of money for you to sabotage the movie," the blacksmith explained. "I'm here to tell you it ends now."

Try as he might, Creed knew he couldn't keep the surprise off his face. How had Barnes found out? But in the end, Creed knew the answer didn't matter. He'd long since cast his lot; all that was left to do was see which way the die landed.

"Who's gonna stop us? You and that retard?" he asked with a chuckle; even Audie laughed at that. "You mighta gotten one over on me before, but you was lucky, and I been itchin' for payback ever since."

"Here's your chance," Barnes said defiantly. "The only way you're going to get to the saloon is through us."

"So be it," Creed said, walking forward as he raised a fist.

Chapter Twenty-six

Cut! Cut! Cut!"

Frank jumped up out of the director's chair so fast it was as if his back end were on fire, looking as if he wanted to come over and take a bite out of Anna, but he only stood and glared instead, running his hands through his hair, pulling at the ends, and leaving it in disarray. Anna couldn't blame him; it was the third time she'd made a mistake since they'd started filming, forcing Frank to stop and start again. But try as she might, she just couldn't concentrate.

At any moment, she expected them all to be dead.

"I'm telling you that she's cursed this whole film!" Joan shouted. "Need I list all the things that have gone wrong since that *hussy* showed up here? How much more of this are we going to take before someone finds a little backbone and puts her on the next train out of town?"

"Oh, please do shut up, Joan," Montgomery chided the

older actress. "You forget that I was around when you were coming up and I seem to recall plenty of times when you flubbed a line or two. It happens to everybody."

"I was nowhere near this bad!"

"If you truly believe that, then your ring wasn't the only thing stolen; your memory was taken right along with it."

"Now, now, everyone," Samuel said, stepping between them to act as a peacemaker yet again. "We're all on edge but it'll just get worse if we start pointing fingers at each other. Let's all take a deep breath and five minutes."

Holding Anna gently by the arm, he steered her away from the crowd and over to the far end of the refurbished bar. Looking at her with genuine concern, he asked, "Are you sure you're steady enough to do this?"

Anna stared at him blankly. She couldn't tell him the truth: that she felt claustrophobic, as if she were already in her coffin, petrified with fear that the building was about to collapse. It was only a couple of minutes before noon, the appointed time for the sabotage to take place. All she wanted to do was run screaming into the afternoon sun, but she couldn't. It was a struggle, but she continued to cling to her belief in Dalton, that he'd make it right, just as he'd promised. She had to trust in him.

"I'm...I'm just a bit out of sorts, that's all," she said.

"If you want, you can step out and get some air," Samuel suggested. "We can manage without you for a while."

Searching the producer's face, Anna couldn't help but try to find some hidden meaning in his words, her paranoia getting the better of her. Was he trying to warn her away because of what was about to happen? Was he showing her mercy? Had she misunderstood the type of man he was from the very beginning?

But then, just as Dalton had expected, the truth revealed itself.

Behind her, Anna heard the unmistakable click of a pocket watch being closed. "Truth be told, I'm not feeling very well myself. If it's all right, I'm going to go outside for a bit," a man's voice said.

Slowly, Anna turned around, her eyes wide with shock and disbelief. In that instant she knew, she *knew* that the person behind the sabotage, the mastermind who'd orchestrated the fire, the destruction of the film, the theft of the ring, and possibly even her attack, had just revealed himself.

It was Montgomery.

The first punch split Dalton's lip and the coppery taste of blood flooded his mouth. Creed had walked toward him, then feinted slightly to his left before straightening and throwing a quick right hand, which snapped back his opponent's head. Instantly Dalton realized that he'd been lucky back in the alley, that the only chance he'd had was to catch Creed off guard. This time, the man was prepared.

The second punch, a vicious left hook to Dalton's ribs, sent pain arcing through his body. His legs trembled; try as he might, he couldn't remain upright and he dropped to one knee in the dirt. When he glanced up at Creed through sweat-stained eyes, he saw that the man was smiling. Dalton had thought he was prepared, ready to brawl with the Cobb brothers and stop them from carrying out their murderous orders, but he'd underestimated them. Now he was going to pay for it. Anna and Walker, too.

"You shouldn't never have come here," Creed growled.

A boot caught Dalton in the side, dropping him onto his face, and forcing the air out of his lungs. If he didn't mount some sort of comeback soon, the fight would be over fast.

Through the swirling dust, he saw that Walker was having a better time of it with Audie, though he was no closer to besting his man than Dalton was. Before they'd walked away from the saloon, Walker had snatched up a thick plank, hiding it behind his leg. Now he darted in and out like a pesky fly, swatting at Creed's brother as hard as he could, but the big man didn't seem the least bit bothered. Dalton had noticed Audie was limping, which further limited his mobility, but all it would take would be for him to snatch the plank or for Walker to stray too close and everything would change in an instant.

Keep focused! You've got big enough problems of your own.

"You ain't gonna be able to save that cooze you're sweet on," Creed said with a chuckle, pulling back his foot in preparation for another kick. "And you sure as hell ain't gonna be able to save yourself."

But just before the blow came, Dalton grabbed a fistful of dirt and flung it into the man's eyes. Creed whipped up his hand to block it, but it was still enough to slow him. Hissing because of the pain shooting through him, Dalton still managed to stumble to his feet and land a blow of his own. His fist struck high on Creed's cheek, splitting the skin and sending a trickle of blood oozing down his face. His second attempt, a left aimed for Creed's chin, was partially blocked, but still hit cleanly enough to make Vernon's thug stumble a couple of steps back. Angrily, Creed spat into the dirt.

"Only punches you're gonna get," he snarled.

"We'll see about that."

Over Creed's shoulder, Dalton saw that Audie had managed to snag Walker's piece of wood and had yanked it out of the smaller man's grip. Now the bruiser was swinging it with abandon, forcing Walker to stay well back. Neither man said a word as they circled each other, one because he couldn't, the other because he chose not to. It seemed that whatever slim chance Walker might have had, it was now gone.

The other thing that caught Dalton's attention was that Creed still hadn't let go of the oilcloth. It was still clutched in his left hand. If he hadn't dropped it, allowing him to fight with both hands, it had to be important. Dalton knew he had to find out what it was.

When Creed came forward to attack, Dalton pretended he was about to make the same mistake and again fall for the fake, but he slid back at the last second and easily pushed the thug's punch aside. Grabbing the sleeve of Creed's shirt, Dalton pulled him closer and drove his knee sideways into the man's breadbasket hard enough to lift him from the ground. As quickly as he could, Dalton swatted at the cloth; Creed had been weakened enough that he couldn't hold on, and the package fell, opening as it hit the ground.

Dalton couldn't believe what he was seeing. It was dynamite.

"Have you lost your mind?" he shouted.

"It ain't nothin' but business," Creed groaned.

"It's murder!"

"Depends on which side you're standin' on."

Desperation fueled Dalton forward. He had to stop Creed before he used the explosive. He *had* to! With Creed still bent over from the knee to his gut, Dalton wound back to throw a bone-crushing right but, just as he let go of the punch, Creed's head moved as fast as a viper and Dalton struck nothing but air. He'd been playing possum. Before he knew it, Dalton had taken a shot to the jaw, a pile driver to the stomach, and another to the nose. Stars danced before his eyes. One more blow to the chest and he went down, crashing onto his back. Turning his head, the muscles aching, he saw Walker get tossed into the side of a building as easily as if he was a rag doll.

It was over. They'd been beaten.

Above him, Creed gloated. "I said you weren't gonna hit me no more." Bending down, he picked up the dynamite, its long fuse trailing behind it. Slowly, enjoying himself, Creed pulled a pack of matches from his pocket, plucked one, and struck its head ablaze.

"You weren't never gonna stop this."

When Creed touched the match to the fuse it hissed to life.

* * *

Anna followed right behind Montgomery as he crossed the rebuilt tavern and headed for the door. Stepping over wires and track, then weaving around a sound man, Anna's pursuit never wavered. With every step, her mind swirled, thinking back on everything Montgomery had done for her; rehearsing their lines before her first day of shooting, defending her from Joan's verbal attacks, and coming to her rescue when Milburn ambushed her in the street. He couldn't be the saboteur. He just couldn't be!

Montgomery walked briskly out of the saloon, made his way down the rickety steps and out into the street with an unconcerned air. When he heard Anna approaching, he turned to look at her, the surprise on his face lasting for an instant before he managed to replace it with a smile.

"It looks like you're not the only one coming down with a touch of something," he said, adding a cough into his fist for good measure. "I can only hope that a touch of fresh air might perk me back up."

"Tell me it's not you," Anna insisted, stepping close to him, not buying his illness for a second. "Tell me I'm jumping to conclusions, that it's just a coincidence that you looked at your watch and came outside when you did. Look me in the eye and tell me I'm wrong!"

"About what, my dear?" Montgomery asked. His eyes narrowing with concern, he added, "You might be more ill than you think. Maybe we ought to call the doctor and have him come take a look at you."

It wasn't much that gave him away, just a twitch of his lip as he tried to feign ignorance, but Anna saw it nonetheless. While her career in acting was nothing compared to his, she'd been on the stage long enough to know when someone was playing a role. Montgomery knew *exactly* what she was talking about. *He* was the mastermind behind the sabotage. A weight of disappointment crushed her. Tears sprang to her eyes and her voice caught as she spoke.

"Why?" she asked accusingly. "How could you do it? You stood there in the middle of the street and fought the very same fire you'd ordered to be lit! Why would you do such a thing?"

"Anna, please," Montgomery said. When he reached out and took hold of her hand, she snatched it away angrily.

"Don't you dare touch me!"

"You're imagining things, my dear."

"I saw the letter!" Anna shouted. "The one you slid under Vernon Black's door! I know that you're going to have this building destroyed at noon! I know that you paid to have the film destroyed! I know every terrible thing you've done, but for the life of me, I don't know why!"

And then, as she watched, Anna saw Montgomery change. Gone was the friendly, smiling older man who kept protesting his own innocence. His eyes narrowed; he seethed with an anger that frightened her. She'd thought his transformation into her character's father had been impressive; if this was the *real* Montgomery Bishop, then the man he'd been portraying since she'd arrived in Redstone was his greatest work yet.

"It should've been me," he snarled. "*I'm* the one who put in his time working for this damn studio, making picture after picture after picture for less when money was tight. I should've been the one making all of the decisions instead of toiling away doing bit parts in the middle of nowhere. Not him!"

"This...this is all because of Samuel...?" Anna responded.

"You're damn right it is," Montgomery snapped. "He was always such an opportunist, waiting for his chance to grab the golden ring, climbing the ladder without a care about who he stepped on to get there! The next thing I knew, everything I'd spent years working for was given to *him*! He ruined every plan I'd made. Everything! So I decided to return the favor."

Even though her suspicion had been confirmed, Anna was completely dumbstruck. All she could do in the face of Montgomery's ravings was to cautiously back away, a half-step at a time.

"This movie was Samuel's dream project, the film he's been going on about for years," the actor continued, following after her. "It cost Valentine a tremendous amount of money. If the company lost all of it, if the publicity was bad, if things on the set were such a mess that the movie couldn't even be made, then he'd be tossed out on his ear! All I had to do was find some local thug willing to carry out my every destructive desire. I learned a long time ago that with enough money, anything is possible. Once Samuel was out of the way, I'd get my chance!"

"Even if you had to kill to get it," Anna snapped.

"It could've been me," Montgomery explained, placing his hand on his chest. "I had to put myself at risk for it to be convincing. I had to be above suspicion. That's why I passed buckets during the fire. That's why I comforted Joan when her ring was stolen. I even put my life on the line when Milburn was shot. It could just as easily have been me that took the bullet."

"Or me," she reminded him.

Montgomery hesitated, his face softening. "I didn't want that," he said. "I tried to tell you to leave, that it wasn't safe, but you wouldn't listen. You don't have anything to do with this."

"Neither do most of the people inside that building!" Anna pleaded, pointing toward the saloon.

"It's Samuel's fault that it's come to this! I thought that the production would've been stopped by now, but he's too good a manipulator for that! He's talked the investors back in Hollywood into pressing forward. After this, they'll have no choice but to make me the producer. Samuel will be in a coffin!"

"Not if I warn them first." But just as Anna started to walk away, Montgomery grabbed her arm and held her fast. No matter how hard she tried to shake free, she couldn't.

"It won't do any good," he told her. "It's too late. It should happen any instant now. If you go in there, you'll just get yourself killed."

"But if I survive, I'm going to tell anyone who'll listen

about your plan. You'll go to jail for the rest of your life for what you've done."

Montgomery shook his head. "No one will believe you," he said. "It'd be your word against mine." With a chuckle, he added, "I suppose I have Joan to thank for that. After what happened in the dressing room, there's no shortage of people who think you're unhinged. Why would anyone believe your word when weighed against that of a respected actor like me?"

Anna knew he was right. While Montgomery was a legend in the business, her reputation had been damaged by Joan's self-inflicted injuries. Even Dalton and Walker had no real evidence. Without the incriminating letter, which still had no direct link to Montgomery, they were stuck with coincidence and rumor. It was their words against his.

Montgomery sneered, knowing that he had the upper hand. "Who knows," he said. "If you manage to keep your mouth shut, I might cast you in another movie as a reward."

Anna's temper flared. "You can go straight to—"

But before she could finish, the hot afternoon was split by the shuddering boom of an explosion, so loud and terrible that Anna felt it in her bones.

It was too late.

Dalton lay in the dirt, his body aching, blood dripping from the cuts on his face, dizzy from the beating he'd taken. Creed loomed above him, but Dalton's eyes were riveted on the sizzling fuse of the stick of dynamite. In all of his wildest guesses as to how Vernon Black was going to carry out the plan to destroy the old saloon, he never would have guessed he'd try to blow it up.

"You best cover your ears, boy," Creed said with a sneer.

Pushing through the cobwebs in his head, Dalton lashed out with his foot, catching the back of Creed's knee and toppling the man. In a heartbeat, Dalton was on him, raining down punches as fast as he could throw them. Both fear and desperation fueled him. For every blow that Creed managed to fend off, another one landed: on his chin, against his temple, flush with his ear.

But then, just as Dalton was beginning to think he was going to get the better of the fight, Creed bucked him off. Even as Dalton landed on his back, Creed pressing his advantage by leaping on him, he felt a small sliver of hope; the dynamite lay on the ground behind him.

"You ain't leavin' this alley alive," Creed snarled.

Dalton was too busy fighting to reply.

Back and forth they rolled, their muscles straining, teeth gnashing, each trying to get the upper hand. From somewhere, Dalton heard Audie roar in pain; Walker must have made a comeback of his own. After driving an elbow into the center of Creed's chest, Dalton yanked him over; when he did, he caught sight of the dynamite. To his horror, the fuse had burned through half of its length. Momentarily distracted, Dalton wasn't looking when Creed threw a shot of his own, taking a fist to his chin, and reversing their positions.

"Come on, Barnes," Creed said through blood-stained

teeth. "You ain't barely puttin' up more fight than your girl did in her hotel room. Damn shame you come along when you did. I was about to show her what a real man can do."

Instantly Dalton became nearly blind with rage. He'd had his suspicions about Creed's involvement in Anna's attack, but here was the proof. That a piece of trash like Creed had put his hands on her, had intended to violate her, made him sick. He'd end this here and now, no matter what it took.

Instead of trying to push Creed off, Dalton brought the crown of his head up and smashed it into the thug's face. He did it once, twice, and then a third time, the air filled with the sounds of the sickening crunches. Even though he was hurting himself, Dalton knew Creed was getting the worst of it. Glancing up through blood and sweat, Dalton saw that his opponent teetered on the edge of consciousness.

"That's twice I've bested you, you son-of-a-bitch!"

Dalton's punch snapped Creed's head hard to the side. It sounded like a gunshot. The man landed on his face in the dirt, unmoving and unconscious.

There was no time for Dalton to savor his victory. Frantically, he searched for the dynamite, unsure of where it was in the aftermath of the brawl. When he finally spotted it a dozen feet away, he froze. The fuse was just about to disappear down into the dynamite. In seconds, it would explode. But Dalton didn't hesitate. Later, he'd think that he, Walker, and even Anna in the saloon might've been far enough away to have avoided any damage, but in that moment, instinct took over. Scrambling forward, he snatched up the stick, planted his foot, and hurled it skyward with all of his might. Three fast beats of his heart later, it exploded. The deafening sound paralyzed him just before the concussive force of the blast knocked him from his feet. He felt as if he'd been kicked by a horse. He lay in the dirt, dazed, disoriented, and unable to tell up from down.

Dalton had no idea how long he'd lain there before he felt a hand on his back, slowly turning him over. Staring up into the sun high above the alleyway, he blinked rapidly, wondering if what he was seeing meant that he'd died in the explosion.

His father stood over him.

"Are you all right, son?" George asked, wearing a worried expression.

"What . . . what are you . . . ?" was all Dalton could say.

"I opened the letter. I reckon my curiosity got the better of me."

Dalton nodded; maybe that's what he'd hoped for all along.

With his ears still ringing, Dalton propped himself up and looked around him. His father had gone to the sheriff and managed to prod the lawman into action; he was handcuffing Creed. Walker stood over the man's fallen brother; Dalton didn't know if his friend had subdued Audie on his own or if the explosion had floored him. Either way, Walker gave him a weary nod.

They'd done it.

Or had they? Even as his father tried to keep him down,

to tell him that he wasn't in any shape to be walking around, Dalton was scrambling to his feet. He had to know if Anna was safe. If she wasn't, if he'd failed to keep his promise, he'd spend the rest of his life wishing the dynamite had exploded in his hand.

Fear seized hold of Anna, digging its claws in deeply, as the explosion echoed across Redstone. Looking back at the saloon, Anna expected to see the old building collapsing in a torrent of wood and glass, expected the afternoon to be filled with the sounds of the wounded and tears shed for the dead, but much to her pleasant surprise, everything looked the same, as run-down as ever.

Dalton did it... he saved us all...

Samuel, Frank, Joan, and the rest of the cast and crew ran outside, their faces shocked, looking up into the sky as if they expected to find thunderclouds. Murmurs coursed through the crowd, full of questions about what they'd heard. Many were looking at Anna and Montgomery expectantly, as if they'd have the answer. Anna did and she wasted no time in giving it.

"Samuel!" she shouted. "I know who was behind the sabotage! It was Montgomery!" she claimed, pointing at the actor. "He was behind the whole thing!"

When Anna looked at Montgomery, she saw that he'd once again transformed into the man she thought she'd known. Gone was the hateful scowl and spiteful eyes, replaced with a smile and a look of pity; for a man of his talent, it was as simple as changing a coat.

"I'm afraid our young Miss Finnegan isn't well," Montgomery said calmly. "She followed me outside and started leveling the most ridiculous accusations. No matter what I say, I can't seem to dissuade her."

Ignoring him, Anna proceeded to tell Samuel everything. She laid out what she and Dalton had found, including the letter that ordered the destruction of the saloon with everyone inside. She then repeated everything Montgomery had told her, up to and including his obscene offer in exchange for her silence.

"With you out of the way," she said to Samuel, "he thought that he'd take your place as producer. It was his jealousy that caused all of this."

"You know me far too well to believe any of this nonsense," Montgomery offered in his defense. "It's preposterous! Clearly she needs to see a doctor. After what happened with Joan and now this, I'm beginning to worry that the poor thing might be a danger to herself and others."

Suddenly Anna had an idea; strangely enough, Montgomery had been the one to give it to her. Joan stood near Samuel, as stunned as anyone by what she'd just heard. Ever since Anna had arrived in Redstone, the older actress had done everything she could to ruin her. She'd been snippy, rude, condescending, and as friendly as a rabid dog. But now she might be Anna's best hope.

"Joan," Anna called; when the older actress heard her name, she flinched. "You and I both know what happened in the dressing room," she said. "I don't care about an apology or an explanation, but I need you to tell Samuel the truth. You're the only person who can give him a reason to believe me."

Joan looked as if she'd been slapped. For someone who craved the spotlight so much that she'd go to any lengths to keep it, she seemed more than a little uncomfortable with all the attention she was suddenly receiving. When she opened her mouth, no sound came out.

Samuel broke the silence. "Did Anna really attack you?" he asked.

Joan looked away, unable to meet the producer's eyes as shame reddened her makeup-heavy cheeks. "Not...not exactly..." she stammered, causing a gasp to rise from many in the crowd.

"That still doesn't prove a thing," Montgomery said. "She's lying about me and no one can claim otherwise."

"Don't go countin' your chickens."

Every face, including Montgomery's, turned to see a man step out of the shadows of a nearby doorway and start their way. Anna recognized him immediately; it was the reporter from the *Movie Land News*, the one who'd ambushed her and Dalton a couple of days before. She was shocked by the bandages and bruises on the man's face, but also by his smile; he looked like the cat that'd just eaten the canary.

"What do you know about all of this, Mitchell?" Samuel asked.

"Glad you asked," the reporter crowed. "See, a little birdie told me that if I waited out here today, I might hear somethin' worth printin', and boy, was that right on the button. One gem after another, each tidbit juicier than the last." Turning to Anna, he smiled and added, "Your fella's all right by me, darlin', even if he did bust my beak."

"What did you hear?" the producer prodded.

"It went just like the doll said. Old Monty Bishop here confessed to the whole sordid thing." Looking down at his notepad, he said, "I was so busy scribblin' it all down in shorthand that I darn near got a cramp. If you'd like, I could read it back word for word."

"It's more lies, I tell you!" Montgomery roared, but Anna could see his carefully applied veneer start to crack. He was no longer confident, no longer in control. Despite all his precautions, his plan was crumbling into dust.

"Yell all you like," Mitchell said. "I'm gonna print it just like it happened. Even if you keep yourself out of a cell, you ain't gonna work another day in front a the cameras as long as you live." With a wink, he added, "Although I'm bettin' you're gonna sell me one hell of a lot a magazines."

As happy as Anna was with what the reporter had to say, it dawned on her that he could have spoken up at any time. Instead, he'd left her on the end of the rope, the noose tightening, trying to convince Joan to tell the truth. Undoubtedly he'd been after more gossip.

"Samuel," Montgomery pleaded. "This is all a big mistake. You've got to believe me."

The producer stared coldly at the man. "I don't," he replied coolly, "but it's not up to me to decide. It's for the law." Turning to a couple of nearby crew members, he said, "Grab him and don't let him go. We'll let the sheriff sort it out."

And just like that, it was finally over.

* * *

Once Montgomery had been hauled away, still proclaiming his innocence with every step, Anna began to search for Dalton. Everywhere she looked, people milled together in groups, gossiping about what they'd just witnessed; every face showed excitement mixed with disbelief. But no matter where she turned, Anna still couldn't find him. But then, just as she was about to give in to her rising panic, there he was. He and Walker came out of the alley beside the saloon. Relief flooded her. The blacksmith had his arm around his friend's shoulder, helping Walker get along as he favored his leg. When Dalton looked up and saw her, he grinned, and Anna's eyes filled with tears. Without a moment's hesitation, she began to run. When she reached him, she threw herself into his embrace, wrapping her arms around his neck as the emotions she'd struggled to hold back finally broke through.

"I thought something had happened to you," she cried into his neck.

"Hush now," he soothed. "I'm just fine."

"I was so scared!"

"It's all over now. We did it, just like I promised we would."

"When I heard that explosion, I thought..."

"You just put all of that worry away," Dalton insisted. "Walker and I kept them from what they intended. We beat them."

It was then that Anna looked up, gasping when she saw

how steep a price Dalton had paid to stop the Cobb brothers. His face was a mass of cuts and bruises. One gash along his cheekbone still oozed blood, while another had split his lip. Dark bruises discolored the corner of his mouth and a knot was growing on his temple. Glancing over at Walker, she saw much the same. Both men looked exhausted. If they were the two left standing, she could only imagine how much worse the culprits looked. Still, it pained Anna that he'd been hurt on her behalf.

"Oh, Dalton," she said. "Are you all right?"

"It's not so bad," he answered before wincing as she touched his cheek. "Most places, anyway," he added.

"I know just what might make it better," Anna said, rising to kiss him. She was surprised when he stopped her halfway.

Dalton looked around at the crowd. Most every head was turned in their direction. "Are you sure you want to do that just now?" he asked. "Maybe sometime once we've got some privacy might be better..."

For your career is what she knew he'd left out.

"I don't care who's watching."

Anna knew that Hollywood expected certain things from its stars; a glamorous look, an air of class and mystery in how they carried themselves, but also, ideally, for them to be romantically involved with other actors. It was part of playing the game. But having spent her whole life in search of stardom, Anna had found that what she really wanted was love. And she'd found it here, in a little faraway corner of Texas, with Dalton. No one, not a movie star nor a gossip reporter nor a photographer, was going to keep her from him.

With that, she rose and, as gently as she could, touched her lips to his. He pulled her close, holding her tight. She felt safe, happy, in love. It was better than she would have expected. Somehow, some way, they'd found each other, had overcome their differences, beaten those out to do them harm, and started down the road to a future as bright as the summer sun.

Just like in the movies.

Epilogue

Aɴɴᴀ sᴛᴏᴏᴅ ᴏɴ the balcony and stared into the night. The city spread out below her, smaller than she had imagined but hardly sleeping, the lights of the thousands of automobiles, houses, and street lamps bright enough to dim all but the most brilliant of stars. A soft wind rustled the hem of her dress and stirred the blond hair cascading across her bare shoulders. Behind her, the loud din of the ballroom leaked out the edges of the closed door, the sounds of music and laughter mingling. She knew that there were people waiting for her, producers with offers of more films, other stars wanting to wish her well, waiters looking for an autograph, but she made no move to rejoin the party. For the first time in longer than she would've liked, she was happy to be out of the spotlight.

Maybe being a star isn't all it's cracked up to be…

It had been a week since *The Talons of the Hawk* had made its debut. The crowd at the premiere had been be-

yond anyone's wildest expectations. Lines had stretched
around the block, with searchlights swiveling in the sky
and everyone dressed glamorously. Anna had stared up
at the marquee for a long time, unable to believe that it
was her name she was seeing. Sitting in the front row of
the packed theater, watching herself up on the big screen,
larger than life, Anna had been so nervous she could hardly
sit still. Worry gnawed at her. This was the first time anyone had actually *seen* the movie. What if it wasn't any
good? What if her acting was at fault? What if she'd ruined
everything just as Joan had warned? She fretted that people
would start booing at any moment. But when at last El Halcón and Claire had ridden together into the sunset, and the
house lights had come on, people were on their feet, cheer-
ing and clapping.

"It's a hit!" Samuel had crowed.

And he was right.

It had taken a while for Anna to understand that all of
the problems they'd faced in Redstone had played a role in
building interest for the film. Because of what Montgomery
had done, and especially because of what had been written
about it in the *Movie Land News* and every other Hollywood
gossip magazine, anticipation for the film grew by the day.
Even her infamous run-ins with Joan seemed only to stoke
the fires of interest. In the end, demand had become so
great that Samuel had forced Frank to hurry his editing so
that the film could start being readied for ticket buyers.
So far, the film seemed to have paid off, and everyone connected to the movie had had their lives changed overnight.

Joan's once-fading career had been revitalized by all that had happened. Whatever shame she'd felt for lying about Anna attacking her in the dressing room hadn't lasted long. She was soon just as dramatic and overbearing as ever. But fortunately, a kind of truce had been declared between them. While they'd never be friends, they were no longer enemies. Once, near the end of shooting, they'd even shared a laugh on the set. When Joan had finally reclaimed her stolen ring, Anna had been happy for her.

Milburn's star had also been polished a little bit brighter. Though he'd spent the rest of the scenes acting on his back, he'd taken Anna's threat as a warning and kept his hands to himself. When his gunshot wound finally healed, he'd bragged about his bravery and manliness to anyone who would listen. Screams from smitten women had followed Milburn through the doors of the premiere, proving that he was still as big a heartthrob as ever. Anna would bet that it was only a matter of time before his lecherous ways caught up with him and took his blossoming career down in flames. When she'd told Samuel about Milburn's unwanted advances, the producer had promised never to hire the man again.

While completing his dream film had been far more challenging than he'd expected, Samuel was now reaping the rewards. In every interview he gave, the acts of sabotage he described seemed to grow bigger and more dangerous, but Anna understood; Samuel was a showman who knew that the more interest he could drum up, the more money would be made, and there was talk that he might be made a partner in Valentine Pictures, yet another feather for his cap. Now every time she saw him, he was holding forth to a spellbound audience, flashing his brilliant smile. Frank was often at Samuel's side, looking forlorn and out of sorts as if he loved creating the spotlight but hated being caught in it. She almost felt sorry for the director.

One person who would never receive Anna's pity was Montgomery. Thinking about how his jealousy had nearly been the death of them all still frightened her. But the most horrifying thing of all was that he would never spend a day in jail for what he'd done. Once the actor had been detained by the sheriff, his room had been searched from top to bottom, but nothing that might have incriminated him had ever been turned up. There had been a considerable amount of money stashed in a satchel at the back of a drawer, but that by itself wasn't enough to tie him to the sabotage. The thugs he'd paid to carry out his revenge had never actually met him, so they couldn't drag him down with them.

But that didn't mean that Montgomery was going to get away scot-free. Mitchell Hubert had ended up doing the damage the law could not. He had written his article just as he'd promised, detailing Montgomery's confession and effectively ruining his career in Hollywood. It had become a nationwide story, splashed across the headlines; when Anna read the words Montgomery had spoken to her, she was surprised to see that the reporter hadn't embellished them. If Montgomery had wanted to sue, it was two against one. Eventually, the actor had been put on a train out of

Redstone. The sheriff and Samuel had accompanied him to the depot; no one dared ask what had been said between them. Montgomery hadn't been seen since. Anna, watching him act alongside her up on the silver screen, had shivered.

The criminals who'd carried out Montgomery's scheme of revenge had paid their own steep price. With Creed and Audie Cobb locked behind bars for having tried to blow up the saloon, everyone's attention had turned to Vernon Black. The small-town businessman had pleaded ignorance; the Cobbs were similarly unhelpful, refusing to say a word. A search of Vernon's office had turned up nothing; whatever payments he'd received from Montgomery had surely long since been hidden. But then something changed. When it had finally dawned on Creed that he and his brother were going to jail for most of the rest of their miserable lives, he'd suddenly started talking. In exchange for a bit of leniency, he detailed all he knew about Vernon, particularly about the letters' arrivals, and succeeded in placing his former boss in the cell beside him. None of the three would taste freedom any time soon, if ever.

"You're going to catch a cold out here."

Anna turned as a man stepped out of the shadows near the door and approached her, two drinks in hand. Unable to hold back her smile, she beamed as brightly as the city below, still struggling to believe that all of her dreams had somehow become real.

"I've been waiting for someone to come out here and warm me," she answered with a little sass.

"Looking for anyone in particular?"

"Not really," Anna replied. "Were there any handsome waiters inside?"

"I could go take a look."

"Would you?"

Dalton stepped into the light and shook his head. Handing her a glass, he began to tug uncomfortably at the collar of his tuxedo, attire that she found dashing on him but he felt made him look like an ox in an accordion.

"I can't wait to get out of this thing," he grumbled.

"On that, we can both agree."

When the movie left Redstone, Dalton had faced an important decision; whether to come with Anna or stay behind. Her heart longed for him to be by her side, but she tried not to get her hopes up, fearful that she was asking too much. Surprisingly, he seemed to make up his mind rather easily. Even though he'd railed against Hollywood, bad-mouthing anything and everything associated with the place, claiming that he'd be miserable in a city, he'd packed up his things and agreed to join her in California. Of course, the decision had been made a little easier to swallow when Samuel offered him a position with Valentine Pictures, helping to build sets and repair any damaged props. He'd been pleasantly surprised by the town, but Anna had noticed him looking a bit down from time to time; she had a good idea why.

It had been hard for Dalton to leave his parents and Walker behind. With Vernon locked in a jail cell, George's gambling debt was erased. Still, she understood why Dalton worried; his father's addiction was so strong that it

wouldn't take much to pull him back in. But after the
fight with Creed, when George had come to Dalton's aid,
they felt somehow they might be able to repair some of
what had been damaged between them. For her part, Betty
had encouraged her son to go with Anna, hoping that he,
too, would become a movie star. Walker's reaction was different; he was disappointed that he had to stay behind.
Maybe if Dalton thrived at Valentine and he could pull a
few strings, his friend might join them.

But not too soon…

Every moment that Anna spent with Dalton felt better
than the last. Listening to the sound of his voice, looking
up at his smile as she wrapped herself in his arms, even lying in bed and feeling the rise and fall of his chest as he
slept, everything about him enchanted her. Sometimes she
felt as if he was a matinee idol and she was the swoon-
ing fan. But she knew that not everyone saw it that way.
She'd heard whispers about the two of them, little snippets
of gossip that wondered what she was doing with a rough-
around-the-edges sort when she could have had anyone
she wanted. But she ignored it all. It didn't matter. If being
with Dalton meant that she'd damaged her career, that was
a price she was willing to pay. Ever since he'd come into
her life, she'd had to face the fact that what she'd considered important, to be famous, to see her name in lights,
hadn't been so important after all.

What she'd needed was love, and Dalton had given it to
her.

As he slipped his arm around her shoulders, pulling her

close, his touch warm on her skin, Dalton looked up at the sky and groaned.

"What's the matter?" she asked.

"It's too darn light in the city," he explained. "This time of year, I used to like to go out to the bridge and watch the shooting stars streak across the sky. That's never going to happen here."

"Why did you want to see one?"

"To make a wish."

Anna smiled. "I'm sure there's one up there but we just can't see it," she suggested. "More than we can count."

"So go ahead and wish."

She did as he asked, closing her eyes, her head pressed against his chest, listening to the strong rhythm of his heartbeat. "Done," she said.

"What did you wish for?"

"I'm not telling."

Anna had expected Dalton to press her, to try to get her to reveal it, but he had fallen silent, pulling her tight and giving her a gentle kiss on her forehead.

She'd wished for happiness and love.

Her wish had already come true.

ABOUT THE AUTHOR

Dorothy Garlock is one of America's—and the world's—favorite novelists. Her work consistently appears on national bestseller lists, including the *New York Times* list, and there are over fifteen million copies of her books in print translated into eighteen languages. She has won more than twenty writing awards, including a *Romantic Times* Reviewers' Choice Award for Best Historical Fiction for *A Week from Sunday,* five Silver Pen Awards from *Affaire de Coeur,* and three Silver Certificate Awards—and in 1998 she was selected as a finalist for the National Writer's Club Best Long Historical Book Awards. Her novel *With Hope* was chosen by Amazon as one of the best romances of the twentieth century.

After retiring as a news reporter and bookkeeper in 1978, she began her career as a novelist with the publication of *Love and Cherish.* She lives in Clear Lake, Iowa. You can visit her website at www.dorothygarlock.com.